DOROTHY GARLOCK

A Novel
of the
Tumultuous
1930s

With Song

WARNER BOOKS

ISBN 0-446-60588-3

$6.99 US / $8.99 CAN.

❧

"Mol–ly, sweet Mol–ly, don't let a thing ever change you."

He sang in a soft whisper along with the recording.

Even knowing that he was just flirting, Molly's heart thumped in a strange and disturbing way as she struggled to get sufficient air into her lungs. It seemed to her that the music would never end, but it finally did and they stopped. She made an attempt to move away from him, but he held tightly to her hand and his arm tightened around her. His dark eyes fastened to her face.

"You're a sweet armful, Molly, darlin'."

"You're flirting, Mr. Dolan," Molly said lightly.

Bertha had wound the machine and put another record on the turntable. The song was a slow romantic tune.

The thought struck Hod that he held a treasure here in his arms. He had never felt this way about any woman. He was as happy as he'd ever been; with this girl in his arms, dancing in a darkened room.

Molly's breath quickened and the cheek pressed to his moved slightly. Hod Dolan, you're playing with fire. This slip of a girl could break your heart . . .

❧

"Garlock tackles Depression-era Oklahoma with wit, freshness, and memorable characterization . . . creates people and places with a tart honesty."
—*Publishers Weekly*

Turn the page for more praise for Dorothy Garlock's previous 1930s novel, With Hope . . .

Books by Dorothy Garlock

Almost Eden
Annie Lash
Dream River
Forever Victoria
A Gentle Giving
Glorious Dawn
Homeplace
Larkspur
Lonesome River
Love and Cherish
Midnight Blue
Nightrose
Restless Wind
Ribbon in the Sky
River of Tomorrow
The Searching Hearts
Sins of Summer
Sweetwater
Tenderness
The Listening Sky
This Loving Land
Wayward Wind
Wild Sweet Wilderness
Wind of Promise
Yesteryear
With Hope

Published by WARNER BOOKS

DOROTHY GARLOCK

With Song

WARNER BOOKS

A Time Warner Company

WARNER BOOKS EDITION

Cover design by Tony Greco

Warner Books, Inc.
1271 Avenue of the Americas
New York, NY 10020

Visit our Web site at
www.warnerbooks.com

 A Time Warner Company

Printed in the United States of America

First Printing: May, 1999

10 9 8 7 6 5 4 3 2

For an unflagging optimist
my good friend

RICHARD EFTHIM

The best way to know a bunch of people is to go and listen to their music.
    —**Woody Guthrie, Woody Says, 1975**

The Ballad of Molly McKenzie

The sun it was shining that day in late June,
And Molly was singing a popular tune.
She looked out the window and saw the men go,
Then went down the stairs and found carnage below.
Her mother and father lay still on the floor,
Shot dead by gunmen as they tended the store.

Molly, sweet Molly, singing no more.
Molly, sweet Molly, swore to even the score.

A G-man named Hod came to her with a plan.
He asked her to say she remembered each man,
To tell a reporter who'd publish her claim
And lure the men back like moths to a flame.
The G-man named Hod looked deep in her eyes.
The response that she felt took her by surprise.

Molly, young Molly, agreed to be bait.
Molly, brave Molly, tempting cruel fate.

She opened the store every morning at eight.
She scanned the dirt road for killers in wait.
Would they come when night fell—the perilous dark?
Should she fear the next car that drew up to park?
Hod Dolan, she thought, must be watching somewhere,
The look in his eyes—she knew he must care.

Molly, strong Molly, are you doubly in danger?
Molly, dear Molly, risking love with a stranger.

Some troubles grow from the seeds sown by hate.
Some troubles come from the need for a mate.
Some love sweet Molly with hearts that are pure,
Some nourish hate and claim love is the lure.
In and around the town they call Pearl,
Surely there's love that will save a young girl.

Molly, oh Molly, like flow'rs seek the sun,
Molly, wise Molly, you'll choose the right one.
                                             —F.S.I.

Chapter
One

Seward County, Kansas—1935

> *"My baby don't care for shows.*
> *My baby don't care for clothes.*
> *My baby just cares for me—"*

The girl sang in a loud clear voice as she came into the back of the store with an armload of sun-dried clothes.

"What kinda song is that?" her father asked.

"A good one. Wanna hear more?"

"Not if I don't have to." A mock frown covered his usually smiling face.

"You don't know good music when you hear it. All you listen to is that old Doc Brinkley down in Del Rio playing cowboy music," she teased.

"Don't be knockin' old Doc. If his goat glands can do what he says they can, I'm thinkin' of makin' a trip down to Texas to get me some before the crowd gets there and they run out of goats."

"You'd better not let Mama hear you say that. She'll whop your backside."

"I'll whop him if he shoots off any more of those blasted firecrackers." Molly's mother set a basket of clothes on the floor beside a table and began folding towels. "He threw one behind me, and I almost jumped out of my skin."

"You're in trouble now." Molly danced up to her father and kissed his cheek. *"I wanna be loved by you, nobody else but you—Boop Boop A Doo!"* She laughed gaily when he made an attempt to avoid a second kiss and ran up the stairs to the living quarters.

Roy McKenzie shook his head. It was good to have his girl home again. She brightened the place like an electric lightbulb.

Down the road, a hundred yards from the store, the driver stopped the big Oldsmobile and slipped the gearshift into neutral. The engine purred impatiently.

"Just sittin' there. Ripe for pickin', ain't it?" The man removed his hat, swabbed his face with a handkerchief, and glanced at the man who lounged beside him holding the butt end of a cigar between his teeth. "I could use a orange soda pop right about now." *Didn't the bastard ever sweat? He looks cool as a cucumber while I'm sweating like a nigger at an election.*

Eyes, so light blue that they appeared to be colorless and as cold as chunks of ice, turned to the driver. The man spoke with the cigar butt clenched between his teeth.

"What ya waitin' for? Get on down there before we'll use up what gas we got left just sittin' here." He took the butt from his mouth and held it between his thumb and forefinger as he leaned forward to scrutinize the building they were approaching.

The store was typical of many scattered over the Kansas plains. Painted above the slanting roof on the porch that stretched across the front of the two-storied frame building was a sign: McKENZIE GENERAL STORE. And in smaller letters beneath it: GROCERIES-FEED-GAS.

On each side of the lone Phillips 66 gasoline pump, posts were sunk into the ground to protect it from careless drivers. Tin signs advertising everything from Garrett's snuff to P&G soap were tacked to the front of the store. On the screen door a big white sign outlined in red advertised NeHi SODA POP. A few shade trees were scattered to the side and behind the building. All was still except for the snap of the clothes that fluttered gently from a clothesline situated to catch the southern breeze and the buzz of the bees hovering around a clump of honeysuckle bushes.

The cold eyes took in everything about the place. When the car stopped beside the tall gas pump in front of the store, the man stepped out and looked back through the cloud of dust that hung over the long flat road. He saw no sign of another car approaching. He dropped the butt of his cigar on the ground and smashed it into the dirt with the sole of his highly polished shoe.

"Need gas?" The words followed the slamming of the screen door.

A plump man with sparse gray hair and a white apron tied about his waist waited at the top of the steps.

"Yeah."

Roy McKenzie came down the dirt drive to the gas pump. Its glass cylinder, marked like a beaker to measure gas, seemed empty; but Roy pumped the lever, and gas poured in.

"How much?" he asked, pulling the handle back and forth.

"Fill it."

"These big cars have a way of eatin' gas." Roy unscrewed the cap and let the gas run down the hose and into the car tank. "I 'spect it's pretty hot travelin'. 'Fraid it's goin' to be a scorchin' summer."

As he waited for the tank to fill, Roy glanced into the back window of the car. On the backseat the muzzle of a shotgun protruded from under a blanket. His eyes shifted to the men. They stood at the front of the car watching him. *City men. A fast car. A shotgun.* Apprehension rose in him as he waited for the tank to fill.

The pump registered seventeen gallons when the storekeeper hung the hose back on the pump and put the cap back on the tank.

"That'll be three dollars and six cents. Gas goin' up every day. I'm still holdin' at eighteen cents."

"Got any cold soda pop?"

"Sure do. Iceman was here yesterday."

Roy's feeling of apprehension escalated. The hair seemed to stand on the back of his neck as the two men followed him out of the bright sunshine and into the store. His eyes met those of his wife in the back of the store where she was folding the clothes she had brought in from the line.

"I've got orange, grape, and strawberry."

"Orange."

Wishing the men would leave, wishing his wife would go upstairs to their daughter, Roy took a bottle of pop from the chest cooler and wiped the water off it with a cloth.

"That adds another nickel to your bill."

"Got any SenSen?"

"How many?" The storekeeper moved down the counter and took a cardboard box filled with small paper packets from a shelf.

"The whole box."

"The . . . whole—" The bullet that cut off his words went through his chest and into a can of peaches on the shelf behind him. He was flung back, knocking over tins of baking powder before he sank to the floor.

"Take care of her." The cold-eyed man jerked his head toward Mrs. McKenzie, who stood frozen in horror, her hand over her mouth.

"Ya . . . know I ain't got no stomach for killin' women."

"Do it, goddammit, 'less ya want the Feds down on ya. She got a good look at your ugly face." The gunman jerked open the cash drawer and pulled out a few dollar bills. "Shit! Not enough here to mess with." He lifted the change tray and found a stack of tens and twenties. "That's more like it, but still chicken feed."

The sound of the shot that killed the woman filled the store. The man stuffing the bills into his pocket didn't even look up. He took the box of SenSen and headed for the door.

"Come on. We got business in KC."

"I'm goin' to get me a couple bottles of sody pop."

Keeping his distance from the dead storekeeper and his wife, the man hunched his rounded shoulders, gathered several bottles of pop from the cooler, and hurried out of the store. His companion glared at him with cold eyes over the top of the car.

"You're as bad as a goddamn kid 'bout that soda pop."

In the living quarters upstairs, Molly McKenzie was making the bed with fresh sheets she had brought in off the line. She smiled and shook her head when she heard the loud pops. Her daddy was teasing her mother with the firecrackers again. He was just like a kid about the Fourth of July. The shipment of fireworks had come in that morning, and he had to try them out.

A minute or two later when she heard the screen door slam, Molly went through the rooms to the front, pulled back the lace panel, and looked out the window. Two men in white shirts and brown felt hats were getting into a big black car. One looked across the top of the car toward the store. His face was swarthy, his lips thick.

"You're as bad as a goddamn kid 'bout that soda pop. Let's get the hell outta here." His voice was thin and reedy for such a large man.

The driver of the car folded his long lanky body under the wheel, started the motor, and revved the engine. The wheels skidded, stirring a cloud of dust as the car pulled out of the drive and took off down the road at high speed.

Molly let the curtain drop. She hadn't heard a car pull in. Had it arrived while she was listening to *Ma Perkins*?

Roy McKenzie enjoyed meeting strangers who came from the road as well as his regular customers. Over the past sixty-five years almost everyone within a hundred miles had come to the store her great-grandfather had opened back in the 1880s, and those who hadn't come knew about it.

Roy was fond of saying everyone had to eat, and as long as there were people, he would have customers. Times were hard. The dust storms had taken a toll on the wheat farmers, but if they had eggs or butter to trade, he would supply them with flour and sugar.

Molly had spent a year and a half in Wichita at business school, learning typing and shorthand so that she could get a job as a secretary. After the course, she had wanted to come home for a while before looking for the job she was sure she would hate. Her parents had insisted that she get out, spread her wings, as they had put it, see some of the world other than Seward County. She had lived here all her life. In fact, she had been born in the bed she had just made. She loved the smell of the store, the excitement of new goods, the involvement in the small community.

It was grand to be home!

Chapter
Two

Molly stood on the porch of the store and looked down the flat road that stretched to the horizon. The Kansas sun sent shimmering heat waves over the fields of wheat that struggled to survive.

The Fourth of July had come and gone.

Most of the shipment of fireworks her father had ordered for the celebration had either been sold or given away. Molly had tucked packages of sparklers in with the orders of several families who had been hit hard by the dust storms and the drought. Their children had gazed at the fireworks longingly, knowing better than to ask for something so frivolous.

In the weeks since her parents were killed, Molly had been asked almost daily if she was going to sell the store and move away. Her answer was always the same.

"Why would I do that? This is my home. There's been

a McKenzie here for fifty years. I'll run the store as my father did."

Bertha McKenzie, wiping the sweat from her face with a handkerchief edged with lace tatting, came out onto the porch. Roy's elder sister had come from Wichita and announced that she was here to stay. She had never lived at the store her grandfather built, but she was as familiar with it as if she had. A saintly looking woman with a plump rosy face and a large bosom, Bertha was as strong in mind as she was in muscle. She didn't hesitate to say what she thought and had shared her hard-won wisdom with Molly since the day she arrived.

"That preacher that was here this morning ain't what he's cracked up to be. He's got more on his mind than tryin' to comfort one of his *flock*. He's thinkin' to get you to comfort *him* and to take care of that parcel of younguns of his'n, and he'd get his hands on this store to boot."

"For crying out loud, Aunt Bertha! He's at least thirty years older than I am." Molly shifted her gaze from the horizon to her aunt.

"What'd that make him? Fifty somethin'? Fiddle! Didn't you say he'd had four or five wives and got a batch of younguns off all of them. It's a wonder he's got any hair on top. I'd a thought he'd of wore it off on the head of the bed."

"Aunt Bertha, I swear!"

"It's true. Mark my words. Didn't you say his woman died around Christmas last year? By now he's raunchier than a two-peckered billy goat."

"Mama and Daddy were members of his church. That's why he comes here."

"That may be, but he's got his eye on you, too. His mouth waters ever'time he looks at you."

"How do you know that?"

"Mark my words! That ain't all! You know that farmer that comes in here most every day, the one that doesn't bother to tie his shoelaces and has only one button fastened on the shoulder straps of his overalls?"

"You mean George Andrews?"

"He was givin' you *and* the store the once-over."

"George has been coming here for years. I've not said any more than 'hello' and 'good-bye' to him. He's got about as much personality as a wet rag."

"And he ain't used one in a month of Sundays. Smelled like he'd been sleepin' with the hogs. What I'm tellin' you is that both of them birds has got fornicatin' on their minds. Fornicatin' and gettin' a meal ticket. That Andrews looked at you like a dyin' calf when you wasn't lookin'."

"George raises hogs. That's why he smells like one." Molly gave her aunt a look of exasperation. "Two men are after me; both old enough to be my father."

"Age hasn't anything to do with it as long as a man's under eighty. I ran a boardin'house for ten years. I know what's on their minds . . . and what's in their britches."

"Aunt Bertha! You're not shocking me. I got used to you when I stayed with you in Wichita."

"Oh, love, I got used to you, too. It was so darn lonesome when you left."

"Have I told you how glad I am that you came to stay with me?"

"A time or two. I've only been here a few weeks. Wait until I've been here a year. You'll be tyin' a can to my tail and sendin' me back to Wichita."

"Don't count on it." Molly hugged her aunt and turned away to hide the tears that sprang to her eyes. "Will the hurt ever go away, Aunt Bertha?"

"Not entirely. But it will lessen in time. Grief has a way of doing that."

"To lose both of them . . . and so senselessly—"

"I know. I lost my love during the War. I was sure that I'd die of grief. He died of influenza on the way to France. We never even got to sleep together. Oh, we wanted to, but we thought the decent thing to do would be to wait until we were wed. I wish to hell we hadn't waited."

"You loved him a lot?"

"You bet your buttons. He didn't want us to marry until he had something to offer me. Then the war came along, and he thought it his duty to go."

"Do you have a picture of him?"

"I'll show you someday. He was a handsome Irish lad with black curly hair and eyes that had the devil right in them."

"And you never met anyone else you could love?"

"All men paled when compared to Mick Shannon."

Bertha fanned herself with a cardboard fan. She loved Molly as if she were her own. The girl needed a good man to take care of her, but from what Bertha had seen so far, the pickings here in Seward County were slim, very slim.

"Do you think they'll ever catch the men who . . . did it?" Molly asked with her back to her aunt.

"I don't know, honeybunch. The sheriff said that he'd been contacted by a Federal man, and he was coming here to talk to you. I wish you hadn't told him you got a look at those fellers."

"But I did, Aunt Bertha. I'll never forget their faces. One was kinda stocky with big jaws and thick lips, and the other one was taller and skinny, but he had a big head."

"How come you remember all that?"

"I don't know. After some of the shock of finding Mama and Daddy wore off, I began to remember things. The thin man had several bottles of soda pop, and the other one had an oblong box in his hand. I'm sure it was the box of SenSen that came in a few days earlier. I remember Daddy saying a hundred packets would be a year's supply. People around here don't buy stuff to cover up bad breath when they have hardly enough to eat."

"The sheriff said they were probably big-time gangsters travelin' to Kansas City and saw the store as an easy stick-up."

"They're cold-blooded killers, not stick-up men. If the marshals catch them, I want to be there when they're hanged." Molly turned a cold, set face to her aunt. "I mean it, Aunt Bertha. I want to be there. I've got a right to be there after what they've done." Her voice wavered, and her lips began to tremble.

"There's been a lot of killin' around here the last few

years. They've not caught whoever killed that man and woman down around Liberal or the old man over near Meade."

"I saw the ones who killed my mama and daddy, and I intend to make sure that they pay for it."

"Come on in out of the heat, honeybunch, and I'll pour you a glass of lemonade. You've worked yourself into a lather."

No more than a week later, a car came off the road and stopped a short distance from the porch. Molly felt an instant of panic before she spotted Sheriff Mason's tan Stetson hat. She could see nothing of the driver. They were waiting, she guessed, for Mr. and Mrs. Bonner and their children to leave the store.

Mr. Bonner had led his team to the side door and had unloaded several bags of sweet corn and was lifting a fifty-pound sack of flour and one of sugar into his wagon. Along with the corn he had brought in five pounds of fresh butter to trade. It was already in the icebox.

"Tally up the difference, Miss McKenzie. I'll pay soon as I can."

"I'm not worried, Mr. Bonner. You've traded here for ten years. Your credit is good."

"I'm thankin' ya, ma'am. I wasn't sure now that Roy's gone."

"I know I can't take his place, but I'll do the best I can."

"That's good enough for me, miss." Mr. Bonner cleared his throat and spit more out of embarrassment than need. "If there's anythin' I can do for ya, let me know. Hear?"

"Yes, and I thank you."

"I'll be bringin' ya in a load of stove wood."

"I'll be needing it, Mr. Bonner. We'll make a trade."

The children came out of the store licking peppermint sticks and climbed into the wagon. Aunt Bertha must have given them the candy; she couldn't resist little kids, Molly mused. At the urging of their mother, the children sang out in unison, "Thank you, Miss McKenzie."

"You're very welcome. 'Bye, now. Come again."

She watched the team pull the wagon out onto the road and waved at the children before she went back into the store.

"Aunt Bertha, the sheriff is here. I think the Federal man is with him."

Bertha put aside the wet cloth she'd been using to wipe the shelves. Since the dust storms had begun a few years back, keeping the store clean had become a never-ending chore. Sometimes it seemed to her that all the three hundred million tons of topsoil blown from Kansas, Texas, Oklahoma, and Colorado during April and May had settled here in the store.

Molly positioned herself behind the counter. She had already decided that she wasn't going to like the Federal man. If he was really interested in catching the men who killed her parents, he would have been here before now.

Sheriff Mason plodded into the store, his bootheels resounding on the wooden floor. He removed his hat and wiped his forehead with the sleeve of his shirt.

"Howdy, miss. It's hotter than blue blazes out there."

"Hello, Sheriff. Aunt Bertha is making a pitcher of iced tea." As she spoke, Molly's eyes shifted to the man who came in behind the sheriff. He was definitely not what she had imagined a Federal agent would look like. He loomed over the rather chubby sheriff. A big man in a rumpled dark suit and a white shirt, he had removed his felt hat when he came in the door, revealing a head of thick black hair that curled and twisted in complete disarray. His nose leaned to one side, his mouth was hard, and a thin white scar slashed across his broad forehead and ended with a nick out of the end of one thick dark eyebrow. He had high cheekbones, and his flat cheeks were creased in deep grooves on each side of his wide, full-lipped mouth.

Deep, dark eyes met hers. They held the combination of sharp intelligence and quiet strength. She was right in thinking that she would not like him. He was too cold, too controlled to understand the pain of loss she was suffering.

"This is the agent I was tellin' you about. Mr. Dolan wants to talk to you about . . . what you saw that day."

The man stepped forward and held out his hand.

"Hod Dolan, Miss McKenzie. I'm sorry about your parents."

His hand was rough and strong and warm, but not sweaty.

"How do you do? We can talk in the back of the store. Would you like a glass of iced tea?"

"A glass of tea would be hard to turn down." His mouth didn't become much gentler when he smiled.

Hod Dolan was a man with a photographic mind. He would remember with clarity for the rest of his life this first meeting with Molly McKenzie. His eyes swept over the girl, locking into his memory the dark brown hair that hung to her shoulders, the slender, graceful body and the skirt of the neat gingham dress swirling around her sun-browned bare legs at mid-calf. Her movements were coltish. But it was her eyes that fascinated him. They were an unusual color: deep violet-blue. He felt something akin to an electric jolt when he looked into them.

"This is my aunt, Miss McKenzie." Molly looked over her shoulder and spoke to the agent, then to her aunt, "Mr. Dolan, Aunt Bertha. You know the sheriff."

"Yes, I know the sheriff. Howdy to you, mister. Do you take sugar in your tea?"

"No, ma'am."

"It's hotter than an oven in here." Bertha had wrapped a cloth around the sweating glasses on the table. "Take your tea out back. I'll watch the store and see that the sheriff don't snitch a cracker or get in the pickle barrel."

"If someone comes in for gas, call me."

"I'll pump it," the sheriff said. "Go on and have your talk with Dolan."

"Don't you want to sit in?" Molly asked, reluctant to be alone with the G-man with the unwavering stare. There was something harsh, almost brutal about him.

"No. This is out of my control—Fed business now. Just tell him what you told me."

"I'd rather we be out of sight, Miss McKenzie. I don't want it known that I was here."

"Why?"

"I'll tell you in good time."

Molly shrugged and led the way out the back door, across the porch and into the yard toward the screened gazebo her father had built back in the twenties before the dust storms. She paused beside her mother's small rose garden.

"Beautiful roses." Hod reached down and touched the petal of a cabbage rose.

"My mother's pride and joy." Molly batted the moisture from her eyes. "It isn't as clean in here as it was before the dirt storms," she said as she opened the screen door and went inside. "But it's shady, and the flies can't get in." She took the cloth from around her glass and wiped off the bench.

Hod set his glass on the bench, removed his coat, and looked around for a place to hang it.

"There's a nail in the post beside the door."

After hanging his coat, he unbuttoned his shirt collar and loosened his tie. His shirt was wet with sweat, and she now could see that he wore a gun in a brown-leather shoulder holster. He rolled back the cuffs of his shirt, exposing forearms covered with fine dark hair. Then he stood silently, drinking his tea and looking at her. His eyes gleamed darkly from between a brush of thick lashes. His look was so long and so intense that she began to be irritated.

"What do you want to know? I need to get back to work."

"I imagine Mason and your aunt can tend to the store."

"What do you want to know?" she asked again.

"Everything. Start from when you first got up in the morning."

"I had biscuits and grape jelly. Will that help you catch the men who killed Mama and Daddy?"

He ignored her sarcasm. "Who all came into the store that morning?"

"The Browns, the Sadlers, and the Folkmanns. A couple stopped for gas. They were from around here, too. Daddy knew them."

"Did you see the car drive in?"

"The . . . gangsters' car? No. I didn't even hear it. I was listening to *Ma Perkins* on the radio."

"What time was that?"

"Ten-thirty."

"How long after that did you hear the shots?"

"A minute or two. I heard what I thought was . . . firecrackers. Daddy got in a shipment . . . that morning. When the screen door slammed, I looked out the window and saw the men. The stocky man had a high voice—almost like a woman's. I thought at the time the voice didn't go with the size of the man."

Hod nodded. "What did he say?"

"He said something to the other man about him being like a kid about his blasted soda pop. Only he didn't say blasted."

"The sheriff said one of the men left with something. Tell me about that."

"The stocky man had a box in his hand. I didn't realize it at the time, but it was the new box of SenSen Daddy just got in. There were about a hundred packets in it. Later I looked for the box, and it was gone. The . . .

killer . . . had taken it. Will knowing that help?" She turned her face away and cleared her throat.

"You bet. One has a fondness for soda pop, the other uses SenSen. I know exactly who they are."

Thank goodness! "That's a relief. When you catch them I want to be there when they're hanged."

"Knowing who they are and catching them are two different things."

Hod watched the changing expressions drift across her face. She wasn't picture-perfect, but pretty. Very pretty and totally feminine, but he suspected that a rod of steel lay alongside her backbone. He watched as she swept the rich dark brown hair from her neck with a nervous gesture. Her deep violet-blue eyes shone with tears that would haunt his thoughts during the days and nights to come, even more than her boyishly thin body and the small pointed breasts that nudged the bodice of her dress. A man would have a sweet armful when he held her. Hod frowned, annoyed with the direction his thoughts were taking him.

Sitting on the bench, legs crossed, Molly was acutely aware of being scrutinized by the intense dark eyes. She remained silent, but the swinging of her sandaled foot revealed her uneasiness.

"Well?" she finally said.

Hod cocked a brow. Her features were tranquil, but he felt the tension in her. Had she sensed his distraction? He was accustomed to being on guard, weighing his words, but somehow this situation seemed to have knocked him out of kilter. He mulled over the best way to approach her with the plan he had in mind. The success of it would depend on her trust in him.

Molly considered him thoughtfully as she waited for him to speak. Daddy would like him. He was a man who would be able to handle any situation he found himself in.

"Do you really want to catch the men who killed your parents?"

"That's a ridiculous question." She rose abruptly to her feet. "If your parents had been killed, wouldn't you want the men who did it caught and punished?" Anger made her eyes shine. Molly felt the moment freeze into silence.

"Of course, I would." He spoke softly, breaking the tension between them. Then, with his eyes holding hers, he lifted the glass and drank the last of his tea.

"Well?"

"I need your help."

"I've told you everything I know."

"There is more you can do. I would like for you to talk to a reporter from the *Kansas City Star* and tell him that you got a good look at the men who killed your folks and that you can identify them." His dark gaze met hers evenly.

"They would print it . . . and the killers would see it." She spoke without the slightest bit of emotion.

"It would be dangerous. They will want to . . . eliminate a witness."

Molly was silent. She looped a strand of hair behind her ear, an acknowledgment of her inner turmoil, but she answered without hesitation.

"You . . . want to use me for bait?" She smiled. "It's all right. I'll do whatever it takes."

"You'll have as much protection as I can give you."

"I'd do it without your protection. I've got Daddy's shotgun. If I get either one in my sights, they'll get both barrels."

His answering smile lent a fleeting warmth to his features. He studied her for a long moment. She faced him, refusing to look away. *She may think that she could shoot a man now, but could she, if push came to shove? It's hard to take a life, even that of scum like Pascoe or Norton.*

"It's not a sure thing that they'll come," he finally said. "But I'd bet on it."

"I don't want Aunt Bertha to be here."

"That's up to you . . . and her. I'd send you both away, but someone in the area may know someone in KC and pass the word that you're not here. The paper could get hold of it."

"And they'd print it?"

"Hell, yes! They want to sell papers and don't give a damn if I make an arrest unless it's a blood-and-guts shoot-out they can spread over the front page and print out in an extra."

"They had extras sometimes in Wichita. It was kind of spooky to wake up in the night hearing: 'Extra, extra, read all about it.' I always thought the worst had happened."

"Like what?"

"Oh, that the world was coming to an end or . . . something." Long slender fingers plucked at the collar of her dress near where the pulse beat rapidly in her throat. "I'm not leaving here. You'd better understand that right now."

"I didn't think you would." Hod took his coat off the nail and slung it over his shoulder.

"When can I expect the reporter?"

"I'll call him tonight. It'll be a week or so. He'll want a picture—" He cut off his words at the loud blast of a car horn. "Who is that?"

"Sounds like Walter, the iceman. He comes about this time of day."

"What's his name?"

"Walter Lovik. Why?"

"Who else comes here on a regular basis beside the postman?"

"The soda-pop man comes on Wednesdays during the summer."

"Where do you get your goods?"

"From a wholesaler in Liberal."

"Do you call in the order?"

"We mail it in, and it's delivered when they have a load coming this way." Molly drew in a shallow, aching breath. "Daddy went down there . . . sometimes."

"So you own a truck?"

"Yes."

"Is there enough room in that shed for another car?"

"Yes."

"How many on your telephone line?"

"Maybe twelve or fifteen. Some have had to drop off, because money is so tight. You ask a lot of questions."

"It's my job. I don't want the iceman to know I'm here."

"Then I'd better get in there. He's a talker and will want to shoot the breeze for a while."

"Molly," he said as she passed him, "this is our chance to get two killers put away. I'll do my best to keep them from getting to you."

She shrugged as she looked into his eyes. This close she could see small specks of light in the black. *What kind of man is he? What does he do when he's not hunting gangsters? Does he have children? Does his wife worry about him?*

"I mean that." He spoke quietly and sincerely, his hand resting for a minute on her shoulder. Her pale, calm face was turned toward him. He felt as though he were drowning in her magnificent eyes, the waters closing over him.

Molly left the gazebo quickly. She looked over her shoulder once on the way to the store. Hod Dolan had come out and was watching her. The man confused her. Had he sensed the tempestuous spin of her thoughts during that last moment?

Hod stared after her feeling that they had shared something warm and intimate. It was ridiculous, but he'd sensed a kindred spirit in this woman he scarcely knew. He'd not felt anything near that with any other woman, even those with whom he'd been physically intimate. He shook his head more to clear it than to deny his thoughts.

Molly came into the back of the store shortly after the iceman entered by the side door. He was a feisty young man with bright red hair and merry blue eyes. The sleeves of his shirt were cut off near the shoulders, showing thick muscular arms. One hand grasped the handle of the ice tongs. The iron fingers of the tongs gripped the large block of ice he carried on his back. The heavy leather shield between him and his burden had a pocket on the bottom to catch water dripping from the ice.

"Hi there, sweetheart," he said to Bertha, who had moved out of the way to let him pass. "Look at this nice clean piece I picked out just for you. Not a speck of sawdust on it."

"Hello, yourself. You're an hour late."

"Howdy, Sheriff. You here lookin' after my girl? How are ya, sugarpuss?"

"Just a holdin' my breath till you got here," Bertha answered easily.

"I'm here now, honey. Ya gonna give me a kiss?"

"I sure am, *honey*! Right up the side of your head with this wet dish towel."

"Now, sugar, that ain't nice a'tall. You don't need to be in a snit 'cause I'm a little late."

Walter swung the heavy block of ice off his back and set it on the edge of the cooler. With a large hand he scooped out the small chunk of ice that remained and slid the fifty pounds in place.

"I've been saving a nice big bucket of chips for ya, darlin'. Will that rate me a glass of tea?" With a pick, he split the small chunk of ice so it would fit alongside the big one.

"It depends on how big a bucket of chips," Bertha shot back sassily.

"You're a hard woman, love. Do you need a chunk for your icebox?"

"Twenty-five pounds should take care of it."

The sheriff stood back, waiting for the young iceman

to return from the truck. This was a side of Bertha McKenzie he'd not seen on his two previous visits to the store. She was bantering with Lovik as if she'd known him all her life. Had she known him before she came to the store a few short weeks ago? The sheriff frowned. Was she one of those women who preferred younger men? He turned his head when Molly moved up beside him. Then shifted his glance to the empty doorway.

"Hi, Walter."

"Molly, love. Bertha's bein' mean to me today."

"Not too mean to bring a pitcher of tea to the porch. Huh, Aunt Bertha? It's cooler out there."

"Give me a bucket, Molly darlin', and I'll get you some nice clean chips."

"Here's one." Molly grabbed a new bucket and blocked the aisle leading to the back of the store. "We appreciate that, Walter." She shoved the bucket into his hands.

"Enough to let me take you to the picture show down at Liberal on Saturday?"

"You're flirtin' again. I don't think your wife would be too pleased about that."

"She'd not know it, or care if she did, love. She packed up and went home to her mama."

"I'm sorry, Walter."

"Don't be, sugar. It was bound to happen." He held his arms out wide. "I'm available, girls. Now don't both of you rush at me at once!"

"Get the chips, Romeo," Bertha said drily, but managed a smile.

"I'll bring 'em in." Mason followed Walter to the door. "And *Romeo* can go around to the porch and sit with Molly."

"Bertha's my girl." Walter playfully slapped the sheriff on the back as they left the store. "Are you tryin' to cut me out?"

As soon as Walter and the sheriff left the store, Hod Dolan slipped in the back door. Bertha opened her mouth to speak, but closed it when he shook his head. Molly pointed toward the storage room, and Hod disappeared inside.

"What's goin' on?" she whispered.

"Tell you later," Molly whispered back. "He doesn't want *anyone* other than you, me, and the sheriff to know he's been here."

"Lord o'mercy. Why is that?"

"Tell you later."

"For crying out loud—"

"He has a plan to catch the dirty devils who killed Mama and Daddy, and he wants me to help," Molly whispered.

"Help him . . . catch— I hope I didn't hear that right."

"Give me the tea. Walter's coming back in."

Chapter
Three

Bertha backed her new '34 Ford out of the shed behind the store. She had been driving since the early twenties, but this was her first new car. She had bought it when she sold her house in Wichita. The shiny black two-door sedan was her pride and joy. Bertha stopped in front of the store and waited for Molly to hang out the CLOSED sign and lock the door. After checking the lock on the gas pump, Molly got into the car.

"It's a shame everything has to be locked up nowadays. Daddy always left the gas pump unlocked in case someone ran out of gas. I don't remember anyone ever taking any and not leaving the money."

"Times have changed, sugarfoot. World's getting meaner." Bertha eyed with approval the round lace-edged neck of her niece's flowered dress and the short puffed sleeves. "You look might pretty this morning."

"I don't feel very pretty." Molly straightened her

small-brimmed hat and smoothed her skirt over her thighs with white-gloved hands. "I'm worried because we haven't heard from Mr. Dolan or his reporter."

"Oh, you'll hear from him. Can't say that I think much of a man who'd set a girl up as bait to catch a murderer." Bertha sniffed in disdain.

"He said I'd have protection. Besides, if he can catch them, it may save the life of someone else." Molly looked over at her aunt's rosy face and down to the locket that rested on her ample bosom. Inside was a picture of the lover she had lost so long ago. "I wish you'd go away for a while, Aunt Bertha. I couldn't bear it if something happened to you."

"Are you out of your mind? I'm not leaving you here by yourself, and that's that."

When her aunt got that stubborn look on her face, Molly knew that there was no use arguing . . . for now, and changed the subject.

"I'm not looking forward to sitting in a hot church for a couple of hours."

"When that old windbag gets to rantin', he don't know when to quit. If he had any sense at all, he'd cut it short on these hot days."

"You just don't like him."

"I don't. His eyes are too close together."

Molly laughed. "Good enough reason, I guess."

The brimstone-colored road cut a path between golden fields of wheat. A ghostly hand waved to them as they passed a tan glove tied to the head of an iron bed frame that served as a gate to the Andrews farm. Against a far horizon, under a blue sky of low-flying clouds, was a long mountain ridge that, in outline, was broken and crumbled.

Beyond the fields, a sea of short, dried grass rolled back on each side of the road. No trees grew this far back from the river, and the shadows of clouds created dark patches on the open, sun-yellowed grassy plain. Molly and Bertha might as well have been traveling across a space as empty and limitless as the sky except for a small cluster of cattle and a windmill silhouetted against the blue.

They turned off the main road into Pearl, Kansas. Set well back from the bank of the Cimarron River, it was a scant four miles from the McKenzie store. It had been a typical hell-raising frontier town in its heyday, but the population of five thousand of fifty years ago had dwindled to less than half that number. A dozen buildings lined each side of main street. The newest in town was a square two-storied schoolhouse built by the WPA. Scattered around the business district were plank houses, most weathered to a dull gray. Those on the outer edge had a few chickens picking in the yards and a cow staked out nearby.

The town dated back to the day when a preacher, heading for Santa Fe, had camped along the riverbank in a grove of cottonwood trees. While there, his wife was bitten by a rattlesnake and died. He took that as a sign that the Lord wanted him to build a church right there and that a town would follow. First came a saloon, then another and another. Soon the town became a watering hole for travelers heading for the Sante Fe trail. Later a post office was established to serve the wheat farmers and ranchers in the area and the town was officially named for the preacher's wife.

One of the saloons now had become a billiard parlor and the other one a restaurant. Although Congress had legalized the sale of 3.2 beer in 1933, Kansas remained a *dry* state by statute of local option.

Alongside the road near the church, a big yellow dog lay stretched out in a puddle of shade. He closed his eyes when they passed and didn't open them again until the dust from their passing had drifted away. Bertha angle-parked the Ford alongside a few other cars and short-bedded trucks. A few families from the surrounding farms and ranches had come to church in wagons. The teams were staked out beyond the small cemetery behind the church. Molly took a moment to gaze at the impressive monument that identified the McKenzie block of lots in the cemetery. The sight of the two ungrassed graves of her parents brought a shine of tears to her eyes.

"Looks like there's a good crowd today," Molly remarked as she got out of the car.

"What else is there to do on Sunday around here?" Bertha swiped at the dust on the radiator cap with her handkerchief. "I'll have to wash the car when we get home," she grumbled.

"On Sunday?" Molly teased.

"I'll put a sack over my head, and the Lord won't know it's me."

Molly wiped the smile from her face as she entered the church. She and Bertha slipped into a pew near the back and sat down. They were scarcely seated when the congregation stood to sing. Bertha opened the song book and shared it with Molly. The pianist played a short prelude, then the song-leader burst forth in song, waving his arm in time with the music. The voices of the congregation filled the small church.

"Shall we gather at the riv . . . er. The beau-ti-ful, the beau-ti-ful riv . . . er. Gather with the saints at the riv . . . er, that flows—"

Molly sang without looking at the hymnbook. She had been coming to this church all her life and knew most of the songs. She also knew most of the fifty people who made up the congregation . . . some better than others. Across the aisle her best friend, Ruth Hoover, a high-school teacher, was trying to catch her eye. *Talk to you later*, she mouthed. Molly nodded. The two had been friends since grade school. Ruth had come out to the store when Molly's parents were killed and stayed with her until her aunt arrived.

The song ended. Molly and Bertha sat down. In front of them young Matthew Klein decided that he no longer wanted to sit quietly in his mother's lap and struggled to get down. She held him and whispered urgently for him to be quiet. Finally, she took a cracker from her pocket and gave it to him. The child settled back and munched on it quietly.

At the front of the church, the minister's children were preparing to sing. The girls wore white stockings and pink hair ribbons. The boys, with slicked-down hair and wearing freshly ironed shirts, looked as uncomfortable as if they'd been asked to swallow a frog. In the front pew twelve-year-old Otis held his baby brother while Charlotte lined the other children up according to height. As distasteful as it was to sit and hold his baby brother, Otis had far rather be doing that than lining up with his siblings to sing. *Thank goodness old Aunt Gladys had convinced their father that she was ailing this morning and unable to come to church.*

The pianist played a few notes and the youngsters began to sing. *"Jesus loves me, this I know. For the Bible tells me so. Little ones to Him belong. They are weak, but He is strong."*

Preacher Howell's elderly sister had come to stay with the family after his wife died, but the bulk of the responsibility for the children rested on young Charlotte's thin shoulders. The preacher's household was well organized. Molly had to give him credit for that. All of the children had responsibilities matched to their abilities. They were kept clean and well fed. The ones in school were good students, according to Ruth.

Molly's thoughts wandered during the rest of the service. It had been ten days since Hod Dolan had been to the store, and she had heard nothing from the reporter who was to interview her. Hod Dolan didn't seem to be the kind of man who would start something and not follow through with it.

She had thought about him quite a lot. His face was sharply etched in her memory. His dark eyes beneath black, level brows had seemed to see right into her mind. His mouth as much as his eyes had set the tone of him. It was firm and unsmiling. He was hard and tough. He would have to be, Molly thought with a pang, to do the work he did. Her instincts told her to trust him to set the trap that would catch the killers of her parents, but she was impatient for something to happen.

"You're twitching like a nervous cat," Bertha whispered, and looked at the watch pinned to the bosom of her dress. "And I've got an itch I can't scratch. Isn't that windbag ever going to run out of air? It's a quarter after twelve."

"All stand for the final hymn."

Finally the service was drawing to an end.

"It's about time," Bertha murmured loudly enough for everyone around her to hear. She got stiffly to her feet.

During the final chorus of the hymn, the preacher walked down the aisle to the door so that he could greet each of the worshipers as they left the church. Molly and Bertha, the last to arrive, were the first to leave.

"Miss McKenzie, it's good to see you." The minister clasped Bertha's hand.

"Shouldn't be any surprise to you. I been here every Sunday for the month."

"Yes, yes, so you have." His eyes had already dismissed Bertha and settled on Molly. "Dear child, how are you? You're looking rather peaked. Are you not sleeping well?"

"I'm fine." Molly tugged on her hand, but he held it tightly.

"I worry about you being out at that store . . . all alone."

"I'm not alone. Aunt Bertha is with me."

"It's not a safe place for you, my dear. Times being what they are."

"Good-bye, Reverend. I enjoyed the sermon." Molly had pulled her hand from his, crossed her fingers, and stepped outside the church before she told the lie.

The Reverend Howell was pudgy with an appealing, soft-featured face, twinkling blue eyes, and a sweet smile showing surprisingly good teeth. His thick, light wavy hair, brushed back from his forehead, rose in a high pompadour. He was at least thirty pounds overweight, a testimony to the fact that some of his parishioners tithed with vegetables, meat, and eggs, and he ate well. At one time he had been a barber, but now he leased the front part of the shop out on a percentage and kept the back part for his clock-repair business. He had found that being a barber required regular hours, and he cherished his free time.

Aunt Bertha was right, Molly thought. His attitude toward her had changed of late. She hadn't noticed earlier because she'd had so much on her mind. The idea of his thinking that she'd be interested in him! Not in a million years! The thought of having those soft fat hands touch her made Molly's stomach queasy.

"I'll be out to see you soon," Preacher Howell called.

"I just bet he will," Bertha snorted.

"Wait a minute, Aunt Bertha. I want to see Ruth."

While they waited for Ruth to make her way through the line, a man leading a horse came from the back of the church. Molly glanced at him, then looked back. She'd never seen him before. He was not young—late twenties, she guessed. He wore tan pants, a striped shirt, and a string tie. He was stuffing a white handkerchief in his pocket when his dark eyes met hers. He put his fingers to the brim of his Stetson hat in acknowledgment and swung into the saddle.

"He's a new face around here, isn't he?" Molly asked, as Ruth walked up beside her.

"Yes. He just got here. He stays out at Morrison's ranch. Mr. Morrison told Daddy that he works for the government."

"Can't the government afford for him to have a car?"

Ruth shrugged. "Guess not. He rides that horse everywhere he goes. He's not bad-looking."

"Probably has a wife and six kids stuck away someplace. Hard as nails or I miss my guess," Bertha said. "Not a man to be tied down."

"I didn't know you knew so much about men, Miss McKenzie. Tell me more so I can get one." Dimples appeared in both of Ruth's cheeks when she smiled.

"I ran a boardinghouse for twenty years. I know enough about men to fill a book. That'n would be a hard nut to crack."

"Hey, you all. I'm not setting my cap for him. Although he's the most interesting thing to come around in a while. The pickings are slim here."

Ruth was a curvaceous, hazel-eyed girl with dark blond hair that she wore in a straight short bob, parted on the side and held back with a single barrette. She had given up trying to be willowy like Molly and was content with herself the way she was. Ralph Hoover, her father, one of the few ranchers in the area who hadn't succumbed to the temptation to plow his virgin range to grow wheat and cash in when the prices were high, had been able to send his only daughter to teacher's college.

She had returned to teach in the Pearl school. Some said it wasn't fair for her to take a job when there were others looking for work who didn't have a well-to-do daddy to take care of them. All had to admit, however, that Ruth was an excellent teacher. Some students had stayed in high school this past year because of her encouragement.

"I wanted to tell you about the dance a week from Saturday night." Ruth's voice trailed off as a man and a girl came out of the church and headed for a car parked across the road.

Molly's heart went out to Ruth. She had been in love with Tim Graham since high school. They'd gone together for a year before she went off to college. When she returned two years later, he was going out with one of the Bruza twins, a tall, slender dark-haired girl who was the complete opposite of Ruth. Jennifer was a conniver, and sweet only when it suited her purpose. Ruth was independent and self-reliant.

Teetering on high heels and clinging to Tim's arm, Jennifer, better known as Jen, smiled sweetly at Molly and Ruth as they passed. Tim tipped his hat and would have paused, but Jen tugged on his arm.

"Come on, sugar. Mama's waitin' dinner."

"She looks like the cat who swallowed the canary," Bertha remarked.

"I heard that they're engaged." In spite of herself, Ruth couldn't keep the echo of pain from her voice. "If he had to choose one of *them*, why couldn't it have been Janythe. She's the virgin. Jen's the slut."

"Who said they're engaged?"

"Jan told Gloria at the beauty shoppe."

"Oh, well. It's not official. I'm sure Tim will see through her and realize that she's a selfish little . . . little—"

"—Skinny, nasty bitch!" Ruth said angrily. "If he's such a weak fool, he deserves her. About the dance and barbecue. It's being put on by the Cattlemen's Association. They're going to pit-cook a steer and bring in a band from Liberal. Proceeds will go to the library. Want to come?"

" 'Course, we do," Bertha said quickly. "How much are the tickets?"

"Two for a dollar, and it includes the food. I'm selling. If I sell twenty, I get in free."

"Count on us," Bertha replied, as Molly began to protest.

"Aunt Bertha, I don't think—"

"You need to get out and mix with the young folk. So do I. I'm not all that dang old, you know."

"I don't feel much like . . . mixing."

"Your mother and daddy would be the first to tell you that you can't grieve for them forever. You're young and pretty and smart—"

"—You're saying that because you love me. But—"

"No buts." Bertha dug into her purse and shoved a dollar bill in Ruth's hand.

"I like this woman." Ruth tore two tickets from a roll and gave them to Bertha. "Uh-oh! Old Archie's getting rid of the last of his congregation, and he's got his eye on us. Or rather, you, Molly. We'd better get out of here."

Ruth hurried to where her parents were waiting, and Molly and Bertha climbed into the car. The preacher reached the sidewalk as Bertha was backing the Ford out onto the road. He stood watching them drive away, his hands on his hips. Looking straight ahead and refusing to wave, Molly failed to see the flash of anger that came over the preacher's usually smiling face. It remained only an instant, and when he turned to speak to one of his "flock," he was smiling again.

"Told you that old fool had an eye on you." Bertha stepped on the gas, stirring up a cloud of dust.

"I feel sorry for Charlotte. She's only fourteen. If he doesn't marry again soon, she'll be stuck there taking care of her brothers and sisters and miss the chance of having a life of her own."

"How many kids did you say he has?"

"Ten, including a set of seven-year-old twins. Two older brothers from his first marriage left home years ago. I didn't know them. They were a lot older than me."

"Horny old cuss, ain't he?"

Molly took off her hat, let the wind whip her hair, and stared out the window. Would the soreness in her heart ever be healed? She dreaded going back to the empty rooms above the store. What would she do with the rest of the day? She would scrub the floor while the store was closed if not for the fact that her father had frowned on working on Sunday.

"Sunday is a day of rest," he had told her. "No work will be done in this store unless someone comes in who is out of gas."

Bertha slowed the car. "Now what the heck does he want?"

George Andrews had stepped out from the iron bedstead that served as a gate leading to his ranch. He waved to them.

"Someone may be hurt."

"He doesn't act any too smart to me."

"Daddy said he was smart as a whip. I'll admit that he doesn't look it. But I'm sure he's harmless."

When the car stopped, George stood where he was and stared at Molly for a long moment. He was a man in his late thirties, but he looked older. He dressed the same on Sunday as he did on a working day. His overalls, however, were fastened on both shoulders today. The long-sleeved underwear he wore beneath the overalls had been washed with something red that had faded it to mottled pink. The small cuts on his weathered cheeks suggested that he had scraped off his whiskers with a dull razor.

George and his sister, Gertrude, were a strange pair. Little of their homestead, set well back from the road and surrounded by a grove of cottonwood trees, was visible from the road. Gertrude was much older than George. She was never seen in public. Molly had heard her parents say that Gertrude, many years ago, had returned home in disgrace.

"Hello, Mr. Andrews. Is something wrong?" Molly doubted that she had ever exchanged a dozen words with the man away from the store other than "hello" or "goodbye." He'd been coming there ever since she could remember, but he had never tried to engage her in conversation when they met in town.

"Miss Molly." He put his fingers to the bill of the flat cap he wore. "I . . . thought ya ort to know . . . there's a feller sittin' in a car up at the store." When George talked his lips barely moved so that his words came out in a murmur.

"Has he been there long?"

"Since right after ya went by goin' to church."

"What kind of car?"

"Old beat-up Model T. Radiator was boilin' over."

"Why'd you go to the store if you knew we'd gone to church?" Bertha leaned over so she could look at him.

"I been . . . huntin' for my dog. She went off to have pups."

"How is your sister, Mr. Andrews?" Molly asked in an attempt to soften Bertha's sharp inquiry.

"All right. Ya can have one of Stella's pups if ya want."

"I don't know. I've been thinking about getting a watchdog, but I need an older dog."

"Stella'd make ya a good watchdog."

"I appreciate the offer, Mr. Andrews, but I don't need a litter of pups."

"I'll take the pups soon as they're weaned, and if I tell Stella to stay and watch out for ya, she will."

"I'll think about it. Thanks for the warning about the man at the store. He could be gone by now, or maybe he's out of gas."

"I'll go up there with ya—"

"I don't think that's necessary, but thanks."

Bertha moved the car ahead slowly at first, then increased the speed.

"Might be you should've taken him up on his offer."

"Robbers won't come to the store in an old beat-up car with the radiator boiling over. It's probably someone out of gas."

"From now on, I'm carrying that pistol of Roy's in my purse."

Bertha slowed the car as they approached the store. A topless Model T Ford was parked in the shade of the huge elm tree. All they could see were two long legs hanging over the door on the driver's side.

"We better stay in the car till we find out what this bird is doing here." Bertha eased the car up alongside the Ford.

A man lay asleep on the front seat. The shoes at the end of the long legs hanging over the door were well worn, as were the tan britches he wore. His open shirt exposed a hairless chest, but there was a stubble of whiskers on his face. Light blond hair glistened with sweat.

When Bertha pressed down on the horn, the man came up out of the seat as if he'd been stung by a wasp. It was no wonder. The blast of the extra loud horn that Bertha had insisted be put on her new car made Molly clap her hands over her ears.

"Golly, Aunt Bertha! That horn's loud enough to wake the dead!"

The man sat up and rubbed his hands over his face and his fingers through his hair. He buttoned his shirt and crammed it down into the waistband of his britches before he climbed over the closed door of the car. He was tall . . . very tall and very thin. He had long arms to go with his long legs. His shoulders were narrow and his hands big.

"What'er you doin' here?" Bertha demanded.

"Waiting for Miss Molly McKenzie. Do you know when she'll be back?"

"I do."

"Well—?"

Molly opened the door and got out. "I'm Molly McKenzie. Who are you?"

"Clyde Floy from the *Wichita Eagle*."

"How do we know that?" Bertha grumbled. "You don't look old enough to be out of high school."

"It's a problem I face all the time." The grin that spread over his boyish face exposed white teeth, one with a gold cap. "I'm here to interview Miss McKenzie and take her picture."

"I was told that a reporter would come from Kansas City," Molly said.

"You'll have to make do with me. The *Star* picks up my feature stories from the *Eagle*."

"Come on into the store."

He stood with hands on hips looking at Bertha's car.

"Dandy car. I see you got it from Lee's Ford in Wichita. How fast will it go?"

"I had it up to seventy-five once or twice coming over here."

"I get forty out of my old T." He reached into the back of his car and picked up a notebook.

When Clyde Floy climbed up the steps to the store, Bertha was right behind him. She wasn't letting Molly go into the building alone with this stranger even if he did look like a wet-eared kid.

"Can I buy a bottle of pop?"

"Sure. But you're welcome to have dinner with us. We've got lemonade in the icebox."

"To tell the truth, I'm starved. There's not much open between here and Wichita on Sunday."

"Aunt Bertha cooks up something on Saturday so that we don't have to bother on Sunday. It won't be fancy, but it'll be filling." Molly took off her hat and led the way to the stairs in the back of the store.

The quarters above the store were divided into four large rooms. The parlor across the front, two bedrooms in the middle, and the kitchen across the back. The toilet and the bathtub were downstairs in the storage room as was the new Maytag washing machine Roy had bought his wife for a birthday surprise the month before he was shot.

"Go on into the front room," Bertha said. "You get a breeze from three directions in there. I'll spread a cloth on the library table, and we can eat in there."

Molly saw the newspaperman looking around the room, noting its lace panel curtains and comfortable chairs. The radio cabinet stood against the wall, the antenna wire extending out the window. He walked over to peer into the glass-fronted bookcase beside the Victrola. At one side of the couch, a small round table, covered with a long silk-fringed scarf held an electric lamp with a square stained-glass shade.

"Sit down, Mr. Floy. Turn on the radio if you like. I'll help Aunt Bertha."

In the kitchen, Molly flipped open the top of the small icebox and chipped off enough ice for three glasses. She filled them from the pitcher of lemonade.

"What do you think, Aunt Bertha?" Molly murmured.

"Well . . . I think he's all right. Doesn't look mean."

"I thought Mr. Dolan was going to send a reporter from Kansas City."

"Well, you got one from Wichita. Here, spread this on the library table." She handed Molly a cloth. "I'll bring in the potato salad and the sandwiches."

Molly decided that she liked Clyde Floy. While she talked, his pencil flew across the page, taking down her words in fluid shorthand. Having completed the shorthand course at the business college, she appreciated his proficiency.

"That's all I can tell you," Molly said, after she had covered what had happened that hot June day, omitting the details about the pop and the SenSen as Mr. Dolan had instructed. She described the men and repeated several times that she could identify them and hoped to see them hanged.

"Do you plan to stay here and run the store?"

"Yes, I do. I was born here and have worked in the store since I was ten years old. I plan to stay in business as long as I can."

"Do you have help?"

"Only my aunt, who came here from Wichita to stay with me."

"Off the record." He looked earnestly into her eyes. "You're asking for it, you know."

"I know."

"I'd not run this if Dolan hadn't asked me to."

"I know," she said again.

"I want to take your picture standing on the porch. The sun is about in the right spot for a good picture."

"All right. I'll comb my hair."

After the picture session the reporter sat on the porch and told them some of his interesting experiences. He seemed reluctant to leave. It was late evening before he packed his camera equipment in his car.

"I'd rather drive at night," he said. "It's cooler and easier on the T."

"Will you get all the way to Wichita on one tank of gas?"

"I know a fellow in Pratt that'll open up for me. I'll sleep awhile there," he said as he filled his gas tank.

"Send me a paper."

"I will. Dolan's counting on the story getting a front page slot in the *Kansas City Star*. I'll send a copy." He hesitated then said, "What's the address here?"

"Route number one, Pearl."

"You're a sitting duck out here, you know."

"I know."

"Dolan's a good man. He knows what he's doing, but I'd hate like hell being a part of getting you ladies killed."

"How well do you know Mr. Dolan?" Molly asked.

"Only by reputation. He was in on the capture of the Barrow gang down in Louisiana last spring. I don't know if he was in on the ambush, but he was responsible for tracking them. Frank Hamer, the famous lawman, says Dolan's one of the best."

"We ain't gonna be sittin' here on our hands waitin' for 'em to shoot us. Soon as Molly gives the nod that it's them, I'll be blastin' away with that old blunderbuss."

"I'll not be comin' 'round here for a while," Clyde said with a laugh.

"Don't worry, Mr. Floy. We'll be careful. I just hope they take the bait, and we get a chance at them. How did you happen to get so chummy with a Federal man?"

"Hod saw some of the pictures I took after what they call Black Sunday. He stopped by and we talked. He's got family on a farm in Nebraska and a brother down in Oklahoma. Guess they're all just holding on, hoping Roosevelt's New Deal will make things better.

"Black Sunday. Lordy! I'll never forget April 14. It was bad enough in Wichita, but my brother said that here it was a nice clear day. Then suddenly a black blizzard appeared on the horizon, moving toward them. There was no sound except for the nervous fluttering of birds, no wind, as the solid wall of darkness approached. When the cloud of dust engulfed them, it was as dark as night at four o'clock in the afternoon.

"I had holed up in Pratt. The next day I went down to Liberal and then on to Guyman and took pictures. One is of a house with sand drifted up to the middle of the door. A woman holding a baby and frightened children clinging to her skirts are standing in the yard. Another is of a long line of just the tops of fence posts, a confused chicken hawk sitting on one. Darn good pictures, even if I do say so." He grinned. "I'm trying to record a pictorial history of this era because there's never been anything like it."

"I wonder if it'll ever be over."

"Oh, yes. They are sowing grass seed and letting the land go back to what it was . . . pasture and range land. I give Roosevelt credit for pushing through reforms that should pull the country out of the Depression."

"Well, you can't give Roosevelt credit for these sandwiches. Here's a couple to eat along the way." Bertha handed him a package wrapped in a Colonial bread wrapper. "If I was still in Wichita, I'd fatten you up, boy. Where did you say you were staying?"

"At Mrs. Beams' Bed and Board at Kellogg and Twenty-second."

"It's no wonder you're skinny as a rail. Bessie Beams is known for setting a stingy table."

"I might just have to come back here for another story." He grinned his boyish grin.

"Do that, sonny." Bertha lifted her brows. "I saw a lot of things while I was running my boardinghouse. Too bad you're not writin' for the funny papers."

"I might give it a shot if I could get someone to draw the pictures." His boyish grin appeared again. "As much as I'd like to stay and mooch another meal, I'd better be on my way. Good-bye and good luck, ladies." He waved as he drove away."

"Nice boy," Bertha said.

"I have the feeling he's not a *boy* even if he does look like one."

"He was giving you the eye."

"Come on. He wanted to get his story."

"He's still a man."

"A second ago you said that he was a boy." Molly laughed, and put her arm around her aunt. "The baited hook is out there, Aunty. Now we'll see if we reel in anything."

* * *

In Kansas City Hod Dolan lay on his back and watched the swishing blades of the ceiling fan stir the hot dry air. Sundays were boring. The chief of his division insisted that his staff do as little work as possible on Sunday. After morning mass there was not much to do. Hod had been lying on his bed for an hour, hands behind his head. Thinking.

Today Clyde Floy was going to Pearl to interview Molly. He didn't know when he'd stopped calling her Miss McKenzie in his mind. Dear God! Had he done the right thing? He would have called off the whole plan after he met her if the chief hadn't insisted that he go through with it.

Pascoe and Norton are holed up somewhere in the area. They know that the woman is the only thing tying them to the killings. It's all we've got, and if she's as smart as you say she is, she'll be all right with you there to see to it.

Hod was unable to explain to himself—why after a half hour of conversation with her he was overcome by the desire to know everything about her. Everything.

It was really more than merely wanting to know. It was a compelling need, and it was crazy. He was twenty-eight years old and acting like a damn fool. She was constantly in his thoughts, and he was more than a little ashamed of this budding obsession. He would be concerned for anyone being put in her position, he reasoned silently, but his excessive concern told him that he was more than casually interested in her, and not as a witness, but as a woman.

The thought struck him with the force of a kick in the stomach.

With each visit to his brother's home in Oklahoma, he had come away with a hunger to have what Tom had with his wife, Henry Ann. Tom's eyes sought his wife's when he entered a room. He managed to touch her when she was near. Tom had given his heart wholeheartedly to his Henry Ann as had Mike, their older brother who lived in Nebraska, given his to his Lettie.

It seemed to be the trait of the Dolan men. When they loved a woman it was an all-consuming love. Would it be the same with him? Was he in love with this slip of a girl? He'd not spent more than an hour alone with her.

Naw. Love didn't happen that fast.

The tightness in his chest was caused by worry about keeping her safe . . . and from the pleasant anticipation of seeing her again.

Chapter Four

To the Reverend Archie Howell anger was a waste of time and energy; still he was not at all pleased that old Mr. Yeager had held him in conversation, delaying him so that he'd not been in time to catch Molly before she left the church. The poor old man did not have much in his life to talk about other than his ailments, and he was hungry for sympathy. It was a shame, Archie mused, a puredee shame. *Why was life allowed to go on when it had no meaning?* As far as Archie was concerned, old man Yeager's useful days had ended. Just taking up space, the Reverend Howell thought, as he headed for home.

The Howells lived in a sprawling old ranch house with a porch on three sides. The town in its boom days had spread out until the house was less than a half mile from its edge.

The noon meal was over. The children, having changed into their everyday clothes, were going about their assigned tasks. No work was done on Sunday after the kitchen was tidied, nor were the children allowed to play boisterous games. There was no laughing or loud talk. During the afternoon the children were to sit quietly and read or sing hymns. Charlotte and Otis were responsible for keeping their young siblings quiet.

Archie walked across the kitchen to stand in the doorway of his sister's room. The small room off the kitchen was slightly larger than a pantry, but large enough to hold a single bed and a small chest. Gladys, Archie's senior by a dozen years, sat in a rocking chair beside the window, cooling herself with a cardboard fan. Gladys's life had not been happy, and she lamented about it constantly. She had never married, and since the deaths of their parents she had made her home with first one sibling and then the other. Opinionated and ill-tempered, with an attitude of self-pity, she was not pleasant to be around.

"Is the kitchen cleaned up yet? Did they get dishwater all over my clean floor?" Her sparse gray hair was pulled back into a tight knot at the back of her head. The hairy upper lip of her small mouth was constantly raised as if she were smelling something unpleasant.

"Charlotte will see that it's clean."

"Well . . . if they don't do a better job than they did this morning, I'll have to do it over." Her face puckered as if she were sucking on a sour pickle.

"If it wasn't cleaned properly, why didn't you tell me before we left for church?"

"You were reading your Bible and Charlotte was gettin' the kids ready. She don't pay no more attention to me than she would a stump. Thinks she's runnin' thin's 'round here. I ain't doin' nothin' to suit her and ain't since I come here," Gladys whined, and her shoulders rose and fell dejectedly.

"Has she been sassin' you?"

"I come here to take care of the baby, not be a slave," Gladys said, ignoring the question. "I ain't strong. Never was . . . not even in my prime. My back got broke-down long ago toting water and slopping hogs. Times my back and legs hurts so bad I can't stand it. I'm doing the cookin', and the ironin', 'cause I can sit down to do it. She ort to do the rest." Gladys worked the fan swiftly, creating a breeze that stirred the hair that had come loose from the knot at the back of her head.

"She's doing the washing . . . and the cleaning."

"Fiddle! She puts on a show when you're here. When you ain't, she gets her head in a book, and the younguns could tear down the house for all *she* cares. I ain't knowin' how long I'll be able to hold out. Nobody cares if *I'm* wore down to a nub. Nobody a'tall. You just try and get a woman to come here and do what I'm doin', and you'd be payin' out a pretty penny, I tell you."

Archie looked at his sister and wanted nothing more than to get her out of his house and never have to see that pinched, sour face or hear her whining voice again. *She wasn't well! Bullshit!* She was strong as a horse and ate like one. She didn't do anything if she could get one of the kids to do it.

"I just got my wind up . . . and had to have my say." Gladys dabbed at her eyes and let her lips tremble.

"I'll talk to Charlotte."

He backed out of the doorway and went to inspect the

kitchen. The girls had done a good job of cleaning up after the noon meal. They knew that they'd get the strop if they didn't. The rest of the house was clean and quiet. On the porch the girls were gathered around Charlotte. She was reading a story. The baby lay on a blanket, and Clara was fanning him with a straw hat. They were good children, he mused. Why wouldn't they be? He had trained them himself.

He had called on Gladys to come and stay after each of his wives had died, and she had stayed until he took another. Now just the two of them were left out of a family of six children, and there was nowhere else for her to go. Even when he took another wife, he was stuck with her . . . for as long as she lived.

It was a depressing thought.

"I'll be gone for a while, Charlotte. Keep the children quiet. Your aunt says she doesn't feel well."

"I will, Daddy."

Archie patted his eldest daughter on the head as he passed her. He doubted that she had sassed Gladys. Charlotte had developed into a lovely young lady, and woe to any rutting youth who tried to take her away from the family. She belonged here with her brothers and sisters. He supposed that she would have to quit school and take over if . . . something should happen to Gladys.

He was thinking more and more about Molly McKenzie. When he did, his pulse raced. When he took a wife this time, he'd not pick one that was used. His last wife, the mother of his three younger children, had turned to fat after her first child. He was glad to be rid of that one.

The preacher heard a giggle as he passed the shed and stuck his head in the door.

"What are you boys up to?" he demanded.

The two small boys standing beside Otis spun around fearfully.

"Nothin', Daddy." Otis turned and held out the thin skin of a rattlesnake. "I was explaining how snakes shed their skins."

"Where did you get that?" Archie frowned.

"I found it and thought it was something the boys should know about."

Archie's face relaxed. "That was thoughtful of you, Otis. You're a chip off the old block. I'll be gone for a while. First thing in the morning I want you boys to grind up that corn Mr. Brady brought over. We need chicken feed. The grinder's in good shape, isn't it? You cleaned and greased it?"

"Yes, sir."

Otis turned his back. "I ain't no chip off ya, you old . . . shit," he muttered as soon as his father left the door.

One of his brothers stuck out his tongue, the other put his thumb to his nose and waved his fingers.

"You guys better watch it," Otis cautioned. "If he catches ya, he'll beat the daylights outta ya."

"I'm goin' to run away when I get big," Harley, one of the seven-year-old twins declared.

"You got to get big first." Otis placed the snakeskin down on the box. "We 'bout got caught this time. Look and be sure he's gone."

The youngest boy peeked around the side of the shed and watched his father drive away.

"He's gone. Now can I look at the picture?"

"Don't tear it, and don't let Aunt Gladys get wind we got it. She'll tell Daddy. It'd tickle her to see us gettin' a whippin'." Otis pulled a page torn from a movie magazine out of his shirt and smoothed it out on the top of the box. The boys gazed down at the picture of a girl with spit curls and a Cupid's-bow mouth. Her dress was cut low, showing a generous amount of cleavage. She was posed with one foot on a chair showing her leg to mid-thigh. "Her name's Clara Bow. You can almost see her titties."

"And her twat. Golly! She's pretty. Has Charlotte seen it?"

"Where'd you hear that word?"

"Twat? I hear things," Harley said. "Boys at school talk about twats and peters."

"Holy cow!" The six-year-old looked at his brother with admiration.

"Charlotte told me to get rid of it. She said that if Daddy or Aunt Gladys found out about it, there'd be hell to pay."

"Did she really say . . . hell?"

"She did, but don't you be sayin' it." Otis looked sternly at the six-year-old. "You might slip and say it in front of someone."

"I won't." The child shook his head fearfully.

"Where'd ya get it, Otis?" Harley was thin and freckle-faced.

"Carl Palmer slipped it to me after Sunday school."

"Can I have it when you get through with it?"

"No. I'm going to tear it in little pieces after I show it to Alfred Wesson. Don't tell anyone about it, and don't let Charlotte know I showed it to you."

"How many more weeks until school starts?" Harley asked.

"Three."

"I'll be glad. I hate it here."

"Me too," his younger brother echoed.

"Well, ya just got to put up with it till I get old enough to get a job, and I'll take ya with me."

"Ya'd do that, Otis?"

" 'Course, I would. You're my brothers, ain't ya?"

"Charlotte said we got brothers older'n her. Why'd they leave? Why didn't they take us?"

" 'Cause ya wasn't born yet, silly."

"I wish they'd come back."

"I wish our maw hadn't died," Harley said wistfully.

"Why? So he could whip her legs with a willow switch? She didn't have no say." Otis folded the picture carefully and tucked it inside his shirt. "I think *he* was glad she died. He never cried 'cepts when someone was around to see him, and it didn't take him long to get another woman and more kids."

"Do you think he'll get us another maw?"

"I'd bet on it. He don't like sleepin' by hisself."

"Why?"

" 'Cause, well . . . 'cause he likes to make kids."

"Ya mean he likes to get hung up in 'em like those dogs did when they come smellin' 'round Daisy?"

"Somethin' like that."

"Golly-bill, Otis. I'd like to see it," the younger boy exclaimed.

"Don't be talkin' about that now."

"I won't. Otis, do you think God likes him and Aunt Gladys?"

The Reverend Howell hummed as he drove down the dusty road toward the farm where Walt Yeager had lived all his life, scrounging out a living on sixty acres. He had a few cows, a little corn patch, six head of hogs, and a garden. He had been alone since his wife's death more than ten years earlier. The couple had lost a son in France during the war and a daughter had left home never to be heard from again.

Mr. Yeager tithed ten percent of his meager earnings to the church, paying mostly with hog meat and chickens. That was all right with the preacher. Cash money was scarce, and he had a large family to feed.

Poor old man, the preacher mused. His plumbing had gone rusty on him. Archie chuckled at his assessment of Mr. Yeager's ailment. What in the world did he have to live for? When a man could no longer get it up to pleasure himself with a woman he might as well be dead.

The Lord giveth life and the Lord taketh it away.

The lane leading up to the small clapboard house was rutted. Dry lemon yellow weeds stood between the tracks. Flourlike dust, stirred by the wheels, swirled behind the car. The heat was wicked. It rolled up from the dusty road, giving the preacher a powerful thirst.

Archie pulled into the yard and turned off the motor. A few chickens scattered, then went about the business of finding something to eat. The squeaking of the windmill was the only sound other than the buzz of June bugs around the honeysuckle bushes.

Archie helped himself to a drink of water from the pump, then went up onto the porch and knocked on the door. He knocked again when he got no response, and called out.

"Mr. Yeager, are you here?"

"I'm here. Come in. I was just takin' a little nap." The old man held open the screen door, a smile of welcome on his whiskered face.

"I was a little concerned about you, Mr. Yeager," Archie said smoothly. "Thought I'd stop by and visit a bit."

"Good of you. I ain't been well. Got a misery in my shoulders, and my stomach ain't been right. Not been able to sleep nights either for getting up ever' whip-stitch to let water. I tell ya, my parts is all wearin' out. I ain't knowin' what I'll do when I can't do for myself no more."

"Don't worry about it now. And don't use up your strength standing. Sit down. I'll take a chair over here. We'll pray about it before I go."

"I don't know, Preacher. It just seems like ever'thin' piles on at once. Coons got in my cellar and just tore up jack. Wolves brought down two of my calves. I'm thinkin' that the good Lord is tryin' me."

"He does that sometimes, but He never piles on more than a person can bear, Mr. Yeager. And when He does, He finds a way to deliver you from it."

"I keep a hopin' that."

"You're a good man. You ready to meet your Lord?"

"That I am. I never cheated a man outta a dime. I ain't never hurt no livin' soul that I know of. I never lusted after no woman but my missus."

"That's saying a lot, Mr. Yeager. You are very well thought of in this community."

Archie watched the smile come to the weathered face, then got up and walked about the room, more sure than ever that the Lord had sent him here this day.

"You've let your clock run down." Archie opened the glass door, wound the clock and the chimes with the key and started the pendulum swinging. He turned the hands to the correct time, then went to look out the front window.

"I ain't had a good night's sleep since Black Sunday in April, Reverend Howell. I'm always thinking the dirt storm will come in the night and I'll be suffocated."

"If it comes, you'll be safe. You've nothing to worry about," Archie said patiently. He went slowly behind the chair where the old man sat resting his head back against a pillow.

"I'm glad ya come, Preacher. You always make me feel better."

"You'll get a good sleep tonight, Mr. Yeager."

Archie looked down on the near-bald head and to the work-worn hands that gripped the arms of the chair. He patted the old man's shoulder sympathetically before he snatched the pillow from behind his head and clamped it down over his face.

Archie was stronger than he looked. He wrapped his arms around the pillow and held on while Mr. Yeager thrashed his life away. Within minutes it was over. The old man's lifeless body went limp. Archie removed the pillow, let it drop to the floor, and moved around to look into the old man's staring eyes. Gently he closed the lids.

"Now you are at peace, my friend. You'll not hurt or be scared of the dust storms anymore."

With the body draped over his shoulder Archie carried it to the bedroom and placed it on the bed. He straightened the limbs, removed the worn boots, then knelt beside the body, clasping one of the old man's hands.

"Dear Lord," he prayed in his most humble voice, "I've brought you Mr. Yeager, who in life had nothing but pain and heartache. His life had no meaning, and he longed to be with his Savior. I did my best to see that he didn't suffer as he passed over. I'm asking you to open the Pearly Gates and take him to his heavenly home, where he can be once again with his wife and son. I'm asking this in Jesus' name. Amen."

Archie soothed the thin gray hair back from the lined weathered face and folded the gnarled hands on his chest.

"Taking your afternoon nap, Mr. Yeager? I know you're thanking me. It's all right. I was glad that I could take you from your misery to that joyous reunion in the sky. No, no. Don't thank me. I'll see that you get a real cryin' funeral, my friend."

Archie left the quiet house and went to the pump for another drink of water before he got in his car and headed back to town. There was always such a feeling of peace when he helped someone to get to the "other side." The kindness he had extended to Mr. Yeager would earn him another star in his crown.

He sang softly, *"When they ring those golden bells for you and me."*

After a while he sang more loudly in a clear baritone.

> *"Don't you hear the bells now ringing?*
> *Don't you hear the angels singing?*
> *Singing glory hallellujah . . . jubilee—"*

The evening service on Sunday was held after an hour-long meeting of the young people of the congregation. The discussion that evening, led by the choir director, Miss Armstrong, concerned how to raise money to pay for new hymnbooks.

"How many books do you want to buy?" The question was asked by Tim Graham.

"Forty to start, and they cost two dollars each."

"If we raise ten dollars a week over the next two months—"

"—Ten dollars!" Twelve faces turned toward Jen Bruza as if she had said a swearword in church. She clasped Tim's arm and looked as if she would cry.

"I . . . just thought—"

"You may as well ask us to raise a hundred." The young man who spoke was holding tightly to the hand of the girl he had been engaged to for a year and had been unable to wed because of the hard times.

"Jen was just making a suggestion." Tim patted the girl's hand.

"It's all right with me if she raises ten dollars. I'll be lucky if I raise one."

Charlotte glanced at her father to make sure he hadn't turned around to look at her before she whispered to her friend, Margaret, "Are you going to stay for church?"

"No. I came to see you."

"I'm not staying. One of the kids threw up, and Daddy said I could go home. Aunt Gladys says she's sick," Charlotte added, and wrinkled her nose. "I don't believe it. She just didn't want to come."

"Do you have to go straight home?"

Charlotte saw her father get to his feet and answered her friend without turning her head.

"Not . . . right away."

"Now, now," Preacher Howell said in a placating tone as he held his hands up to get attention. "We're making too much of this raising money for hymnbooks. We don't want it to be a burden on anyone. When I was down in Oklahoma preaching under a brush arbor we raised money by selling watermelons, sweet corn—"

"Preacher Howell, can I have a word with ya?" A man in overalls came hurriedly down the center aisle.

"Of course, Mr. Romig. Is something wrong?"

The man came close and spoke to the preacher in low tones. Preacher Howell's brows came together in a deep frown.

"No. Ah, no," he muttered. "Poor old man."

"Herman, his nephew, said to tell you he'd like to hold the service day after tomorrow here at the church."

"I'll announce it tonight. Thank you for coming by."

The Reverend Howell waited until Mr. Romig had left the church before he spoke. He clasped his hands together, held them up, and rested his chin on them for a moment, then lifted his head and looked at the ceiling. He longed to take credit for the extreme kindness he had extended to Mr. Yeager, but he knew that these unenlightened people would not understand. It was best to let his good deed go unheralded.

"Mr. Romig brought the news that our dear brother, Mr. Yeager, passed away this afternoon. He was here in church this morning and said that he had been under the weather lately. He asked me to stop by and look at his clock. He wasn't feeling well, and I didn't stay long. I advised him to take a nap, and that is where they found him. He died peacefully in his sleep. He will be missed, but we must take comfort knowing that he is in a better place.

"Service for Mr. Yeager will be held here at the church on Tuesday morning. Now, out of respect for a man who has been a member of this church for forty years, I think we should dismiss. Evening service will be held in an hour."

"Can you go now, Charlotte?"

"I'll have to tell Daddy first. I'll meet you outside."

Charlotte went to stand beside her father and wait until he turned to acknowledge her.

"I'm going home to see about Hester."

The preacher put his arm across her shoulders and tilted his head to gaze fondly at her.

"God gave me a treasure." He smiled at Miss Armstrong, who had been asking about the music for the funeral. "I don't know what I'd do without her. Go on home, honey. I'll be home as soon as the service is over."

Charlotte was glad to make her escape. The act her father put on about loving his children made her sick. She knew that he didn't mean a word of it. Outside she searched for Margaret and found her standing beside a tall boy wearing a dark blue shirt and a flat-billed cap.

Wally Wisniewski.

Her heart gave a frantic leap. Her father didn't like Wally or his mother. They didn't go to church, and Mrs. Wisniewski wore long earrings and loud clothing. They were foreigners, he said, even though Wally's grandparents were born in this country. She hesitated. If her father looked out the door and saw her talking to him, a whipping was sure to follow.

They were looking at her. She waved to Margaret and went quickly down the road and around the corner out of sight of the church. She stopped and waited, almost breathless, not daring to peek around the clump of honeysuckle bushes to see if Margaret had gotten the message. When she appeared with Wally strolling along beside her, Charlotte was tongue-tied.

"Hi, Charlotte. Why'd ya run for?"

Wally was a good-looking boy with wild dark hair and gray eyes. He and his mother had come to town several years ago and opened the restaurant. He usually wore a teasing grin on his face. His attitude was plain to all. They could like him or leave him—it made no difference to him. He had no special close friends and was terribly protective of his mother, spending long hours helping her at the restaurant.

Charlotte was startled to find his eyes locked on her and a teasing smile on his face. A rosy blush lit her suntanned cheeks.

"Ya don't want your old man to see you talkin' to me? Is that it?"

"Well . . . he just . . . don't think I'm . . . old enough—"

"How old are you?"

"Almost fifteen."

"Hey, I gotta go." Margaret began to back away. "See you both later."

" 'Bye, Marg. And thanks," Wally called.

"Why are you thanking her?"

"Don't you know? I'll walk you home, Char. A pretty girl like you shouldn't be out here in the dark by herself."

"It isn't completely . . . dark." Lack of breath was making her giddy, but she gathered her wits and began to walk down the road.

"It will be in a minute or two. Why don't the preacher like my mother?" The question came abruptly and surprised Charlotte.

"How do you know he doesn't like her?"

"He never comes into the restaurant, and he snubs her when he meets her on the street or at the post office. I thought preachers were supposed to like everyone."

"I'm . . . sorry—"

"Hey, it's not your fault. You never come in the restaurant, either."

"I never get to town . . . by myself. I've always got the kids."

"Are you coming to the cattlemen's dance?"

"Heavens no! Daddy would never let me."

"I wish you were." Wally took hold of her hand.

"I wish so . . . too."

The lights of an approaching car appeared. Charlotte tried to pull her hand from his, but he held on.

"Are you afraid to be seen with me?"

"It isn't that—"

"Squat down like you're tying your shoe. I'll stand in front of you."

She knelt, letting her hair fall over her face. The car passed.

"Who was it?"

"The Byingtons."

"Oh, no! If she recognized me, she'll tell Daddy. I've got to get home." She took off running down the road.

"Char! Char!" he called, but she didn't answer.

Charlotte lay in the bed and listened for the sound of her father's car. When it came, she closed her eyes and trembled with fear. Rigid with anxiety, she listened for his footsteps coming toward the room she shared with her sisters. Seconds after he entered the house he was at the doorway of their room.

"Charlotte! Charlotte, come out here," he called.

"What is it?"

"Get up and come out here."

"I'll get dressed."

"No need for that. I've seen you in your gown before."

Charlotte slid out of the bed, careful not to wake her sleeping sisters, and grabbed an everyday dress off the hook. She slipped it on over her head and followed the light to the front room. Her father stood in the middle of it.

"You were seen with that . . . that boy from the restaurant. You told me you were coming home to take care of Hester. You . . . lied!"

"No. I came home. Ask Otis. I . . . just happened to meet Wally—"

"Don't you dare lie to me," he shouted. "You were on the road in the dark with that . . . that . . . trash! Did he feel you up? Did you let him kiss you?"

"No! He just walked with me. Please, Daddy—"

"You lying little bitch!" He took her arm and pulled her toward a chair. After sitting down, he jerked her until she fell facedown across his knees. He lifted her dress, then her nightgown, until her bare bottom was exposed.

"Please don't—" Charlotte was sobbing.

His hand came down hard on her buttocks. "I'm disappointed in you." *Swat.* "You've always been such a good girl." *Swat.* "I'll not have you corrupted by that riffraff. You're pure, and you'll stay pure." *Swat.*

Charlotte was so immersed in humiliation that she was unaware when the slaps stopped.

"My dear little girl, I had to do that. It's my duty as your father." He hugged her and pressed her head to his shoulder. "You are precious to me, Molly. It hurts me when you cry. I just want to hold you for a while. I've wanted to for a long time. My sweet and pretty Molly—"

Charlotte remained very still for a long moment, shocked into silence by her father's words, then she pulled away and stood.

"I'll go to bed."

"Go on, honey. In the morning you'll see that I did what I had to do."

Back in bed Charlotte pressed her tear-wet face to her pillow. Little Hester moved over, snuggled up to her back and wrapped her arm about her waist.

"Did it hurt, Char? What did you do?"

"Nothing bad. Go to sleep," she whispered miserably.

Oh, she hated him. He had dirtied one of the nicest things that had ever happened to her. She had done nothing wrong, nor had Wally. He had only held her hand. She laid her cheek against the palm he had held, and tears rolled from her eyes.

Why did he call me Molly? Was he thinking of Molly McKenzie when he held her on his lap after he'd spanked her? Was he thinking to marry Miss McKenzie and bring her here?

Oh, if only he would—

Chapter
Five

A week after Molly had given her story to the reporter, a sudden dust storm swept across the plains. Molly saw the black cloud rolling in from the southwest and ran into the house to warn her aunt. Bertha placed damp cloths on the windowsills and around the doors while Molly, with a handkerchief tied over her nose and mouth, went out to pen the dozen hens that roamed the yard and to close the doors to the shed and the well house. Stella, George Andrews's dog, who had given birth in the shed, was with her puppies and looked at Molly with calm, wise eyes, as if to say she knew enough to stay with her offspring.

In the store, even though they covered as many counters and bins as possible with old sheets and blankets, a thick layer of dark red dust sifted in during the daylong storm. It was stifling hot in the store with all the doors and windows sealed. Molly and Bertha passed the time by fanning themselves and watching out the window to see if anything passed on the road.

When the dust storm was over, they had the chore of clearing the dirt away. The two women spent the next two days cleaning when they were not waiting on customers.

Each day George brought food scraps for his dog. Stella was a big, white shaggy dog of undetermined ancestry. The father of her brood must have been dark. Some of the pups were black with white spots and some were white with ugly brown or black spots. Molly thought them adorable. She spent time each morning and evening cuddling them. Stella watched with a wagging tail and waited for her own pat on the head.

George lingered in the store for a while each morning and each afternoon, saying little or nothing. He usually bought something: a can of peaches or a can of sardines. He had a fondness for canned fish. He always paid in cash. As far as Molly knew he had never run a bill.

Bertha didn't hesitate to call on him when there was something heavy to move, and he seemed to be more than willing to oblige. Molly ignored him for the most part and went about her work as if he weren't there, but from time to time she would turn and find his eyes on her. It made her feel slightly uncomfortable but in no way threatened.

The day after the storm, the Reverend Howell came to the store as she was filling out a bill for a customer.

"Are you all right, my dear?" He squeezed behind the

counter where she was scooping pinto beans out of a barrel. "I was worried about you. I should have come out during the storm." His hand gripped her shoulder in a gesture of intimacy.

"Why in the world would you do that?" Molly moved away. She glanced at Mrs. Finklestein and saw the interested look on her face. She was stirred to anger. "Excuse me, Reverend Howell. I'm waiting on a customer."

"Of course, dear. I was just so anxious to see if you were all right."

"That's kind of you," Molly said coolly. "Did your children and your sister come through the storm all right?"

"Yes, of course they did, but we don't get the full blast of the storm in town like you do out here in the open."

"That's mighty strange, Preacher. I didn't realize the wind blowing that dirt skipped over town." Bertha came to the front of the store wiping her hands on her apron. "Can I help you with something?"

"No, thank you, Miss McKenzie. I'll get gasoline before I leave," he said curtly. *You'd better realize, you old busybody, that I'll not stand for your interfering between me and Molly.*

"How's your family? I 'spect Charlotte has her hands full taking care of all those younguns."

"Charlotte realizes her responsibilities and tends to her own business."

Not only the words, but the cold, calculating look in the preacher's eyes sent a shiver of apprehension up Bertha's spine and made her more determined than ever to stay close to Molly while he was in the store.

Mr. Finklestein came in through the side door. He had loaded sacks of chicken feed into the bed of his wagon. Molly moved down the counter and began to add up the bill. The Reverend Howell pretended an interest in the canned goods on the shelf.

After the Finklesteins left, Molly came from behind the counter.

"I'll get your gas now, Reverend Howell." She went past him and out the door and onto the porch.

George came around the corner of the store carrying two of Stella's pups.

"Preacher want gas? I'll pump it, Miss Molly."

"Thank you, George. Put the pups here on the porch. I'll watch them."

"How much you want?" George asked grumpily.

"Three gallons." The preacher answered in a responding tone.

When the gas was in the tank, the Reverend Howell came to the porch and pressed a silver dollar in Molly's hand and closed her fingers over it.

"I'll get your change."

"Don't bother, my dear," he said softly so that the others couldn't hear.

"No," Molly said firmly. "I'll get your change." She hurried into the store. When she returned, she dropped the change in his outstretched hand so she wouldn't have to touch him. "Thank you, Reverend. Tell Charlotte and the young ones hello."

"You could come out and do that yourself. You're welcome anytime."

"I don't have a lot of time to go visiting."

"I'll come get you on Sunday afternoon."

"No. No, thank you." Molly turned and spoke to George. "I think that Stella must have something in her paw. I saw her limping."

"I done took care of it, Miss Molly. She had a sticker-burr 'tween her toes."

Archie Howell waited a minute or two, then, realizing he would have no time alone with Molly, tipped his hat, got in his car, and left. The three in front of the store watched him leave; Bertha and Molly with relief, George with a puzzled frown.

The iceman came Saturday morning. Walter was his usual cheerful self and teased Molly and Bertha about taking them to the dance that night.

"Why, sugar, if you do that, you'll have to bring me home about nine o'clock." Bertha liked the cheerful red-headed man and enjoyed what she called "shooting the breeze" with him. "Won't that put a crimp in your evenin'?"

"Nine o'clock? You're just a killjoy, Bertha darlin'. At least promise me a dance."

"You can have all of 'em, darlin'!"

"Now, now. I got to be spreadin' myself around and keep *all* the ladies happy." His laughing eyes flashed at Molly, and he winked. "Ain't that right, Molly, with the prettiest eyes a man ever looked into?"

"You're full of blarney, Walter Lovik." Molly couldn't help laughing at his foolishness.

Shortly after Walter left the postman came into the store with two large packages of goods from a wholesale house in Kansas City. Bruce Paonessa had been delivering the mail for nearly twenty years. Mr. Bruce, as he was called, was tall, thin, and storklike, with a hawkish nose, big ears, and red-rimmed eyes. He was a quiet man, and it was a good thing because he knew almost as much about the business of folk along his route as they did, with the exception of George Andrews.

Mr. Bruce had delivered the dreaded death notices during the war and the news of the stock market crash of '29. He'd brought the news that this area was not the only one devastated by the dust storms, but that portions of the surrounding states were as well. He delivered the tax eviction notices and bills stamped "final notice" as well as *True Love* magazines to lonely women out on the ranches.

Every week or two George Andrews mailed a package to a store in Wichita and, as regularly as clockwork, received a package in return. It was none of Bruce's business, but he had a healthy curiosity about what was in the packages and the big envelopes that came from places like New York and Chicago.

"Where do you want these, Molly?"

"On the counter."

"You've got a Kansas City and a Wichita paper. You're on the front page of both."

Both Molly and Bertha hurried forward when Mr. Bruce opened the papers and spread them on the counter.

"Oh, my goodness!" Molly felt her face grow hot when she saw a four-column-wide picture of herself standing in front of the store. The headline was spread across the top of the *Kansas City Star.*

GIRL CAN IDENTIFY KILLERS

The story beneath the picture read:

Molly McKenzie, in the rooms above the country store owned by her parents, heard what she thought were firecrackers. She looked out the window and saw two men getting into a big black car. She gave Federal officers a description of both and is sure that she can identify them.

Miss McKenzie told the officers . . .

Molly quickly scanned the rest of the story. The reporter had written it exactly as she had related it to him.

"Well . . ." She let out a deep breath. "That's that."

"That should draw them out of the woodwork," Bertha said.

"Is that what you're up to?" Mr. Bruce's face wore a deep worried frown. "Good grief! They'd just as soon kill you as look at you. You women are no match for gangsters."

"Maybe not, Mr. Bruce, but Daddy's old shotgun is."

"And I'll be holding a Colt .45," Bertha added pertly.

"You should get a lawman out here."

"No!" Molly said quickly. "That might scare them off. If they're caught, I want to testify at the trial. If they come here, and I see them first, there'll be no need for a trial. One way or the other they'll pay for what they did."

"You don't know what you're up against. They could come with machine guns and shoot up the place like they did in the Kansas City train station. Times have changed, girl. People aren't just ornery anymore. They're down-right mean. I remember when your daddy never even locked that gas pump out there."

"I know." Then in an effort to change the subject, she said, "I sure hated it about poor old Mr. Yeager. He was a nice old man."

"Sure was. He complained a lot, but he worked like a horse. I was surprised that he went so fast. Guess I shouldn't be. A half dozen folks on my route have just keeled over the last couple of years."

"Reverend Howell blames it on the dust storms."

"Bullfoot!" Bertha snorted. "I don't believe anythin' that old windbag says."

"Got to be goin'. You women be careful." The postman shook his head. "I don't know what the sheriff is thinking of. If anything happens to you women, he'll be run out of the county."

"We'll be all right, Mr. Bruce."

"I hope they know what they're doin'. Next month, I'll be buying my gas here, Molly. Got to spread my business around," he added on his way to the door.

"I appreciate that," Molly called, then her eyes went back to the papers spread on the counter, and her mind went to the man who had been in and out of her thoughts for the past several weeks.

I'll do my best to see that they don't get to you. I mean that.

She had spent no more than fifteen minutes alone with Hod Dolan, yet his face had stayed in her mind's eye, and she remembered with clarity the sound of his voice. A connection had been forged between them. Just what it was she didn't know. It was something that went beyond his grim, dark face, his piercing, knowing eyes and lean strength that had caused her to trust him with her life.

He had promised to protect her, and she believed him.

For thirty years it had been the practice to keep the McKenzie General Store open until nine o'clock on Saturday night. Occasionally they closed an hour early, as they did this night so that Bertha and Molly could attend the cattlemen's dance. It was just getting dark when Bertha brought the car to the front of the store.

"I'm not sure that this is a good idea." Molly opened the door and got into the car.

"Are you worried we'll be gettin' company?"

"The paper was dated day before yesterday. The gangsters have had time to get here, if they're coming."

"Look under that quilt in the backseat, and you'll see the shotgun. It's loaded and ready."

"I hadn't thought of it."

"I did. We'll be all right at the dance. It's coming home that worries me some."

"Maybe we shouldn't go."

"This may be our last outing for a while. I'm going to eat my half dollar's worth of barbecue."

When they reached Pearl, the aroma of smoke and cooking meat was extra pleasing after the last few days of dust-filled air. Beneath strings of lights, people were dancing in the marked-off section of the street in front of the store and the barbershop. The six-member band had set up on a makeshift stage one cement block high and floored with wide planks lent by the lumberyard. A male trio with stringed instruments hanging from cords around their necks were singing "*When I Grow Too Old to Dream*," and couples were swaying to the slow music.

After leaving the car, Molly and Bertha walked down the crowded sidewalk toward the dance area, passing families who had come from every direction just to hear the music and watch the dancers.

"Miss Molly! There's Miss Molly—" The childish voice reached Molly, and she turned to see the Bonner family sitting on a bench in front of a vacant brick building. They were dirt-poor, and Molly was sure they had not come to eat barbecue, but to watch.

"Hello, Becky. Hello, Willy."

Mr. Bonner got politely to his feet as the women approached. The little girl jumped from her mother's lap and hurried to Molly.

"Daddy can sing some of those songs," the child announced proudly, and grabbed Molly's hand.

"Well! What do you know about that!"

"Me'n Willy was good all day, so we could come."

"I just bet you're good every day. How are you, Mrs. Bonner?"

"Fine . . . and you?"

"Aunt Bertha and I've been busy cleaning up after the storm." She looked up at the man in the clean, but patched overalls. "I hope you folks haven't bought your tickets yet."

"Well . . . ah . . . no, ma'am."

"Mr. Bonner, the store bought two extra tickets to the barbecue to give away to a valued customer. My aunt and I would like for you and Mrs. Bonner to have them. I'm sure they'll pile enough food on the plates for the children, too."

"Well . . . ah . . ." The man stammered again, looked at his wife, then back to Molly. "That's mighty kind of ya, but . . . we et 'fore we left home and . . . we didn't bring no plates."

"That's no problem," Bertha said. "We didn't figure whoever . . . we found to give the tickets to would have plates. I brought extras. I'll just dash back to the car and get 'em."

"Are we goin' to eat the . . . barb-cue, Daddy?" Willy came to stand beside his tall father. Molly's heart melted at the look of longing in the child's eyes.

"The store always buys extra tickets to . . . things, Mr. Bonner. It's our way of saying thank you for your business."

"But . . . my tab . . . at the store—"

"Times will get better, and you'll pay up. I'm counting on that stove wood you promised. Daddy always said you cut and stacked the neatest stove wood he'd ever had."

"Well, I do thank ya, ma'am."

"No thanks are necessary." Molly hugged little Becky to her side. "I'll swear, Becky, you get prettier every time I see you."

"Here ya are, folks." Bertha arrived with the plates and handed them and the tickets to Mrs. Bonner. "When you're finished with the plates, leave them on the hood of my car. Sure glad we ran into you folks and got rid of those tickets. Now we can enjoy the dance."

"Thanky." Mrs. Bonner shyly hung her head.

As Bertha and Molly walked away, Molly murmured. "Thank you, Aunt Bertha."

"Bullfoot. I did have my mouth set for barbecue, but . . . what the heck. It won't hurt me to miss a meal or two," she said, patting her round stomach.

"They're so poor . . . and proud. I just couldn't stand the thought of those children watching other folk eating . . ." Molly paused, then added, "I've got a dollar, we can get a couple more tickets."

"Maybe we can buy some and take it home."

"There are a lot of strangers here tonight," she added as they approached the restaurant.

Molly glanced at a young man standing against the wall of the bank building. His hat was pulled low on his forehead, and a knapsack hung from his shoulder. His clothes were worn, and he needed a shave.

"That'n's a bum," Bertha commented. "Part-Indian from the looks of him."

"Twenty-five percent of men are out of work, Aunt Bertha. That's a lot of men."

"There you are." Ruth came out of the crowd gathered on the corner of the dance area. "I've been looking for you." She was wearing a light green dress with a gathered skirt and puffed sleeves. Her dark blond hair was pulled over to the side and held with a large bobby pin decorated with a small ribbon bow that matched her dress.

"Don't you look pretty. New dress?"

"Yeah. Don't you recognize the pattern? It's one I borrowed from you. Come on. I want you to meet someone. Oh, shoot! Here comes Tim and the slutty twins."

"Janythe isn't slutty. She's not like Jen."

"I know. That wasn't fair."

"Hello, Molly," Jennifer called. "If you're alone, you can join us. I've got to share Tim with Jan. She didn't get a date. I'll share him with you, too."

"That's very generous of you. But no, thanks. We'll not be staying long."

"Saw your picture in the paper. I wish I'd been there. I'd have told you to not wear that light-colored dress. White . . . or green dresses"—she glanced at Ruth—"always tend to make you look . . . fat."

"Jen!" Janythe frowned at her twin. "Molly wouldn't look fat in a bedsheet. I thought you looked pretty in the picture, Molly."

"Thanks. I wasn't posing for a magazine."

"Let's go." Ruth pulled on Molly's arm.

"I'll let you have a dance with Tim . . . later on, Ruth."

"Now why would I want to do that?" Ruth said sweetly, but her lips were curled contemptuously. "I like to dance with a *man*, one who can *lead*, not one who follows along like a puppy dog on a string." She watched Tim's face turn a dull red before she turned away.

"Well said," Bertha commented when they were out of earshot of the trio. "You two go on, I'll go in the restaurant and visit with Catherine. I doubt she'll be very busy tonight."

"I'll meet you there later."

"We'll come for you when we're ready for the barbecue," Ruth said.

"We're not eating. At least I'm not. How about you, Aunt Bertha?"

"I'll eat at Catherine's if I eat anything."

"Just a minute, you two. Where are the tickets I sold you?"

"We don't . . . have them. Come on. Whom did you want me to meet?"

Ruth reluctantly walked along beside Molly. "Where are your tickets?" she asked again. "I know you well enough to know you didn't lose them."

"We . . . gave them to someone. I'm not hungry anyway. Whom did you want me to meet?" she asked for the second time.

"Molly McKenzie, you're generous and downright sweet!"

" 'Course, I am."

Three pairs of male eyes followed the progress of the two girls as they threaded their way through the crowd. One of the males moved slowly along the walk, keeping them in sight. He bumped into a heavyset woman carrying a basket.

"Well, I never!" she sputtered.

"Sorry, ma'am," he murmured, and moved on.

The band was playing *"I'm Confessing That I Love You."* The crowd standing around inside the roped-off area began to dance, and couples outside the ropes slipped under them to reach the sawdust-slicked surface.

"I wondered where you'd run off to." The voice was deep and had a ripple of laughter in it. Molly wasn't sure the man was speaking to them until she heard her friend's low laugh.

"There aren't many places to run off to in this town."

"That's true."

He dropped his cigarette and smashed it with the toe of

his boot. He wore a white shirt and string tie as he had done the day Molly had seen him at the church. His black, wide-brimmed hat was anchored firmly on his head.

"Keith, this is my friend Molly McKenzie. Molly, Keith McCabe. Don't believe a word he says, Molly. He's Irish and full of blarney."

"How do you do?"

"Pleased to meet you. I saw you at the church."

"I remember. Strangers stick out like sore thumbs around here."

"I've been compared to much worse."

"I didn't mean . . ."

"I know. You're right, Ruth. She is prettier than that picture in the paper."

"I told you, Molly! Keith is a ladies' man. Don't let him turn your head." Ruth's eyes shone with laughter when she looked up at the tall man.

"I'm not having much luck turning yours."

"—And I don't intend to let you."

"Why not? I'm a nice fellow."

"I've not heard anyone saying so . . . but you." Ruth appeared to be supremely happy. She turned to Molly. "Keith thinks you were out of your mind to tell that reporter that you can identify the men who killed your parents."

Molly lifted her shoulders in a shrug and turned when someone called her name.

"Molly, darlin'."

"Hello, Walter."

"I've been lookin' for you and thinkin' that if you

didn't come to town tonight, my heart would break for sure."

"—And heal as soon as you saw another girl. You know Ruth."

"Sure. I know every pretty girl in the county."

Molly rolled her eyes. "Well, Walter Lovik, meet Keith McCabe."

"Howdy." Walter extended his hand. "I ain't sure we'll get along, McCabe. I ain't likin' you cornerin' the two prettiest girls here and keepin' 'em all to yourself."

"I've been lucky . . . up to now."

"I'll be takin' one of 'em off your hands if Miss Molly will dance with me."

"What will your other girls think, Walter?" Molly took his hand. He lifted the rope, and she ducked under.

"They'll be jealous," he said as he took her in his arms. "But they'll just have to live with it."

Walter was an excellent dancer. After a few minutes he began to sing softly in her ear. *"I'm in the mood for love. Simply because you're near me—"*

Molly enjoyed the dance even if she wasn't in much of a mood for dancing. She knew Walter for exactly what he was, a flirt, and wondered why his wife had stayed with him as long as she had. When the dance was over, he squeezed her hand tightly and led her back to where Ruth and Keith stood just outside the dance area.

The three pairs of male eyes stayed on Molly as Walter led Ruth to the dance floor. One pair of eyes narrowed angrily as she laughed up at the tall man in the black hat.

"I'm afraid I'm not much for dancing," Keith said, as they watched Jen and Tim dance by. "I'd step all over your toes." Jen smiled sweetly at Keith over Tim's shoulder. He didn't appear to notice.

"My parents loved to dance," Molly said. "Daddy would put a record on the Victrola, crank it up, and they'd waltz. They could even tango."

"You're lucky to have fond memories of your parents. I don't remember mine."

"Oh, I'm sorry—"

"No need to be sorry. I'm used to it." He grinned down at her. "I hope you know what you're doing . . . announcing that you can identify the killers of your folks."

"They won't come back here. They're probably in Chicago by now and have banks or bigger stores to rob."

"I hope you're right. But it depends on who they are, I guess."

"Will you be here long?"

"I'm not sure. I work for a cattle company that wants to put grass back on the plains to hold the topsoil. I'll be coming out your way to look over the land one day soon. We're interested in the land that lies between the main road and the river."

"Daddy had a section. He leased it to a rancher."

"To plant?"

"For his cattle when there was grass. He paid Daddy usually with beef. I got awfully tired of canned meat. Mama wouldn't stand for anything going to waste."

"Have you lived around here for a long time?"

"All my life."

"Did you know Jackson Howell, the preacher's son?"

"Not well. He and his brother were quite a bit older and out of high school when I got there. They left here years ago and as far as I know they've not been back."

"I met him in Texas. I remembered that he was from around here. Said his daddy was a preacher."

"You went to his church."

"Yeah, I did. It was hard to believe that he was Jack's pa. They're certainly nothing alike." Keith McCabe's eyes were following Ruth as she danced with Walter. He looked back down at Molly and grinned. "Jack said the old goat had been married twice since his mother died and had lost both wives. It don't appear the preacher has much luck with his women."

"I think Jack has lost count. My daddy said that the preacher had been married briefly after his first wife died. The woman up and left and never came back. The preacher appeared to be brokenhearted. It was about that time his boys left home. But his broken heart didn't keep him from marrying right away after he got the divorce papers."

"What'a ya know. A divorced preacher."

"It wasn't held against him because she deserted him."

"He's had five wives, and I haven't even had one yet."

"Poor Keith." Molly laughed. "Do you have horns under that hat?"

"Not that I've noticed." He grinned at her, then turned to watch Ruth as she and Walter came toward them.

He really is a nice man, Molly thought. *Maybe something will develop between him and Ruth. I think she's finally over Tim.*

*   *   *

Archie Howell looked out of the attic window of the barbershop and gritted his teeth in frustration. He had been
in the stuffy attic for several hours watching the activity
on the street below. He had seen Molly talking to the
farmer in front of the vacant store, then watched as she
cuddled up with that redheaded iceman. Now she was
with McCabe, the newcomer living out at Morrison's
ranch. All he seemed to do was ride around out in the
country on his horse.

The preacher's obsession with Molly had begun
months before his last wife died and before Molly went
to Wichita to learn to be a secretary. He worried that she
would meet someone, marry, and stay in Wichita. He had
debated about helping one of her parents to the other side
so that she would come back home. As things turned out,
he hadn't needed to interfere.

The problem was that she didn't seem to realize that
they were destined to be together, to raise the children he
had and have more together. The palms of his hands
began to sweat, and he felt a swelling in his britches at the
thought of having her naked in bed. This fierce, consum-
ing yearning for her went beyond anything he'd ever
known. It consumed him, like a sickness, a sickness from
which he didn't want to recover.

Beneath the attic window, leaning against the wall of the
barbershop, a young man with a knapsack hanging over
his shoulder and several days' growth of beard on his face
watched Molly with Keith McCabe. He had found out a
few things about McCabe, but not enough to satisfy his
curiosity.

Molly was pretty. They had told him she was. She wasn't silly-pretty like some girls, but quietly pretty in a dignified kind of way. The eyes that had flashed at him as she passed were fringed with dark lashes, her skin was clear and lightly tanned. He'd not been able to see the color of her eyes, but he knew that they were an unusual deep violet-blue.

He knew a lot about her. She had been to business school in Wichita and would be twenty one years old in a few weeks. Her body was slender as a reed and had the grace of the wind on the grass of the plains. There was quality there, too. She reminded him of his sister, Henry Ann, down in Oklahoma.

Damn, but that barbecue smelled good. His stomach was protesting the fact that he hadn't eaten much for several days. He wished that he could buy a plateful or two. But he was supposed to be a bum. Bums didn't spent money on barbecue. Someone would be bound to notice.

The third pair of male eyes watching Molly left her long enough to search the area carefully. The watcher was used to observing and storing away in his memory what he saw.

A bum was standing in front of the barbershop beneath the window where the preacher was peering down at the crowd thinking he was hidden from view. The Bonner family lined up to get barbecue. The man watching was sure where they had gotten the tickets. He had seen Molly and her aunt stop to talk with them. Molly's generosity didn't surprise him at all.

When Walter Lovik and Molly finished the dance, they

went back to where the teacher and McCabe waited. Walter then led the schoolteacher to the dance floor. The watcher's eyes rested on Molly and McCabe. She was laughing and talking. He liked to see her laugh. She'd not had much to laugh about lately.

It was time to go. The man realized that he had to make haste. He stepped behind a building and disappeared into the darkness.

Chapter
Six

WITH SONG

The car headlights cut a swath through the darkness. It was nearly midnight, and neither Molly nor Bertha voiced the anxiety they were feeling as they neared the store. Both dreaded the time when they would leave the car. Bertha turned into the driveway, drove past the gas pump, stopped, backed the car so the lights shone on the shed, then backed again so that the lights illuminated the farside of the store.

"The car can sit out tonight," she announced as she parked beside the porch and reached into the backseat of the car for the shotgun. "Let's get inside."

The two women went up onto the porch. With the shotgun in her hand, Bertha faced the road while Molly unlocked the door. Once they were inside Molly switched on the light, turned, and locked the door.

In the deep shadows beside the honeysuckle bushes a man moved back when the car came into the driveway in front of the store. He nodded in approval as the head-lights were shone on both sides of the building. He watched as the women went cautiously up onto the porch and entered the store, and he lingered until the lights went on in the upstairs window. When he got to his feet, he stretched his tired muscles and looked up at the sky. Millions of stars blazed from horizon to horizon, beautiful and unreachable, shedding very little light on the plains that surrounded the store.

The watcher waited a few minutes, listened to the sounds of night, and heard nothing out of the ordinary. Then he moved slowly toward the back of the store. He paused at the gazebo, turned, and gazed for a long moment at the lighted window, rubbing his hand lovingly down the barrel of the shotgun cradled in his arms, and walked away.

On Sunday morning Molly awakened the instant a hand touched her shoulder. In the light of early dawn filtering through the window, she saw her aunt hovering over her.

"What is it?"

"There's a car out back. It came in about thirty minutes ago with the lights off. That big old white dog came out of the shed and growled, then went back in to her pups."

"Some watchdog she is. Heavens! Why didn't you wake me?"

"I was watching to see if anyone got out. No one has so far."

"Get the shotgun."

"I've got it. I've been downstairs to make sure the doors were locked."

"Aunt Bertha, you're the limit. You should have wakened me." Molly hurried into the kitchen to look out the window.

The dark car was pulled up close to the gazebo, where it would not be seen from the road. As Molly watched, a match flared and was quickly extinguished. *Someone is still in the car.* Molly battled the storm of anxiety inside her. She backed away from the window and allowed the curtain to fall back in place. *Is this it? Have the gangsters come to kill me?*

"I'll go down and call the sheriff."

"And wake up all those busybodies on the party line? Besides, it'd take that old fool an hour to get here."

"We can't just sit here and wait for them to come in!" Molly pulled back the curtain a crack.

"I'm thinking that if it was . . . *them* . . . they'd do it in the dark, not wait till daylight."

"You're right. It could be a traveler pulled off the road to get some sleep."

"Then why'er they tryin' to hide?"

"Someone's getting out."

The door on the passenger side opened. Even in the dim light of morning Molly could see that he was short and husky. Wide suspenders held his britches up. He lifted his arms and stretched, then leaned in to say something to the other person in the car.

"Where's he going?" Molly whispered when he headed for the side of the shed.

"He's unbuttoning his britches. He's going to pee."

"How crude!"

"He doesn't know we're watching. Maybe he's got a weak bladder."

"He'd better not do it on my hollyhocks."

"Then you'd better call out and tell him, 'cause that's exactly what he's going to do."

"Heavens! I'll not be able to pull weeds around those hollyhocks for the rest of the summer." *That is if I'm here for the rest of the summer.* "What'll we do if they don't go?"

"Wait."

"I keep thinking that if they were the gangsters, they'd break in here and try to get away before daylight. It's almost that now." Molly pressed her face to the window. "I'm glad they weren't here last night."

"If they'd a been, I'd have turned around and headed back to town. They'd have had a heck of a time catchin' my Ford."

"Come look. Another man's getting out. Well, for heaven's sake! It's . . . It looks like . . . Mr. Dolan." Her heart pounded with relief and something vaguely like excitement. "Why didn't he come to the door?"

"Maybe he thought we'd shoot him."

"Why is he here so early? Oh, I know. He doesn't want anyone to know he's here."

"If that's the case, he'd better get rid of that car. George will be here at daylight to feed his dog."

"That's right. He can put it in the shed."

"I'll put on some coffee. You go down and find out if he's goin' or stayin'."

"Heavens! I've got to dress, wash my face, and comb my hair."

"You don't need to get all gussied up."

"Not gussied up. Just presentable. I can't go down and meet strange men in my nightgown."

Molly hurried into her room and, reluctant to turn on the light, fumbled in the semidarkened closet for her blue-and-white-checked dress. She pulled the wide sash off the hanger, wrapped it tightly around her narrow waist, and tied it in a bow. She ran the brush through her hair and tied it back with a blue ribbon, then moistened her suddenly dry lips with a tube of Tangee lipstick.

Downstairs she turned on the light in the storage room, used the toilet, and waited after she flushed it for the water to stop running before she went to the back door, unbolted and opened it.

The fresh air of morning washed over her. She breathed it in deeply as she stepped out onto the porch. There was no one standing beside the car. The yard was empty. Puzzled, she turned to go back into the store.

"Oh! Oh . . ." Her hand flew to her throat. "You . . . you scared me!"

"I should hope so." Hod Dolan moved away from the wall beside the door. "I heard you fumbling with the lock. I didn't know who was in there." Another man stepped up onto the porch from the other side. Hod continued to look at Molly, his dark brows puckered in a frown. "It was foolish to open the door and step out without knowing who was here. Don't do it again."

"I knew it was you. I saw you from the upstairs window."

"You couldn't be sure from up there." There was a hard edge to his voice. His eyes continued to roam her face.

Looking at her almost made his heart stop. His lips were dry, his palms sweaty. The realization of how badly he wanted to see her again, utterly ridiculous, of course, began to surface in his mind, and it made him angry.

"Oh, for goodness sake! Come in. Aunt Bertha's making coffee."

"I'll bring in your gear, Hod, then be on my way."

"You're staying?" Molly's voice rasped hoarsely. Her startled eyes went from the man leaving the porch to the Federal man. His face was just as she remembered it; full-lipped, rough-hewn, with a jaw set at an almost brutal angle. Large slanting eyes gleamed from beneath a brush of brows as dark as his wild, jet-black hair.

"For a while. I brought a cot to set up in your storage room."

"No need for that. There's an extra bed upstairs." She hoped desperately that he didn't know how nervous she was.

"Thanks, but the storage room will be fine."

"Suit yourself." She went past him to the door. "Aunt Bertha's making coffee. Your friend is welcome to have some before he leaves."

"He'd like that. It's been a long night."

The man returned and set two canvas bags on the porch. He grinned at Molly.

"Morning." Molly was glad her manners hadn't deserted her.

"Mornin', miss. Bob Walker." He put his fingers to the brim of his brown felt hat.

"Molly McKenzie."

"I know. Saw your picture in the *Star*."

Molly grimaced, thinking of Jen's remark that the light-colored dress made her look fat.

"I'm beginning to think that was the most harebrained idea I ever had," Hod growled.

"Be glad to trade places with you and spend a week with this pretty little thing." Bob's homely face split into a grin.

"A week?" Molly's violet-blue eyes met Hod's.

"Sorry to have to tell you, but it could be longer, or shorter, depends—"

"On what?"

"On when this case is completed."

"—And you catch them?"

"There's no guarantee they'll come here."

"But you think they will."

"I'd not be here . . . otherwise." Irritated with himself for the foolish feeling of elation that had washed over him at the first sight of her, his tone of voice was harsher than he realized.

"Well. I'm sorry to be such a bother to you. It was your idea to use me for bait. Not mine." *I'm beginning to think that I don't like this man at all!*

"You're right. It was. And I'll give you as much protection as I can."

"I didn't ask you for that, either."

"Right again. But you're getting it."

Bob Walker gaped at Hod in disbelief. He had known and worked with him for several years. This was a side of him he'd not seen before—irritable and sharp with this sweet-faced girl who had put her life on the line to catch two hardened killers.

"Howdy." Bertha's stocky figure filled the doorway.

"Morning." Hod spoke, then picked up one of the bags.

"Put your things in the storage room, Mr. Dolan." Molly turned her back on him and smiled at Bob Walker. "This is my aunt Bertha, Mr. Walker. She makes awfully good biscuits. Do you have time for breakfast?" Molly was torn between good manners and anger at the big dark man with the scowl on his face.

"Nothin' I'd like better, ma'am, but I'm thinkin' I'd better get on down the road to Pearl. I'll get a bite there if there's anything open."

"You're out of luck there," Bertha said. "That town closes up tighter than a drum on Sunday."

"You could put your car in the shed, but our neighbor, George Andrews, will be here sometime this morning to feed his dog."

Hod's head jerked around and his brows beetled.

"His dog? What's his dog doing in your shed?"

"Having pups."

"Why *your* shed?"

"Ask her. I don't know."

"How often does he come here?"

"The dog is a . . . she," she said in a deliberate attempt to further irritate him. *I'm sure now that I don't like him and that it is going to be a long week.*

Hod's eyes narrowed. "How often does the neighbor come here?" He asked with mock patience.

"Two or three times a day and . . . he stays awhile each time."

"Is he courting you?"

Molly's mood changed in an instant. Her eyes lit up with laughter, and she struggled to suppress the giggle that almost choked her. She didn't speak, but Bertha did.

"Of course not!" She spoke sharply. "I'll put my car in the shed. You park yours out front by the gas pump, Mr. Walker. Folks that pass will think you're getting gas."

"How about the neighbor?" Hod spoke to Bertha.

"He won't come in. The store's closed on Sunday. But we'd better get crackin'. He's usually here shortly after daylight."

Thirty minutes later, the four of them were sitting at the kitchen table, where Bertha had dished up hot biscuits, sausage, and gravy. The men had already drunk one pot of coffee, and another was perking on the burner.

"You always get the cushy jobs." Bob speared another biscuit and grinned at Hod. "Why can't I stay here and you do the roadblock for Pascoe and Norton?"

"Because the chief said for me to stay and that if anything happened to the girl, I was fired." Hod kept his eyes on his plate.

Bob sent Molly a quick glance and took a gulp of his coffee.

The girl! Molly felt the blood come slowly up from her neck to redden her cheeks. She was embarrassed not only at being referred to as *the girl*, but at the thoughts she'd had about this man between the time she first met him and this morning when she opened the back door. She had even been excited when she saw him get out of the car. She chided herself harshly for being so stupid. To him she was a means of keeping his job.

Hod saw the look on her face and was more angry with

himself than he could ever remember, but training prevented even a flicker of his emotions to show. His heart thudded with slow and heavy thumps, weighed down with regret for those few unguarded words.

When she spoke, Molly's voice was quavery. "I'll be careful. I would hate for you to lose your job because of me." With eyes threatening to well with tears, she got up from the table without excusing herself and went to look out the window. "George is here."

Bob hurriedly left the table, a biscuit in his hand.

"Come on. We'd better get downstairs." Bertha led the way to the stairs.

Hod came to the window immediately and looked out over Molly's shoulder. George was at the water pump filling a bucket. He carried it into the chicken house. For a couple of weeks now he had done the chicken chores when he came to feed Stella.

Molly stared out the window. She felt trapped between the window and the tall, hard body just behind her. She held her breath. Her shoulders tensed.

"Where does he live?" Hod's words were spoken close to her ear. A strand of her hair caressed his nose.

"About a half mile across the field." Her voice was cold, her body rigid.

"I didn't come here just to keep from getting fired," he murmured. She was staring straight ahead, scarcely breathing. He was acutely aware that although she was slender and in some ways as delicate as a flower, she was nevertheless as fierce and tough as a willow switch. His eyes took in every detail of her set profile. "I would have come here without pay to protect you. I'm sorry that you thought that I only came to keep my job."

"I don't like you very much, Mr. Dolan. I want the men who killed my parents to pay for what they did, and I'll do whatever, put up with whomever I have to, to see that it's done."

"How long have you known that man out there?"

George had come out of the shed with his arms full of pups. He lowered them gently to the ground and stood watching them scamper about. Stella stood proudly near-by.

"As long as I can remember. I'm going down to talk to him." Molly sidestepped in order to keep from touching him and headed for the door. As she reached it his words stopped her.

"Be careful what you say to him."

She turned and looked at him. "I'm not the complete fool you think I am."

Hod watched her leave, heard her footsteps on the stairs, then turned to the window to watch as she crossed the yard to talk to the neighbor.

Damn, damn, damn! I can't put into words what I feel for you, Molly McKenzie, because I don't know what it is. I don't even know you very well. But you've stuck in my mind like a burr since the day I met you, and it makes me damned mad to think that you could break my heart if I let you.

"Morning, George."

"Mornin', Miss Molly. Ain't ya goin' to church?"

"Not this morning. We may go to the evening service."

"Your picture was in the paper. Be careful 'bout goin' out nights." George never looked directly at her when he spoke to her.

"You think the killers will come here?"

"It's what that newspaper feller wanted, ain't it?"

"Well . . . yes, I guess so."

"Be careful. Hear?"

"I will. I've got Daddy's shotgun."

Molly looked up from the pup she held in her arms and caught him looking at her. He quickly averted his eyes. He was dressed as usual: overalls and faded shirt. But this morning he had something large in the bib of his overalls.

"The pups are old enough for you to take home." Molly searched for something to say, and this was all that came to mind.

"I reckon I'll leave 'em for a while."

"You don't need to come over every day. I'll feed Stella our table scraps. She'll get plenty to eat."

"And get lazy. She be gettin' out of the habit of huntin' for herself."

"Well." Molly set the fluff of fur down on the ground. "I'd better get back in."

"Big car out there . . . at the gas pump."

"Aunt Bertha's taking care of him. He's on his way to Pearl and was afraid he'd run out of gas before he got there." She glanced up at the kitchen window, knowing that Hod Dolan was watching her. She lingered deliberately.

George was on his knees cuddling one of the squirming puppies. His big rough hands stroked the tiny creature. She had known him for as long as she could remember, but she had never really looked at him or thought about him as a person. He had thick reddish-brown hair, high cheekbones, and deep-set eyes. Hard work had made his shoulders wide and his arms thick with muscles. She guessed him to be a little younger than her father who was forty-two when he was killed.

It occurred to Molly that George had been young once and possibly full of dreams. Because he was quiet and never participated in any of the community activities, never offered help to anyone nor asked for any, he was what her daddy had called an *invisible* man. People overlooked him. He was just George, that odd fellow out on the old Andrews place.

"How is your sister?"

George looked up, surprised by the question. Molly saw that his eyes were green with amber flicks.

"She's all right."

"I haven't seen her in years. Does she ever go to town?"

"No. Don't want to." George gathered the puppies up in his arms and stood. "Better get on back. I'll come and fork up the rest of your potatoes in a day or two."

She started to refuse the offer but changed her mind. "I'd appreciate it."

"I'll have some pretty good corn to pop. I'll bring you some."

"I'll take it on trade."

"No. I ain't wantin' nothin' for it." He walked into the shed.

After a few minutes, when he didn't come out, Molly turned and went back into the store. The front door of the store was open to allow air to circulate. Hanging on the screen door was the CLOSED sign. Bob Walker squatted on his heels behind the counter, eating a biscuit.

"Is he coming in?"

Molly shook her head and went to the front door. George was coming around the side of the building. He paused to look at the gas pump, then the car. Molly unlatched the screen and went out onto the porch.

"Ever'thin' all right, Miss Molly?" With a slight movement of his head he indicated the car.

"Of course. Aunt Bertha had to go upstairs and get change." Behind her the door opened. Bob came out with Bertha behind him.

"Thank you, ma'am." Bob hurried down the steps.

"Welcome. Have a safe trip." Then, "Mornin', George. Goin' to be a scorcher today."

"Yes, ma'am." He watched as the car pulled out onto the road. "I best be goin'."

Molly and Bertha watched him cross the side yard and head across the field.

"George isn't stupid. He saw that the lock was still on the pump and the cylinder was dry."

"The lock is always on the pump on Sunday. I could've locked it after I pumped the gas." Bertha wiped her face on the end of her apron. "If he did notice, he'd not say anything."

"I don't like having to hide things."

"You may not like it, but if Mr. Dolan thinks it necessary—"

"Mr. Dolan doesn't know everything."

"Maybe not, but now that the story has been in the paper, he's all that's standing between us and the killers."

"I wouldn't say *all*."

"Well for Pete's sake." Bertha's face took on a worried expression as she studied the set, stubborn look on her niece's face. Then she said, in an attempt to change the subject, "That Walker fellow is an eater. I packed him a half dozen biscuits with sausage to take with him."

"Did he pay for it?"

"I didn't ask for pay."

"They are not our guests, you know."

"What's got you stirred up? Oh, I know. The remark Mr. Dolan made about he didn't want to come here, but had to or get fired. Sounds reasonable to me. It was his idea, and it's his duty to see that nothing happens to you."

"I don't think I'll be able to have him here in my house for a week. We'll have no privacy at all."

"It'll probably be more'n a week. Mr. Walker said that sometimes these stakeouts, as he calls them, last for several weeks. If that happens, he and Mr. Dolan will take shifts. We should have thought of that before we started this thing."

"It's a relief to know that he'll not be here all the time. He's a know-it-all."

"It's his business to know it all, honey. I don't understand. This is what you wanted, isn't it?"

Molly turned and went back into the store without answering.

Chapter Seven

Molly walked through the store to the back door. As she passed the storage room she could see Hod taking a gun out of a canvas bag. It had a handgrip under the barrel, and in front of the grip was a round drum. Although she had never seen one, she'd seen pictures and knew that it was a machine gun.

"It's a machine gun," she said the words as she was thinking them.

Hod looked up. "Thompson submachine gun, better known as a tommy gun." He wiped the barrel with a soft cloth.

"Gangsters use them."

"And lawmen."

"I've heard about them. Machine Gun Kelly . . . Dillinger—"

"Bonnie and Clyde Barrow."

"Is that the kind of gun that killed them?"

"I suppose so."

"Were you there?"

"At the ambush? No."

He placed the tommy gun on the canvas cot and began to wipe the barrel of a rifle. When he didn't look up, Molly went out the back door and walked quickly to the outbuilding that Granddaddy McKenzie had built to use as a barn. It now served as a shed for a 1926 truck and Bertha's new Ford. The side door of the shed was propped open so Stella could go in and out.

Coming out of the bright sunlight, Molly blinked to adjust her eyes to the dim light of the shed. The dog stood over the straw nest where her pups were climbing over each other to reach her teats. She was ignoring them. Her nose was pointed toward the far corner of the building that held old store equipment as well as household castoffs accumulated over the years.

"Hi, Stella. Why don't you lie down, girl, and let your babies have their dinner?" Molly's words were greeted with a low growl. "Hey, now. You've never growled at me before." She reached to stroke the dog's head. Stella didn't give her as much as a wag of her tail in appreciation. The low growls continued to come from the dog's throat. "What's the matter? Are you afraid—"

Molly's gaze followed that of the dog and saw the shape of a man's wide-brimmed hat and a face looming up over the bottom part of an old kitchen cabinet. The shriek that tore out of her reflected the lightning stroke of fear that knifed through her. Stella broke loose from the pups hanging on her teats and ran several yards toward the man, barking furiously. Molly darted for the door and sprang out into the sunlight as Hod was leaping from the porch of the store with his gun in his hand.

"In there! A man," Molly gasped.

"Get in the house!" Hod dashed past her and flattened himself against the wall beside the door.

Stella's barks had turned into vicious snarls.

Molly's feet seemed to be rooted in the ground.

"Goddammit! Get in the house!" Hod yelled.

"Hod! Hod! It's me. Call off the damn dog!"

"Good Lord! Is that you, Johnny?"

"Get this dog off me. I don't want to shoot her."

Molly crowded into the doorway behind Hod. "You know him?"

"Yes, I know him."

"What's he doing sneaking around in my shed?"

"Call off the dog," he said impatiently in answer to her question.

"Stella," Molly called, and moved around in front of Hod. "Come here, Stella. Don't you dare shoot her." She glared at the man holding a canvas knapsack between himself and the snarling dog. "She's got more right here than you do."

The dog backed away and, keeping her eyes on the stranger, sidled over to Molly, who knelt.

"Go see about your babies. No one is going to hurt them." Molly stood, and Stella leaned against her legs. She stroked the dog's head.

"I've had a hell of a time dodging the farmer that was just here." The stranger removed his hat and wiped his sweat-drenched face on the sleeve of his shirt.

"Glad to see you, Johnny. I didn't expect you so soon."
Hod stepped forward and held out his hand.

"I've been hanging around town for a couple of days."

"Is it too much to ask what is going on?" Molly asked
with a heavy tone of irritation in her voice.

"I guess not," Hod said, almost smiling. "Miss
McKenzie, meet Johnny Henry, your new helper."

"How do you do?" Molly controlled her frayed nerves
and held out her hand. Manners came first. Then she
turned on Hod. "What do you mean . . . my helper?"

"Every store needs a chore boy. Someone to mop, load
feed sacks, pump gas. You just hired Johnny."

"I did no such thing. We hardly make enough to keep
us going—"

"No pay is required. He works for me."

"For you? Doing what?"

"Lookout. Backup. He looks like a kid, but he can handle himself. He's been on jobs with me before."

Hod's takeover attitude rankled Molly.

"Folks around here know that I don't make enough to
hire extra help. And if I did, it would be someone from
around here."

"Tell them that he's working for board. They'd understand that."

"They'll not understand my taking in a stranger."

"Tell them he's kinfolk."

"They know all my kin, for heaven's sake. I've lived
here all my life."

"Well, tell them he's your aunt's kin. Someone from
Wichita."

"You're determined, aren't you?" Molly's tone reflected her exasperation.

"Yes, I am." Hod went to the door and looked out. "Will that farmer be back today?"

"He'll be back, and his name is George Andrews. He's a nice man. He . . . he cares about his dog."

"Then why doesn't he take her home?"

"He thinks I need a watchdog."

Hod snorted. "Fine watchdog. She didn't make much racket when we came in this morning."

"Enough to let us know you were here." *To let Aunt Bertha know anyway.*

The young man looked from Hod to the girl they had come to protect. It was evident that the two of them didn't like each other. Why? Hod was a man of few words, yet here he was, bickering with this woman.

Johnny Henry had known Hod for several years. Hod was a brother to Tom Dolan, who had married Johnny's sister Henry Ann. Listening to Hod talk about the law and his job as a Federal Marshal had fascinated Johnny. Because he was familiar with southern Oklahoma territory, he had helped Hod locate the farmhouse where Machine Gun Kelly had held the kidnapped oil man, Charles Urschell. That had earned him a job as deputy Federal Marshal. He and Hod had tracked the Barrow gang, established their pattern for Frank Hamer, the famed former Texas Ranger who was responsible for ending their crime spree.

Hod had requested that Johnny be pulled from another job to assist him and Bob Walker on the Pascoe-Norton case. His chief, feeling uneasy about setting a girl up as bait to catch two notorious criminals, had agreed.

"Am I going or staying?" Johnny asked. "It's damned hot in here."

Molly turned her attention to him. He was average height and whiplash thin, a handsome young man of obvious Native American heritage.

"You were in town last night."

"Yes, ma'am," he answered, although she hadn't asked a question.

"Have you had breakfast?"

"No, ma'am."

"Come in, then. We give every bum who comes to our door at least one meal."

"I'm not a bum, ma'am."

"Don't get on your high horse. I didn't say you were."

"Am I staying?" Johnny looked at Hod.

Hod had been watching Molly during the exchange with Johnny. Despite her show of outrage at having strangers take over her store and her home, she was too intelligent not to understand that it was necessary in order to save her life and to catch the killers of her parents. She would come around once she had time to stop and think about it.

"Ask the lady," Hod finally replied.

"It seems I have no choice." Molly bit off each word.

Hod's black eyebrows shot up. "You had a choice. I didn't twist your arm to get you to let the reporter interview you."

"I was waiting for you to throw that up to me." She

turned her back, dismissing him. "Come in, Mister . . . what did you say your name was?"

"Johnny Henry. Call me Johnny."

"Come in, Mr. Henry." Molly stepped out of the shed and headed for the house. Johnny lingered to speak privately with Hod.

"Hell's bells, Hod. Are we going to have trouble with her?"

"When the chips are down, she'll do what she's told. It's probably my fault that she's got her back up. I was sharp with her when we first got here." Hod stepped to the door to watch Molly cross the yard. He was impressed with her spunk despite himself. He was convinced now that she'd not keel over at the first sign of trouble. He turned back to Johnny. "Come on in and meet Molly's aunt. She makes the best biscuits I ever ate."

George walked slowly across the field toward the dreary homestead where he had lived all his life. He wasn't looking forward to what awaited him there. Gertrude would be in a foul mood because he hadn't killed the old red rooster she wanted for the pot. Instead he had brought in a younger chicken. She hated Old Red because the rooster had pecked her legs a time or two while she was hanging clothes and insisted on coming up on the back stoop to do his business.

He liked Old Red. He was a tough old bird who had lived through the dust storms even when he'd been blown out of his favorite roosting spot in the apple tree beside the barn and carried out into the middle of God only knew where. He had found his way home late the next day. George figured he had earned a better fate than to have his head chopped off and be put in the cookpot.

Gertrude was getting harder and harder to live with. She had always been a little crazy, but now she was seeing things that weren't there. One day she stood on the porch and talked to a man in a black suit and brocade vest, so she said, and told him that her mama was out gathering eggs. Mama had been dead for twenty years or more. One day while he was in town to see the doctor to get a boil lanced, she told him a preacher had come to the house and told her that he was bound for hell. When pressed for details, she clammed up. He figured it was another one of her imaginary visitors. It was all right, as far as he was concerned, for her to live in her imaginary world. He had his.

George didn't know what to do about Gertrude. She wouldn't move a hundred feet away from the house. She hadn't been to town or to church in years. What's more, she didn't want anyone to come to the house, which was not a problem because no one ever came. She had made it plain to visitors, for as long as he could remember, that they were not welcome.

He went straight to the wooden chest when he reached the barn, unlocked it, and put away the heavy pistol he took from the bib of his overalls. He lingered a moment as he always did when he opened the chest, and gently fingered a few of the prize possessions he kept there for his eyes only. He thought of the big old box as his treasure chest. After closing it and snapping the lock in place he went to stand in the doorway of the barn and look back across the field toward the McKenzie store. As he stood with his shoulder against the doorjamb, the far cry of a whippoorwill came low and sadly from across the field. It seemed to mourn a lost loved one.

Something was going on over there that they didn't want anyone to know about. That black car in front of the store had been parked behind it for a while, judging by the oil spot on the grass. It had been moved to the gas pump, but no gas had been pumped. And that young fellow who had been in town last night had slipped into the back of the shed and hidden. Anyone with half a brain could tell that he wasn't a bum. His boots were too new. He wasn't a gangster either. They'd not send a wet-eared kid to do away with an important witness.

If he had been sent to guard Molly against the gunman who killed the McKenzies, he was mighty young for the job. Unless . . . he was not the only one there. George decided to go back over there after a while and study the footprints around that oil spot on the grass, and then he'd know.

"Why'er ya standin' 'round out there lollygaggin' for?" Gertrude had come out of the house with the broom and chased Old Red away from the stoop. "Why didn't ya kill that old fool?" she demanded.

"I didn't want to," George replied, and went past her into the house.

"Ya don't do nothin' I want ya to do." Gertrude came in the door behind him. "Eats are ready. Ya better eat so ya can get back over to that store."

George could hardly remember when Gertrude had been young and agile and laughed and played with him. She had been bright and pretty, but the hard passage of time had done away with that brightness. Her fair hair was still parted down the center, but now it was thin and streaked with gray. Her shoulders were rounded, her breasts sagged, and her stomach protruded. She had lost most of her teeth, and her shrunken mouth gave her face a pinched look. All vanity or desire for simple pleasures had been expunged from her long ago.

He stood inside the door for a moment and let his eyes adjust to the gloom of the kitchen after coming in out of the sunlight. Blankets were nailed over the two windows, and the only light came through the door, which was closed most of the time. The few times he had reached up and turned on the light that hung from the ceiling in the middle of the room, Gertrude had turned it off.

"Foolish wastin' money on the electric. 'Sides, it hurts my eyes," she'd say, then rant on for thirty minutes about her ailments.

Over the years George had come to realize that it was easier just to give in to her.

They had not sat down to eat a meal together in years, and he didn't expect to now. He usually dished himself up a plate of food and took it to his room or the back stoop. It was the same every day of the week. He now filled his plate with boiled chicken and dumplings. Gertrude was clean with her cooking even if the rest of the house did look like a cyclone had hit it.

Today he unlocked the door to his room and took his plate inside, closed the door, and threw the bolt. Gertrude was not allowed in the room. He had put the lock on the door to keep her out. It was sweltering hot in the closed-up room. He had made it as tight as possible by stuffing rags around the windows to keep the invading dust at bay. George opened windows on two sides to let in a breeze, then sat in a chair beside a rolltop desk to eat. George's eyes roamed his sanctuary, from the bookcase filled with books to the pictures on the walls.

This was his private world. He thought of it as his picture gallery. He could sit for hours looking at the pictures on the walls. He had an old Wells Fargo safe that sat beside the desk. He kept it covered with a tapestry he had bought during his one and only trip to Kansas City. The lamp on the desk had been ordered from a catalog as had the telescope he used to look at the stars.

The RCA radio came from Sears. It sat on a table beside his bed with the wire extended out the window to connect with the antenna fastened to the top of the house. It was his window to the outside world. He listened to President Roosevelt's fireside chats. He didn't understand how the Social Security Act was going to help matters. Roosevelt wanted to give folks over sixty-five a pension. *Where in the world was the money going to come from?*

He listened to the radio as he ate his meal. They were still talking about the death of Will Rogers and Wiley Post in an airplane crash in Alaska a week or two ago and about that fellow Hitler over in Germany. He was raising Cain again. Maybe somebody ought to shoot him before he did too much damage, George mused. If they'd shot the Kaiser, it would've saved the Germans and a lot of other folks a world of trouble.

His peaceful time was interrupted by a pounding on the door.

"Why'd ya go in there for?" Gertrude yelled from the kitchen. "I know. I know why ya go in there. You want to listen to that blasted radio. Mama told me this mornin' that ya warn't ever goin' to amount to doodly-squat. She said Papa ort to take a strap to yore behind. Ya ain't got no business listenin' to that jibber-jabber all day and half the night. Ya ort to be out there workin' with Daddy's hogs, is what ya ort to be doin'. Winter's goin' to be comin', and we ain't goin' to be havin' no hog meat."

George let her sharp words roll off his back unanswered.

"I'm goin' to Kansas City tomorrow. Ya can jist cook yore own vittles. 'Fore I go I'm goin' to get me a gun and kill that red devil that shits on my porch. I done kilt that bitch dog a yours. She ain't round here no more. My man's comin' for me and . . . I'm goin' and I ain't comin' back."

George reached over and turned up the volume on the radio.

Bertha took to Johnny Henry right away.

"Well, we can't pass ya off as kin. Your mama or your daddy was Indian or I miss my guess."

"Yes, ma'am. My daddy was Cherokee."

"Thought so. He must have been a good-looking devil. Why don't we say, if anyone asks, and I'm sure they will, that I knew you and your mama in Wichita. Leave it to me. I'll spin them a yarn."

Hod looked at Molly. "That all right with you?"

Molly lifted her shoulders in a noncommittal gesture. "Where is he going to sleep, Aunt Bertha?"

"Not in the storage room. Not you either, Mr. Federal Man."

"No more of that," Hod said quickly. "Call me Hod. Why not the storage room?"

"Good reason. The toilet is in there. Do you think I want to get you up in the middle of the night and send you out into the store so I can use it?"

Molly felt the heat rush to her face. She had wondered about that, but hadn't dared to voice it. Leave it to her aunt. Plain talk came naturally to her.

"I hadn't thought of that," Hod said, keeping his eyes on the iced-tea glass he was turning around and around on the kitchen table. "We won't be sleeping at the same time anyway."

"I'll share Aunt Bertha's bed, and he can use mine." Molly resented being left out of the decision making.

Hod watched her intently. Since morning he had been alert to her every move, every glance in his direction. She didn't smile. Her face was set in a blank mask; her lashes veiled her eyes, allowing only a thin glimmer of violet-blue color to show between her lashes.

I'm sorry we got off to a bad start, pretty little woman. I'd like nothing more than to sleep in your bed . . . with you in it. He cursed himself silently. *Good Lord! What had brought that thought to mind? I've not even kissed her and probably never will.*

She'd had a hard time lately and had endured better than most. She'd not be interested in a rough man who made his living catching or killing criminals. He had been living in a rooming house and out of a suitcase for so long he was almost convinced that he'd be unable to settle down to life with a wife and family.

"It won't be necessary for you to give up your bed. We'll manage." When he spoke his voice came out unnecessarily gruff.

"Do you think they'll come at night?"

"It's hard to tell. One thing in our favor . . . a big thing, is that we're sitting out here in the open, and it's not likely they'll come here on foot. They're more likely to drive in here and spray the place with a tommy gun."

"But what if we've got customers?"

"It will not matter to those gangsters if they can get you."

"For crying out loud! Why in the world did you set me up if there was the possibility of innocent people being killed?" Anger made her eyes sparkle.

"There's a good chance they'll not get this far. The lookouts on the road will spot them, and if they don't stop them, the gunfire will alert me and Johnny that they're on their way."

"I'll never forgive myself if I'm responsible for getting an innocent person killed."

"I feel the same. You are their target. I want you to stay off the porch and away from the front of the store. I don't think they could get close enough to pick you off with a rifle, but I don't want to take the chance."

"Pleasant thought. Thanks for reminding me."

"I want you to be aware of the danger."

"Don't worry about that. Believe me, I'm aware. Why else would I tolerate two strange men living in my house?"

Hod looked at her for a long moment. She looked back, too proud to let him know how scared she really was.

"What do you know about this George who comes to feed his dog?"

"I don't know him very well. No one does now that Daddy is gone. He's always lived nearby. Daddy said more than once that George was no dummy. They talked about a lot of different things. Daddy thought he was pretty smart."

Bertha snorted with disbelief. "He don't act smart to me."

"Did he come to the store as often when your daddy was here?"

"I've been gone for a year so I don't know how often he came here lately."

"There's something I intended to mention, Hod." Johnny spoke with the slow drawl of southern Oklahoma and Texas.

"Yeah. What's that?" Hod pulled his eyes away from Molly to look at his young partner.

"The farmer has a Kodak in the shed. I saw him take it from the top of a rafter, take out the film, and put in a new roll."

"George has a Kodak in the shed?" Molly asked, her eyes locked on Johnny's face. "Oh, I bet he was taking pictures of Stella's puppies. He's very fond of his dog."

Hod's eyes went back to Molly. "Do you trust him. Has he ever made a move that . . . that you didn't like?"

"What do you mean?"

"I know what he means," Bertha said. "The man's got a crush on Molly, but he keeps his distance."

"Aunt Bertha! That's the silliest thing I ever heard. My gosh! He's old enough to be my father."

"I don't think he's as *old* as you think he is," Bertha retorted. "And what's that got to do with anything? That preacher that keeps coming around is older than George, older than your daddy, and has children older than you. He looks at you like you were a bone and he was a starving dog."

"Well for goodness sake, Aunt Bertha. You don't have to tell everything you know."

Hod's eyes narrowed, and his expression became blank. "How many other suitors do you have coming here regularly?"

"Dozens and dozens," Molly snapped.

"I can see why fellers would have a crush on you." Molly's eyes turned on Johnny when he spoke. She smiled. The look that passed between them was not lost on Hod.

Good grief! Is the boy falling for her . . . too?

"Thank you . . . I think. It was supposed to be a compliment, wasn't it?"

"It sure as heck was."

Hod cleared his throat. Molly turned her magnificent eyes on him, and tension drew his nerves tight.

"Back to the farmer. Do you trust him?"

She raised her brows. "I've never had a reason not to."

"I'll have a talk with him. If he's as smart as you think he is, he's seen that oil spot out back where we parked early this morning and will wonder what's going on."

"I'm almost sure he saw me in the shed, yet he didn't

turn a hair. I wasn't too anxious to tackle him. He looks as strong as a bull."

"That doesn't speak well for him. He didn't know what you were up to."

"Do you want George to know why you're here?" Molly addressed her question to Hod.

"I don't want him to know, but it looks like I'll have to tell him."

"I'll talk to him."

"I'd rather do it," Hod said, and turned his eyes away from her. "I'll be getting calls from the Bureau. They'll pretend they are a wholesale house in Kansas City. Write down whatever the caller says and give it to me. There's another thing I want you to know. You'll be paid for our food. I can even arrange for you to be paid for preparing it."

"Whoa now." Bertha held up a hand palm out. "The groceries you eat will come from the store. The store is Molly's. That's one matter. The other is that I'm so damn glad you're here that I'll take no pay for fixing meals."

"That's good of you, Miss McKenzie—"

"Call me Bertha. I'm not all that damned old." She reached over and swatted him on the shoulder. "How do you feel about a batch of cookies?"

"It's too hot to use the oven, Aunt Bertha." Molly picked up her iced-tea glass and Bertha's and took them to the kitchen cabinet.

"I cook them on a griddle like a flapjack. Run down and get me a cup of raisins, sugarpuss, and I'll get started." Bertha pushed her chair back from the table and stood.

"Sugarpuss?" Hod smiled. His dark eyes shone with pleasure. Shiny black hair tumbled down on his forehead, making him look incredibly young and handsome.

A sudden paralysis kept Molly rooted to the spot. A poof of air came from her parted lips.

"Well?" she said, not understanding why she said it.

"Fits," he mouthed, still smiling.

"Smart aleck," she mouthed back.

He chuckled, a sound she'd not heard before. To cover her confusion, she scooped up a tin cup and hurried downstairs, unable to keep the smile off her face.

Chapter Eight

After the noon meal, the Reverend Howell got into his car and drove toward the river. His Bible was on the seat beside him should a member of his congregation discover him parked in his favorite spot in the shade of the cotton-woods that grew along the riverbank. He could tell them that he needed a quiet place to prepare his sermon. In reality, he was seeking a quiet place to think . . . about Molly. She had not been to church that morning. It had been almost more than he could manage to keep the smile on his face as he shook hands with the worshipers as they left after the service.

Molly, Molly, why can't you see that you are my only love? The others meant nothing. God took my rib and made you . . . for me. It is HIS will and mine that we be together always.

Just for an instant he stroked the hard bulge in his britches. He knew it was a sin to relieve his aching loins by that method. He had done so a few times lately, and the guilt had plagued him for days. Now he clasped his hands behind his head to remove the temptation to touch himself.

He was getting impatient. Gladys, he decided, was a big stumbling block. As long as his sister was with them, he would never get Molly to see how much he needed her. That was the ploy he had used to approach his last two wives. He had made them aware of how desperately his children had needed a mother.

After he married, his wives usually served him nicely, except for one . . . the bitch! She had become disobedient and had not even given him any children. She had been of no use to God or man!

His fourth wife had had an aging mother whom he had helped get to the other side to be with her family and friends. It had cleared the way for the one who became the mother of Charlotte and Otis. The mother of the twins and Danny had been a disappointment to him and refused to give him the proper respect despite the many switchings he had given her.

Molly would be no different from the other women. She loved children; she always asked about Charlotte and the little ones. She would be docile and loving once she was broken in. Also standing in the way was that smart-mouthed aunt of hers who had come from Wichita. She was of little consequence. Later, he could take care of her, but first he had to do something about Gladys. School would start tomorrow. If Gladys should meet with an accident, it would force Charlotte to stay at home, which in turn would generate a large amount of sympathy for the family . . . and for him.

Since seeing Otis in the barn with the snakeskin, an idea had been brewing in the back of Archie's mind. Just in case he should act on the idea, he had placed some supplies under the seat of his car. He got out, lifted the seat, and took out a pair of heavy leather gloves, a forked stick, a stick with a wire loop on the end, and a gunnysack. Humming softly to himself, he began to search up and down the riverbank.

Dear sister, I would much rather just take your breath away and let you make a painless journey, but I dare not use that method again so soon. I'm sorry that you will be frightened and will suffer, but you'll forgive me once you're with Ma and Pa and walking the streets of gold.

Archie thought back to his conversation this morning with Dr. Markey; the only doctor within thirty miles of Pearl. He was going to Guyman, Oklahoma, that afternoon and wouldn't be back until late the next night.

There was time. Plenty of time.

In the front room of the living quarters above the store, Hod sat in a chair beside the window, looking out over the porch roof to the road beyond. On the floor beside him was the tommy gun and leaning against the wall was a high-powered rifle. Molly had been shocked at seeing the display of weapons, but said nothing. It seemed strange having men in her home and stranger still having one she was as conscious of as she was of Hod Dolan.

Bertha brought the oscillating electric fan from the kitchen, plugged it into the wall socket, and turned it toward Hod.

"That feels good." His forehead was beaded with moisture. A rivulet of sweat rolled down the side of his face. "Don't you need the fan in the kitchen?"

"I've done all the cooking I'm doin' today. We usually have a cold supper on Sunday and listen to *Lux Radio Theatre*."

"The farmer is back." Johnny came to the door and spoke to Hod. "He's out there with the pups, but I saw him eyeing that oil spot and the tire tracks."

"You take over here. I'll go have a talk with him."

"I'll go with you." Molly waited, sure that Hod would rebuff her offer, but he surprised her.

"Good idea." He waited for her to lead the way.

"Are you going to tell him everything?" Molly asked, as they went down the steps and into the store.

"I haven't decided yet."

As Molly pushed on the screen door at the back of the store, Hod put his hand on her shoulder.

"Just a minute." He went outside ahead of her, scanned the area with squinted eyes, then said, "Come on out."

George looked up when he heard the door squeak. He kept his eyes on the big, dark-haired man as he came off the porch, Molly beside him. Not a flicker of expression crossed his face.

Molly came to him, bent, and scooped up one of the puppies.

"George Andrews, meet Mr. Hod Dolan. He's a Federal Marshal. I think you know why he's here."

"Howdy." George held out his hand. After the hand-shake there was a silence Molly felt compelled to fill.

"The puppies are growing. You haven't named them yet."

"You said you had names picked out." George's gaze left Hod to look at the pup who was trying to lick Molly's face.

"You'll let me name them?"

"Don't you want to?"

"Of course." Molly laughed and held the pup away from her to look into its face. "You're a wiggler, is what you are. Maybe I'll call you Wiggy."

Hod noticed that George's eyes devoured Molly's face when she wasn't looking at him, and he was very adept at not letting her catch him.

Good Lord. The man was head over heels in love with her and she hadn't the slightest clue. Poor miserable cuss.

"I understand that you come over several times a day to look after your dog."

George turned his head slowly, looked at Hod, and nodded.

"Have you seen anything unusual or anyone hanging around that you don't know?"

"Only the man in the shed this morning."

"Why didn't you let Miss McKenzie know that a strange man was in the shed?"

"I figured he was one of the lawmen come to protect her."

"How did you know that?"

"His boots. He was in town last night. Bums don't wear brand-new hand-tooled cowboy boots."

Hod grinned. "You spotted the oil on the grass and the tracks when the car was moved to the front of the store."

"I'd have to be blind not to notice that."

"Still you didn't alert the women."

"Nope."

"Why not?"

"Miss Bertha knew. It ain't right that ya set Miss Molly up like you done."

Molly was surprised by the way George stood up to Hod. It was a side of him she'd not seen before. She was anxious that Hod not be sharp and overbearing with him.

"You're carrying a gun in the bib of your overalls." Hod's eyes never left George's face.

"Yes," George said simply, offering no explanation.

"Would you use it on a man?"

"If I had to."

Hod nodded. "We'd like your help here."

"All right."

"Don't you want to know what's going on before you agree?"

"No."

"All right." Hod looked steadily at the man. George looked steadily back, waiting for the lawman to speak. "I figure the back of the store can be seen from that stand of trees." Hod pointed to a line of scrub oak about a half a mile across the field. "A man with a rifle and a scope could pick off anyone coming out of the store."

"Guess he could."

"Do you live beyond that point?"

" 'Bout quarter of a mile."

"Do you have a telephone?"

"No."

"Well." Hod ran his forked fingers through his damp hair. "Let's get out of sight and have a talk."

"Where?"

"The shed."

George scooped up three frolicking puppies. Molly headed for the shed. Hod placed his hand on her shoulder to halt her while George went through the doorway. He shook his head when she looked back at him. He lifted the puppy from her arms.

"I think I can handle this," he said softly.

"In other words, get back to the store." Her expression mirrored her resentment.

"Something like that."

"Don't you hurt him!"

"Hurt him? Godamighty! It'd take a tornado to hurt that big . . . buffalo."

"He's not a . . . buffalo!" She stared him in the eye.

Hod couldn't believe his ears. "I'll not *hurt* your little pet!" he snarled.

"You'd better not!" She closed her eyes briefly as if she couldn't bear to look at him, then went swiftly toward the store, her back straight, her head high. She entered the building without looking back.

You stubborn little mule! If you only knew how many nights I've lain awake thinking of you—

Hod turned to see George standing in the doorway watching her. An unfamiliar feeling stirred in his chest. *I can't be jealous of this man!* He was sure Molly didn't have romantic feelings for the farmer, but she was showing more consideration for him than she was for the man trying to save her life.

"Why is she mad?"

"She's afraid I'll *hurt* you," Hod growled.

"Hurt . . . me?" An expression of disbelief flickered across George's rough features. When at last he spoke again, his voice was quivery.

"She . . . said that?"

For the remainder of the day Molly had involved herself in a frenzy of activities to keep her mind off the dark, quiet man sitting beside the window in the front room. He had not told her about any arrangement he had made with George, but after he left the shed, he'd had a long conversation with Johnny.

In the late evening it cooled down, and Bertha served a cold supper of egg salad sandwiches, iced tea, and cookies. She placed it on the library table in the living room. The fan stirred the breeze making it the coolest room in the house.

Johnny ate hurriedly, then took several cookies and went down to the back porch. He moved over the floor and down the stairs as soundlessly as a shadow in the soft Indian moccasins he had worn since coming into the store.

Bertha announced that she was going to take the bath that she'd missed the night before. Left alone in the near-dark room with Hod, because he had asked that there be no light, Molly turned on the radio. The set crackled and finally a familiar voice came from the speaker.

"*Good evening, Mr. and Mrs. North and South America and all the ships and clippers at sea. Let's go to press . . . FLASH.*" The sound of tapping telegraph keys in the background lent drama to Walter Winchell's fifteen-minute program, which concentrated mainly on personalities and gossip. By the time the program was over, static made listening impossible, and Molly switched off the set.

"There must be a storm somewhere near."

Hod had been stealing glances at her while they listened to Winchell. She moved her hands restlessly, hooked her hair behind her ear or drummed her fingers on the arm of the chair. She wasn't indifferent to him. His presence made her uncomfortable and cross for some reason. He'd be damned if he could figure it out. Hell, you'd think that she'd be glad he was here.

"I hope it's a rainstorm." Her voice came softly and unexpectedly from across the room.

"It could be an electrical storm without rain clouds."

"It's all we've had lately."

"What did you think about Clyde Floy?" He wanted to keep her talking.

"The reporter? He was all right. He said that his main interest was photography."

"He's good at that. Did he show you the pictures he took after Black Sunday?"

"No. But he told us about them. I was impressed with his shorthand. He's fast. I never had to repeat a word."

"I understand you went to business school."

"For a little more than a year. Daddy insisted I get my certificate."

"Did you like it?"

"Not really. I don't like living in a big city. I never want to be someone's secretary or be in a typing pool."

"Why not? It's a good job for a woman."

"I've got a job here."

There was a long silence, and Hod was afraid she would leave the room. He asked the question that he'd been thinking about most of the day.

"Are you sorry now that you agreed for Clyde to come interview you?"

Molly thought for a moment before she answered. "Nooo . . ."

"I thought maybe you were," Hod said softly, his dark eyes piercing the gloom in the room to discern the expression on her face.

"I didn't realize that it would be quite like this."

"I should have explained to you that there would be two men here at all times. Johnny and I will give you as much privacy as we can."

"Have you done this before?"

"Guarded a witness? Not quite like this. I'm usually out in the field. The Bureau doesn't do much of this. What they've done in the past is stash witnesses away someplace until they need them to appear in court. This situation is entirely different. We have reason to believe that Pascoe and Norton have robbed six country stores between Amarillo and Kansas City. There may be others we've been unable to tie to them."

"I hope they come soon, and we can get it over with."

"I do . . . and I don't." *Now why in the hell did I say that?*

"You don't? I thought you wanted to catch them."

"I do want to catch them, but I don't want you to get hurt."

"Or . . . you'll get fired."

"No! Dammit! If they get through the roadblocks, they could come here, spray this place with machine-gun bullets or throw in a firebomb. I'd like to hide you and your aunt away someplace until this is over."

After a silence Hod heard a soft giggle.

"What's so funny about me wanting to hide you away and keep you safe?" he said almost angrily.

"I was thinking that you could dress up like Aunt Bertha. Johnny could wear one of my dresses—"

In spite of himself Hod laughed. "Now that would be a . . . sight—" His words trailed. He stood and peered out the window.

"Is someone coming?" Molly came to stand beside him.

He breathed deeply, then said curtly, "Car. Coming slow. Without lights. Go to the back rooms. If I yell 'drop,' drop flat on the floor."

Molly moved quickly to the small hallway separating the two bedrooms, her heart beating so hard that she was sure he could hear it. She listened for the rat-a-tat-tat sound of a machine gun she had heard in the movies.

Oh, God! Don't let this be it. They'll kill him!

The silence was broken by a faint clicking sound. Hod had picked up the tommy gun. Then the awful silence again. It went on and on until Molly thought she would scream. How does he stand this pressure? How could a woman endure knowing that the man she loved waited beside a window expecting it to be sprayed with a machine gun that fired 450 cartridges a minute?

I would never let myself fall in love with a man in such dangerous work. I'd never know when he left me if he would ever return, and I would die a little bit each time.

This time the silence was broken by the sound of Hod's voice.

"They went on by. Damn fools out driving without lights. Good way to get themselves killed. Molly . . ." Silence. Then, "Molly . . . ?"

He heard the soft closing of the bedroom door.

Dawn finally came.

Molly had spent the long night hours sleeping only a scant hour at a time. The tension of the day had left her in a state of nervous exhaustion. During the waking hours she had sorted through every scrap of conversation that had passed between her and Hod Dolan over the past week. Her thoughts had been unpleasant company. The man evidently thought her a dumb country girl.

There were many things about the Federal man that she didn't understand. She'd had absolutely no experience with a hard-edged man like Hod. She had seen him looking at Johnny with genuine affection. He had been gentle with the puppies, polite to a fault with her aunt, and yet, when he handled the machine gun, his face was hard as a rock. She had no doubt that he'd cut down a man without a thought of mercy should he be acting in the line of duty.

She knew nothing about his personal life, how he lived or where he lived or if he was married. Did he have a wife and children waiting for him in Kansas City? He'd said nothing one way or the other about . . . *that*. For heaven's sake! She wasn't interested in him in a *romantic* way! It wasn't every day a girl had a real live G-man in her house.

One thing in his favor: Aunt Bertha liked him, and she was an excellent judge of people . . . especially men.

Damn you, Hod Dolan! Get out of my mind!

Molly got out of bed and dressed quickly. With a jerky motion she ran the brush through her hair, steeled herself to face him, and opened the bedroom door. She passed through the kitchen to see Hod and Bertha sitting at the table.

"Morning," she murmured, and headed for the stairway, praying that Johnny was not in the storage room that also served as the bathroom. He wasn't. She could see him sitting in a chair beside the front door of the store.

She closed the storage-room door behind her and leaned against it after she had turned the key in the lock. Johnny's shiny new cowboy boots sat beside his pack.

Hod Dolan's black-leather suitcase and canvas bags were stashed in the corner.

Molly pushed herself away from the door and used the toilet. When she finished she reached up to pull the chain to flush it. The chain broke up near the tank attached high on the wall above the stool and no water came down into the toilet.

"Damn!"

Molly looked at the chain dangling from her hand and at the nasty-looking waste in the toilet. She had to get rid of it fast. The stench was filling the room. She grabbed a bucket and began filling it with water from the spigot they used to fill the washing machine. When it was full, she dumped it into the toilet and was relieved to see the waste disappear.

She still had to do something about the stench. She would die a thousand times if Hod or Johnny came into the room before it disappeared. She found the matchbox, struck several sticks, and waved them around the room. The thought of Hod using the toilet and reaching for the chain that wasn't there brought a smile. It would serve him right!

She looked at her pale face in the mirror above the sink. The sleepless night had taken its toll, leaving dark smudges beneath her eyes. She opened them wide and looked at the sprinkling of freckles across her nose. She hadn't bothered to use any bleach cream or lemon juice since she had come home from Wichita.

Her mother hadn't been here to remind her.

She bared her teeth and grimaced at her reflection. Her eyes felt as if they were full of sand, and her mouth tasted as if an army had marched through it during the night. She'd gone right to bed last night and had not come down to brush her teeth. She did that now. Then she removed her dress, washed herself thoroughly, dipped into her jar of deodorant and smeared it under her arms before pulling her dress back over her head.

Well, what the heck! she thought as she looked at herself critically in the mirror. *I'm not going to town. This is a workday.*

She ran the comb through her hair, slipped a narrow ribbon beneath it, and tied it in a bow on top of her head. She dreaded going back upstairs, but knew that she must.

The telephone was ringing as she opened the door. She paused for it to ring again. It was their ring, two shorts and one long. She went behind the counter and picked up the receiver.

A hand came around from behind her and covered the mouthpiece before she could speak. *Where had he come from?*

"Careful." Hod grasped her wrist and held the receiver away from her ear, putting his face close to hers. His body was hard and warm and big. She tried to lean away from him.

"Molly? Molly, is that you? Say something. Oh, shoot—"

"Ruth?" Molly jerked her hand from Hod's grasp and put the receiver close to her ear but far enough away so that he could also hear. "Ruth, I . . . wasn't sure if it was our ring." She forced a lightness into her voice.

"Two shorts and a long, or have you forgotten?" Ruth laughed merrily. "I heard receivers go up all up and down the line. Hear ye, hear ye, everybody. You may as well hear what I've called to tell Molly—Gladys Howell, the preacher's sister, died last night. She was bitten by a rattlesnake."

"Oh, the poor woman," Molly exclaimed. She turned her back on Hod, but he continued to stand close to her.

"My goodness. Ruth, this is Doris Luscomb. What in the world happened?"

"Hello, Doris." Ruth wasn't the least surprised when another voice came on the line. "Are you there too, Pat?"

"I'm here."

"Figured you were. How about you, Mrs. Secory?"

"Mama isn't on, but I am. I'll call her."

"Susie Secory! Today's the first day of school. You'd better be getting ready."

"I will, Miss Hoover . . . in a minute."

"Ruth, tell us what happened," Molly said.

"Well, the way I heard it, the Reverend took his sister down by the river to prepare a picnic for the kids. He left her to spread out the quilt and went back to the car for the basket. When he returned the snake had wrapped itself around her and bitten her on the neck."

"How in the world could a snake jump up and wrap itself around the neck of a grown woman?" Molly asked.

"Preacher said she was on her knees on the quilt and screaming her head off."

"Who wouldn't be screaming," another voice chimed in.

"That you, Betty?"

"Yeah. Susie said something important happened."

"Poor Reverend Howell. It must have been terrible for him," Doris said after clicking her tongue against the roof of her mouth.

"For him? What about his sister, for heaven's sake? She was the one getting bitten by the snake!" Ruth's voice squeaked in indignation.

"Well, I didn't mean . . . I wonder if I should go out and help with those sweet little kids. I bet the Reverend is beside himself. Why do these things happen to the good people? He is the kindest man I've ever known."

"He got her into town only to discover Dr. Mulkey had gone down to Guyman for the day," Ruth continued. "I doubt he could have done anything anyway. The venom went right into the artery."

"The Lord certainly does try that man," Doris murmured.

"Oh, come on, Doris." Betty had a slight lisp. Probably didn't have her teeth in. "He loves every minute of the sympathy he gets."

"Betty Secory! You should be ashamed of yourself."

"Molly," Ruth broke in, "I've got to get going. School starts today. The reason I called was to ask if you wanted to send some food to the house. If so, I'll ask Keith to come pick it up."

"Are you keeping company with that man out at Morrison's, Ruth?" Pat chimed in before Molly could speak.

"I'm not sure I know what you mean by *keeping company*, Pat. I'm not sleeping with him, if that's what you mean."

"Forever more! You know I didn't mean . . . *that*."

"Of course we'll send something," Molly hurried to say. "I'd appreciate it if Keith would pick it up. I'm expecting a shipment today. It'll be hard for me to get away. Will the funeral be tomorrow?" She shrugged off the hand Hod placed on her shoulder.

"At two o'clock. Poor Charlotte. I suppose she'll not get to go to school now. She was one of my best students. If you want to feel sorry for someone, Doris, feel sorry for Charlotte."

"Maybe Mr. Howell will find another wife soon. He doesn't seem to have much trouble getting them. But he does seem to have a problem keeping them. Doris, do you or Pat know a single woman who is looking for a husband and won't mind being number five . . . or six?" Molly asked.

"That's not funny, Molly. You should be ashamed. That man has had more grief in his lifetime than any ten men."

"I'm ashamed, Doris," Molly said drily. "Truly, I am."

"It's not very smart to be saying such things on the party line." Doris said huffily. "There's no telling who's listening in."

"Ain't it the truth? You two thrash it out. Pat, you and Betty referee. I've got to go. Maybe I'll see you tonight, Molly."

" 'Bye, Ruth."

Molly hung the receiver in the cradle attached to the side of the wall phone and, without looking at Hod, moved out from behind the counter and away from him.

"Who's coming?"

"Keith McCabe. The preacher's sister died. I'll send a

pound of coffee or something to the house. The funeral is tomorrow."

"Who is this McCabe?" He had the dead-serious, no-nonsense look on his face.

"He is a friend of my friend Ruth Hoover. She teaches in the high school. I've known her all my life. He's staying out at Morrison's ranch. He'll come and take our donation out to the preacher's house, where the neighbors will be feeding the family until after the burial. That's all there is to it." She recited the monologue patiently as if she were talking to a child.

"I don't enjoy prying into your affairs, Molly. I do so only to be as sure as I can be that nothing unexpected happens here."

"I know. If anything happens to me, you'll get fired."

"You're not going to let that go, are you?" When she didn't answer, he said, "You look tired, Molly. Didn't you sleep well? Is that why you're so cross?"

"I slept all right, and I'm not cross. Just tired of having to explain every move I make. How did *you* sleep?"

"Fine. As you know, Johnny and I take three-hour shifts at the upstairs window. We're used to sleeping in short intervals."

Molly stared at him, pondering how he could look so refreshed with so little sleep. He had shaved, his midnight black hair, resentful of brush and comb, fell down on his forehead. His shirt was clean but wrinkled. He was a big, attractive man, clearly intelligent; his dark eyes seemed to absorb everything, his mind was quick and alert. She couldn't deny that her heart fluttered more quickly in his presence. It was a natural reaction, she reasoned.

"What are you thinking, little Molly?" he asked softly, searing black eyes holding hers.

"I was . . . wondering if your wife worried about you," she answered honestly, miserably conscious that his eyes had lowered to her lips.

"Would you . . . if you were my wife?" He grinned with a devastating charm that made his rough features beguiling.

"I suppose," she said with cool indifference.

"If you were my wife, would you want me to give up this work and do something else?"

"I'm not your wife, so the question is moot." In order to have something to do, Molly picked up a rag and ran it over the smooth surface of the counter.

"What made you think that I was married?" He leaned against the counter.

"I've not given it a lot of thought. I just assumed that a man your age would be."

"I admit that I'm old enough, but I don't have a wife. I've never even come close to getting one."

Molly continued to wipe the counter as if the task was the most important one in the world, hoping to hide the sudden elation that swept over her.

"I can understand why," she murmured.

"You can't imagine a woman wanting me. Is that it?" She looked at him and saw the grin on his face. It irritated her and prodded her to speak words she instantly regretted.

"No. Some women will take anything."

"Whoa! The lady has a sharp tongue this morning."

"I'm sorry. I didn't mean to be insulting. I just don't

think you'd be very good husband material." Molly felt the hammering of her heart against her breast.

He reached over and took the rag from her hand, and looked down into her face. His dark eyes glittered with amusement; and when he spoke, it was with smiling lips.

"Why not?"

"Well, you wouldn't be home much, you're bossy, and . . . your work is dangerous."

He rubbed his chin. "I was afraid you were going to say it was because I was pig-ugly."

Unexpected laughter burst from her lips. "I was just getting ready to add that. Are you fishing for a compliment?"

"I'll give you one if you give me one." Hod's mouth spread wide with a grin.

Laughing, he is handsome as sin!

"It would take me an hour to think of one"—her eyes shone with laughter—"and I've got work to do."

Hod couldn't drag his eyes from her face.

Sweetheart, you could break my lonesome heart.

"It'd not take me but a half a second. But never mind now. Are you going to open the store?"

"Anytime now. Daddy opened as soon as he'd had breakfast. Sooner if someone came."

"Run up and get your breakfast—"

The telephone rang again. Two shorts and a long. Molly glanced at him and went to the phone. He was beside her when she lifted the receiver.

"McKenzie Store."

"This is the long-distance operator. I have a call for Molly McKenzie?"

"This is Molly McKenzie."

"This is your party," the operator said in a singsong voice. "Go ahead, sir."

"Miss McKenzie?"

"Yes."

"Ellis Dalton from Dalton Wholesale in Kansas City. Your order has been held up in Topeka. I'll know by late this afternoon when it will be shipped."

"All right. Anything else?"

"No nothing."

"Thank you for calling."

Molly hung up the phone and turned to Hod. "You heard?"

"Every word. I need to speak to Johnny."

Chapter Nine

Would you mind if Johnny used your truck?"

Both men had come down from the living quarters and stood at the foot of the stairs. Molly was washing the front of the icebox.

"No. But it hasn't been started since Daddy died. Aunt Bertha's car is behind the truck, but there's a door at the back of the shed. Daddy usually went out the back way and circled around." Molly took keys from a nail beside the back door and gave them to Johnny. "You might have better luck than I did."

"That thing won't start," Aunt Bertha came out of the storage room. "I tried it one day. Take my Ford, Johnny. If you put a scratch on it, I'll break both your legs."

"Thank you, ma'am. It'll be a pleasure to drive that car, and I'll sure be careful." Johnny smiled. "I'm not wantin' to get my legs broke."

Johnny was a breathtakingly handsome young man.

His golden skin was smooth, his teeth even and white. Inky black brows hovered over deep-set dark eyes. Molly glanced at Hod. He was watching her and didn't turn his eyes away when they met hers. What was *he* thinking for goodness sake? She was the one to break the contact.

Bertha watched until her car turned down the road toward Pearl.

"Isn't she a beauty?" She exclaimed, beaming with pride. "I'd not lend her to anyone else. I like that kid. 'Sides, if something happens to it, the government can buy me a new one." She picked up her dusting cloth and went to the front of the store.

"I'll stay down here until Johnny gets back," Hod said. "If someone comes that you don't recognize, make for the storage room."

"I recognize this bird comin' in now." Bertha looked out over the spool cabinet. "It's that smilin', little fat preacher. What the heck is he doin' here? You'd think he'd be home with his younguns today of all days."

"Is he the one who just lost his sister to snakebite?"

"That's him," Bertha said drily. "He's pie-eyed over Molly. Looks at her like a dying calf."

"Aunt Bertha! I wish you wouldn't say things like that."

"It's true, honey, and you know it. Something about the smiling little toad makes my skin crawl."

"Has the preacher taken a shine to you?" Hod asked.

"For heaven's sake! He's old enough to be my father."

"What difference does that make? A lot of women go for older men."

"Not me. Thank you."

"He's a man, and you're a pretty girl." He saw the color rise in her cheeks.

Damn, but you're pretty . . . and fresh. Molly, sweet Molly, your eyes are like spring violets.

"He'll wonder what you're doing here."

"Don't worry." He stared into her remarkable eyes as if he could never get enough of looking at her. His lips quirked. "I'll think of something."

The preacher stopped the car beside the gas pump, got out, and tossed his hat on the seat. Before stepping up onto the porch, he smoothed down the sides of his hair with his palms. When he opened the screen door the bell jingled merrily.

"Morning, Reverend," Bertha said as soon as he stepped inside the store. "Sorry to hear about your sister."

"Morning," he answered, moving past her. His eyes were on Molly in the back of the store filling a glass jar with penny candy. He stopped directly in front of her. "Morning, Molly."

"Morning, Reverend Howell. I'm sorry about your sister."

"Thank you, my dear. I came to you because I knew that you would feel my grief deeply."

"The entire community feels your grief as they do for anyone who loses a loved one."

"I take it you heard what happened."

"Ruth called this morning. She said Dr. Markey was out of town. How unfortunate."

"Yes. I'm not sure he could have saved her had he been here. I'll not forgive myself for leaving her alone while I went to get the picnic basket."

"You shouldn't blame yourself. These things happen."

"Ordained by *God. He* has a plan for all of us, Molly. *He* decided that it was time for Gladys to come home."

"Still, it's a pity. I know that you'll miss her."

"The children are suffering, Molly. They had looked forward to the picnic. Now poor little Charlotte won't get to go to school."

"That's a shame. Can't you find someone to watch the little ones? Ruth says that Charlotte is an excellent student."

"I just don't know what in the world to do. My dear little children lost first their mother and now their aunty." The eyes that were fastened on her face were shiny with tears.

"I understand that the service will be held tomorrow afternoon."

"Molly, dear, I was wondering if you would come out to the house today. The children love you. You would be such a comfort to them . . . to all of us. Please, please come." He came close to her and put his hand on her arm.

"I . . . don't see how I can do that, Reverend Howell. The store . . ." Molly shrugged his hand away, picked up a box of jawbreakers, and began to fill another jar.

"Your aunt would be here, dear. I'm sure that she could take care of things. Isn't that why you brought her here?"

"No, I'm sorry. I can't leave."

"Please reconsider, Molly. The children need you. I . . . need you."

"Do you *need* gas, Reverend?" Molly asked pointedly.

"Are you sure you can't come home with me?" He allowed his voice to quiver.

"I'm sure. Very sure."

"Well, I do need gas, my dear."

"I'll get it, sweetheart."

Preacher Howell had not noticed Hod standing back among the brooms and shovels hanging from the ceiling. At the sound of Hod's voice, he spun around. When he saw the big black-haired man, he backed up a step.

"Reverend, this is—"

"Hod Dolan." Hod stepped forward and stuck out his hand. "I'm Molly's soon-to-be-husband," he said while shaking the preacher's hand vigorously.

Archie Howell's mouth hung open; and, as the realization of what the man was saying sank into his mind, color came up from his neck to turn his face a dull red.

"You're . . . goin' to marry . . . him?" he croaked, looking first at Molly then back to Hod.

"We've been engaged for several months now. Molly wanted to wait about making the announcement because of the death of her parents." Hod turned to the stunned Molly. Her hands clung to the top of the glass jar. "Honey, you kept the secret better than I thought you would."

Hod's sharp eyes saw the hot anger that washed over the preacher, watched his nostrils flare and a muscle jerk in his fat cheek. For an instant a murderous rage flashed from eyes that settled on Hod's face. The red that colored Archie's cheeks faded as quickly as it had come, leaving his soft face inordinately pale and expressionless.

"Well, now, this is a . . . surprise—"

"Did you say you needed gas? I'll get it. Stay inside, sweetheart. Did you know that you're getting freckles on your nose?" Hod's arm was across Molly's shoulders. He hugged her to him and dropped a kiss on her nose.

"Hod, be . . . have," she croaked.

"Molly and I haven't decided where we'll be married. Could be here, could be Wichita. She has a lot of friends here, but we have a lot in Wichita, too."

Archie Howell turned pale blue eyes on Molly. As their eyes met, color came again to his face making it beet red except for the white around his mouth.

"I'm sorry, Molly. It would have been so . . . wonderful." There was regret on his face and his shoulders slumped.

"I'm sorry about . . . your sister, Reverend Howell." A puzzled frown puckered her brows. She was suddenly grateful for Hod's big warm body close to hers.

"Yes, so am I."

"It is too bad." Hod continued to hold Molly close to him. "Damn, but I hate snakes. Molly said it was a rattler. A full-grown rattler or a cottonmouth bite is deadly."

"Snakes are dangerous," Archie said calmly, even though the eyes turned on Hod were cold as an icy pond. "I'll be getting back to my children. Good-bye, Molly."

"Good-bye."

Hod followed the preacher through the store and out onto the porch. When the screen door slammed behind them, Molly hurried to look out the window.

"Why would he think I'd go to his house? There must be a dozen women there by now."

"I've been trying to tell you, honey. That man's got what I call a fixation where you're concerned," Bertha said.

"What in the world do you mean by that?"

"It means that he's obsessed with you and thinks he has a chance of having you."

"Well, for heaven's sake! That makes me want to—"

"—Throw up? Maybe now the pious preacher will set his sights on someone else. That was quick thinking on Hod's part."

"Too quick. How'll I get out of it without having everyone think that I was jilted?"

"We'll think of something."

George came around the corner of the store, Stella beside him. The big white dog growled low in her throat. George reached down and gave her a pat on the head.

"Morning, George," Hod called.

"Mornin'. Preacher want gas?"

"Yeah. I'll get it." Hod began pumping the gas into the cylinder while chatting with George about the electrical storm that had failed to produce the much-needed rain.

Archie noticed the obvious friendliness between the two men. At first, chafing under the humiliation of Molly's rejection, his mind had whirled in confusion. Now, however, he could think clearly.

George Andrews has never been that friendly with him or anyone else except for Roy McKenzie. If that's the way the wind blows, so be it. I've survived disappointments before. I chose you, Molly, but you rebuffed and embarrassed me after I paved the way for us to be together. This citified blowhard cannot possibly give you the pleasure I would have given you. But . . . too late now. The die is cast, and you're all bound for hell.

God, I've been your good servant and helped the poor,

the miserable, and the ill cross the great divide to rest in Your arms. Why, oh why, did You let this happen? An eye for an eye. A tooth for a tooth. Molly, Molly, you'll be so sorry.

"How much?" Archie was jarred from his thoughts when Hod spoke to him.

"Two gallons." Archie dug in his pocket for the thirty-six cents.

The big white dog left George, went up onto the porch, and lay down. George waited beside the pump. An uneasy silence ensued while the gas went into the tank.

When Hod cut off the gas flow, and screwed the cap back on the tank, Archie dropped the change in his hand and got into the car.

"Good day to you," Hod called, as the car shot away from the pump, turned, and headed down the road toward town in a cloud of dust. He had the uncomfortable feeling that the preacher was not what he pretended to be. He had to give the man credit though. He was furious when told that Molly was to be married. It showed for only a second, then he covered it up admirably.

"Do you go to his church, George?"

"No. Don't like him."

"I don't think I do either. Does he come around here much?"

"Three, four times a week since Roy and Velma died."

"Miss McKenzie said he had been hanging around after Molly."

"Yeah. He's been doggin' her."

"You knew that?"

"I was watchin' it."

"Did he come here at night?"

"A time or two. Sat on the porch. Miss Bertha stayed put."

"Good for her."

"If he'd a tried anythin', I'd a stopped it."

Hod's head swiveled around so he could see the big, quiet man who stood with his thumbs hooked in the pockets of his overalls. The outline of the pistol was in the bib.

"Had you decided what you were going to do?"

"Yeah." George glanced at him, then down at Stella. "He warn't goin' to have her."

"I told him I was going to marry Molly. It made him madder than a peed-on snake."

One of George's rare grins appeared on his face. "Bet it did."

"What if I told you that I might really want to marry her?"

"Wal . . ." George took off his hat and slapped at a big horsefly buzzing around his face. "I'd study on it. You ain't had a bunch of wives and a sister what up and died suddenly."

"No. Are you trying to tell me something?"

"Nothin' ever'body don't know." He watched as Johnny drove Miss Bertha's car in and stopped in front of the shed.

"Keep a watch on the road, George. If you see anything coming from either direction, give a whistle." Hod met Johnny at the dock where feed sacks were loaded.

"Found Bob down the road. He went to the telephone office to call the chief."

"Something's happened. Could be that he's pulling us in."

"He'd not leave these women out here unprotected . . . would he?"

"No. He'd send someone else." The thought of not being here when Molly needed him made Hod's stomach lurch painfully.

A minute or two later a loud whistle came from the front of the store. Hod and Johnny sprang up onto the dock and into the open doorway. At Hod's signal, Johnny took the stairs two at a time to take up the position at the front window with the tommy gun.

"Back room," Hod barked. The two women obeyed as he hurried to the front window.

George was sitting on the porch step. As the car slowed to turn in at the store, he got up and casually moved to the side of the porch, stooped, and brought out something in a gunnysack. From the shape of what was in the sack, Hod had no doubt what it was. *Godamighty! The man is either fearless or a stupid son of a bitch if he thinks to go against a tommy gun with a shotgun.*

The flashy car that jerked to a halt beside the porch steps stirred up a cloud of dust. It was tan with a black top that sloped down to a trunk attached to the back. A fancy ornament adorned the hood. The man who flung open the door wore a white shirt, a bow tie, a straw Panama hat, and polished cowboy boots. He ignored George and came into the store.

"Morning." Hod stayed behind the counter.

"I'm looking for the Morrison Ranch," the man said curtly without bothering to return the greeting.

"Sorry. Can't help you." Hod's tone was equally curt.

"It's a big ranch, and you don't know where it is?"

"It's what I said."

"For chrissake! Don't you ever get outta this place?" The man tipped his hat back and looked at the goods hanging from the ceiling with his upper lip raised as if he smelled something foul.

"We went to town last Christmas." Hod's eyes widened as if he were imparting important news.

When the obnoxious little "rooster" got the message that Hod was making fun of him, he squared his shoulders and stomped to the door, the heels of his boots echoing loudly on the wood floor.

"Folks around here aren't very friendly," he declared.

Hod followed him to the door. "Not when some inconsiderate son of a bitch drives in, skids his car to a halt, and stirs up a cloud of dust."

Ignoring the remark, the man said, "Do you know a man named Keith McCabe?"

"Never heard of him."

"He's been here a month or two."

"It's a big country."

The screen door slammed. Heading to his car, the man spotted George at the side of the porch.

"Hey . . . hey, you. Do you know the way to the Morrison Ranch?"

"Yeah."

"Well . . . where is it?"

"South and west of Pearl."

"Do you know if Keith McCabe is still there?"

"Might."

"Well." The man dug into his pocket and flipped a coin to George. He caught it in his big hand, looked at it, and flipped it back. The man failed to catch it. It hit the car and fell into the dirt. He left it there.

"Don't know."

"Thanks for nothing, hayseed. If you see him tell him that his cousin, Martin Conroy, from *Conroy*, Texas, is looking for him."

Hod had come out onto the porch. He leaned against a post and watched the car skid out onto the road and head for town. It took a full minute for the dust to clear. During that time, Hod wished he had the little pipsqueak's neck in his two hands.

"Ya reckon the little bugger has a town named after him?"

"It'd have to be a turd town," George said without cracking a smile, and sat back down on the porch.

The bell tinkled when Johnny came out onto the porch and stood with hands on his hips looking down the road toward town.

"I know that little son of a gun. He was a brother to Emmajean, Tom's first wife. What the hell is he doing up here?"

"That name sounded familiar. I was just beginning to sort it out in my mind. He's the one Tom thought set fire to his house, though he couldn't prove it."

"He wouldn't even go to his own sister's funeral. The family was ashamed of her because her mind wasn't right. I wonder what he's doing up here," Johnny said again.

"He's looking for his cousin, Keith McCabe."

"Keith McCabe? That don't say much for McCabe."

"You can't choose your relatives, Johnny." Hod stepped off the porch and went around to where George sat, his hand stroking the head of his dog. The bitch's head rested on George's knee. "Are you planning on using that shotgun you've got in the gunnysack?"

"It ain't there just to look at."

"The men, if they come, will be well armed. They'll be coming with tommy guns, dynamite sticks, and heaven knows whatall."

"Yeah?"

"Doesn't that scare the hell out of you?"

"Yeah."

"Well?"

"Well what?"

"They'll kill you, dammit!"

"Not if I can help it."

Hod threw his hands in the air. "I give up. Come on in. Let's have a cold soda pop."

George drank his soda pop and left a coin on the counter. As soon as he went out the back door, Molly turned on Hod.

"Why did you tell the preacher that . . . that we're engaged?"

"I was letting him know that you're taken, and he could look elsewhere for a girl. I thought you'd be glad."

"Well, I'm not!"

"I also thought it would be a reason for me being here."

"How will I explain when you leave? Tell all my friends that my beau from Wichita jilted me?"

"Tell them you jilted me, that you tied a can to my tail, and sent me on down the road."

"Bullfoot! Who'd believe that?"

"You mean that I'm so handsome, such a good catch, your friends wouldn't believe it?"

"Talk sense or not at all!"

Molly grabbed a broom and began to sweep the floor even though it had been swept once that morning. Monday was always a slow day at the store. When her parents were alive, her father would clean the store and her mother would do the washing.

With the two men underfoot, Molly wasn't sure what to do. One of them stayed in the front of the store, the other sat in the upstairs window. Bertha, however, seemed to enjoy having them around.

In the middle of the morning a man with a bag slung over his shoulder walked in from the road. Hod went to the porch to look him over. He was ragged and thin. Gray whiskers covered his sunken cheeks.

"Howdy."

"Howdy. Ya mind if I have a drink a water?"

"The well's out back. Help yourself."

"Thank ya kindly."

Hod went through the store to the back door.

"A lot of tramps stop by here." Molly's soft heart ached for those without a home. "I'll fix something for him to eat."

"Hadn't you better wait until he asks?"

"Why make him beg?" Her eyes stared defiantly into Hod's. "He's probably got nothing left but his pride, if he's got that."

Molly, sweet Molly, you're too good to be real.

"You're right. Fix something and I'll take it out."

Hod stood at the back door. The man had thrown off his old felt hat and stuck his head under the water pouring from the pump spout. Poor devil. At least the weather was warm. It must be hell to be without a home in the winter.

Molly came from the living quarters and went to the front of the store. She put a package of soda crackers and a couple cans of sardines in a sack and added sandwiches of bread and jam she had made while in the kitchen. Hod was tempted to kiss her when she handed him the package.

"You're a sweet woman, Molly McKenzie." He went out the door, not wanting to see the look on her face. He didn't understand why he had voiced his thoughts, but he was glad that he had.

The postman drove in and Molly went out to get the mail.

"Morning, Mr. Bruce."

"Mornin'. Did you hear about Reverend Howell's sister?"

"Ruth Hoover called this morning. It isn't often a person gets bitten by a snake around here. Although there are plenty of snakes down by the river."

"Are you goin' to the buryin'?"

"I'm not sure."

"Did the law send anybody to look after you women?"

"Well—"

"I'm sayin' that it would be a hell of a note if they set you up out here and didn't do anythin' to protect you." He saw her anxious look back toward the store. "Ya don't have to tell me nothin', Molly. I notice George is hangin' around a lot more. Good man, George, even if some folks think he's kinda queer. He ain't no fool, I'll tell ya that."

"Daddy always liked him."

"Yeah, well, I got to be gettin' on."

" 'Bye, Mr. Bruce."

Hod met Molly at the door. "It scared the hell out of me when I saw you at that car. Then I realized it was the postman."

"Don't you think I've got more sense than to go out to a strange car? I've known Mr. Bruce all my life. He was pretty upset about the article in the paper. He thought I had lost my mind to allow it."

"Does that flirty iceman come today?" Hod said, ignoring her outburst.

"How do you know he's flirty?"

"He was here the day I came to talk to you. At the time I thought that you deliberately kept him here so that I'd have to stay in that hot storage room."

"You can't hurry Walter. He flirts with everyone. It's just his way."

"Does he come here the same day every week?"

"He comes on Tuesdays and Fridays in the summertime."

"How long has he been on the route?"

"He was doing it when I came home in May."

"How often do you get soda pop?"

"The pop man comes on Wednesday." Molly set aside the letters for her aunt and thumbed through the wholesale catalog. "I've got to order chicken feed and lamp oil.

Not many folks have electricity; just those in town and on this road. Daddy usually went down to Liberal about the time school started and brought back a couple of barrels of oil and a load of feed."

"In that truck in the shed?"

"It might not look so good, but he had a new engine put in last winter."

"Car comin'," Johnny called, and a minute later, "It's Bob."

The big sedan pulled in and stopped at the gas pump. Bob Walker and another man got out. Hod met them on the porch.

"They got Floyd Pascoe up in Topeka. Norton got away."

"Kill him?"

"Deader'n a doornail." Bob mopped his forehead with his handkerchief. "They held up another store. Killed the owner and as they were leaving a rancher drove up. They shot at him, wounded him, but he pulled out a Smith & Wesson and killed Pascoe. Chief thinks Norton's headed for Chicago. He's not one to act alone. Pascoe was the brains of that outfit."

"What are we to do here?"

"Hod, you lucky dog, you get to stay here with this pretty woman." Bob's homely face split in a grin. "Johnny, you're to report to the Federal Marshal in Ardmore, Oklahoma, and the rest of us are to be back in Kansas City by tomorrow noon."

"If the chief thinks Norton won't act alone, why does he want me to stay here?"

Bob recited the chief's message, word for word:

"If anything happens to that woman after that spread in the paper, the Bureau will be crucified by every reporter on the radio from H.V. Kaltenborn to Walter Winchell and every newspaper in the country. The *Star* would delight in spreading it across the front page. It was Dolan's idea. He's to stick to that woman like glue and see that nothing happens to her. It'd be just like that Norton to hire someone to do his dirty work for him."

"Poor old Hod." Johnny slapped Hod on the back. "It's a shame, is what it is. You've got to stay here, eat Aunt Bertha's cooking, and look after the prettiest woman I've seen in a month of Sundays."

"Did he say how long I was to stay here?" Hod asked, ignoring Johnny's teasing.

"He didn't say how long. He did say for you to call the first chance you got. But I'd think you'd stay until we got Norton and found out if he'd hired someone. You'll just have to suffer it out, son."

"Are you leaving me a car?" Hod asked, determined to keep the pleased smile off his face.

"Nothing was said about it. You've ridden with the Texas Rangers, haven't you? You'll just have to find ya a horse."

"You're very funny, Bob."

"By the way, Pascoe had the newspaper clipping in his pocket. They might've been on their way here."

"It was not one of the best ideas I've ever had."

"Glad to hear you admit it. We've got to be going. We'll drop Johnny off in Wichita to catch the bus to Ardmore after we stop up the road and send Clarence and his partner on up to Tokepa. You'll be the chief in charge here, old hoss."

"You fellows are just jealous because you'll be sweating in that hot car and eating dust, while I sit here under the fan eating Miss Bertha's cherry pie and looking at a pretty woman."

"Yeah. Some fellers have all the luck."

Chapter
Ten

It was Johnny who told Molly and Bertha the news that he was leaving and Hod would be staying.

"I'll ride with Bob to Wichita and take the bus down to Ardmore." He had come out of the storage room with his knapsack. "Hod has all the luck."

"You just wait right there," Bertha said, then on the stairs to the kitchen, "I'll get you something to eat on the way. I made an extra big batch of those flapjack cookies."

"Which one of the gangsters was killed?" Molly asked.

"Pascoe. Norton usually drove the car."

"I wish they'd killed both of them," she said angrily. "Neither one was fit to live."

"I'll agree with you there."

"If you're ever this way, Johnny, come back to see us."

"Thank you, Miss Molly. I'm hoping to get my ranch in shape so I can make a living and quit this work except to help Hod out now and then."

"Is your ranch in Oklahoma?"

"Right on the Red River. It doesn't amount to much now, but with luck and hard work it could someday."

"It will. Thank you for coming here and helping to look out for us."

"It was my pleasure, Miss Molly."

Bertha came down the stairs with a paper sack.

"Here ya are, kid. You take care of yourself. Hear?" She reached up and kissed him on the cheek. "I could'a had a boy 'bout your age, if I hadn't a been so blasted goody-goody." She rolled the top of the sack down and put it in his hand.

"Thanks, Miss McKenzie. 'Bye, ladies."

"Bye, Johnny."

When Bertha went upstairs to fix a noon meal, Hod sat on the porch talking to George. He filled the tank on the big touring car with gas for his fellow officers. Then Bob Walker went in to pay and bought cheese and crackers to eat on the way to Wichita. When George left to go home, Hod went into the store.

Molly was eaten up with curiosity. Why was *he* staying? Did he ask to stay? How long would he be here?

"I guess Johnny told you what happened in Topeka."

"He said one of the men was killed."

"I'm to stay here for a while."

"He said that, too."

"You'll be paid for my board."

She shrugged, then asked, "How long will you be here?"

"Until they catch Norton and find out if he paid one of his pals to do the job. They think that he and Pascoe were on their way here when they decided to rob a store. A rancher drove in and killed Pascoe."

"It's what Johnny said. Now that half the danger is gone, there's not much of a reason for you to stay."

"You don't like having me around, do you?"

"It . . . isn't that—"

"Then why are you on the defensive every time we talk?"

"Well . . . I get the impression that you think I'm just a country twit and that this is just a run-down old country store and . . . you'd rather be someplace else."

He turned to face her more directly. A shaft of sunlight sifting in through the window shone on her face, so that her eyes seemed especially bright.

"I don't know what gave you that idea," he said softly, his eyes holding hers.

Molly, disturbed at the way he looked at her, felt uneasy in the region of her heart. She shrugged again.

"It isn't important."

"To me it is." Suddenly it was of great importance to him that she not resent him. "I'll try to keep out from underfoot."

"Dinner's ready anytime you can eat it," Bertha called from the top of the stairs.

"Go on up. I'll be here if someone comes in." When she hesitated, he said, "I'll not get in the cash register and I'll not eat the raisins or candy sticks or jawbreakers or cheese—"

"I counted the raisins. If you take even one, I'll know

it," Molly said severely. Then light, spontaneous laughter burst from her lips. His nonsense had had the desired effect on her, and he could only stare at her and wonder at the power she had over him.

Molly, sweet Molly, you're turning my life upside down.

"Keith is here," she said when a car came to a stop beside the steps.

Apprehension washed over Hod at the familiar way she used the man's name. Then he cursed himself for being so distracted by her that he hadn't even been aware a car was approaching.

"Has he been here before?" he asked almost angrily.

"No. But he's nice. Ruth really likes him."

"And . . . you?"

Molly didn't answer. She walked to the door to meet Keith McCabe.

The sleeves of his white shirt were rolled up for coolness sake, and he took off his black Stetson hat as he entered the store.

"Hello, Mr. McCabe. Ruth said you'd be by."

"I thought we were finished with that *mister* stuff. How are you, Molly?"

"Just fine. I'd like you to meet Hod Dolan. Hod, Keith McCabe."

"Pleased to meet you." Keith held out his hand. The men were of equal height although McCabe was heavier.

"Likewise." Hod was used to taking a man's measure. Keith McCabe appeared to be a man who had been over the mountain, as his grandfather used to say about a man who had been tested. Tested, yes, but Hod wasn't sure yet which side of the mountain Keith had come down on. He'd have to wait and see.

"Ruth said you'd be by to pick up something to take out to the Howells'. I've got it ready." She slipped a sack of Cain's coffee into a paper bag.

"Mr. Morrison lent me his car, and Mrs. Morrison said that as long as I was coming here I should pick up some things for her. She made a list." He took a paper from his shirt pocket and handed it to Molly. She slid along the shelves and set items from the list on the counter.

"Do you live around here, Dolan?"

"No. I'm from Wichita."

"Just passing through?"

"I'm here to see my girl."

"I see." Keith's eyes darted toward Molly at the end of the store, where she was reaching into the icebox for cheese.

"By the way, there was a man here this morning looking for the Morrison Ranch and for . . . you."

"Yeah?" Keith's head turned toward Hod. "What'd he look like?"

"A jelly bean. He said he was your cousin. His name was Martin Conroy, from *Conroy*, Texas. He made sure we knew that."

Keith swore under his breath. *I wonder what the little son of a bitch wants this time?*

"Jelly bean fits him, but horse's ass fits him better."

Hod grinned. "If he carries that uppity attitude with him all the time, it's a wonder he still has teeth."

"I've been tempted to loosen a few myself. Where did he go?"

"Off down the road. A fellow that was here told him the Morrison Ranch was south and west of Pearl."

Keith chuckled. "It's north and east of Pearl. He must have got the fellow's dander up."

Molly finished filling the order and moved up the counter to write out the bill. Hod watched her add the column and put the groceries in a sack. Keith took bills from his pocket, and Molly gave him change.

"Too bad about the Reverend's sister. No one has been killed by snakebite here for several years."

"Too bad, too, that the doctor was out of town."

"The preacher was here this morning. He doubted the doctor could have saved her. The snake bit her in the neck. Right on an artery."

"That's strange." Keith's face registered puzzlement. "Did the snake jump up and bite her on the neck or sneak up on her while she was lying down? Usually a rattler makes plenty of noise and coils before it strikes. She wasn't deaf, was she?"

"I never heard anyone say that she was."

"Does the preacher usually do his trading here?"

"Some of it."

"He didn't buy anything this morning," Hod said, darting a glance at Molly. "He wanted Molly to come out to his place and comfort his kids. I suspect he was the one looking for comfort," he added drily.

"Hod!" Molly wanted to kick him.

"Yeah. Ruth said he had a crush on Molly."

"Well, I fixed that." Hod grinned at the red-faced Molly. "I told him our news, didn't I, honey?"

"Hod, don't you dare!"

"She doesn't want to announce our engagement. She's afraid folks will think it too soon after she lost her folks."

"Well, congratulations. The way Walter Lovik was acting the other night, I thought that he was in the running for her hand."

"I'll set him straight about that." Hod's tone was belligerent.

"No!" Molly turned on Hod.

"Does Ruth know about this?" Keith asked.

"No," Molly said again, and glared at Hod. "You make me so . . . mad! Keith, he—"

"Honey, honey," Hod said quickly. "Don't deny it. It'll only make it worse. I'm sorry I let the cat out of the bag. But that blasted preacher got *my* dander up this morning. Aunt Bertha was right . . . he looked at you like a sick calf."

"You don't even know what a sick calf looks like, Hod Dolan."

"Sweetheart! Have you forgotten that I was raised on a Nebraska farm?"

"More than likely you were raised in the barn!"

Hod looked at Keith and winked. "She likes me."

Keith chuckled. "I've got to be going. I'll go by the preacher's and take Mrs. Morrison's offering and yours. Ruth said something about coming out tonight. Has she cleared it with you?"

"She mentioned it this morning. She knows that she doesn't have to wait for an invitation."

"See you tonight. Will you be here, Dolan?"

Hod moved over, slipped his arm around Molly, and grinned down at her. "You bet. I'll be here."

Molly stood ramrod stiff until Keith got into the car, then pushed away from Hod.

"This playacting has gone far enough."

"Can you think of a better reason for me to be here?"

"The truth for starters."

"Even at that, folks would talk about a big, handsome man like me staying nights with *two* single women." His eyes danced with deviltry. "Me being your intended and your Aunt Bertha here as chaperone, folks will know that things are on the up-and-up. Come on. Admit that it was good thinking on my part."

"You've got everything figured out, haven't you?"

"I try to. I slip up every once in a while."

"I'm relieved to know that you're not perfect."

He laughed. *Molly, sweet Molly—*

The party line was busy with talk about the death of Gladys Howell. The telephone rang a dozen times during the afternoon, but only once did it ring two shorts and a long. Molly answered.

"McKenzie Store."

"Is Keith McCabe there?"

"No. He was here about noon."

"This is his cousin. You can tell that hayseed who sent me off on a wild-goose chase looking for the Morrison Ranch that it wasn't a damn bit funny. I drove all over the damn county. I'm back in Pearl at the . . . Main Street Cafe."

"I don't know what you're talking about."

"Did Keith say where he was going?"

Molly was silent for a minute, then said, "Not exactly."

"Jesus Christ! If he comes back there, tell him where I am. I want to see him right away, and I don't have all day to wait on him."

"I doubt if he'll be back. Good-bye." She hung up the receiver.

"What was that about?" Bertha asked.

"Somebody looking for Keith McCabe. We've sold a lot of gas lately. I'm going out and measure the tank."

Molly went out the side door and down the steps of the loading platform. She reached underneath it and pulled out a long rod, laid it on the platform, and wiped it with a cloth.

"Goin' to measure the tank?" George came from the back of the store.

"I didn't know you were here, George." Until the last few days she had always called him Mr. Andrews. Somehow now it seemed perfectly natural to address him by his given name.

"I'll do that."

George took the heavy rod and went to the front of the building where, out about six feet from the porch the gas tank was buried in the ground. He had to lean the rod against the porch and use both hands to remove the heavy cap on the tank. He slid the rod into the tank, pulled it out, and showed Molly the wet end.

"Eighteen inches left in the tank."

"Then I'd better call the gasoline company soon."

"It ain't good to let it get too low. Ya'd be suckin' up the water that settles on the bottom."

Molly looked at him in surprise. "There'll be water in the gas?"

"Yeah. Condensation."

"I never knew about that."

"Warn't no reason for ya to."

"Thank you for telling me."

He put the rod back under the platform, then the cap back on the tank. Molly walked beside him to the back of the store, where the puppies frolicked in front of the shed.

"I'll take a couple of them home."

"Oh, do you have to?"

"They've got to be weaned. Stella's skin and bones from feedin' them."

Hod came out the back door, a frown on his face making him look sinister. He strode across the yard and stood before Molly.

"I thought you were in the store."

"Well, I wasn't. I had to measure the gas tank."

"Warn't nobody around," George said.

"A man with a rifle in the woods yonder could pick her off."

"I went there 'fore I come here. No tracks."

"Did you see anything of that bum that was here this morning?"

"Walked on past, heading for town."

"He seemed harmless, but I wasn't sure."

Molly looked from one man to the other. Irritated with both of them for ignoring her, she went up onto the porch and strode into the store.

Keith McCabe left the preacher's house after dropping off the food donations. A half dozen church women were fussing over the children, preparing food and doing whatever they could find to do to justify their being there. The preacher, they said, had gone to his room to grieve in private. Keith had been glad of the excuse to visit the Howell home.

He was still puzzled at how Miss Howell could have been bitten in the neck by the rattlesnake. A rattler was not a tree snake and wouldn't have fallen out of a tree and wrapped itself around her neck. Had it been on the ground, coiled to strike, the rattles would have warned her. Even if she hadn't heard the rattles, the snake would have been more likely to strike at her leg. In that case, she could have possibly been saved if a tourniquet had been applied.

It was a suspicious circumstance. Yet, why would the preacher want to get rid of his sister?

At the Morrison's he found the message that Marty was waiting for him at the cafe in Pearl.

Jim Morrison was a big, weathered, gray-haired man, seasoned by many years on the cattle ranch. He had contempt for the shortsightedness of the wheat farmers who had plowed the land, causing tons of topsoil to be blown into the surrounding states by the blustery winds.

"How did Conroy know you were here?" Jim asked, as Keith deposited the groceries on the kitchen table.

"Damned if I know."

"As I recall the gossip, that kid had the brains of a flea. Old Martin Conroy was smarter, and I've heard that he wouldn't have been so bad if he hadn't married that snooty bitch from Wichita Falls."

"He died a couple years ago. Now Marty is *the* Conroy. He feels pretty important."

"I hadn't seen old Martin since he was a boy. Heard about 'em through folks we've known in Conroy. We was kind of shirttail relations, like you. Your mama being a second cousin to old Martin makes you about a third cousin to young Marty."

"I'd just as soon you didn't bring it up."

"Being as we're shirttail relation to *your* daddy, Marty probably doesn't even know there's a connection between us."

"It's none of his business anyway."

"Anythin' new on this other matter you're lookin' into?"

"A few things. I want to go write everything down that I've heard while it's still fresh in my mind. Then I'll go to Pearl and find out what's on the little turd's mind. I have to get him out of town before he has time to screw things up."

Keith drove the Morrison car back to town because he had a date to pick up Ruth after school. Later, they would go out to Molly's. When he came up here from Texas, he hadn't planned on finding a woman as interesting as Ruth Hoover. Not a raving beauty, but she was smart, spunky, and fun. Having been raised on a cattle ranch as he had been, she was no shrinking violet, that was sure.

The night of the dance, he had been jolted to realize that he was irritated when that fellow Lovik kept coming back to dance with her. After about the third time, he'd been tempted to punch the iceman in the nose.

Unconsciously he smiled, thinking about it.

A black-and-tan Oldsmobile was parked in front of the barbershop when Keith reached Pearl. It was the fanciest car most of the residents had ever seen. Several of them stood on the sidewalk and gawked at it. Keith spotted it as soon as he turned the corner and entered town. He parked behind it and went into the cafe.

"Afternoon, Mr. McCabe." The dark-haired owner of the cafe called from the door of the kitchen. She was a small attractive woman in her mid-thirties. Her hair was caught at the nape of her neck and cascaded to the middle of her back. Large gold hoops hung from her ears.

"Howdy, ma'am." Keith hung his hat on a rack beside the door and sat down at a corner table. "I'll have coffee, Mrs. Wisniewski."

"Mr. Conroy said that if you came in to tell you he was at the barbershop."

"I'll wait here. When he wears out his welcome there, he'll be back."

The twinkle in the eyes of the woman who brought his coffee told him that she understood what he meant.

"This is the most excitement we've had in one day since I've been here. The preacher's sister dying from snakebite and the little big shot in his fancy car honoring us with a visit."

"Lord it over you, did he?"

"Well, he made sure that I knew he was from Conroy, Texas, the town named for his granddaddy."

"I just bet you that if his granddaddy knew how he'd turned out, he'd rise up out of his grave." Keith looked toward the door as Marty flung it open and came in.

"Jesus Christ, Keith. I'd never have known you were here if the barber hadn't spotted Morrison's car. Where the hell have you been? I've been all over this damn county looking for you."

"It's none of your business where I've been. What do you want?" Keith asked bluntly.

"Where can we talk?"

"Right here."

"But . . ." Marty jerked his head toward the kitchen.

"Spill it, Marty. She's not listening."

"I had a hell of a time finding out where you went. I had to go to Lubbock and find out from your grandma."

Keith half rose up out of his chair. "Goddammit!" he swore. "You have a nerve bothering her—"

"Don't get in a sweat. I knew you'd not go off without letting her know where you were headed."

"What did you say to wheedle it out of her?" Marty's face turned a dull red. "Goddamn you! What did you tell my grandma?" Keith demanded.

"I said . . . I said that there had been a misunderstanding and that the . . . Texas Rangers were looking for you for questioning." He finished quickly. Keith stared at him so intently and so angrily, he rushed to explain. "I told her that I had to warn you so you could turn yourself in and . . . tell your side of . . . things."

"You worthless, no-good pile of horseshit. I should break every bone in your rotten, cheatin', lyin' body. Grandma will be beside herself with worry." Keith's voice was getting quieter and quieter, a sign that his anger was rising.

Marty knew that his distant relative was angry enough to bite the head off a snake. He hadn't counted on Keith's getting in such an uproar over what he had told the old lady. He seemed to have put his head in the lion's mouth, and now he had to figure a way to get it out.

"Calm down, Keith. I had to find you. You'll be glad I did."

"Don't count on it, you rotten son of a bitch."

"You're interested in making a lot of money, aren't you?"

"What harebrained scheme have you cooked up now?"

"Oh, I know what you're up to, Keith." Marty laughed. "You might have been able to fool your granny into thinking you were coming up to visit the Morrisons, but not me. You're looking for a gasfield out here in the middle of nowhere."

"Now aren't you smart? You'd make a top-notch detective." Keith's voice was heavy with sarcasm. It failed to register with Marty.

"You didn't think I'd find out, did you?" Marty sat back with a smirk on his face. "Well, I did, and I've talked to Simon in Dallas, Kennedy in Midland and Efthim Drilling in Houston. Richard Efthim told me that they would consider drilling when you say the word. How is that? You find the gas, I find the backing."

Keith stared at the cocky little man, his anger and disbelief building.

"You've got a good reputation, Keith," Marty continued confidently. "I only had to mention your name, and I got the ears of really big-time investors. How about it? What say we form a partnership?"

"Marty, I don't know what to say to a stupid, clabberhead like you." Keith spoke softly. "This may come as a surprise to you, but if I were building a shithouse, you'd have about as much chance of being my partner as you'd have standing out there on the street and pissing all the way to Wichita."

"Now, Keith, I know you're upset because I found out what you're up to, but think about it. That gasfield up at El Dorado is making money hand over fist. This one could be even bigger. Think of the money—"

"You think, Marty. Think of what you'd look like without any teeth, with your ass kicked up between your shoulders, and your head screwed on so you'll see where you've been and not where you're going."

"Why are you so damn mad? We're kinfolk, and kinfolk should stick together."

"You sure stuck to Emmajean. The whole damn Conroy family turned their backs on her, and she was your sister, for God's sake."

"She was crazy as a loon, and you know it."

Keith got to his feet, walked to the counter, and placed some money in the dish sitting there.

"Thanks, Mr. McCabe." The voice came from the kitchen.

Keith took his hat from the peg, slammed it down on his head, and pushed Marty out the door ahead of him.

"Now get your hoity-toity little ass back in that car and get the hell out of here or I'm going to go through you like a hot chili pepper through a *gringo*! Get out of this town, out of this county, out of this state, or I just might pound you into the ground."

"I'd . . . have you arrested."

"I don't think so." He gestured toward the onlookers. "I think you've been here long enough to piss off enough people that they'd get a kick out of seeing me bust your head and be willing to swear you started it."

"You're going to be sorry about this, Keith. I was willing to help you do something really big. You go ahead and find that gasfield; you'll get no help from me getting backing."

"Marty, that purely breaks my heart. Now get the hell out of here; and if I hear of you meddling in my affairs again, I'll come looking for you and cut you down so low you can walk under a toad without taking off your hat."

Several people, including the barbers, had come out onto the sidewalk to look over the fancy car. A number of them heard what Keith had said. Some of them grinned.

Red-faced, Marty climbed into his car. When he took off, he deliberately skidded the wheels and threw gravel on the Morrison car parked behind him.

Keith turned to go to his car and came face-to-face with Jennifer Bruza.

"Well . . . hello—" Jennifer was a pretty girl, very pretty. Ruth had told him that she and her twin lived with their widowed mother. Their father had died several years ago, leaving his family comfortable, if not well-off.

"Ma'am." Keith tipped his hat.

"What are you doing in town this time of day?" Jennifer's big brown eyes caressed his face. It was a look she had practiced before the mirror of her dressing table.

"I had business—"

"With the man in that . . . gorgeous car?"

"Him and others." Keith had met her type before. She was a born flirt, but even knowing that didn't keep him from being amused by her obvious attempt to attract him.

"You didn't ask me to dance . . . the other night." She pouted prettily.

"I don't dance."

"Don't dance? I'll teach you. Jan and I are having a party Saturday night. Please come. Everybody will be there."

"I don't know. Ruth and I had planned to go to Liberial to the picture show."

"Oh, well—" Her eyes turned frosty for a second or two. "If you change your mind and want to do something that's fun, you've got a standing invitation."

"Thanks. I'll tell Ruth."

He grinned as she spun around on her high heels and sashayed down the walk.

"Mr. McCabe?" Wally Wisniewski, the son of the woman who owned the restaurant, stopped beside Keith.

"Who was that?"

"The lady? Miss Bruza—"

"No, the man in the fancy car. He'd have to be rich to drive a car like that."

"He's someone I knew down in Texas. School out already?"

"Yeah. You waitin' for Miss Hoover? She's keepin' a couple of smart-mouth kids after school. Miss Hoover don't take no sass."

"I imagine not. She's got good kids in her class, too, hasn't she?"

"Some." Wally grinned. "We've only got twenty-two in our high school this year. Miss Hoover said Charlotte Howell won't be coming back now that her aunt died.

She'll have to stay home and take care of her brothers and sisters. Don't seem hardly fair. Char liked school."

"Maybe the preacher will find someone to come live in and take care of the kids."

"I hope so. I only get to see Char at school. Her old man won't let her go to anything but church. Margaret, one of her friends, told me that she got into a lot of trouble because I walked home with her one night after early church. Someone saw us and told the old Bible-spouter. He gave Char a spanking."

"How old is she?"

"Fifteen this week."

"I'd think that was a little old for a spanking."

"She didn't do anything. When the Byingtons passed, she took off down the road like a turpentined cat. She was scared to death. I knew then that that old son of a bitch was mean to her."

"I take it you don't like the preacher?"

"You take it right. He don't like us, either."

"Why is that?"

"He tried to keep Mama from getting the cafe going."

"What did he do?"

"For one thing, he said Mama was bound for hell for smoking cigarettes. And having her here wasn't a good influence on the women in the town."

"A lot of women smoke cigarettes nowadays."

"Not here in Pearl. He told folks that we were foreigners, and if we didn't have any business, we'd close up and go back where we come from. We might be foreigners in Pearl, but we wasn't in Chicago. It's all the same country, isn't it?"

"It was the last time I noticed."

"I think he don't like us 'cause he kind of shined up to Mama when we first got here and she'd have nothin' to do with him. Mama can get pretty feisty at times." The boy grinned. "She told him in front of the barber to keep his damned hands to himself or she'd use a meat cleaver on them."

"That would do it." Keith smiled at the thought of that tiny woman swinging a meat cleaver.

"Mama and I don't understand why the people in this town think he's so great. Don't they wonder what happened to all those wives he's had?"

"I've not heard that there's anything suspicious about their deaths, Wally. The doctor certified all of them died of natural causes. Folks figure he's had bad luck with his womenfolk."

"Bad luck, my hind leg. He's not at home like he is in church. He rules those kids with an iron hand. They hate him."

"Charlotte say that?"

"No. Otis. He's a couple years younger than Char. He's going to run away when he gets a little bigger. He and his little brothers have been doin' most of the work out at that place since we came here. They're treated like the hired hands. I'm surprised the old preacher lets Otis come to school."

"Wally," his mother called from the doorway of the cafe. "Come move some things for me."

"Be right there, Mama."

"Sounds to me like those kids need a friend, Wally."

"Old preacher don't want them to have friends."

"Wally—"

"See ya, Mr. McCabe. My mama is such a little bitty thing she depends on me a lot." He grinned proudly.

"I bet she does. She's lucky to have you."

"See ya," he said again. "Your girl will be along soon." Wally winked at him and disappeared inside the cafe.

Keith went to the car. It was nice, real nice, to have Ruth referred to as *his* girl.

Chapter
Eleven

It unnerved Molly to have Hod constantly underfoot and it irritated her that her aunt agreed that it was a good thing to let people think he was her fiancé. Obviously, the man thought that it was pretty much a joke that he had proposed marriage to her. She mulled over her conclusions as she restacked cans of Bon Ami and bars of Lifebuoy soap to make room for the new shipment of Ipana toothpaste and Colgate tooth powder.

Several neighboring ranch families had come to the store during the day and, after being introduced to Hod, had congratulated him and told him what a good, sweet girl she was and that they knew her parents would be happy she had someone to look after her.

Hod was attentive when customers were present. He never missed the opportunity to put his arm around her and to act the loving husband-to-be. He was a good actor, she told herself. He would do anything to keep her safe and to . . . keep his job.

In the late afternoon, Bertha went upstairs to rest before preparing the evening meal. Hod sat on a stool behind the counter and watched out the window. Only two customers stopped for gas. One was a couple with two small children, obviously no threat.

The other was a lone male. Hob scrutinized him carefully when he stepped up onto the porch, and came into the store. He decided that he was what he appeared to be, a traveler, especially when he saw that there was no place he could conceal a weapon unless it was strapped to his inner thigh.

Molly stayed in the back of the store while Hod pumped gas, collected the money, put it in the cash drawer, and returned to his stool beside the window. She dusted and rearranged the goods on the shelves that her father had laughingly referred to as Molly's Beauty Supplies: Tangee lipstick, rouge, Pond's face powder, cold creams, and hair oils. As she wiped off the bottles of thick, gooey hair-setting lotion and the box filled with cards of bobby pins, her mind was on the man sitting beside the window.

Hod's mind was on her. He had tried for a week to analyze his feelings toward Molly McKenzie. His obsession with her worried him. It was not that he was desperate to get her into bed—although last night while sitting in the dark beside the upstairs window, he had thought about how it would be to bury himself in her soft, naked body. That alone wasn't unusual. He was a normal, healthy male and had all the natural mating instincts.

This was different. It was much more than the desire for relief of the moment. He wanted someone . . . her . . . to belong exclusively to him, to care for him. He wanted the kind of love his brother Mike shared with his wife, Letty, and Tom had with his Henry Ann.

You're not good husband material. He had been annoyed with himself for the leaden feeling that weighed on his heart on hearing her words. Thinking about it, his insides churned. That first day, when he met her, he had known that he would have to be very careful. Yet he had gone full tilt ahead, paying no heed to the warning signals, and allowed himself to daydream about her.

His first mistake was getting the bright idea of using her for bait. His second mistake was putting the idea to his chief, and his third was sending the reporter out here. He should have called this whole thing off after he met her.

Molly McKenzie was not for him, he reminded himself sternly. His brain knew that, but his body and his emotions refused to accept the idea. She was young, sweet, innocent, totally unaware of how sordid the world had become. He, on the other hand, was cynical and guarded after years of having to deal with robbers, rapists, and killers. Nothing that these criminals did shocked him anymore.

For the past year he had longed to live a quieter life. He didn't want to walk into another bank, another store, another house and look at a bullet-riddled body. He wanted to come home at night and have a sweet woman in the kitchen, standing at the stove, waiting for him. She would be smiling and—

"Mr. Dolan . . . Hod?" Molly had come to the front of the store while he had been daydreaming.

Hod drew a deep, steadying breath and turned to her. They looked at each other for what seemed a long time before he spoke.

"Is it time to close the store?" His voice was strained.

"We don't close until dark in the summertime. Aunt Bertha called down that supper was ready. You go eat. If anyone comes, I'll come get you."

"You go ahead and eat first."

"I'm not very hungry."

"You should eat more. You're too thin." He saw the tightening of her mouth and realized that he had said something stupid. "I'm sorry. It isn't any of my business how thin you are."

"No it isn't," she answered frostily.

"Why is it that almost every time we talk we strike sparks off each other?"

"For one reason, almost every time we talk, you criticize me for something."

"I didn't realize that and . . . I'm not sure it's true."

"What do you call that last remark? And"—she interrupted when he started to deny—"you made fun of me because Reverend Howell was . . . well, thought I would welcome his—"

"—Courtship." He finished for her. "I was not making fun of you, Molly. I wanted to punch the old fool in the nose for even thinking that you'd be interested in him."

"That isn't the way it appeared to me. And you made up that utterly ridiculous story."

"Do you think it ridiculous that you and I could be engaged? Am I lumped into the same category as the preacher?"

"Now you're really being ridiculous!" She turned and went quickly to the stairs leading to the living quarters.

"You run away every time you start to lose an argument."

"See?" she turned. "Another criticism. I wonder why you bother to stay and protect such a stupid, worthless woman."

Molly knew that she was being unreasonable. But . . . damn, damn, damn! Just looking at him made her . . . say and do crazy things!

Charlotte Howell was tired and sick at heart. Today was the first day of school, and she had missed it. She'd never be able to go again unless her daddy found someone to come take care of the kids. The first thing he had said when he came back from town, after he told them that Aunt Gladys had died, was that she, Charlotte, was now in charge of the house. She didn't want to be in charge of the house or the kids. She was glad to turn them over to the women who came today. The kids were glad, too. They were enjoying being fussed over, something Aunt Gladys had never done.

Charlotte wandered out toward the barn, where the boys were squatting under a tree. Her daddy was in his room. She kept track of where he was every minute of the time he was home. Today Charlotte's mind was especially troubled. Why had her daddy wanted to take them on a picnic on Sunday afternoon? A picnic was fun. They were never allowed to have fun on Sunday.

Aunt Gladys hadn't wanted to go on the picnic. She said that her back hurt, and she wanted to rest before going to Sunday night service. Her daddy had insisted that Aunt Gladys go. He even got angry and demanded that she pack a picnic lunch that they would take to a beautiful spot along the river. She could lay out the quilts, he had told her, and unpack the lunch while he returned for the children.

The afternoon had passed slowly while Charlotte and the children waited for him on the porch. Finally, just as it was getting dark, he returned to tell them Aunt Gladys was dead. He didn't seem to be broken-up about it. He told them to go to bed, that they wouldn't be going to church service; he had stopped by and asked one of the deacons to take over. After telling them that he went into his room and closed the door.

"Did you grind the corn?" Otis was sprawled on the grass. The two younger boys sat cross-legged in front of him. They squinted up at their sister.

"Didn't figure we had to work today. We're grievin' for Aunt Gladys."

"Yeah, Char. We're grievin'," Harley echoed.

"It's nothing to make light of, Harley."

"I ain't makin' no light. Why does everybody die? I was just gettin' to like Aunt Gladys . . . a little."

"I don't know, Harley. I guess it's just the way it is."

"I wish it'd been *him* the snake bit." Five-year-old Daniel's large blue, red-rimmed eyes looked up at his sister. He had been crying.

"Don't say such a thing, Danny," Charlotte responded

quickly. "We'd be orphans and have to go to an orphans' home."

"Do they whip you at a . . . orphans' home?"

"I suppose, if you're mean."

"I wasn't mean." Danny's lips quivered, his voice trembled, and his eyes filled with tears. "I spilled the dumb old chicken feed. I didn't mean to."

Otis reached over and removed a cover from Daniel's lap. Charlotte gasped as she saw more than a dozen cut marks from a willow switch on the child's legs. Some of them were beaded with blood. She dropped down on her knees beside him.

"Oh, Danny. When did he do this?"

"This mornin'." Otis answered for his brother. Tears ran down Danny's cheeks. He wiped his nose on the sleeve of his shirt. "He went in the car someplace and when he came back he was mad. When he saw the little pile of chicken feed, he took Danny to the barn."

"Have you put anything on the cuts?"

"I didn't know where the ointment was, Char. *He* was in there, and I didn't dare go in and ask *him*."

"It's on the shelf over the washbench."

"He told Danny to stay out of the house. He hasn't had anything to eat except what me and Harley could sneak out."

"Oh! That makes me so mad! There's enough food in there to last a week. I'll be right back."

The women who had come to help were in the front room cooing over the baby. Charlotte headed for the kitchen. A regular feast was spread out on the table. In a clean dishcloth she wrapped several pieces of fried chicken, two slices of buttered bread, and two deviled eggs. *The mean old thing might make Danny stay out there all night. At least he'd not be hungry.*

After finding the tin of Watkins salve and hiding it under the cloth, she went out the back door and walked leisurely, in case her father was watching out the window, across the yard to where her brothers waited.

"He can't see you from his room, Danny, but—"

"—Why do you think we're sittin' here?" Otis asked grumpily.

"Go to the barn to eat this anyway. I don't think he'll go out there today."

"Maybe he'll die!" Harley said.

Charlotte ignored her brother's outburst and carefully applied the ointment to the switch cuts on Danny's legs. She was putting the lid back on the tin when Margaret Jenson and her mother drove into the yard.

"I don't want 'em to see." Danny became panicky and tried to cover his legs.

"They'll not see." Char quickly spread the cloth over the child's legs. "I'll bring out a pair of Harley's old overalls. They'll be too long, but you can roll up the legs."

Otis reached for the tin and hid it behind him just before Margaret reached them.

"Hi, Char. We missed you at school. You're coming back, aren't you, Otis?"

"I . . . think so."

"Mama brought out some canned meat and a jar of pickled peaches," Margaret announced. "She waited till I got home from school so I could come."

Margaret's mother was a widow. After her husband

died, she went to Liberal to beauty school, came back and opened a parlor in the front room of their home. Margaret had a permanent wave. Her hair lay in deep waves, and the ends curled about her neck and shoulders. Charlotte envied her having a mother who cared how she looked. She had never even dared to set her own hair in spit curls.

"How was school?"

"It was exciting to be back. We missed you," Margaret said again, then whispered, "I've got a note from Wally."

"Don't . . . don't give it to me now," Charlotte whispered hastily. "*He* could be looking out the window. Come in the house with me. I've got to get a pair of overalls for Danny."

Margaret followed her into the house. The two girls slipped silently up the stairs. As they passed a closed door Charlotte put her finger to her lips. She eased open the door to a small room, then silently closed it behind them and leaned against it. Margaret pulled a folded piece of paper from her pocket and handed it to her friend.

Charlotte's heart was thumping like a wild bird trapped in her breast. She went to the one small window and turned her back to her friend to read the few lines on the page.

Char
Miss Hoover says you'll not come to school. When will I see you? I'm sorry you got in trouble last time.
                                        Wally
P.S. I missed you. School won't be fun without you.

Charlotte read the note several times, then folded it into a small square and shoved it down past her ankle into her sock.

"Did you read it?"

"Uh-huh. He said I could. Do you want to send a note back?"

"I'm afraid to."

"I brought a pencil and tablet. Come sit in the car with me like we're waiting for Mama."

"Oh, Margaret. You're the best friend I ever had." Charlotte opened a trunk and took out a pair of overalls.

When they went out into the hallway, her father was standing in the doorway of his room. Charlotte's tongue clung to the roof of her mouth.

"Hello, Reverend Howell," Margaret said pleasantly. "We're sorry about your sister. Mama's downstairs."

"Good of her to come." The Reverend's eyes went to Charlotte. She held up the overalls.

"I had to get clean pants for one of the boys. Otis . . . said he'd a . . . splattered him when he slopped the hogs."

"Good boy, Otis. I'm depending on you and Otis to see that the children stay clean. We'll have a prayer before supper," he said to Margaret. His soft beardless face was without its usual warm smile. The constant movement of his shoulders was evidence that he wasn't as calm as he pretended to be. "You and Mrs. Jenson are welcome to stay and eat with us."

"Thank you. I'll tell her."

"Go on now, Charlotte. Don't forget your duties. You're the woman of the house now."

The girls went down the stairs and out the front door.

"Your daddy scares me. I don't know why."

"He scares me, too, and I know why."

"I told my mother that he spanked you."

"I wish you hadn't. It's so . . . embarrassing."

"Mama says it's a shame you've got to stay home and take care of his kids. She says that this growing-up time should be a happy time in your life . . . meeting boys, going to parties and to school. She thinks your daddy could hire somebody if he wanted to." Margaret giggled. "Maybe he'll get married again."

"I'm hoping he'll do . . . something."

"Wally feels bad. He just wanted to walk with you the other night. He's really very nice. I wish I was the one he liked."

"He is nice," Charlotte murmured.

"He didn't have any idea walking home with you would get you in so much trouble."

"You . . . didn't tell him about—"

"No!" Margaret wished with all her heart that she *hadn't* told him, but it was too late now.

Otis and the boys went to the barn after Charlotte gave them the overalls and she and Margaret went to sit in the car.

"Hurry and write your note. Mama said we'd not stay long. She don't like your daddy much. She's thinking about pulling out of his church and going to that Baptist church out in the country."

"I've never written a note to a boy before."

"You'll think of something. Start with—'Dear Wally'."

"I can't say *dear!*"

Charlotte stuck the pencil in her mouth and wet the lead, then began to write on the tablet.

Wally,
I'm sorry too that I can't come to school. I hope
Daddy finds someone soon to take care of the kids. I
miss everyone.

Charlotte
P.S. Try to have fun.

She tore the sheet out of the tablet, folded it into a small square, and gave it to her friend.

"Tell Miss Hoover . . . I'll miss being in the play this year."

"I will. Here comes Mama. I'll walk out one day after school. Maybe I'll have a note from Wally."

"You are my best friend," Charlotte said for the second time. And under her breath . . . *you and Wally.*

"George is here to keep an eye on things," Hod said to Bertha after he had eaten his supper. "Do you mind if I use your bathtub?"

"Of course not. Light the tank. It'll take about fifteen minutes for it to warm up enough to take the chill off the water. I'm going to wash tomorrow. If you have anything to be washed, lay it out."

"I can do it. I don't want you to see the holes in my socks," he said with a teasing grin as he got up from the table.

"I've washed socks with holes in them big as my fist. I've washed men's drawers, too. I had a rooming house in

Wichita for almost fifteen years. There's not much I don't know about holes in men's socks."

"Fifteen years? You were just a child fifteen years ago."

She chuckled. "Blarney. You're Irish, for sure."

"My granddaddy came from County Cork."

"Mine came from Limerick. He was a pistol. He could drink a jug of Irish whiskey and dance an Irish jig when he was eighty years old. I got most of my bad habits from him."

"I've not noticed any."

"Go on with ya and get your bath. I baked a chocolate cake for when Ruth and McCabe get here."

"Chocolate cake! Will I be invited to the . . . party?"

"I'm inviting you now. Maybe they'll wind up the Victrola and dance. I never heard of an Irishman who didn't like to dance."

"Yeah." Hod laughed. "We all danced at home in Nebraska. There were enough of us to have a set. Papa would play the fiddle and us kids and Ma would dance. An old preacher there used to call us heathens because we were Catholic. He'd say we were dancing our way to hell."

Before closeting himself in the storage room to take his bath, Hod went out and spoke to George.

"If you're going to be here for a while, George, I'll take a bath."

"I'll be here."

"A couple of Molly's friends, McCabe, that fellow that was here today, and a woman named Ruth, are coming out."

"I know who they are."

Hod went to take his bath, and George walked to the front porch.

Molly came out of the store and sat down on the steps beside George, leaving a good three-foot space between them. She had put on a freshly ironed sleeveless dress, brushed her naturally curly hair, slipped a hair ribbon underneath, brought it up behind her ears, and tied it in a bow on top of her head. Her legs were bare, and she wore low-heeled sandals. On an impulse she had dabbed a bit of Evening in Paris perfume behind her ears. She was sorry as soon as she had done it. She never used perfume except on special occasions . . . but *he'd* not know that.

"Mr. Andrews . . . ah, George, you've spent a lot of time here since Daddy and Mama died. I want you to know that I appreciate it, but I don't want you to neglect your own work because of . . . because of my having that story in the newspaper."

George turned his head to look at her. Her feet rested on the step. She had arranged her skirt over her legs and wrapped her arms about her knees. To him, she was the prettiest thing in the world. He had watched her grow up into a young lady . . . as sweet and beautiful on the inside as she was on the outside.

"Somethin' smells good."

Molly laughed. "It's the Evening in Paris perfume that Mama gave me for Christmas last year. I've got to use it up or . . . something in it will evaporate and it'll not smell so nice."

George wanted to hear her laugh again. He longed to be able to talk to her; but his mind went blank when he was around her, and he couldn't seem to say anything that made sense to him. He talked to so few people that he had not learned the art of conversation.

"This is a pretty time of day, isn't it?" Molly said. "It's peaceful and quiet."

"Except when the wind blows."

"It's not very quiet then. There's not a thing out here to stop it. I wish the dust storms would hurry and be over. Do you think they ever will?"

"Not till they stop plowing the land."

"You plow, don't you?"

"Not much."

They sat in silence for a long while. Finally Molly spoke.

"Does your sister mind being by herself? She isn't sick is she? She could walk over here and visit with me and Aunt Bertha."

"She ain't sick. She wants to be by herself. She hates it when I'm there."

"Oh, no! How could she? You're all she has."

He shrugged his massive shoulders. "She imagines things and talks to herself."

"I don't think I've seen her but once or twice."

George didn't want to waste his time with Molly talking about Gertrude. He sat in miserable silence, afraid that she'd take his silence as not wanting to talk to her and would go back into the store.

"George," she said after several minutes had gone by, "do you think it strange that Reverend Howell has such bad luck with his wives? He's had five that I know of. The first one died right after Stuart was born. One ran off.

Charlotte's mother and the twins' mother both died in their sleep. The last one died a few weeks after giving birth."

"Maybe six."

"Six wives? Really?"

"Had one before he come here."

"Where did you hear that?"

"Jackson Howell."

"Well, doesn't that beat all?"

"He was two years older'n Stuart, but they had different mamas." George was glad that he had something to tell her.

"Daddy said the boys were small when they came here and not too long after that his wife died. I guess that would have been Stuart's mother. Nothing was ever said about the boys not being full brothers."

"Jackson knew it. He wasn't no fool."

Molly turned her head to look at him. He was looking off into the distance. Only lately had she come to know him. There had been no chance before. When she had come to the store he always left without talking to her. In his younger days he must have been a pleasant-looking man. His profile was clean-cut. His eyes were a soft brown, with squint lines fanning out from the corners. As long as she could remember she had never seen him in anything but overalls. Years ago all the boys and men wore overalls, but now they usually wore pants and shirts.

You've not had much of a life, have you? You're a good, kind man who has been stuck on that farm taking care of a sister who doesn't want you in the house.

"What do you mean, Jackson was no fool?"

"Said his daddy had a real mean streak. He was smart enough to run off, him and Stuart. Never heard what happened to them. Could be dead by now."

Molly thought about telling him that Keith McCabe had met Jackson down in Texas, but decided that information was for Keith to tell. She wished that George had more friends. She couldn't think of any friends he had other than herself, Aunt Bertha, and now Hod.

"I found a dirtdobber's nest under the eave of the shed. I knocked it down."

"I saw them buzzing around near the gazebo."

"Stay away for a while. They'll leave."

Silence again.

"When I was a little girl, I'd sit here and gaze out over the prairie. Of course, there wasn't anything as far as the eye could see, and there isn't anything now. But I used to imagine that over that way"—she pointed straight ahead—"was the ocean." She swung her arm around and pointed toward the east. "That way were buildings that reached to the sky."

"Are you wantin' to go live in town?"

"Heavens no! I love the wide-open spaces. I was glad to leave Wichita. But I don't know how long I can hold on to the store, times being what they are."

It seemed hours, but could only have been minutes before George spoke. Molly's thoughts had forged ahead to the visit of Ruth and Keith and how she was going to explain to Ruth that she was not engaged to this cold-hearted Federal man who had come down from Kansas City to catch the killers of her parents.

"You'll not have to move from here if ya don't want to." Molly failed to hear the anxiety in his voice. "You can live here," he repeated very softly.

Chapter Twelve

During the evening, Molly discovered a different side of the grim-faced Federal man. He was both friendly and funny. Ruth seemed to like him as soon as Molly introduced him. She had decided to make it clear to her friend why he was here.

"Ruth, meet Mr. Hod Dolan. He's here in case the gangsters who killed Mama and Daddy come back after reading in the paper that I could identify them."

"Keith said . . . that—" Her voice trailed away, and she held out her hand. "I should have known. Glad to meet you, Hod. Glad you're here, too. It was hard to believe that Molly would get herself engaged and not tell me about it."

"Glad to be here, Ruth." His smile made him darkly handsome. A fact that was not lost on Ruth. "You can tell that it rubbed her the wrong way to have folks think she was going to marry me."

"I don't know why. I'd consider you a good catch."

"Why, thank you. Do you . . . ah . . . have a special friend?"

"Yes," Keith said firmly, and pulled a laughing Ruth back against him. "Find your own girl."

"I'm trying." Hod's teasing eyes rested on Molly.

You're really spreading it on, aren't you, Mr. Dolan? You're charming my friend with your big-city ways.

Molly led the way through the semidarkened store to the stairway.

"Go on up, Ruth. Aunt Bertha is fixing iced tea. I'll be there in a minute." Molly hurried to the back door and stepped out onto the porch.

"Where the hell are you going?" Hod was right behind her and grabbed her arm.

"None of your business."

"It's my business when you leave this store."

Molly turned on him. "I want to see if George is still here. If he is, I'm going to invite him to come in and have cake with us."

"He'll not come."

"I'm going to ask him anyway, so let go of my arm."

"Dammit, Molly. He'd rather die than go up there."

"How do you know that?"

"He's terribly self-conscious and shy. He'd be miserable not knowing what to do or say."

"How do you know?"

"I know. You'd know, too, if you'd stop to think about it. He's just now getting to where he'll talk to me. He hardly talks to you—"

"He talked to me tonight. He told me . . . things."

"Not about himself."

"He did. He said his sister didn't want him in the house. I want him to come in."

"Molly, use your head. You can't just spring that on him all of a sudden. Don't ask him in when you have company. If you did shame him into coming in, he'd be mortified because he'd not know how to act or what to say."

"You've got all the answers, haven't you?"

"No, I don't. But trust me on this."

"He needs friends. He's not so old that he couldn't . . . find someone. Be happy."

"If it's your plan to soften him up so you can match him up with someone, my advice is to start slow. Invite him in for a glass of tea. Your aunt said that one night before I go we'll make ice cream. Ask him to come turn the crank. Make him feel you need him. Ease him into being sociable. Don't embarrass him by asking him to do something that will humiliate him."

"And where did you learn to handle this type of situation? From the gangsters you associate with?" Molly knew that he was right, but it was hard to back down.

"The gangsters I associate with would rather shoot him than look at him. He's crazy about you, you know."

"I don't know any such thing!"

"It would be hard for him to refuse you anything."

"He feels that because he and Daddy were friends, he should look out for me and that's all."

"Molly, darlin'," he said in a heavy Irish drawl, "there are times when you're dumber than a doorknob."

"Well! Thank you for the compliment. That's the nicest thing you've said to me yet. A doorknob is essential to a door."

His grin infuriated her. "Exactly."

Molly went back into the store. She heard Hod close and lock the door as, back straight, head up, she hurried up the stairs. She didn't understand why he made her so angry and made her say such stupid things.

The chocolate cake sat in the center of the kitchen table. Laughter and music came from the living room. Records had been her mother's weakness, and she had a large collection. Kate Smith was singing.

"When the moon comes over the mountain—"

Molly paused in the doorway. The song was her mother's favorite. She hadn't played it since that terrible day in June.

Hod was behind her. When he put his hand on her shoulder, she shied away. He went past her and into the room.

"We'll have to turn off the light or stay in the kitchen."

"Oh, but—" Molly stammered.

"There's exposure here from three directions," he said patiently. "I'll not risk it."

Without a word, Bertha turned off the lamp with the square glass shade. The room was not completely dark because she had left the light on in the stairway leading down into the store.

Molly's eyes quickly adjusted to the semidarkness. "Is this necessary?"

"It is," Hod said tersely.

"It's a great idea." Keith's voice came from the far corner of the room.

"Why . . . you . . . masher! You pinched me." Ruth was bubbling with laughter.

"It wasn't me. Was it you, Hod?"

"Wasn't me. I'm way over here and about to pinch Molly."

"Well, for heaven's sake!" This came from Bertha. "Isn't anybody going to pinch . . . me?"

"I'll pinch you, Aunt Bertha."

"Thanks, love. But it wouldn't be the same."

"I don't know what this is." Ruth put another record on the Victrola. "I can't read the label. Come on, cowboy. I'll teach you to dance. It's dark, and no one will see that you have two left feet."

"But . . . Ruth, I told you—"

"—That you don't dance. But you can learn. Don't be bashful. It'll be fun."

"Well, all right. You'll probably leave here tonight with broken toes."

The library table and the chairs had already been pushed against the wall. Keith put his arms around Ruth and they stood in the middle of the floor for a long moment swaying to the music and the low seductive voice of the vocalist.

> "Stay as sweet as you are. Don't let a thing ever
> change you.
> Stay as sweet as you are. Don't let a soul
> rearrange you."

Keith's arm locked Ruth to him and he suddenly began to dance. After Ruth realized how good he was, she began to sputter. He laughed.

"Why you . . . polecat! You can *dance*. Why did you tell me you couldn't? I'll get even with you for this."

He chuckled. "I had lessons since Saturday night. Now stop sputtering and dance."

Ruth stopped and refused to move. "Did you take Jen Bruza up on her offer to teach you?"

"Who's that?"

"The flirty twin who asked you to dance about a dozen times the other night."

"Oh, her. Naw. I went out to Hollywood and got some lessons from Fred Astaire."

"Be serious."

"Sweet schoolteacher, I've been dancing since I was knee-high to a frog. Have you ever known an Irishman who didn't like to dance?"

"Why wouldn't you dance the other night?"

"I wanted to watch the crowd. That's another one of my bad habits. I'm a crowd-watcher."

Hod waited until Keith and Ruth began dancing again, then held out his hand.

"Molly?"

Molly had no choice but to let him pull her into his arms. His hand was warm and firm. The arm around her waist drew her close to him. She could feel the hardness of his chest and his breath on her cheek. He lowered his head and pressed his cheek to hers. When he moved, she followed on instinct, her feet feeling as if each weighed fifty pounds.

"Mol—ly, sweet Mol—ly, don't let a thing ever change you." He sang in a soft whisper along with the recording.

Even knowing that he was just flirting, Molly felt her heart thump in a strange and disturbing way as she struggled to get sufficient air into her lungs. It seemed to her that the music would never end, but it finally did, and they stopped. She made an attempt to move away from him, but he held tightly to her hand and his arm tightened around her. His dark eyes fastened to her face.

"You're a sweet armful, Molly, darlin'."

"You're flirting, Mr. Dolan," Molly said lightly. "Have you been taking lessons from Walter?"

She glanced at Ruth and saw her laughing up at Keith and wished with all her heart that she could be as casual with Hod.

Bertha had wound the machine and put another record on the turntable. The song was a slow, romantic tune.

> *"Are the stars out tonight? I don't know if it's*
> *cloudy or bright—*
> *'Cause I only have eyes for you, dear—"*

The thought struck Hod that he held a treasure here in his arms. He knew with certainty that he would stay here for weeks if necessary, until he determined if they had a future together.

By God, he would!

He had never felt this way about any woman. He was as happy as he'd ever been, with this sweet girl in his arms, dancing in a darkened room. He chuckled to himself and caressed her hair with his lips. At times she was as prickly as a burr, but it only added to his fascination with her.

"I only have eyes for you—" He sang the words with his lips close to her ear. The only indication that she heard them was that her breath quickened, and the cheek pressed to his moved slightly.

At first she had been stiff as she followed his steps. She had relaxed some, but not enough. He wanted her to lean on him, put her arms around him, and lay her head on his shoulder. He wanted her to enjoy their closeness and absorb the music with him. He was tempted to run his hand up and down her back, but he didn't dare. This was far more than he had expected, and it would have to do for now.

The music ended. She moved away, and he let her go but held tightly to her hand. He pulled her over to face the fan. He stood behind her, and wisps of her hair blew back in his face, catching on the rough stubble on his chin.

Hod Dolan, you're playing with fire. This slip of a girl could break your heart. Another voice inside his head said, *Enjoy it while you can. If you miss this chance to catch the brass ring, you'll be going back to that goddamn lonesome life you've had for the past five years.*

Hod lifted her hair from her neck and turned her back toward the fan. He knew that it would be hard for her to believe that at times he was so damned lonesome that he thought every chamber of his heart was empty. His was a solitary existence, even though his days and some of his nights were spent amid a crowd of people. He worked with men who knew that when the job was finished, they would go home to a family who loved them, worried about them. When his job ended, he went to the rooming house, stretched out on the bed, and stared at the ceiling.

Molly was facing him. They looked steadily at each other. Even in the darkness, the force of her eyes held him as firmly as his arms had held her while they danced.

"It feels good, but we shouldn't hog the fan."

"Look." Hod moved his shoulders so she could see. Keith's shoulder was against the wall, his body shielding Ruth. His head was bent and they were murmuring to each other. "I don't think they even know it's hot or that we're here," Hod whispered, his head bent so that his lips touched her ear.

"I hope she's not falling in love with him. She doesn't know anything about him."

"You don't know anything about me."

"But I'm not—"

"—I know all I need to know about you."

"You can't. You've only known me for—"

"—Ever. I feel like I've known you for years and years. You've got to admit that we dance as if we've danced together for years."

"It must be pretty dull around here for you," she said in an attempt to change the subject. "No bright lights, picture shows, or honky-tonks."

"Doesn't Pearl have a honky-tonk?"

"Nothing that even resembles one."

"Well, doggone!"

"They have one in Liberal."

"How far is that?"

"About twenty-five miles. I used to go down with Daddy."

"You and your daddy went to the honky-tonks?" His eyes teased her.

"No. To the wholesale houses."

"Aren't you due to make another trip?"

"I can't go and leave Aunt Bertha here alone. I'll have the supplies delivered."

"Won't that take a hunk out of the profit?"

"Yes, but even if I could go, I'd have to have someone work on the truck first. It's not been driven since . . . June."

"Didn't I tell you? I'm a first-class mechanic. Maybe not first-class," he amended. "My brother, Tom, is first-class. He likes to tinker with motors of any kind and taught me a little. I'll take a look at it. If it runs, we could go at the end of the week."

"I'll not leave Aunt Bertha."

"She could go to town and stay with a friend. George could run the store for a day. You trust him, don't you?"

" 'Course, I trust him, but all he's done up to now is pump gas."

"I think he'd be proud to help out. Think about it. I'll take you to a honky-tonk," he promised with a teasing smile.

"Oh, boy! I've been to one honky-tonk in my life, and I didn't like it much at all."

"Picture show?"

"I love picture shows. While I was in Wichita, Aunt

Bertha and I went to see *It Happened One Night* with Clark Gable."

"I suppose you only had eyes for Gable. When I saw it, I only had eyes for Claudette Colbert."

"You would." She laughed.

The softness of Molly's laughter stroked Hob like warm fingertips. He couldn't take his eyes off her. Her mouth was parted, and he felt her warm breath on his lips. The happy light in her violet eyes did strange things in the area around his heart. Somehow she had seeped into the secret recesses of his being, and it was going to be difficult, if not impossible, to get her out.

"Are you young folks going to stand there looking at each other or are you going to come in here and eat cake?" Bertha had entered the room without their being aware of it.

An instant later the unmistakable sound of a gunshot and the whine of a bullet as it passed to thud into the opposite wall stunned everyone but Hod.

"Down!" he yelled, as he shoved Molly to the floor. "All of you lie as flat as you can . . . and stay there."

He made a dash to the hall, grabbed the tommy gun as he passed the library table, and made for the stairway. When he reached it, Keith was behind him.

"I told you to stay put."

"I can handle myself, but I'll need a weapon."

"Rifle beside the back door. We'll go out that way. The shot came from the southwest." Hod switched off the light in the stairway. They felt their way down the stairs to the back door, where Hod picked up a flashlight and handed Keith the rifle.

The first thing Hod saw was Stella standing at the side of the porch. The hair stood up on the back of her neck and low growls came from her throat. Hob went one way, Keith the other. Hod sidled along the building, his eyes searching the darkness thirty yards out. He reached the front of the store and met Keith coming from the other side.

"A car without lights took off down the road . . . fast. I'll try to catch him," Keith said.

"They may be trying to draw us away."

"That's why I should go."

"Watch yourself, they may have a tommy."

"If they'd had one, they'd have used it instead of a rifle."

Keith backed the car with a jerk and swung out onto the road. Only then did Hod stop to realize how automatically he had accepted the man's help. Who was this guy? He certainly had seemed to know how to handle himself.

Obviously the shooter, whoever he was, was not a professional. He had shot with only a window as a target. Norton would have waited until he'd had Molly in his sights or sprayed the place with a tommy. If he had hired an assassin, he'd picked a poor one.

Stella had come around to the stand beside Hod. She was still looking off down the road.

"They didn't come in close enough for you to get their scent, did they, girl?" Hod patted the dog on the head and hurried to the back of the store.

*　　*　　*

In spite of her fear and the absolute idiocy of lying flat on the floor in her living room, Molly giggled. She wasn't sure if the giggle was caused by hysteria or nerves. It was impossible to have coherent thoughts.

"Aunt Bertha? Are you all right?"

"Right as rain. This is a barrel of fun," she added drily.

"Ruth?"

"I'm all right, too. Can we get up now?"

"Let's go to the stairs." Bertha had started wiggling toward the hallway. "Hod told me once that the stairway was a good place to be if bullets started to fly. Ah . . . shoot! I'm all out of practice crawling on the floor. Ain't done it for a year or two."

A minute later the three women were sitting in the pitch-dark landing leading to the floor below. The shock of hearing the shot and being shoved to the floor had evaporated. Molly had never really believed that this would happen. But it had. Someone out there wanted to kill her. Hod had gone to find him. *Oh, dear God! Don't let him get shot!*

"Keith took off after Hod," Ruth said worriedly. "He pulled me to the floor, hopped over me, and was gone."

"Hod was right to turn off the light, but it put everyone else in danger. I couldn't stand it if one of you was shot because of me. Aunt Bertha, please go to town until this is over."

"And miss all the fun? Forget it, sugar. I'm staying right here, and when Hod gets his hands on that bird, I plan to put in a few good licks with my iron skillet."

"Are they leaving us here . . . alone?" Molly asked, as she heard the sound of a car starting.

"It's Keith. That's his car, or rather, the one he's using." Ruth tried to keep the panic out of her voice.

A minute later they heard steps on the back porch, then the door opened.

"Don't shoot, ladies. It's me," Hod called.

"We're here on the stairs," Molly said. "Did you see anyone?"

"Where did Keith go?"

"Can I turn on the light?" Bertha asked.

"Not yet." Hod came toward them with the beam of his flashlight directed to the floor.

"Where did Keith go?" Ruth asked again.

"He went to take a look down the road. He'll be right back. Are you ladies all right?"

Hod came up the stairs and stopped a few steps below Molly, so that his face was level with hers. She could feel his eyes on her face, and when he reached out his hand, she mindlessly put hers in it.

"We're all right." Reaction had set in, and Molly's voice quivered.

Hod wanted to pull her into his arms and never let her go. This close call had made him aware of just how dear she was to him. The realization that had lurked in the back of his mind came forward with soul-crushing force. *I've fallen in love with this slip of a girl. Oh Lord. What can I offer her?*

"Stay here," he said softly. "I want to go up and assess . . . the damage." He squeezed her hand before he released it, and took the stairs two at a time.

The bullet had passed through the window screen, crossed the room, and slammed into the wall about six inches from the ceiling. The shooter had been some distance away but near enough to hear the music from the Victrola and know they were in the room. On a still night sound carried and might be heard for three hundred feet or more. Had he and Molly still been dancing, more than likely one or both of them would have been hit because the bullet that came through the window screen had angled upward.

Hod had not really believed that Norton would undertake the assassination without Pascoe. Tomorrow he had to get into town and call headquarters.

Keith drove with reckless speed, hoping to get a glimpse of the car ahead. It didn't make much sense to him that this was an act of a person whose mission was to eliminate a witness. Marty Conroy, however, was known to do stupid things. If Marty had followed him out of a need for revenge and had shot into the darkened room, he would beat him to within an inch of his life.

The night was still, and road dust hung in the air. When Keith reached Pearl there were a half dozen cars in the two-block business area. One, a Model A truck with no muffler, pulled away from in front of the dry goods and grocery store raising a fresh cloud of dust. Keith cruised the two blocks, turned, and came back to stop a few car lengths from the cafe. Mrs. Wisniewski and her son were cleaning up.

"Hi, Mr. McCabe," Wally said when Keith opened the screen door. "You looking for something to eat?"

"Not tonight. Did you see any strange cars in town this evening?"

"No. Did you, Mama?"

"The only stranger I've seen all day was that little duded-up squirt that was in here today. He hasn't been back that I know of."

"Did any car come into town during the last . . . say ten minutes?"

"We were in the kitchen. I heard Ollie Johnson's old truck start up a while ago. It's been parked down by the post office since suppertime."

"Thanks, Mrs. Wisniewski."

Keith went out and stood in front of the cafe.

"Something wrong, Mr. McCabe?" Wally had come out to stand beside him.

"Nothing important. I thought I saw someone I knew." Keith's eyes were on a car coming slowly toward them down the street. "Who's this?"

"That's the old preacher snooping around," Wally answered with disgust before Keith recognized the driver.

The preacher gave them a friendly wave as he passed.

"Is he usually in town this late?"

"He owns the building the barbershop is in. He has a room upstairs where he tinkers with clocks. He's up there sometimes at night."

"Where does he park his car? He came from around the corner."

"Usually out behind. He sneaks in and out hoping to find someone wallowin' in sin so he can preach a hellfire-and-brimstone sermon Sunday morning."

"Isn't his sister's funeral tomorrow?"

"Yeah. Mama had me take a couple cans of peaches

out to the house today. There was a bunch of women there. I didn't see Charlotte or Otis, so I didn't stay."

"Folks usually rally around when there's a death."

"There's a lot of gullible fools believin' in that preacher," Wally grumbled.

"I'd better be going." Keith's hand came down on the boy's shoulder. " 'Night, Wally."

On the way back to the store, Keith's heart thudded slow and heavy with the suspicion that the bullet that crashed into the living room at the store might have been meant for him. Damn it to hell! Would Marty go that far to get even with him?

For the first time in his life he'd found a woman who consumed his thoughts even after he left her. He wanted to see more of her and to explore the possibility that she was the one his granny had said would come into his life and fill it with her presence until there was no room for anyone else. He would love her to distraction, Granny said, and build his future around her.

"Son of a bitch," he swore, and pounded his fist on the steering wheel. He was crazy for thinking about a woman when his life was up in the air like it was.

Keith drove the car into the area in front of the shed and hurried into the back of the darkened store, wanting to be near her and make sure that she was all right.

Chapter Thirteen

George, are you sure you don't mind staying here at the store while I go to Miss Howell's funeral?" Molly had walked out to where George was filling the trough with chicken feed.

"I don't mind."

"I can't leave Aunt Bertha here alone. Especially after what happened last night. Besides going to the funeral, I need to go into town to the bank."

"I'll be here."

"Mr. Dolan is going with me."

"He said that."

"He told you what happened. He wouldn't let me come outside until you got here to tell him there was no one back in the woods."

"Ain't nobody there. I always look."

After the talk she'd had with Hod about George, Molly

was seeing him with different eyes. She looked into his face, but his eyes evaded hers.

"I feel so fortunate having you for a neighbor and appreciate your taking over the chicken chores and helping to look out for those crooks. As soon as this is all over we'll have a big dinner, a picnic or something to celebrate. You'll come, won't you?"

"I dunno." He picked up a bucket and went to the pump. Molly followed.

"You don't have to decide now. Think about it."

"All right."

"Oh, yes, I forgot to mention that Aunt Bertha wants to make ice cream one night soon. We'd like for you to help us."

"Doin' what?" He moved the handle on the pump up and down.

"Turning the crank."

"Hod'll do it."

"He may not be here."

George's head came up. "He's leavin'?"

"He can't stay here forever."

"Why not?"

"He's got a job in Kansas City."

"He likes it here."

"You're wrong. He'd not live here. Not enough happening. He'd be bored in no time at all."

"I ain't knowin' 'bout that."

"Oh, well, I've got to go get my hat and gloves. Aunt Bertha is ironing Hod a shirt to wear to the funeral."

Molly went into the back of the store. Hod came down the stairs wearing a white shirt and a tie, the ever-present gun in the shoulder holster. He carried his coat and his hat.

"It'll be hot wearing a coat."

"It's necessary, and I'm used to it."

"George said he didn't mind staying with Aunt Bertha. I hope he comes inside."

"He will. I told him to sit there in the window and give everyone who comes in the once-over, and if he didn't know them, get the shotgun out from under the counter."

"You better get goin'. Here's the bank deposit." Bertha handed a canvas bag to Molly and keys to her car to Hod. "I'm going to get caught up on book work today."

"I couldn't have managed if you'd not come to take over that chore, Aunt Bertha."

"I'm better at the business end of this store than I am at meeting the customers."

"We'll not be gone more than a couple of hours." Molly kissed her aunt on the cheek.

"I can't believe they left me here without a car," Hod grumbled, and followed Molly out the door. "I'll get one in a day or two if I have to buy it myself."

In the close confines of the car, Molly sat silently with one hand in her lap, the other holding on to the brim of her straw hat. The windows were down, and a good breeze was blowing into the car. She watched Hod's hand as he worked the gearshift between them. He was an excellent driver. The car didn't jerk at all when he shifted the gears. She glanced at his profile, then away before he could catch her looking at him.

She hadn't gone down to the bathroom this morning until she saw him out in front of the shed talking to George. He had moved the cot he had slept on back into the storage room and placed his belongings on it. *He was neat as a pin. Her mother would have loved him.* They had been at breakfast when he asked her if she wanted to go to Miss Howell's funeral.

"I won't be expected to be there because of the store."

"It would be a good idea if we're seen together. We don't want folks to think you're hiding me." His eyes held hers, and she realized he was serious.

"It's a silly reason for going to a funeral."

"I need to make a call from a private line," he'd said quietly. "I've made arrangements with George to stay here while we're gone."

Bertha had agreed with Hod, and there was nothing to do but get ready to go. Last night's event had affected all of them, made them realize what could have happened if Hod had not insisted that the lights be turned off.

Unable to think of anything to say to him, Molly looked out the window and read each line of the jingle nailed to fence posts as they passed. *She put a bullet— through his hat—but he'd had closer—shaves than that. Burma Shave.*

Molly considered that jingle hers. The man who put up the sign several years ago had stopped at the store and let her pick it out from a half dozen that he was putting up between Pearl and Liberal.

"I better put on my coat before we get there."

Hod stopped the car in the shade of a huge cotton-wood, stepped out, and quickly slipped into his coat. When he got back into the car he turned to Molly, reached over, and took her hand out of her lap. He held it tightly, giving her no chance to withdraw it.

"I know you're afraid after what happened last night."

"Not any more than I was before."

"I don't think it was Norton that shot into the house. It's not his style. He would be more professional than to warn his target with a random shot."

"If not him, who was it?"

"He could have hired some thug to do it for him." He turned her hand over and rubbed his thumb along her knuckles. "The thug may have given it a token try so he could collect his money."

"Then it's over?"

"We can't be sure. I'm going to talk to my chief. If he calls me off, I'll try to get a leave to stay here. If I can't get time off, I'll quit the Bureau."

"Oh, no. I don't want you to lose your job because of me. I'll close the store. Aunt Bertha and I will go to Wichita."

"That wouldn't solve anything, Molly. If it's Norton, you'd still be a witness wherever you are."

"What do you mean *if* it's Norton?"

"Of course, it's Norton or one of his fellow thugs. I'd give anything if we hadn't started this thing." He laced his fingers with hers, and looked squarely at her. "But then, I wouldn't have met you, or had an excuse to stay here and get to know you."

"You wouldn't have had to stay at a country store, eat road dust, and be bored silly," she said with a breathless tremor in her voice.

"I'm a country boy. I told you that I was born and raised on a farm in Nebraska. I wish you could meet my brothers, Tom and Mike. Both are crazy in love with their wives. Mike almost grieved himself to death when he thought Letty had died. I'll tell you the story sometime." He smiled into her eyes, and the thought registered in her brain before it filled with turmoil that he planned on there being *time* to tell her the story.

"I'd like to hear it."

"Both of them live on farms and have no desire to do anything else, even during these hard times. Tom is married to Johnny's sister. He still has a love for motors and does some mechanic work on the side."

"Johnny told me about Henry Ann. I doubt that I'll ever meet them." She lowered her chin and looked down at the hand that lay in his. He was rubbing the back of it with his thumb. "We'd better go, or we'll be late for the funeral."

"Molly, we'll have to act as if we're in love if we expect folks to believe we're engaged." His eyes never wavered from her face. "Otherwise, you'll be talked about for having a man staying out at the store. It gives me a legitimate reason to be there."

"But you may leave soon, and then what'll I tell them?"

"We'll think of something when the time comes. You'll have to introduce me—"

"I know."

"They won't believe it if you do it as if you just bit into a sour apple." He squeezed her hand and smiled. She smiled back with her mouth closed and dimples appeared in her cheeks.

"I'll try to look like I bit into a Baby Ruth candy bar."

"Fair enough." He reluctantly released her hand and started the car. For an instant longer he looked at her. Her eyes were brilliant. "You've got the most beautiful eyes I've ever seen."

The compliment caught her by surprise. She shook her head in denial. But she couldn't look away from him.

"They're just . . . a different color."

"Beautiful," he said softly, then repeated, "Beautiful."

Hod parked the car in front of the bank. He stood just inside the door and endured the curious glances of the teller while Molly made her deposit. With banks going broke every day, he wondered how solid this one was. Bertha had told him that they had an account in Liberal as well as this one in Pearl. She didn't believe in putting all her eggs in one basket, she'd said.

The service was about to start when Molly and Hod arrived at the church and crowded into the last pew. She sat close to him, with her shoulder tucked behind his. He reached for her hand, brought it to his thigh, and covered their entwined fingers with his hat.

Too rattled to think clearly and trying to analyze the words Hod had spoken a few minutes earlier, Molly heard only half of what was being said by one of the deacons. He was reading a sermon prepared by the Reverend Howell because, the deacon said, the preacher was too *broken-up* to deliver it himself. After the short message, a few hymns were sung. Miss Armstrong, the choir director, sang "The Old Rugged Cross," and suddenly the service ended.

The preacher, his soft-featured, slightly pudgy face arranged in lines of sadness, came down the aisle. Molly felt the flesh creep on the back of her neck when his clear blue eyes focused on her and Hod and stayed there overly long. He stood at the door while the simple casket containing the body of his sister was carried down the aisle, followed by his children—the girls in white dresses, the boys in white shirts.

When it came time to leave, Hod moved to the end of the pew, and Molly, ignoring the curious glances of the mourners, walked out ahead of him. She breathed a sigh of relief to see that the preacher was not standing at the door as he usually did after church service. She and Hod went out into the sunlight.

The casket was being carried to the burial ground behind the church. The preacher and all of his children followed, even to the baby, who was carried by Charlotte. The sad picture brought tears to the eyes of some who had not even known the deceased. Molly and Hod moved with the crowd, her hand tucked in the crook of his arm.

"Molly? I'm glad you could get away from the store for a while." The woman's eyes went questioningly to Hod.

"Hello, Doris. Aunt Bertha is at the store. Meet Hod Dolan, my . . . fiancé. Hod, Mrs. Luscomb."

"Fiancé? Oh, my goodness. How do you do? When did all this take place?" Doris had stopped in her tracks, and the crowd went around them.

"Hello, Mrs. Luscomb." Hod transferred his hat to his other hand and took the hand she offered. "It isn't as sudden as it appears. Molly has been reluctant to announce our engagement so soon after she lost her parents." He lied so smoothly that Molly almost believed it herself.

"Velma mentioned that you had met a nice man in Wichita. She didn't say it was . . . ah . . . serious."

"It certainly is serious . . . on my part. How about you, sweetheart? Are you seriously considering marrying me?"

Molly smiled sweetly, her eyes shining into his. She circled his arm with her two hands so that she could pinch him.

"There's nothing I want more."

"Oh, isn't this sweet." Doris gushed. "When is the big day? We'll have to plan a bridal shower."

"We've not set a date, Doris."

Most of the mourners had already gathered at the gravesite when they reached it. Molly and Hod stood on the fringe while the short service was conducted. Hod held Molly's hand in the crook of his arm by pressing it tightly to his side. Not wanting to stand in line to pay respects to the family, she tugged on his arm, and they started walking back to where they had left the car as soon as the last words were said.

The Bruza twins intercepted them. Jen grabbed Molly's arm.

"Molly! I didn't expect to see you here." Jen, in a yellow print dress with a round neckline, held on to Molly's arm, but her bright interested eyes were on Hod.

"What's so strange about my coming to a funeral?" Molly said, then spoke to the other twin. "How are you, Janythe? Are you still planning on going to secretarial school?"

"Mama is making arrangements for me to go to the same school in Wichita that you went to."

"I think it's a waste of money." Jen was smiling flirtatiously at Hod, but she still managed to say something negative. "You're not using typing and shorthand at the store, Molly, and Jan won't use it either. She'll marry a farmer or a rancher and have a dozen kids."

Molly ignored Jen, which didn't seem to bother the girl at all. She was concentrating all her attention on Hod. When it became apparent that she wasn't going to be introduced, she spoke directly to him.

"Do I know you?"

"I don't think so. I'm Hod Dolan."

"Hello, Hod Dolan. I'm Jennifer Bruza." Jen held out her hand. Hod touched it briefly. "Are you one of Molly's long-lost cousins?"

"No, thank God. I'm the man who's going to marry her."

Jen's mouth dropped open, then snapped shut. Her eyes, round with surprise, went from Hod to Molly.

"You're joshing me!"

"I don't josh about serious matters," Hod said coolly.

"You're marrying Molly?" Disbelief was in her voice.

"Yes, I'm marrying Molly!" Anger was in Hod's.

"Well, what do you know about that? Our little Molly has a beau! I can't believe it."

"Jennifer!" Jan exclaimed. "Hush up!"

"Don't pay any attention to my twin, Hod. My sister is always telling me to hush up."

"You'd do well to listen, but you won't, will you?"

"Of course not. I can't get over Molly having a beau. The only men I've seen her with were Keith McCabe and Walter Lovik. Everyone at the dance thought she was trying to take Keith away from Ruth. Poor Ruth can't keep a boyfriend. They always stray after a prettier girl. I have to admit that Molly is prettier than Ruth."

"Let's go, Jen. Mama's waiting."

"Mama's always waiting," Jen said with a frown on her face.

"We agree on one thing, Miss Jennifer. Molly is pretty." Hod smiled adoringly down at Molly. "In fact she's the prettiest, sweetest, and *nicest* girl I've ever known. There's not a mean, jealous bone in this delectable body of hers. And I'm crazy about her."

"Who'd have thought it?" Jennifer raised her brows.

"I'm so glad for you, Molly." Janythe hugged Molly's arm.

"Thank you," Molly murmured.

"We're having a party at our house Saturday night." Jen continued to flirt with Hod, tilting her head and giving him sideways glances. "We'll roll up the rugs and dance. You like to dance, Hod? We've got a new Benny Goodman record."

"Saturday?" Hod shook his head. "Molly and I plan to

go to Liberal Saturday and pick out Molly's engagement ring."

"I'll be eager to see it." Jen stroked her hair back over her ears and straightened her shoulders so that her breasts pushed at the bodice of her dress. She looked at Hod, smiled, and winked. They walked away with Jan talking angrily to her twin.

When Hod laughed, Molly could feel the chuckles against the hand he had pressed tightly to his side.

"Brassy little twit. She must be the town vamp."

"She is, but Jan, her twin, is nice. Jennifer likes to think that she's irresistible to men, and to some, she is."

"She's as easy to read as a book. I pity the poor man who marries her."

"You didn't need to spread it on so thick."

"Maybe I meant every word of it."

"Oh, yeah?" Molly laughed. "And maybe the moon's made of green cheese."

"Isn't it?" A muscle twitched in the corner of his mouth, but there was no amusement in his eyes. "I always heard that it was." They reached the car, and he opened the door for her. "I like being with you, Molly." He closed the door before she could reply and went around to slide in under the wheel. "Let's go on over to the telephone office so I can make my call, then we'll go get something cold to drink."

The telephone operator was busy at the switchboard. They waited behind a low railing until she was free to acknowledge them.

"Hello, Molly. Been to the funeral?"

"We just came from there."

"Big crowd?"

"Average, I'd say. Fleeta Mae, this is my fiancé, Mr. Dolan."

"Your fiancé? Congratulations, Mr. Dolan. I've known Molly since she was knee-high to a duck. You couldn't have found a better-liked girl in the state of Kansas."

"I realize how lucky I am."

"He wants to make a call, Fleeta Mae."

"And he doesn't want everyone on the party line listening in. Can't say as I blame him."

Fleeta Mae's blond hair was always finger-waved, the scallops around her face were held in place by heavy wave-set that had dried, leaving her hair as stiff as a board. The headset seemed not to touch a hair on her head. Although she was middle-aged, the woman held one of the most coveted jobs in town. She was head operator of the small independent telephone company that serviced Pearl and a few ranches on the main roads.

"Give me the number you want to call, Mr. Dolan, and take a seat in that booth over there. It'll be plenty hot if you close the door. Leave it open, and Molly can turn the fan your way."

"Charge the call to the other end." Hod took a card out of his pocket and handed it to the operator. She read the number, raised her brows, and gave Hod a second look before she turned to her switchboard. Hod went into the booth and closed the door.

Five minutes later he was still talking with sweat running down his face. Molly stood at the counter and talked to Fleeta Mae between her placing or receiving calls.

"Too bad that holier-than-thou preacher had to bury his sister." Fleeta Mae said after she plugged in a call. "I'd not want to hitch up with him and take a chance on being the next one he buries. Operator. Number please."

"I feel sorry for the children," Molly said during the next lull.

"He rules them with an iron hand. The phone's not answered unless he's there. Number, please. It's twenty minutes after four, Mrs. Pierson. I don't know where Mable is. No, she didn't say that she was going to the funeral." Fleeta jerked the plug from the switchboard. "Heavens! I can't keep track of everyone in town."

A few minutes later Hod came out of the booth wiping his face on his handkerchief. He walked over to stand in front of the fan. Molly went to him, turned him around until his back was to Fleeta Mae and opened his coat. His shirt was wet. Holding on to the lapels of his coat, she held it open so that the cooling breeze of the fan could cool him.

"Feel good? You'd better cool off or . . . you'll melt."

"I was about to melt in that booth. What do you think I am? Sugar or butter?" He spoke softly, intimately; his eyes devoured her smiling face.

"I'll have to think on it." She backed away, and he pulled on his coat to cover the holstered gun.

" 'Bye, Fleeta Mae."

" 'Bye, sugar. When's the big day?"

"We haven't decided yet."

"Let me know. Your mama was one of my best friends even if she did get the man I was after."

"Thank you, ma'am," Hod said.

"Anytime." Fleeta Mae plugged in a call. "Number please. Of course, I'm on duty, Clarence, or I'd not be at the switchboard. Did you want to place a call? I've not got time to talk to you now. No, I'll not take time off to go to a picture show. Clarence, do you want everyone on the line to hear this conversation? No, don't call later—"

Hod chuckled when they left the office. "That must be a very interesting job."

"Clarence Hankenson has had a crush on Fleeta Mae for years," Molly confided with a gentle laugh. "You should see him. He's the exact opposite of Fleeta Mae. She's so very thin and a head taller than he is. He's bald and must weigh two hundred pounds."

"Love is blind, so they say."

"Sometimes it's deaf and dumb, too."

"I'll get us a couple bottles of pop and we'll drive out someplace to drink them so I can take off this damn coat."

"I should be getting back to the store. As soon as we get out of town you can take off your coat."

"Come to think on it, I'd rather go back there, too."

He stopped the car in the shade of the cottonwood again to remove his coat. When he got back into the car, Molly asked the question that had been in her thoughts since they left the telephone office.

"Did . . . they pull you off the case."

"Tried to."

"What do you mean?"

"They said that Norton has been seen in Chicago. He

wasn't the one who shot through the window, and the chief didn't think that he'd had time to hire someone else to do his dirty work. The random shooting, they said, should be the concern of the county sheriff and not a Federal agent. They want me to come back to KC."

Chapter
Fourteen

When are you going?"

She felt a little sick and silently prayed that he not see how anxious she was to know the answer to her question.

Hod picked up her left hand and brought it over to place her palm against his right one. Her fingers were white and slender, her nails short and rounded. Suddenly he could picture a ring there, his ring, proclaiming to all that she belonged to him. He gently rubbed his fingertip up and down her ring finger.

While she held her breath and waited for him to speak, a knot formed in her stomach.

"Are you trying to get rid of me?" His voice was strained.

"You know I'm not."

"Did it embarrass you to introduce me as your fiancé?" He looked out the driver's window and swallowed, fighting the tightness in his throat.

"Whatever gave you that idea?" *I was sinfully proud to introduce you as my fiancé.*

"I'm not going." He turned and looked into her eyes.

Molly's first reaction was stunned surprise. When it passed confusion took its place.

"Won't you . . . get fired?"

"I'm not going," he repeated.

"Why not? If there's no longer any danger that someone will shoot me—"

"—I took a month's leave to make up my mind if I want to go back to the Bureau . . . that's what I told the chief. But I already know what I'm going to do." There was a quiet look on his face that she'd not seen before. "I wanted you to know that I'm staying here on my own without the support of the Bureau."

"I'm glad . . . you're staying. But I don't want you to lose your job."

"I'm not *losing* it. They'll take me back if I want to go."

"At the end of the mouth?"

"Anytime. I have a good record." Their eyes caught and held. "I want to be near you, Molly. I can't get it out of my head that sometime soon you'll need me."

"But if Norton has given up on eliminating me as a witness, what else could happen?"

"I've got a gut feeling about that shot that was fired into the house last night." A worried look came over her face, and he could have kicked himself for telling her that. "But then again," he added quickly, "I've been known to have hunches that went absolutely nowhere."

She tilted her face to look at him. Desire surged through him, not lustful desire, but an overwhelming need to protect her. What she said next took him completely by surprise.

"Can you stand sleeping on that cot for a month?"

He smiled at that. "That cot is a feather bed compared to some places I've slept." Then, his dark eyes soberly searched her face. "Do you want your aunt to know that I'm not on *official* duty?"

"I don't like keeping secrets from her, but if we just don't mention it one way or the other—"

"Good idea. I'll have to buy a car. Will you go with me to Liberal to get one?"

"If we drove the truck down, we could pick up the order for the store."

"You can drive the new car back. You drive, don't you?"

"I can drive the truck. I've driven this car only one time. I might wreck your new car."

"We'll go slow and stop often."

Their eyes caught and held. Molly's heart hammered, and a fluttering began in the pit of her stomach. His smile crinkled the lines around his eyes and deepened the indentations in his cheeks, making him suddenly look boyish. She was unaware how brilliantly her violet eyes shone or how radiantly she smiled. She just knew that she was overcome by a surprising, overwhelming burst of happiness.

Holding tightly to her hand, Hod watched her in joyful recognition that her hand no longer lay limp in his but gripped it firmly. The smile that she gave him reached all the way into his heart. He felt as if he had come to a crossroads and that from now on his life would take a new direction.

Molly, sweet Molly, you've stolen my heart.

Hod drove slowly back to the store. He felt light-hearted and young for the first time in years.

"I wonder how Aunt Bertha got along with George." Molly took off her hat and let the wind blow her hair. "She didn't like him at all when she first came here."

"He takes some getting used to. He's a lot smarter than he appears to be."

"Daddy thought so, too. They'd have long talks. George would hang around if there was no one in the store. As soon as folks came in, he would disappear. He never had much to say to me or Mama."

"Have you ever been to his farm?"

"Never. I don't think Daddy had been there for years. George's sister is strange. She doesn't welcome visitors."

"How old do you think he is?" Hod wanted to keep her talking.

"He isn't as old as my daddy, and he was forty-two. I'd say George is someplace between thirty-five and forty."

"That old? Want my guess?"

"Sure."

"I say, he's about thirty-two."

"How are we going to know who is right? Are you going to ask him?" Hod saw the amusement in her eyes when he glanced at her.

"What do I get if I'm right?"

"The teacher used to put a star on our foreheads."

"Come on, Molly. I'm not a little kid," he teased. "Let's make the bet worthwhile."

"A nickel."

"You're a heavy gambler." Hod slowed down to turn in at the store. "Isn't that the sheriff's car?"

"Looks like it. Oh, I hope nothing bad has happened."

As soon as the car stopped in front of the shed, Molly got out and hurried to the back door. Hod caught up with her, and they stepped up onto the porch together. He put his hand on her arm to hold her back while he opened the screen door and walked into the store. A glance told him that things were normal. Bertha was at the old rolltop desk and Sheriff Mason sat sprawled in a chair with his feet up on a box. Hod held the door for Molly.

"Aunt Bertha? Is everything all right?"

"Fine, except that I've been wading through a batch of lies the sheriff's been telling me."

"Your aunt's a real cutup, Miss Molly. How'er ya doin', Dolan?"

"Hot. How'er you doin'?"

"Fair to middlin'. Not much goin' on out in the county."

"If nothin's goin' on, them stories you've been tellin' me is just a bunch of windies." Bertha closed the ledger she'd been working on.

"Not all of them." The sheriff grinned sheepishly. "The one about the feller hidin' in the outhouse is true."

"I'm going to change clothes, Aunt Bertha." Molly started up the stairs.

"I'll chip ice for tea while you change."

Hod pulled off his tie, shrugged out of the shoulder

holster, and unbuttoned the top buttons on his shirt as he walked the length of the store to speak to George.

"Anything happen, George?"

George moved away from the window. "One thing."

"What's that?"

"That little dude in the fancy car came by. Looked the place over but didn't stop."

"McCabe's cousin?"

"Short, mouthy feller."

"That fits him. Well, he's McCabe's problem."

The telephone rang two shorts and a long. Bertha scurried behind the counter to answer it.

"For you, Hod." She set the receiver on the top of the oak box wall phone and moved out of the way.

Hod picked it up. "Dolan."

"Hod, I want to talk to you about this thing." The deep voice was familiar.

"Not now."

"I need you. That bunch down in Oklahoma—"

"Don't say it. I've made up my mind."

"You're a valuable man, Hod. Don't let all that experience go to waste because of a hunch."

"I'll talk to you another time."

"Will you be where I can reach you?"

"Sure. I'll be right here. 'Bye." Hod hung up the receiver and hurried after George, who had gone out the door. He caught up with him on the porch. "How long has the sheriff been here?"

"Hour."

"Was anything said about the shot last night?"

"Didn't hear anything."

"I'm glad of that. I'm not sure yet how much to tell him. Thanks for staying."

Hod stood on the porch for a minute, then turned and went back into the store. George was a man of few words, but a man Hod wanted on his side.

When George stopped at the pump for a drink of water, Stella lay in the shade at the side of the shed. He filled a bucket of fresh water for her, then knelt and patted her head.

"I'm takin' another one of your younguns home, girl. You'll just have one left. Your teats'll be dried up soon, and you won't be tied down so much. You stay here and look out for Molly for me."

George went into the shed, reached up to the rafter for his Kodak camera. He quickly took out a roll of film and replaced it with a new roll. A minute later, with a black-and-brown pup snuggled in his arms, he was walking across the field toward his farm.

Old Red, the tough old rooster, met him when he came into the yard. He ran at George, squawked, and flapped his wings in greeting. He followed him into the barn, where George left the pup in the corner with its siblings, unlocked the heavy wooden box, and put his gun inside.

For the next two hours George did chores, taking his time because he was not looking forward to going into the house and listening to Gertrude's raving. One of his cows was due to drop her calf at any time. He gave her extra rations. He checked his sows, fed the chickens, and repaired a hole in the chicken house. He climbed the windmill with a bucket of grease and spent a half hour greasing all the working parts he could reach.

The days were getting shorter. It was dusk when he washed at the pump, then went to the house. Gertrude was sitting in a chair beside the window. She had pinned back a corner of the blanket that covered it.

"Ya goin' to move yore bed over there?"

"Not planning on it." George took a bowl from the shelf and filled it with beans from the pot on the stove.

"Might as well. I know why you're smellin' 'round over there. You're after that slutty Velma. She switchin' her tail at ya?"

"You don't know what you're talking about." George cut a square of corn bread and put it on a plate.

"If ya ain't after her, yo're after that little gal a hers. Papa'll horsewhip ya if ya get to messin' with her. You ort to be shamed a yoreself."

"Hush your filthy mouth. Velma is dead. I told you that."

"I'm going to Kansas City tomorrow. Mama made me a new dress to wear. Papa gave me money, but I gave it to the postman."

George turned to look at her. Her thin hair was pulled back in a tight bun. She had a full lip of snuff in her mouth and juice ran down from the corners.

"The postman was here?"

"He comes ever'day. Sometimes twice a day. He brought me a letter from Aunt Maybelle. She wants me to come live with her. She's goin' to leave me all her money when she dies."

"Gertrude, we don't have an Aunt Maybelle," George said kindly. He felt pity for his only relative, who lived in a dream world of unreality.

"Damn you! You sonofabitchin' shithead!" Gertrude jumped up out of the chair. "We do, too, have a Aunt Maybelle. Papa! Papa!" she shrieked. "He's tellin' lies. Whip him, Papa. Whip him till he bleeds."

George had thought to sit out on the porch to eat his supper. After Gertrude's outburst, he carried his supper to his room, closed and locked the door, and turned on the light. Before he sat down to eat, he circled the room, looking at the photographs. He always looked at each one as if seeing it for the first time.

It calmed him to be here among his treasures. Breathing a heavy sigh, he sat down to his meal.

Things had not gone as Archie Howell had thought they would, although there had been an outpouring of sympathy for the family. The children had been doted on by the women of the church. He had been praised for "keeping a stiff upper lip." Enough food had been brought to the house to last a week, but Molly had not come near. She had not even offered a handshake at the gravesite.

And . . . all of this had been done for her.

Archie tried not to let anger cloud his mind. He tried to erase the picture of her sitting close to that black Irishman in *his* church. What did she need of that city man, when he was perfectly capable of taking care of her? It was the Irishman's fault that she had turned cold toward him. Things would have worked out if not for him and her snippy aunt. That dolt, George Andrews, was a part of it, too, for throwing his lot in with the interloper.

He looked at his image in the mirror and practiced his warmest smile. He believed that his kindheartedness and his genuine love of helping people was apparent, because strangers usually warmed to him on sight. He smoothed the hair at his temples and leaned close to the mirror to examine his soft-featured, dimpled face and twinkling blue eyes. He spoke to the image.

They don't know who they're up against, do they, Archie? God is on your side. He furnished the serpent that took Gladys out of a life of misery. He will help you get your heart's desire.

Archie left his room and went down the stairs. Charlotte was washing the children's hands and feet, getting them ready for bed. The kitchen was tidy, the leftover food put away. Archie paused in the doorway and admired the little group of his own creation. They were beautiful children. All of them. A child of his birthed from Molly's body would be magnificent.

"What shall we do with Aunt Gladys's things, Daddy?" Charlotte asked.

"I'm not ready to decide that yet, honey."

Archie looked at his eldest daughter with affection. He could always depend on his Charlotte. In a way he was sorry she couldn't go back to school because she had loved it. But it was best to keep her away from the riffraff who would ruin her by putting modern notions in her head. She would be grateful to him someday that she had learned that a woman's duty was to care for her children. It would make things easier for her when she married and had to learn that it was also her duty to serve her husband as he saw fit.

"I'll be gone for a while." He stroked the dark hair of his second oldest girl, Hester, one of the twins. "You must help Charlotte with the little ones, honey."

"I will, Daddy."

"That's my sweet girl." He went to the door and turned. "Have the boys gone to bed?"

"All but Otis. He . . . went out to be sure the chickens were penned and to put some salve on the cow's teat. She must have caught it in the fence."

"Good boy, Otis."

As soon as her father went out the door, Charlotte hurried to the darkened room at the front of the house to peer out the window. She breathed a sigh of relief when he went straight to his car and drove away. Hester tugged on her hand.

"Char, Otis said that he—"

"—Hester! Let's not talk about what Otis said. All right? It'll be a secret between you and me."

"But you lied, Char."

"I know I did, honey. I hope God will forgive me. I just couldn't stand to think of Otis getting a whipping just because he wanted to talk to one of his friends for a while."

"God wouldn't want Otis to hurt like he did last time, would he? Why did Daddy whip him so hard, Char? I hated him and wished he'd die."

"Oh, honey, don't say that." Charlotte rolled her eyes toward four-year-old Clara, who was listening with rapt attention. "We shouldn't want anyone to die and especially Daddy. But we don't have to think that everything he does is right."

"Will he get us a new mama?" Clara asked wistfully.

"Aunt Gladys wasn't like a mama." Hester gave her younger sister a little push.

"Cut that out, girls. You've got to get to bed. Hester has school tomorrow."

Just saying the word *school* made Charlotte's heart ache. She thought of dark-haired Wally and wondered if Margaret had given him the note she'd written. Yesterday he had come out with a food offering from his mother, but her daddy had kept an eagle eye on her, and she hadn't even been able to show herself.

With the children in bed, Charlotte went to the kitchen to wait for Otis. It made her nervous for him to sneak out. He had been getting more and more defiant lately, and she was afraid for him. He was angry because Daddy was making her stay home from school to take care of the kids. Otis had heard Mrs. Wagner tell him that her sister would come and work for board and a dollar a week. He had turned down the offer even after Mrs. Wagner said the church would pay the wages.

Otis had asked her if she had ever thought about when their mother died, and about the mother of the twins, and finding the baby's mother dead in bed. He said one of his friends had told him that his papa thought it was *damned funny*. Charlotte didn't know what he had meant because she didn't think it was funny at all.

She went to the door of the room her aunt had used. The church ladies had cleaned the room. A box and a cardboard suitcase filled with her aunt's belongings sat on the narrow bed. Her aunt hadn't liked her or any of the children. She had told them almost every day that because of them she lived a life of drudgery. As mean as she had been, Charlotte was sorry that she had died.

Her aunt had stormed out of the house that day saying that she didn't want to go on any old picnic. Her daddy had cajoled and promised to show her a beautiful place along the river. Charlotte shivered, thinking about poor Aunt Gladys with the snake wrapped around her neck.

Curiosity drew Charlotte to the box on the bed. The top was folded down. She lifted it and looked inside. The box was half-full of letters and cards, and on the top an old pocketbook. Inside the purse was a handkerchief, a case for glasses, a comb, and a snuffbox. The snuffbox was a surprise. She'd never seen Aunt Gladys dip snuff. Maybe she didn't dare. The preacher was dead set against tobacco in any form.

Charlotte placed the pocketbook on the bed, scooped up several letters, and thumbed through them. They were all old. As far as she knew her aunt hadn't received a letter since she had come here almost a year earlier. The letters all seemed to be from her sister, Berta, who had died five years ago. Charlotte opened a letter that was addressed to Aunt Gladys while she was here in Pearl after her mother and Otis's had died.

Berta wrote about her ailments and about feeding hobos that came to her door. She told Gladys that they'd bought new canvas side curtains for their car. Charlotte skimmed down the page until her father's name caught her eye.

*Sister, be careful around Archie. He's always been
queer acting. Even Mama was scared of him sometimes. He's had three wives and all of them died
quick like. I ain't sayin he had anythin to do with
them dying. Mama said that he had the face of an
angel but there was a devil in him. When he was a
little boy he had a pet cat. He slept with it and carried it around. I saw him with my own eyes kill his
pet. He wrapped a gunnysack around its head and
held the poor little thing till it stopped fightin to
breathe. He smiled while he was doin it. I'll never
forget it. He gave it a burial, sang hymns and cried.
I ain't sayin he would hurt you. I'm sayin that he
does queer things. Just be careful.*

Your sister, Berta

Charlotte's heart was beating as if she had run a mile.
Out of breath by the time she finished the letter, she put it
back in the envelope, slipped it into her pocket, and wondered if she dared tell Otis about it. Being careful to put
everything back in the box, she closed the lid, turned out
the light, and went to the room she shared with her sisters
and now the baby.

When Archie reached the main street of Pearl, it was almost deserted. The cafe and the grocery store were still
open, and a few people lingered in front of each. Archie
turned the corner, went through the alley, and out onto the
road that passed the church. Adjusting the speed until
the car was moving between five and ten miles an hour,

he rested his arm on the open window and enjoyed the wind in his face.

It was a dark night. No stars peeked through the overcast sky. Archie loved being with his children, but he loved more being alone in the velvet darkness. He began to sing in a loud clear voice.

"When the trumpet of the Lord shall sound,
  and time shall be no more,
And the morning breaks, eternal, bright and fair;
When the saved of earth shall gather over on the
  other shore,
And the roll is called up yonder, I'll be there."

As Archie sang, tears filled his eyes. He knew that he was truly blessed. God had given him the ability to extend to others the extreme kindness of helping them reach the golden shores, where love and peace awaited them.

Now his Father in heaven was testing him. In His wisdom God had chosen Molly to be his mate, to comfort him in his later years. God had depended on him to make the miracle come about. He had failed, so it seemed. Now God would help him make sure that she would never belong to another man.

"Praise the Lord!" he shouted. "Show me the way, Jesus."

After he passed the lane leading to the Andrews farm and approached the McKenzie store, he increased his speed so as not to draw attention by driving too slowly. The store was dark, but a light was on in the living quarters upstairs in the back hallway or kitchen. Archie went a mile up the road, stopped, and waited a few minutes before he turned and went back down the road toward the store. This time he drove a little more slowly, his eyes fastened on the upstairs windows.

"She's up there in bed with that son of a bitch!" The words burst from his mouth. Then he pounded the steering wheel with his fist. "No! No! No! The devil wants me to believe that, but I won't. God wouldn't be so cruel to his favorite son."

Archie was tempted to stop. He loved just being near Molly. Better judgment prevailed, and he passed the store. He had to think, to plan, but he had to be very careful . . . this time.

Hod sat on the bench that advertised Garrett's Snuff with his legs stretched out in front of him. When Molly, Bertha, and he had decided to sit outside for a while before going to bed, he had carried the bench from the porch out into the yard away from the store. Bertha had stayed outside for only a short while, then, afraid she'd get chigger bites, had gone inside.

"Why didn't you tell the sheriff about the shooting last night?" Molly asked from the other end of the bench.

"I figured the fewer people who knew about what's going on the better. He couldn't have done anything about it anyway."

Hod tried to keep his mind off the girl beside him, but it was no use. She had seeped into his heart, his mind, and lodged there. He tried to think of something to say that would keep her there. Every time she started to speak he was afraid she was going to say that she was going in to bed.

"Have you ever walked out under the stars with a boy who was courting you?" he asked out of desperation.

"A time or two."

"Did you like him?"

"Enough. I'd known him all my life."

"Is he still around here?"

"No. He went to the CCC camp. His mother said that he's working up in Yellowstone Park."

"Do you keep in touch with him?"

"What is this? Are you asking for the story of my life?"

"If you want to tell me."

"There has been nothing exciting in my life. You'd be bored to death."

"Want to bet?"

"We've already got one bet." In the brief silence that followed, Hod heard the sound of a motorcar. "Get behind the bench," he said quickly. "The car coming now went north about ten minutes ago."

"How do you know?" Molly obeyed, then peeked over the back of the bench to watch the road.

"I recognized the sound of the motor."

"Motors all sound alike to me."

"You'd learn the difference if you'd sat in the dark for hours listening for a certain one." The car passed by slower than the first time. All Hod could see was that it was a dark sedan. Most cars were dark sedans, so that didn't tell him anything. "Did you recognize the car?"

"No. Did you?"

"No. Next time we come out here I'll bring my binoculars."

"Can you see in the dark with them?"

"Pretty well."

They returned to the bench. Hod sat a little closer to her this time. It was a rare, still, dark night. Bertha had said it was twister weather, and Hod agreed. Heat seemed to press down and around them. In the distant southwest faint flashes of lightning appeared.

"Have you ever been in a tornado?" Molly's voice came softly out of the darkness. She knew she was making idle talk, hoping to prolong the enjoyment of sitting here in the dark with him.

"No, but I've been close to one and seen the results afterward. They can be very destructive."

"Aunt Bertha is afraid of storms. So was my mother. Four or five times a year we'd spend the night in the storm cellar."

"And you? Are you afraid of thunderstorms?"

"Not thunderstorms. But anyone would be fool not to be afraid of a twister."

"How long has it been since you've had a good rain?"

"I don't know. It rained a little about the first of June. Another time we had a little rain squall that didn't amount to much. Aunt Bertha called it a spit rain."

Hod's frustration suddenly reached the limit. He was tired of dancing around the bush. She would be going in soon, and he was going to miss his chance to do what he'd been aching to do since he met her. He decided that he might as well "take the bull by the horns" and see what happened. He moved close to her, put his arm around her, and drew her tight against him.

She was so surprised that she didn't resist.

"We're acting like a couple of kids, and I'm not a kid. We're making this foolish small talk because we don't know what else to say. This is what I've been wanting to do since we came out here, and, by God, I'm going to do it, even if you slap my face afterward." She either liked him or she didn't, he decided. It was time to find out if he had a chance with her or not.

"I've never slapped anyone in my life."

"That's good to know, because before this night is over, I'm going to kiss you."

Chapter
Fifteen

Molly sat in rigid silence. Hod's arm had slid across her shoulders and down her back, pulling her to him. For a moment she felt as if she couldn't breathe. Her hip and thigh were pressed to his, her shoulder was under his arm. She could feel his breath stirring the hair at her temples. Paralysis gripped her throat, preventing her from speaking. When her mind cleared and the last words he had spoken registered, she made an effort to draw away from him.

"I'm not . . . I don't—"

"—Don't be afraid of me. I know you don't go around kissing strangers. I'll admit that you don't know much about me, but I'm not a stranger. Relax and let's enjoy being close together. I'll not kiss you if you don't want me to."

The sound of his voice in the warm, dark night was so reassuring she lost her self-consciousness and relaxed against him.

"That's better," he said in a low whisper. "I've wanted to hold you like this for a long time."

"You haven't known me a long time."

"After I met you that first day, I couldn't get you out of my mind."

"You wanted me to help you catch the killers."

"It was more than that."

"You didn't want me to get killed. You'd lose—"

His fingers came up to silence her lips. "My job had nothing to do with it."

"But that's what you said the morning you came here."

"I was running off at the mouth."

"I can't imagine you saying something you don't mean."

"Want the truth? I was so damn mad at myself for being so crazy happy at seeing you again that I acted the fool. I'm twenty-eight years old, Molly, and there I was mooning over a girl with violet eyes, a sweet smile, and beautiful dark brown hair, a girl whose life I had put in danger."

"I'm sorry—"

Without any thought on his part, his hand came up, cupped her cheek, and turned her face to him.

"Oh, sweet girl! You've nothing to be sorry for. I was knocked off kilter that morning and didn't know how to handle it."

His hand moved from her cheek down to her lap. He picked up her hand and laced his fingers through hers. He wanted to tell her that sometimes thinking about her made him feel all mixed-up and shaky inside, and at other times he was surprised by the flood of happiness that washed over him. But he'd never spoken soft words, and he was afraid that he'd make a mess of it.

"You don't really know me."

"And you don't really know me. I could be one of those flimflam men, or an escaped prisoner, or a bank robber—"

"Or you could be married."

"Oh, Lord! You couldn't be thinking that!"

"I'm not." He felt her body tremble with laughter, but the sound was a mere whisper in the night. "If you had been married, Johnny would have told me. So we can mark that off the list of your previous occupations."

"Thank goodness for Johnny."

She felt so strange being this close to him. A curiously warm, exciting feeling fluttered in her stomach. The hand holding hers was never still. His thumb stroked her knuckles, her palm, and her fingertips. Her heart almost stopped when he turned her hand and brought the ridges of her knuckles up to rub back and forth across his lips.

"When can we go to Liberal? I want to take you to a picture show, sit in the dark, eat popcorn, and smooch with you."

"Smooch?"

"Neck. You know what young guys and gals do in movies."

"You just said that you're not a kid." Her voice was a soft happy sound.

"I should have said 'what sweethearts do.' "

"Are you reverting to your childhood?" she asked in a breathless whisper, ignoring his last remark.

"Sometimes I think so. When I'm with you, I get all flustered and say stupid things."

"I'm glad you said that."

"Why?"

"Because . . . it's what I do."

It took a couple of seconds for the meaning of her words to soak into his brain. When he spoke his husky voice had the sound of a plea.

"Do I have to wait to kiss you, sweet Molly?"

"Not . . . if you don't want to," she answered without hesitation.

Her cheek found a place on his shoulder. He pressed a gentle kiss to her lips. It was over too quickly for both of them. The gentle touch of their lips brought a bittersweet ache of passion in its wake. He lifted her arm to encircle his neck, and his arms closed around her. They held her so closely against him that she could feel the hard bones and muscles of his body against the softness of hers. His hoarse, ragged breathing accompanied the thunder of his heartbeat against her breasts.

Hungrily his eyes slid over her upturned face. Their breaths mingled for an instant before he covered her mouth again. He held her firmly but gently. There was no haste in the kiss. This time it was slow and deliberate. He took his time, with closed eyes and pounding heart.

Molly offered herself willingly. Her mouth opened under the gentle pressure, yielding, molding itself to the shape of his. There was a soft union of lips and tongues before their mouths parted briefly, then met and clung with wild sweetness that held still the moments of time. With a sigh Molly gave herself up to the pure joy of kissing and being kissed, to the thrill of wanting and being wanted.

Hod lifted his head and pressed his cheek tightly to hers.

"Molly, Molly," he murmured, his hand stroking the nape of her neck. "Kissing you was even better than I had imagined."

Slowly, he moved his head until his lips touched hers again as if having once tasted them, he couldn't stay away. She was surprised that his lips were so soft, so gentle, surprised at the pleasant drag of his whiskers on her cheeks. He held her head in his large hand, drawing his fingers through her hair while his lips made little caressing movements against hers.

Suddenly his kiss deepened and he dropped his hand from her nape to wrap her tightly in his arms, driven by passion, sparked by the touch of her tongue on his lower lip. He wanted it to go on and on, but knew it had to end.

He drew away slowly, one of the hardest things he'd ever had to do. He wanted more! What had started out to be a chaste, sweet kiss ended in a kiss of an entirely different nature. She was shaken, too. Her head had dropped to his shoulder, and her nose nuzzled his neck.

She became conscious of his hand stroking her hair and his low voice speaking to her.

"I must be careful with you, little darlin'. I want more, much more than your sweet kisses. Don't be afraid of me. I'll never take more than you offer."

Shivers of awareness went through her. She tugged on his hand, lifted it, and pressed his knuckles to her lips. They had spoken no words of love, but love was there throbbing between them. His lips trailed her face, stopping at each closed eye to feel the flutter of it, moved down her nose to lips that waited, warm and eager.

He pressed her head to his shoulder, and they sat in companionable silence and sweet intimacy.

Hod was jarred out of his contented lassitude by a cool gust of wind and a loud rumble of thunder. Glancing skyward, he glimpsed during the flashes of lightning a blanket of dark, rolling clouds.

"It's going to storm, sweetheart."

"I hope the wind pushes the rain clouds our way." Molly lifted her head from his shoulder and looked up at the sky.

Sweetheart. He called me sweetheart!

"We could be in for some high winds."

Molly moved out of his arms and stood. A gust of wind came up under her full skirt and wrapped it around her thighs.

"Ohhhh—" She fought to hold it down while the wind whipped her hair around her face.

"I'd better get you inside." With his arm around her, they hurried up the porch steps and into the store. Hod pulled the screen door closed behind them and latched it. "I left my flashlight somewhere here on the counter."

"I don't need it. I know where everything is."

Hod found the light and flashed the beam on the floor while he closed and locked the door. Molly went through the store to the stairway. The feeling in her stomach was not pleasant; she was afraid that she had been too *brassy*. Hod had used the word to Jennifer Bruza. She had kissed him in a most intimate way, and let him kiss her as if they were truly engaged to be married. What had possessed her?

It had more than likely been an evening of entertainment for him.

"Good night," she called with her foot on the stair.

"Molly, wait." Being careful to keep the beam of light out of her face, he came to her and took her hand. "I didn't want this night to end until we talked about our future."

I can see our future clear as day. You'll go away, and I'll stay here with tonight locked forever in my memories.

"Tomorrow will be soon enough," she answered in a ragged whisper.

He gazed at her steadily. Even in the dim light he saw that she flushed beneath his stare. His gaze moved down over her soft, full breasts and narrow waist, and he wondered how he had kept himself from touching them. He found himself also wondering how it would feel to hold her naked in his arms. He turned his eyes away from her in an effort to rid his mind of the thought.

"Tonight meant a lot to me," he said softly. "I promise you—"

"—You don't have to promise me anything," she said quickly. "We shared a few kisses is all."

"Is that all it meant to you? It meant a hell of a lot more to me." A clap of thunder almost drowned out his words.

"I'd better get upstairs and see if the windows are closed. Aunt Bertha may have gone to sleep."

"Will you kiss me good night?" It was a question he didn't wait to have answered. He pulled her into his arms, kissing her, gently on the lips, not once but several times, then released her, and whispered, "Good night, sweetheart."

"Good night."

Hod shone the beam on the stairs until she reached the top and pulled the chain that connected with the single lightbulb. She glanced down at him before she disappeared.

While she was getting ready for bed, Molly's thoughts churned. She had just spent the most wonderful couple of hours of her life. She could still feel Hod's kisses on her lips. But spiraling around in her mind were the words he had not said. He had kissed her and told her how he had looked forward to seeing her. Earlier he had promised that he would stay for a month because she might need him. That was the only commitment he had made. He had not said he loved her or anything near it.

It was hard for Molly to believe that a man of Hod's obvious experience would seriously be interested in a country girl like her. He must have met many attractive worldly-wise women. She was perfectly aware of how unsophisticated she was. The farthest from home she'd ever been was Wichita. This store, which meant the world to her, possibly meant little to him.

The more she thought about it, the more miserable she became. Finally, weariness overcame her and she slept fitfully, dreaming that a big black car had stopped in front of the store and the men who had killed her parents were coming inside.

She awakened with a startled cry. A dark form was

bending over her. She whimpered and tried to move, but her muscles refused to obey.

"Molly, wake up. We've got to go to the cellar." Hod's hands shook her. "Put something on over your gown while I go wake Bertha."

He switched on the light as he left the room. Molly bounded out of bed, pulled a dress on over her head, and slipped into her shoes. She remembered to snatch up a quilt and a blanket. Above the rumbling thunder, the roar of the wind and the rippling of the tin on the roof as the wind passed over it, she could hear Hod yelling at Bertha.

Bertha, with a robe belted around her chubby body, her hair up in curl papers, and her feet in slippers, was out of her room and headed for the stairs with a scared look on her face. Hod ran through the rooms checking to be sure that the windows were open.

"It's better to let the wind blow through the house than to butt against it. Come on." Almost stumbling over each other, they ran down the stairs to the back door. "Hold on to the screen," Hod shouted. Even as he spoke the wind tore it from Molly's hands and slammed it back against the wall. Hod pulled the door closed and wrapped an arm around each of the women as they headed across the yard to the storm cellar. The wind-driven rain lashed them like needles. Over the deafening noise of the approaching storm she heard Hod yell.

"Look!"

Molly's gaze flashed skyward. Out of the gray mass of roiling clouds snaked a long gray funnel, perhaps a mile long, dangling down from the sky. Leisurely it dipped to the ground and immediately turned black with the dirt and the debris it scooped up. The sound was like a freight train passing overhead.

They ran, Hod pushing the two women ahead of him. At the cellar door Molly shoved the blanket and quilt into her aunt's arms and helped Hod with the door. They had difficulty lifting it. Then the wind caught it and slammed it back. Molly and Bertha scrambled down the stairs and into the cellar. They waited for Hod. When he didn't follow them down, Molly started to go back up the steps. Bertha caught her arm, and they waited in horrific suspense for him to appear.

Molly was seconds away from hysteria and had started up the steps again when Hod jumped into the stairwell, with the pup in his arms and Stella close on his heels. He shoved the pup at Molly and began the battle to close the cellar door. Gritting his teeth and putting all his strength into it, he managed to get the door up off the ground, then ducked into the stairwell as the wind caught it and slammed it shut. He yanked his flashlight from his belt so he could see to shoot the bolt that would hold it closed.

Molly dropped the pup and lit the lantern as soon as she could strike a match without the wind blowing it out. Her eyes were on Hod. His black hair was plastered to his head, his shirt and pants clung to him like a second skin. He was flashing his light on the rock walls and the heavy timbers of the ceiling, then on the floor and under the cots. Molly knew that he was looking for snakes. She remembered her daddy doing that, too.

Something heavy struck the cellar door. They backed

up and sat down on one of the two canvas cots set one across the back and one down the side to form an L.

Stella and the pup came to stand close to them. Hod shook out the blanket and wrapped it around Bertha. For once the older woman was silent. Molly sat down beside him and covered his back with the quilt he had put over her shoulders. He put his arm around each of the women and they huddled together while the storm raged outside.

Molly's hand lay on his thigh. Her face found refuge in the curve of his neck.

"We'll be all right here," he murmured reassuringly, and Molly felt his lips on her forehead.

"Will the twister miss us?" she whispered.

"I don't know, honey. Sometimes they skip around. I should have awakened you sooner. I thought we were going to get a good thunderstorm until I saw those rolling clouds."

Molly tilted her face and whispered in his ear. "I was so scared. You could have been killed getting the dogs."

"I was sure I had time to get them."

At first, Hod thought the whimpering sounds were coming from the pup. Then he felt the violent trembling.

"Bertha? Hey, now. We're safe here." He took his arm from around Molly and wrapped both his arms around the older woman. "I've not heard of anyone being sucked up out of a good storm cellar even if the twister came right over them. Whoever built this cellar built it well. We'll ride out the storm right here."

In the minutes that followed, the storm seemed to intensify. Things were crashing against the cellar door, and the noise was like a thousand roaring thunders. Hod pulled Molly to the floor between his legs, encircled both women in his arms, and hovered over them. They clung to him as if they were drowning.

Then, just as the sound peaked, it stopped. Abruptly. They waited. Listened. The wind had lessened, but thunder still rolled. Something hit the cellar door. Then again and again. Hod got up and went to the stairwell. The thump came again.

"Good God! Someone's out there." He disengaged the bolt and pushed on the door. It was not so heavy now that the wind was no longer holding it down. In the beam of his flashlight he saw a man standing on spread legs, the piece of lumber he'd used to pound on the door still in his hand. "George! Godamighty, man. What the hell are you doing out here in this storm?"

George stood there in the pouring rain without moving. His hair covered his forehead and stuck to his cheeks.

"Get on down here, George."

"Mol . . . ly." The name came out of the big man's mouth like an agonized plea.

"She's all right. Molly's here in the cellar. Come on down." George didn't move or appeared to have heard him.

"Molly!" Hod yelled. "Come hold the door while I get him down here."

It was raining steadily. Molly held on to the door while Hod went out and grabbed George's arm and guided his stumbling steps down the stairs.

"Mol . . . ly," he muttered. He stood in the middle of the cellar when Hod left him to help Molly with the door.

Stella, not understanding his lack of attention, lifted a paw and scratched on his pant leg. He didn't appear to notice.

"What's the matter with him?" Molly asked, then had to repeat the question when a sudden spate of hail hit the cellar door.

The dog looked at George and whined as if realizing that something was wrong. Hod gently tugged the stunned man down to sit on the cot before he answered Molly.

"For one thing, he's been whacked on the head." Blood trickled down the side of George's face. "Do we have anything I could tie around his head to try and stop the blood?"

"We can use the end of my nightgown if you can tear off a strip."

Hod dug into his pocket and brought out a pocketknife.

"Bertha," he shouted over the racket made by the storm, shaking her shoulder, "we need your help. Cut a strip off Molly's gown." He thrust the knife into her hand. "I've got to get the wet clothes off George and wrap him in that quilt. He's lost a lot of blood and could go into shock."

While Molly held, stretched between her two hands, the fabric of her nightdress that hung down below the dress she had hastily put on, Bertha split it with Hod's knife.

"Let me see if it'll tear now, Aunt Bertha."

By the time Molly had torn off a six-inch strip of her nightgown, Hod had removed George's boots and his overalls, piling them on the floor. He pulled off the wet, ragged shirt and quickly wrapped the near-naked man in the dry quilt. Bertha took the blanket from around her shoulders, folded it, and added it to the quilt as Hod wound the cloth tightly around George's head.

"Mol . . . ly." George's eyes opened and he looked around.

"She's right here," Hod said. "Come here, honey. He's worried about you."

Molly knelt beside the cot. George rolled his head and looked at her.

"Oh, George. Why in the world did you come out in this storm? You needn't have worried about Stella. Hod got her and her pup down here before it struck. He went to the shed and got them. Lie still and get warm."

George's eyes drifted shut. Molly looked anxiously at Hod. He squatted beside her and put his arm around her.

"He's worn-out, honey."

"Will he be all right?"

"I don't know, but I think so. The cut on his head is not real deep, but it'll give him a hell of a headache. He was pounded with things picked up by the wind, and he'll be bruised and sore for a while."

"Is there much damage out there?"

"The store is still there, but . . . the back porch is gone. I didn't have time to look around much. We'll have to wait until daylight to see how things are."

"Thank God you were here."

"Amen to that," Bertha said. She seemed to have lost some of her fright and had sat down on the cot and lifted George's feet into her lap. Her hands were beneath the blanket, and she was rubbing his legs. "His legs are ice cold. I'm tryin' to get the blood going."

"That's a good idea, Bertha. I'm afraid he'd not have made if it he'd passed out somewhere out there in the storm."

"I can't imagine why he'd come over here in a storm. He should have known that we'd take care of Stella and the pup." Molly placed her palm on George's forehead, being careful to avoid the cut.

A conspiratorial glance passed between Hod and Bertha. How could Molly be so unaware that the man was devoted to her? Hod had watched George closely since he became aware of the attachment. The man had not made one move to touch Molly or to get her alone. He went out of his way to avoid her, yet Hod had caught him giving her shy glances, and there was . . . the Kodak in the shed.

"Poor George," Molly said. "He's not had much happiness in his life."

"How do you know that, sweetheart?" Hod hugged her to him, placed a kiss on her forehead, and looked directly at Bertha to get her reaction. Molly's face turned a dull red, and she pulled away from him. She had to clear her throat before she could speak.

"Since his folks died, he hasn't been able to do anything. He's had to take care of that crazy sister of his," she said too loudly. "Shouldn't we try to get him to the doctor?"

"Not much chance of that until morning."

"Then we're taking him," Molly said firmly.

"He's warming up and not shaking as much," Bertha announced in the sudden silence.

Hod stood, his head almost touching the roof of the cellar.

"The thunder has moved away, and the wind has let up. I'll take a look outside."

Chapter
Sixteen

The back porch had been torn off by the wind. The chicken house attached to the side of the shed was gone, too. Tree limbs were down and the roof of the gazebo lay in the road in front of the store. The telephone and the electricity were out. Luckily, there appeared to be no substantial damage to the structure of the store itself.

When Molly and Bertha came out of the cellar, leaving George still asleep on the cot, dawn was breaking. The air was fresh and cool. Hod had already told them that the store had come through the storm in pretty good shape, and Molly was surprised at the debris scattered about. Bertha waded through rain puddles to the shed to check on her car. Though a door had been torn off the shed, the car had not even a dent.

Because there were no steps, Hod helped the women up into the back of the store. They left their muddy shoes at the door and did a quick inspection of the downstairs before going up to the living quarters. Rain had blown in through the open windows, and a leak in the roof had left a puddle of water on the kitchen floor.

The first thing to do as far as Bertha was concerned was to put on a pot of coffee. Molly's first priority was to wash and get into dry, clean clothes, which she did in record time. With a ribbon tied about her hair to keep it out of her face, she began a search of her father's things for something George could wear to go to the doctor because she was determined to take him there. She found a pair of overalls, which her father seldom wore, and an old flannel shirt. The overalls would be too short for George's long legs, but that couldn't be helped.

"Coffee smells good."

Hod was in the kitchen with Bertha. He had changed his clothes and toweled his wet hair until it lay in curls all over his head. The eyes that fastened on Molly when she came into the room were like a deep dark well. This morning his features were rough with a day's growth of beard, making him look hard and perhaps a little cruel. She couldn't help but think that the woman who belonged to him would feel either terribly safe or terribly intimidated by him.

"A twister hit the south side of Wichita three years ago. It scared the waddin' out of me," Bertha was saying. "I ain't sayin' what the one last night scared out of me. Oh, shoot! Looks like I forgot to empty the ice pan last night, and it's run over. Oh, well. I'll just mop it up with the rest of the water the rain blew in."

Molly was grateful for her aunt's chatter while they ate toast and apple butter and drank the strong coffee. Hod looked at her often, but addressed most of his remarks to Bertha. Then he addressed one directly to her.

"I can build some steps out the back door if you don't want to replace the porch right away."

"I haven't even thought about the porch. I'm thinking about getting someone out to fix the roof."

"I'll go up there and see what I can do. The wind may have blown the rain in under a seam, and it traveled down a beam to the kitchen."

"I wouldn't think of asking you to do that. We—"

"—You didn't ask. I volunteered."

"Oh, but—"

"No buts, Molly," he said firmly. "As long as I'm here I might as well make myself useful."

"That's mighty decent of you." Bertha refilled Hod's coffee cup. "I swear to goodness. I don't know what we'd have done without you last night."

"Oh, Aunt Bertha," Molly scoffed. "Don't you think we've got sense enough to go to the cellar if there's a storm, without someone here to tell us to?" Hod's words, "as long as I'm here," reverberated in her mind as she spoke.

"If I recall, young lady, you were sleeping when Hod came up and got us. I know I was. A few minutes later, and we wouldn't have made it to the cellar."

Her tone plainly said that she had made up her mind that Hod was the hero of the day, and it was useless to try and change it. Molly wisely switched the subject. *Hero of the day, but where will he be this time next month?*

"I found some clothes for George in Daddy's things. They'll not fit too well, but they'll do until we can get his washed and dried. Aunt Bertha, will you drive him into town to see the doctor?"

"Of course I will, but I'm thinking it'll be afternoon before that road dries up enough for me to get down it. Don't you think you'd better ask him if he wants to go?"

"Surely he will."

"There may be a lot of damage in town. It looked to me like the funnel was headed right for Pearl." Hod drained his cup and got to his feet. "I'll take the clothes out to George, and if he's awake, I'll see if he wants to see the doctor."

Hod picked up the bundle of clothes Molly had left on the kitchen chair. She didn't turn. He paused in the doorway and looked at the back of her head.

Why are you doing this, sweetheart? Why are you being so cold to me this morning? I was sure that last night meant something to you. Have you had time to think about it and regret what happened between us?

After Hod left, Molly rose and refilled her coffee cup. She didn't dare sit for very long—there was too much to do. The sleepless night had made her tired and grouchy.

"I don't know where to start first," she confessed to her aunt.

"From the looks of that road out front, I don't think we're going to be overloaded with customers. The roads are too muddy for cars. The wagons could make it. I'll stay up here and see if I can dry things out. I'll fold back the rug and turn on the electric fan. Oh, fiddle-faddle. I plumb forgot the electric is off. I'll fold it back anyway."

Molly was coming down from the living quarters just

as Hod came in through the back door of the store. He had the clothes that she had given him in his hand.

"George is gone. He got up and dressed and left while we were having breakfast."

"Gone? He was in no condition to go anywhere. We should go look for him."

"He went home, Molly. Stella and the pup went with him. I followed his tracks around the shed. He headed across the pasture. I imagine he was anxious to get home and see about his sister."

"What if he falls in a faint before he gets there?"

"I don't think he'd have been so foolish as to leave if he thought he couldn't make it home. But if you're worried about him, I'll walk over to his place."

"No. He isn't your responsibility."

"He isn't yours, either," Hod said with a touch of impatience, and went through the store and out the front door. He had to figure a way to get the gazebo roof out of the road, that is, when he stopped pondering why Molly was so concerned about George all of a sudden.

George listened to Molly and her aunt talk about him. He was too embarrassed to open his eyes while they were there and let them know that he was awake. He thought his heart was going to jump out of his chest when he realized he was near-naked under the quilt. The events of the night came back to him in snatches. He remembered pounding on the cellar door and Molly fussing over him. He had heard Hod tell her the store had come through the storm. Oh, Lord! He recalled, someone rubbing his legs. He hoped to hell it wasn't *her*.

George was relieved when Molly and her aunt finally left the cellar. He had lain there for a minute, making sure they were not coming back, before he sat up on the side of the cot. At the sudden movement his head felt as if it was going to explode. He touched the cloth that had been wrapped around it and felt the sore spot. Then he sat and waited until his head stopped spinning, so that he could put on his wet clothes and his boots.

Stella nuzzled his hand to get his attention. He scratched her head before he stood.

"C'mon, girl. Call your youngun and let's go."

When he left the cellar, and saw the debris scattered around, George felt sick. The back porch and Velma's gazebo were gone. The chicken house had been blown away. Tree limbs were down. Dead chickens lay in the yard. This place that had been his haven had been changed forever.

He walked across the field. The rain had sunk into the soil where it was sandy and stood in puddles in other places. He squinted his eyes as he approached his farm. The barn was standing, as was the house. A few tree limbs were down, but there was not as much damage as there was at the store.

George went straight to the cellar where he had taken Gertrude, kicking and screaming, the night before. She had not wanted to go, but he had to put her in a secure place so he could go to the store and be sure Molly was safe. He removed a heavy stone he'd put on the door so that she couldn't get out. He opened it and let it fall back on the ground. He half expected Gertrude to come boiling out. She didn't.

"Gertrude," he called, and went down a few steps and peered into the cellar. She was sitting quietly on the built-in cot, with a quilt around her. "Gertrude, come on out."

"Why'd ya leave me here?"

"So you'd be safe from the storm. Come on out now. The storm is over."

"It was dark down here."

"The lantern was lit and it was full of oil."

"A waste of oil. I blew it out 'fore Papa come down."

George's head was aching, and his patience was running out. He went toward the house. Before he reached the door, Gertrude was behind him.

"Ya left me here and went to that slut. What happened to yore head? Did she hit ya?"

George shook the ashes down in the cookstove and put in kindling from the woodbox. When the fire was started, he filled the coffeepot and set it over the open blaze.

"I ain't cookin' nothin'." Gertrude sat in the rocking chair, rocking and humming. "Hear me, George. I ain't cookin'."

He ignored her and carried the teakettle to his room, shut and locked the door. After washing, he put on dry clothes and examined the cut on his head in his small mirror. It looked worse than it was and a little salve smeared on it would do. Barefoot, he walked around his room and gazed at his pictures. The corner of one was curled. He took a small tack and secured it to the wall. He had his favorites and looked at them for an extra long while.

"I'm goin' to town today," Gertrude called through the door. "Ya'll have to hitch up the buggy." She kicked the door. "Did you hear me? Come outta there right now! Come out or I'll get a switch."

George put his fingers on his ears, hoping to drown out the sound of her voice.

There was rejoicing in Pearl. That tree limbs were down, a few porches blown off and privies blown over was a small price to pay for the crop- and grass-saving rain. People gathered in small groups on the street to discuss the amount of rainfall, what sections of the county got the most of it, and what it would do for the price of wheat.

Keith rode his horse into town and went directly to the telephone office. Morrison's telephone was out, and he had been unable to call to see if Ruth was all right. Fleeta Mae was on duty and gave him only a glance when he came in the door.

"The lines are down, Mrs. Nelson. There's nothing I can do about it. You can call in town, but that's all. Yes, well, I know you're worried. If I hear anything about them, I'll let you know. Mrs. Nelson, I must go. I'm terribly busy." Fleeta unplugged the line from the switchboard and turned to Keith. "Some folks think I should go out and climb the poles and fix the wires. Don't that beat all?"

"Sure does. How about the Hoovers? Is their line down?"

" 'Fraid so. If you're looking for Ruth, and I expect you are, she's at the school although not many kids showed up."

"Does anything go on around here that folks don't know about?"

"Not much. Not even the fact that fellow in the fancy car that was looking for you the other day spent the night at Bessie Peterson's boardinghouse. A tree limb fell on his car, and he's fit to be tied."

"Too bad it didn't fall on his head," Keith muttered. "How long do you think it will be before I can call long-distance?"

"Where to?"

"Dallas, Texas."

"Two or three days. Maybe more."

Keith muttered an obscenity. "Have you heard how the McKenzies stood the storm? The funnel was headed that way."

"I've not heard. I did hear that it traveled south of town and came down on the Collins ranch. That would be southwest of McKenzie's. It may have missed them." While Fleeta Mae was talking a dozen lights twinkled on the switchboard. "Operator. Sorry, the line is down. Operator. Sorry, the line is down. Operator—"

Keith mounted his horse and, deciding to get the unpleasantness over with, headed for where he was sure he'd find Marty. He tied his horse behind the cafe and went through the back door.

"Mornin'," Catherine called. She was wearing a long skirt, several strands of beads around her neck and earrings that reached her shoulders. For such a tiny person, she was defiantly a presence.

"Mornin'. How's the coffee?"

"Strong and hot. You want some?"

"Sure do."

"I'd give you a shot of whiskey if I had one. You're goin' to need it." She jerked her head to the front window. Marty was pacing up and down in front of the cafe.

"Great! Just what I need. Maybe I can drink my coffee before he finds out I'm in here."

But it wasn't to be. Marty saw him through the window and flung open the screen door.

"How did you get in here? I tried to call the Morrisons, but the damn line is down. Just what you'd expect in a hick town." He pulled out a chair and sat down as if he had been invited. He lifted his hand and snapped his fingers to get Catherine's attention. "I want coffee if it's fresh."

"How fresh?" Catherine called back.

"Not that two-day old stuff I got this morning." Marty snapped.

"Is one-day old all right?" she asked to the amusement of two men sitting in a booth. She brought two mugs of coffee to the table and winked at Keith. "Is that all, Your Highness?"

Marty looked her up and down, and snarled. "If I'd wanted something else, I would have asked for it. Now go wash dishes or something. I'd like a private conversation with my cousin."

It was one irritation too much for Keith. He stood, grabbed the belt that held up Marty's britches, and hauled him to his feet.

"The lady doesn't have to put up with lip from a two-bit hustler. Now pay her, and be damn quick about it!"

"What are you so fired up about?" Marty hardly had time to drop some coins on the table before Keith was propelling him to the door with his hand gripping the belt at the back of his pants and pulling them up into his crotch. "Stop it! For God's sake. You're about to cut me in two!"

Keith stopped shoving when they reached the walk in front of the cafe, and pushed Marty against the wall.

"You're the most arrogant, overbearing little son of a bitch I've ever known. Has it ever occurred to you that you're not one damn bit better than anyone else? Who the hell are you to talk to the lady like that?"

"Christ, Keith. She's just a hick waitress in a hick cafe in a hick town. What'er you getting so riled up for? Have you been sleeping with her?"

Anger caused Keith to bounce Marty's head against the wall.

"Ohhhh . . . Damnit! Are you trying to kill me?"

"Don't put any ideas in my head." Keith moved away from him for fear that he might crack his head and kill him. "What are you hanging around here for? I told you to get the hell out of this town, out of Kansas, and to stay away from me."

"I don't think you know what's at stake here. We both have a chance to make a lot of money."

"Marty, I'll say this one more time. I'm not here looking for a gasfield, and if I were, I'd have to be out of my mind to do business with you. How much plainer can I make it?"

"I . . . promised some drillers—"

"—You what?"

"I promised them the job. If I go back and tell them you backed out, they'll . . . they might kill me."

"Tell them I backed out? Did I hear you right?" Keith was tempted to wipe up the street with the cocky little bastard. "If you got yourself in a mess, get yourself out of it." He held Marty against the wall with one hand, ignoring the stares of people along the street. Most of them were enjoying the show.

"Let go, Keith." Marty's struggles were useless against Keith's strength.

"Where did you go when you left here?"

"Liberal."

"When did you come back?"

"Yesterday."

"If you're lying, I'll beat you within an inch of your life."

"I'm not lying. Why in hell do you care where I was?"

"Do you have a rifle?"

"I've got a pistol. You don't think I'd drive around here in the sticks without a gun, do you?"

"I'll give you fifteen minutes to get out of town." Keith stepped back and let Marty straighten his clothes.

"All right," Marty snarled, now that he was free from Keith's grip. "If I get killed over this, you'll be sorry."

"Don't count on it. I may give your killer a reward."

"The roads are muddy."

"You'll make it in that high-powered car."

"You'll wish you'd listened to me, Keith."

"Are you threatening me?"

"Just telling you that . . . you'll be sorry."

"Stay away from my grandma, Marty. If I hear of you even speaking to her on the street I'll make you a new asshole. Understand?"

Yes, I understand, you high-handed son of a bitch! Next time I'll get you in my sights before I shoot. But I scared the shit out of you the other night, didn't I? Little old Marty Conroy ruined your party! And you thought you'd catch me in that old car. Ha!

Keith stood on the walk and watched Marty drive out of town. He breathed a sigh of relief. He wasn't sure if Marty knew of his connection in Dallas; but if he did, and he hung around here, he could screw things up royally.

By midmorning the sky was clear except for a few billowing white clouds. The hot sun and a warm breeze were rapidly drying the hard-packed road in front of the store.

The first thing Hod had done was to build a temporary step out the back door. Because of the missing porch, Molly and Bertha had to go through the store and out the front to hang wet clothes, bedding, and rugs on the line to dry, some of which would be washed when the electricity came on. Bertha was especially appreciative of his effort. Molly only nodded her approval. She had been so shy and aloof that Hod had come to the conclusion that she regretted what had happened between them the night before.

Hod picked up debris, laid aside the boards that could be used, and piled the rest with tree limbs to be burned. He was sweating profusely when Keith McCabe arrived.

"Looks like you got your share of the damage." Keith dismounted and led his horse over to the pump to drink.

"We got enough, but we didn't get the full force of it."

"No. South of here Collins lost their shed, the top of their barn, and part of their house."

"As you can see, we lost the porch, the gazebo, and the chicken house. There's some minor damage to the roof. We were lucky."

"I was going to call and see how you made out, but the telephone lines are down all over the county. Anything I can do?"

"I'd appreciate help getting the top of the gazebo out of the road. A couple of cars have gone by and managed to get around it. The road is drying, and traffic will pick up."

After their struggle to get the gazebo roof into the yard at the side of the store, both men were panting.

"Is this far enough?" Keith asked. "If not, we can put a rope on it and the horse will pull it to the back."

"I don't know if Molly wants to rebuild the gazebo or not. It might as well stay here until she decides. How about a good cold drink of water?"

The men drank at the pump, then sat down on the back step. Hod told Keith about George's coming over in the storm and about the head wound that left him stunned but still on his feet.

"This morning we left him sleeping in the cellar, when I went back with dry clothes, he was gone."

"I saw him the night Ruth and I came here." Keith took off his hat and wiped his brow with the sleeve of his shirt. "Big man. Looked like he could whip a bear with a willow switch."

"He'd be a rough customer to tangle with if he ever got his dander up." Hod picked up a stick and wiped the mud from the soles of his boots. "I can't leave the women here alone or I'd go over to his place and see about him. I owe it to him for his help here."

"He lives about a half mile beyond that tree line, if I read the plat book right. Do you want me to stop by there on my way to town and see if he's all right?"

"If it wouldn't put you out. I like the son of a gun. He's strange, but I believe he's trustworthy."

"Molly's aunt said he'd formed an attachment for this place and he's over here every day."

"The attachment is for Molly, the poor cuss. He's crazy about her."

"Doggone! That could be trouble."

"Could be sometime down the road. He's terribly protective of her."

"Hello, Keith." Molly came to the door. "I see Hod put you to work."

"Glad to help." Keith stood and slapped his wide-brimmed hat down on his head.

"Did Ruth and her folks make it through the storm all right?"

"Ruth was in school this morning, so I guess they did. It's hard to know how much damage was done because the telephone lines are down all over the county."

"And the electricity is out. It's strange how you can get so used to something in only a few years so that when it's not there, you really miss it."

When Keith was ready to leave, Hod walked with him to where he'd tied his horse.

"How long are you going to be around?" Keith asked.

"I'm not sure. How about you?"

"I'm not sure either." Keith grinned, aware that each with his own reason for being there, was dancing around the other. "Unless I find your help is needed over at the Andrews', I'll see you in a couple of days." Keith swung into the saddle and lifted a hand in farewell.

Hod watched Keith ride across the prairie land toward the line of trees that separated Andrews' land from McKenzie's. He rode as if he was part of the horse. Something about the man made him seem trustworthy, even though the reason he gave for coming to Pearl didn't hold water as far as Hod was concerned.

Hod was also a puzzle to Keith. Being from Texas, Keith had heard of Frank Hamer, the famed Texas ranger and Hod Dolan, the Federal agent who worked with him on the Barrow case. He had been surprised to meet him in a little country store in Kansas. He was aware now why Hod had come here, and it was becoming increasingly clear why he was staying. George Andrews wasn't the only man in Seward county crazy about Molly McKenzie.

As Keith approached the Andrews homestead he noticed that it was well kept. Fences were mended, outbuildings were in good condition, and the area around the house was clear of debris. The windmill was turning and not a squeak could be heard. The big white dog that had been at the McKenzie store came out and barked a time or two, then went to lie down in the shade. A red rooster ran at him, then backed off after getting within several yards of the horse.

Keith dismounted a good distance from the house and tied his mount to a fence. As he approached the house, the back door opened and a crone stood in the doorway. Her thin, hawkish face was surrounded with tangled, gray-streaked hair. She wore a dark dress and a dirty apron.

"What you want here?" Her voice was shrill and angry.

"Ma'am, my name is Keith McCabe. Is George—"

"—Where'd ya come from? Why'er ya ridin' Papa's horse? He ain't goin' to like it a'tall."

"It may look like your papa's, ma'am, but it's mine. I'd like to speak to George if he's here."

"Did ya come to take me to Chicago?"

"Ah . . . no, ma'am. If George isn't here, I'll—"

"—Get out! Go! Shoo . . . shoo . . ." She made a fluttering motion with her apron as if shooing chickens. "Go on. Get out. Papa won't like you coming 'round tryin' to court me. I already got a beau."

Lord a mercy! She's crazy as a bedbug.

Keith tipped his hat and, reluctant to turn his back on her, backed away, then turned and headed for his horse. He had reached him and was about to mount when he saw George down the lane with a package and letters in his hand, obviously coming from the mailbox on the road. Keith waited.

"Mr. Andrews? I'm Keith McCabe. I was just over to the store and Hod asked me to stop by and see if you were all right. He said you got a bump on the head during the storm."

" 'Twasn't nothin'."

"Hod was worried about you."

"I'm all right."

"Well, I'll be going—"

"—I told ya to get!" The woman came running out the door with a long-barreled gun. "Get, or I'll shoot."

"Godamighty!" Keith exclaimed.

"Ain't loaded," George murmured, and started across the yard toward the woman. "Give me the gun, Gertrude."

"I'm goin' to shoot. He tried to rape me."

"Godamighty!" Keith said again, and mounted his horse.

"I wouldn't let him." Gertrude screeched. "I held him off with the gun."

"Go back to the house," George said calmly, and took the gun out of her hand. "Go on. I'll take care of it."

"Kill him!"

"Go on." George gave her a gentle shove toward the house.

"Papa ain't goin' to like all these men comin' round," Gertrude yelled over her shoulder as she hurried to the house. "I ain't goin' with him. Tell him, George. Tell him I ain't goin'."

After the back door slammed, Keith said, "I'm sorry I upset her."

"Don't matter none."

"Have you considered a doctor?"

"Ain't no use."

"Well . . . good day to you, Mr. Andrews."

George nodded.

Chapter
Seventeen

Hod leaned against the doorframe of the shed and watched Molly take clothes from the line. Despite her attitude today, he was sure that she had been as happy as he was when they sat on the bench with their arms around each other. She was a lovely, sweet woman. He would be the luckiest man in the world if he could have her by his side for the rest of his life. The urge to be near her was so strong that, at times, it gave him an odd, uneasy feeling.

Several of Molly's neighbors, including Mr. Bonner, came in the afternoon and offered their help in replacing the porch and the chicken house. Mr. Bonner was pleased to tell them that his place had escaped the high wind with only minor damage and had benefited greatly from the heavy rainfall. Molly thanked them all and said that she didn't think that she would rebuild the porch right away, but if she did, she would remember their offer.

Molly didn't approach Hod until early evening. She found him at the loading platform repairing a ladder.

"I'm worried about George. He hasn't been here all day."

"Keith was going by his place on the way to town. He must have seen that George was all right or he would've been back."

"Stella went back home, so I guess there's no reason for him to come over every day."

"I guess not."

"Why are you working on that ladder?"

"Because I'm going to need it to get to the roof."

"It won't reach."

"It'll get me up to the roof of the front porch, and from there to the roof."

"You don't need to do that."

He stood the ladder up against the building before he looked at her. He held her eyes briefly before she looked away.

"Why is it that you will accept help from Mr. Bonner and from George, but resent help from me?"

"You've got it wrong. I appreciate all you've done." Her hand fluttered toward the yard. "But you've worked all day. You didn't come here to be a handyman. I can't afford to pay a handyman." Her voice trembled. "I can't even afford to replace the porch."

"That's why you need me. I work cheap." He tried to get a smile out of her and failed. Color rose to tint her cheeks, but when she refused to look at him, he cast about for a reason. "You don't think that I meant any of the things I said last night, do you?"

"I . . . well, I don't know. It's easy to get caught up and say things you don't mean. Oh, you may have meant them at the time, but later, when you think about it—"

"Stop it, Molly. Let's get this straight right now. I don't say things I don't mean."

"Aunt Bertha said to tell you that supper was ready." She turned to go, but stopped and looked back at him over her shoulder. Their eyes caught and held as he sent his silent message.

Molly . . . darlin'! I'll not be frozen out. My future happiness and yours is at stake.

She hurried into the store, and Hod swore under his breath.

Two people drove in for gas. One was Mr. Bruce, the postman. Hod pumped the gas, and he went inside to sign the ticket. The last gas sale of the day was to a rancher and his wife, who were going to town to have supper at the cafe. They were celebrating the rain that saved their feed crop.

The days were getting shorter, and it was dark by the time Molly, Bertha, and Hod sat down to supper. They ate by the light of the kerosene lamp. Bertha was aware of the tension between Molly and Hod and tried to fill the void with idle conversation.

"I'm going to bed early tonight. I used muscles today I didn't know I had. I know you're tired too, sugarfoot. You worked like a beaver all day."

Hod waited for Molly to say something. She didn't, and the silence grew until Bertha filled it again.

"The rug in the living room is almost dry. I folded it back so the floor could dry. I'd hate to have it warp. Nothing I hate more than a bumpy floor. What do you think about getting one of those throw covers for the couch? Might brighten the room up some."

"I hadn't thought about it, but we can look for one in the new Sears Roebuck catalog." Molly spoke without much enthusiasm. Her head was bowed, and her shoulders sagged wearily.

It was hard for Hod to keep his eyes off her. Somehow he knew that she had deliberately made herself as unattractive as possible to show him just how little his presence meant to her. After they closed the store she had put on a faded brown dress and tied an apron made out of a flour sack about her waist. Her hair was tied at the nape of her neck with a string.

"Mrs. Luscomb told me that the house the Bonners lived in was little more than a shack. Poor, but proud, is the way she put it. They just barely scratch out a living, but I guess you knew that."

Bertha continued to chatter. Hod appeared to be listening, but in his thoughts he was talking to Molly.

Being in love is new to you, sweetheart. It's new to me, too. I wish that you'd look at me without that tight, suspicious look on your face. Give us a little time to get used to this wonderful thing that has happened to us, and you'll see how right it is. The realization that, except for chance, I might never have met you purely scares the hell out of me.

When supper was over, Hod excused himself and went downstairs. By the light from the lantern, he washed, then set up his cot out in the store away from the storage room, so that the women would feel free to use it. He instinctively knew that tonight was not the time to talk to Molly. She was too tired and . . . confused. Did she think about the kisses they had shared last night? Or how her fingertips had stroked his cheeks?

Hod drew in a deep, ragged breath and cursed. His hunger for her love was driving him out of his mind.

Molly, sweet Molly, don't turn me away.

"Be good children and learn a lot. Your daddy is proud of you."

Archie Howell watched Otis, the twins, and Danny walk down the road to the school. Charlotte stood on the porch with Clara, the baby asleep on her shoulder. Archie knew that his eldest daughter was sad, but she would soon get used to the idea that her place was to make a home for her orphaned brothers and sisters.

"I'm going to call on the Reynoldses this morning. I heard their cow was hurt in the storm, and they had to butcher it. They'll probably want me to have some of the meat."

"All right, Daddy."

Charlotte hoped that he didn't bring any meat home and expect her to can it. Since the government program of going out to farms and ranches and killing hogs and cattle to bring up the prices had gone into effect, they'd been eating canned meat given by the parishioners until they were sick of it.

Archie got into his car. Before he drove away, he looked at his home. Not a tree limb was down, not a board out of place. The Lord had spared his home because he was his Lord's servant. Archie fervently believed this and drove away humming happily.

The preacher was surprised that Reynolds did not offer him any of the beef he had butchered. The man bemoaned the fact that he had lost a shed and some of his trees were down. He seemed to be anxious to get back to work. Archie stayed only a short while, telling Mrs. Reynolds that he must get back to his children.

It was midmorning when he headed for McKenzie's store. He had not forgiven Molly for rejecting him and accepting another man after he had waited for her to finish school and then paved the way for her to be his wife. None of the women he had wanted and courted had treated him so cruelly. His pride demanded that he avenge his honor. And he would, all in good time, he told himself. All in good time. Miss Molly McKenzie would soon find out that there was a thin line between love and hatred.

George Andrews was looking up at the roof where Dolan was shaping a piece of tin to the peak when Archie parked his car in front of the store.

"Morning," Archie said pleasantly, glad the two would be out of the way. Now if only that snoopy aunt was upstairs, he could speak to Molly alone.

"Ya want gas?"

"Not this morning." Archie went up the steps and into the store.

"Mornin'. What can I do for you?" Bertha rested her chubby elbows on the wooden counter.

"Is Molly here?" He looked around, as if he hadn't noticed as soon as he stepped in the door that she wasn't there.

"Upstairs. She not feeling well."

"Nothing serious, I hope."

"She's feverish. What can I do for you?" Bertha said again.

"Bottle of vanilla flavoring and a pound of cheese," he said abruptly.

"How'd your place weather the storm?" Bertha set a bottle on the counter. "This size all right?"

"Fine. I have a message for Molly from Ruth Hoover. I'll just go up—"

"—No, don't go up," Bertha said quickly. "She's in bed with a sore throat."

"I'm her pastor. It's my duty to go up and say a prayer for a speedy recovery." His voice was even and calm. The only sign of his anger was the slight flush on his fat cheeks and the jamming of his hands in his pockets.

"I think the Lord will forgive you for not doing your duty this time. Molly wouldn't want you to see her. Beside, if she's got something contagious, she would feel terrible if you took it back to your children." Bertha cut the cheese, weighed it, and wrapped it in white paper. "Anything else?"

"That's all," he said abruptly. "What do I owe?"

"Fifty-two cents."

Archie placed the coins on the counter and headed for the door.

"I'll relay the message from Ruth," Bertha called. He ignored her and walked out the door. "Horse's ass," she muttered. "Crazy old lecher didn't have no message."

"You talking to yourself, Aunty?" Molly came down the stairs as Archie drove away.

"You just missed the preacher. I told him you were sick abed, then was scared spitless you'd come down."

"I saw him drive in and waited until he left."

"He's not going to be put off even if you are supposed to be engaged."

"It was a stupid story to put out in the first place. I heard pounding on the roof. Hod's determined to fix the leak."

Bertha didn't answer. Her mind was on the preacher. She had a funny feeling about that bird. Something about him made the hair stand up on the back of her neck.

Archie's mind was on Bertha. He was sure that she had lied about Molly's being sick. The girl was deliberately avoiding him, and her aunt was helping. Which meant that they were aware of his intentions. *Well, my girl, that's all right. There are more ways than one to skin a cat. No one ever humiliated Archie Howell and got away with it.*

He slowed as he neared the lane leading to the Andrews homestead. The gate was open. On impulse he turned in and drove slowly toward the house set back amid the cottonwoods. He had been here only one time . . . years ago. At that time, no one had come to the door when he knocked. He had not come back. The Andrewses were not churchgoing people, and it was foolish to waste his time on them.

Archie stopped the car and surveyed the place. It was a well-kept farm. A big white dog came out of the barn and barked a couple of times, but made no threatening moves. As he approached the house the door opened and a tall, gaunt woman stood there with arms folded across her flat bosom.

"What'a ya want?"

"I came to see you, dear lady."

Archie doffed his hat and put on his most angelic smile, the sweet, cherub smile that caused most folks to warm to him immediately. He had heard that George Andrews's sister was not right in the head, and he used a tactic that had worked for him before.

"What for?"

"Because I wanted to get to know you."

"What for?"

"Well, because I heard that you are a very nice and attractive lady."

"What's your name?"

"My name is . . . Matthew. May I come in?"

"Papa don't allow men in the house."

"Is he here? I'd like to ask his permission to call on you."

"He won't let you court me. He won't let nobody but a rich man court me."

"I'd like to ask him." Archie smiled. "I'm not poor. See my car?"

You poor, dear soul. Your reasoning has left you. But I can see I need to help you find a better life. God sent me to you. Dear lady, you'll soon be with your papa and walking the streets of gold.

"Ya can come in if ya behave."

"I'll behave. I promise."

Archie stood just inside the door. The house was as dark as a dungeon. The only light came through the open door. Blankets covered the windows; the doors leading to the other rooms were closed. The woman stood back with her hands wrapped in her apron, her hawklike eyes, bright as stars, fastened on him. She reminded him of a black raven.

"Where is your papa?" Archie asked.

"Right there." Gertrude pointed to the empty rocking chair.

"Oh, yes. I see him now. How do you do, sir?" He bowed, then turned to Gertrude. "Does your brother live here?"

"George does. He goes in there and won't let me in." Gertrude went to a padlocked door and kicked it with her foot.

"That's not very nice of him."

"He's mean."

"Does he hurt you?"

"He turns on that old radio. I tell Papa, and he whips him."

"It's what he should do."

"He put me in the cellar, shut the door, and went to that slut at the store."

"Oh, my. He shouldn't have done that."

"A man came. He wasn't my beau. My beau is coming tomorrow to take me to Chicago."

"I'm glad I came today, or I might have missed seeing you."

"Do you want to kiss me?"

"Not . . . on our first meeting, dear lady. I'll reserve that pleasure for later. I must be going."

"I'll get my sunbonnet and go with you."

"I can't take you this time. I'll be back."

"When?"

"Soon. Very soon. I promise." Archie backed out the door. She followed him.

"I want to go with you," she called.

"Not this time. I'll be back." He hurried to the car and started the motor. She came toward the car. He waved and drove back down the lane.

Archie was elated. God had shown him the way. He would help the poor demented woman end her misery and earn another star in his crown. At the same time he would accomplish one of his goals. He took his hands from the wheel and rubbed them together. *Thank you, God. Thank you.*

He reached the road, turned toward town and began to sing:

Yes, we'll gather at the river, the beautiful, the
*   beautiful river.*
Gather with the saints at the river that flows from
*   the throne of God.*

"The preacher didn't stay long," Hod said to George as soon as he came down from the roof.

"He wasn't happy when he left. He looked like somebody'd peed in his pocket."

The long speech surprised Hod, but so did the humor and the grin on George's face.

"If he didn't get to see Molly, it'd put his tail over the line."

George placed the tools Hod had been using in a bucket and set it on the loading platform.

"I'll get the keys to Bertha's car so we can get the truck out of the shed. We can work on it out here and still keep an eye on the store."

"Ya think that feller will come for Molly?"

"I'm not sure, and I can't take the chance." Hod hopped up onto the platform and went into the store.

Hod backed Bertha's car out, then he and George pushed the truck out of the shed and under the cottonwood at the side of the store. Molly brought out big glasses of iced tea. She forced one of the glasses into George's hand when he would have turned away.

"Aunt Bertha is making egg salad sandwiches for lunch, and you'd better not run away."

"I'd mind her if I were you, George," Hod teased. "She can be a real twister when she gets stirred up."

"Oh, you!" Molly tossed the words at Hod and went back into the store.

Hod watched the skirt of her dress swirl around her slim bare legs. Her hair shone in the sunlight. Hod stared until she was out of sight. His mind, all his senses were fused to her when she was near. He had known her for such a short time, yet it seemed to him that he had always known that she was his mate, his life's companion.

He leaned against the truck and finished his drink.

"Well, George. We know this old girl won't start. So let's take a look under the hood."

A half hour later, Hod wiped his greasy hands on a rag.

"Everything checks out. It's got to be the battery. We'll have to go into town and get a new one. I'll ask Bertha if I can use her car."

It was apparent to Hod that George didn't know much about cars. He seemed to know the names of the parts, but not their functions. Hod wondered if his knowledge had come from a catalog. He wanted to ask him if he could drive, but didn't wish to embarrass him. The shy man had opened up some, was talking to him more, and seemed to be more at ease around him.

"At the end of the week Molly and I are going to take the truck and go to Liberal to get an order for the store. I'd appreciate it if you would stay here with Bertha while we're gone."

"I'll do it."

"I'm going to buy a car while I'm there. Molly can drive it back."

"She can drive the truck," George said proudly, and looked Hod in the eye.

"A car will be easier for her to handle. Do you have a car?"

"Can't drive."

"I'll teach you to drive mine, if you want to learn."

"I'd buy one if I could drive it."

"We can start the lessons as soon as we get a battery for the truck. I'll put it out back and you can drive it around the pasture. I'm sure Molly won't mind."

Molly came out the side door and onto the loading dock. She called to them.

"Come to the front porch. It's shady there. Aunt Bertha is bringing out sandwiches."

George turned on his heel to walk away.

"Better not leave, George," Hod cautioned. "She'll be after you like a shot. Once she makes up her mind, it's dangerous to buck her."

"I need to go home."

"Come on. Eat a sandwich to satisfy her and save us the trouble of a fuss."

Hod went around to the porch. George followed reluctantly. Bertha came out with a tray of sandwiches covered with a cloth.

"Set there on the edge of the porch. Molly's bringing tea."

The two women sat on the bench. Bertha told about the preacher's visit and how she'd put him off by telling him that Molly was sick.

"He's got a real crush on you, sweetheart." Hod watched Molly's face redden. "I've got to make it clear to him that you're my girl, and he'd better keep his distance."

His teasing fanned Molly's temper. "You're taking a lot for granted, Hod Dolan." She returned his grin with a haughty stare.

"You *are* my sweetheart, sugarfoot. I know it, you know it, and now Bertha and George know it."

Molly refused to rise to the bait and did her best to ignore him. Out of consideration for George, she tried to hide her irritation by making conversation with her aunt and reminding her that the iceman would be there today.

After eating one sandwich, George rose to leave. Molly's voice stopped him.

"George Andrews, don't you dare leave until every last

sandwich is gone from that plate. Egg salad spoils fast in this weather. Besides, you do so much for us, you've got to let us feed you once in a while."

"I told you," Hod said, when George sat back down. "She's bossy as a hen with a couple of chicks."

George had not really wanted to leave. He was amazed at how Hod and Molly talked to each other. He was sure that Hod liked her . . . a lot. Then how could he tease her and make her mad? George looked off toward the horizon, realizing how much he had missed. There was so much he didn't know about being part of a family. Was he too old to learn?

Molly fumed silently. Her brain pounded with a million vague thoughts she couldn't voice. She had always craved the kind of love and companionship her parents shared. She had been lonely since they died and susceptible to Hod's bits of Irish blarney that let him believe that she was fair game for a brief flirtation.

For a moment her eyes, like daggers, stared into the predatory gaze of eyes as black as a bottomless pit. He was a handsome man and a hard one who couldn't possibly be seriously interested in a naive country girl. She had to keep her guard up not only against the preacher, but against him. She was in danger of losing her heart to a man who was here today but might be gone tomorrow.

Molly pulled her thoughts together when she heard Hod speak her name.

"Molly and I will go get one if you will lend us your car one more time."

"I'll only charge you an arm and a leg," Bertha teased.

"I'll stay here. Aunt Bertha can go with you."

"You're my responsibility, you'll go with me. George will stay here with your aunt."

"You arrange everything to suit yourself, don't you?"

"If I can." Amusement glinted in his dark eyes. Suddenly, he laughed.

"I'm glad you're amused," she snapped.

"Amused and pleased, ma'am," he said with mock politeness.

"Pleased because you get your way, no doubt."

"No, pleased because it's becoming perfectly clear that our lives together will never be dull. It's also clear, sweet Molly, that you're going to balk every step of the way, and I'm going to love every minute of breaking you to a double harness."

At that moment, Molly was sure that she hated him. Talking about marriage that way! Then Bertha laughed. It sobered her. She was making too much of this little flirtation. She promised herself to lighten up and not to let him know that when they had sat on the bench with their arms around each other, she had taken his words seriously.

Chapter Eighteen

Molly was amazed at how one night of rain could wash away the dust and leave the trees looking so fresh and green. Oh, blessed rain. How she had missed it!

"It's useless to pout, sweetheart." Hod's deep smooth voice broke into her thoughts. "I couldn't go into town without you. I'm sticking with you until I'm sure you don't have a price on your pretty head."

"I never pout."

"Then why have you avoided me for two days? Are you ashamed of what we did the night of the storm?"

"No."

"Then talk to me. Better yet, move closer to me so I can hold your hand."

"We don't have to carry the charade quite that far." She turned her head, tilted her chin, and gave him a view of her profile.

"Have it your way for now."

His voice was dangerously soft. The smoldering look he gave her when she glanced at him caused a wave of apprehension that sent a shiver down the length of her spine. It was strange, she thought, how the same voice could be so full of laughter one moment and so grating in its harshness the next.

No words passed between them until they reached the outer edge of Pearl.

"Where shall we go for the battery?" Hod asked.

"Turn left at the next corner and go about a block to the Phillips 66 sign. Mr. Wescott is the distributor. We get our gas from him."

Hod stopped the car in front of a small building. At the side was a large steel tank set in a frame five or six feet off the ground. A tank truck was parked nearby. As Molly got out of the car, a man came through the open door of the building.

"Hello, Mr. Wescott. Did you come through the storm all right?"

"Better than some I hear. A few tree limbs down at my place is all." His eyes went to Hod, and Molly was forced to introduce him.

"This is Mr. Dolan. He's . . . helping me get Daddy's truck going and it needs a battery."

"Dolan, huh?" He shook Hod's hand. "I heard you had someone helping you out at the store. Good idey, considering. The day I came to fill your tank you'd gone to the funeral. Now about the battery. Did you bring the old one in? We may be able to recharge it."

"I was going to do that," Hod said. "But when I lifted it out I found that it had split down the side."

"Yeah, well, old ones'll do that. What's that truck? A twenty-six? Roy made many a trip to Liberal in it." He went back into the little building. Hod and Molly followed to the door. "I hate for you to buy a brand-new battery for that old truck, Molly. It's not going to last much longer. I've got one here that's been used, but it's been recharged and has a lot of life left in it." He brought it out and set it on the step.

"It makes sense to me. How about you, honey?"

"If Mr. Wescott thinks it will do."

"How much?"

"Four dollars. A new one would cost you fourteen."

"Sounds fair to me." Hod pulled his wallet from his pocket.

"Oh, no," Molly said quickly. "Put it on our bill, Mr. Wescott, and I'll pay with the next load of gas."

Hod flung his arm around her. "Don't fuss, honey. What's mine is yours." Hod extended a five-dollar bill.

"I'll get your change." Mr. Wescott disappeared into the building.

"You make me so mad." Molly's breath hissed through her teeth. "You're determined that everyone think we're . . . that we're—" She bit back her words when Mr. Wescott returned and dropped a silver dollar in Hod's hand.

"That's a fancy automobile you've got here."

"It belongs to my aunt."

"We don't want to mess it up with battery acid. There's room on the floor in the back. I'll get a piece of cardboard to set it on."

Hod shook hands again with Mr. Wescott when they left. Molly waved.

"That was a bargain." Hod started the car, moved it slowly to the corner, and stopped.

"I'll pay you when we get back to the store." Her voice was louder than she intended and full of resentment.

"Let's get an ice cream," he said, ignoring her outburst.

"If I say no, you'll say yes. So let's get one."

"Now you're getting the idea, sweetheart." He laughed, and, before she could move, he reached over, cupped the back of her head with his hand, and kissed her soundly on the lips.

"Are you out of your mind?"

"I've been wanting to do that for ... let me see ... forty-eight hours." He laughed happily. "Where's the soda fountain in this town?"

"There isn't a soda fountain now. The only one was in the Corner Drugstore and they went out of business. The cafe has ice cream."

"Cafe, here we come."

Hod was happier than he could remember being. He had found the woman who was meant for him. He loved to look at her, to talk to her, to be with her even when she was obstinate as she had been for the last two days. She had responded to his kisses, and he was confident that she cared for him. She was just confused because things were happening too fast.

But ... damn! This can't be easy for her!

Hod had been told by his mother and his brothers that his one redeeming quality was that he was exceedingly fair-minded. He was asking this lovely, sweet girl to turn her life over to a man that she scarcely knew. It was only natural that she would have some misgivings.

These thoughts floated around in Hod's head while he drove to the cafe and parked the car. He took her hand before she could get out and held it between both of his.

"I've embarrassed you, and I'm sorry." There was genuine regret in his voice. "Just because I am so sure that what's happened between us is wonderful and right, I presumed that you would feel the same."

She turned her head slowly. Her round violet eyes were so shiny that he could see his reflection there.

"I understand." Her voice was not quite steady.

"All I'll ask is that you don't shut me out until you've had time to know your heart."

Without realizing it, her hand was gripping his tightly. This feeling of being totally alive when she was with him, even butting heads with him, and seeing his face behind her closed eyelids disturbed her. She wasn't sure that she was ready to give her heart or that he really was offering his. She was quiet for a long while, then closed her eyes and breathed deeply.

"I'm sorry I've been such a shrew. My heart was damaged when I lost my parents. It's mending now. But I fear that you could break it, and it would never mend."

"Ah . . . sweetheart. I've pushed you too fast. I just want to be with you. I've never had anyone of my own before. The possibility of it went to my head, and I acted the fool."

"Hod Dolan, the G-man, acting the fool?"

"I admit it, sweetheart. This is all new to me. I'm learn-

ing as I go." He got out of the car and went around to
open the door for her.

"Walter was put out because you wasn't here," Bertha
said as soon as Hod and Molly walked into the store.

"Who?" Hod asked.

"The iceman."

"That redheaded peacock who came the first time I was
here?"

"Peacock?" Bertha laughed. "That fits him. He was
going on like he always does. George looked mad enough
to clobber him when he kept calling Molly his girl."

"It's just his way," Molly scoffed. "He likes to think
he's a ladies' man. The electricity hasn't come on, has
it?"

"No, doggone it. And it's darker than the bottom of a
well around here at night."

Molly walked over to the telephone and lifted the receiver. "Still no phone either."

"It's like livin' in the olden days," Bertha fumed.
"Folks went to bed at dark. That's why they had so many
kids."

George had gone out the front door as soon as Hod and
Molly came into the back. Hod followed him out and
called to him.

The big man turned, and Hod could see the lump made
by the gun in the bib of his overalls. It hadn't been there
when he and Molly left, which meant he'd had it stashed
nearby.

"How'd it go?"

"All right."

"No strangers?"

"No."

"Iceman got under your skin, did he?"

"Yeah. I'm goin' now."

"I got the battery. I'll have the truck going tomorrow."

George nodded as if the news was of little consequence to him, and struck off across the field.

"Pssst . . . Otis, let me in. He's gone." Charlotte opened the door to the room Otis shared with the younger boys and waited for her brother to tell her she could come in. "He's gone, Otis. Please come out, or let me come in. I've got the salve."

Harley came to the door. Even in the near dark hallway, Charlotte could see that he had been crying.

"He's mad at me. Won't talk to me."

"Oh, honey, he's not mad at you," Charlotte whispered. "He's hurting and he feels shamed that Daddy whipped him. Is Danny in there?"

"Danny's scared. Otis yelled at him."

Charlotte pushed the door open and went into the room. Otis, naked from the waist up, was lying on his stomach on the bed, his face buried in his arms. She dropped to her knees beside the bed and made a little moaning sound when she saw the red, angry-looking welts on his back made by the strop.

"Oh, brother!" She laid her head on his arm and kissed his tear-wet cheek. "Harley, run downstairs and get a wet towel. Hester will help you wring it out. Danny, stop crying. We've got to help Otis."

"Why's Daddy so mean?"

"I don't know. Otis, I'm going to put some salve on your back. If I hurt you, let me know. I'll try not to rub hard. He went to Bible study and won't be back for a couple of hours. Oh, brother, I told you to get rid of those movie-star pictures."

"He did," Danny said. "He got some more at school today and Daddy looked through his tablet and found them. Daddy said they were naked . . . sluts."

"What? They were naked?"

"They had clothes on, but . . . you could almost . . . see their titties. Daddy said if boys looked at 'em, they'd play with their peckers and it would make them go blind or crazy."

"Hush up, Danny," Otis growled.

"Me and Harley said we didn't see them . . . but we did." The child began to cry again. "Otis got the strop, 'nd we didn't 'cause . . . we storied."

"He'd a whipped Otis anyway, and maybe harder if he knew he'd showed the pictures to you and Harley. Otis, honey. Sit up and wipe your face. Harley brought you a wet towel."

Otis sat on the side of the bed and held the towel to his face. Charlotte knew that he was ashamed of crying. She wanted to put her arms around him, but was afraid to touch his poor back.

"I'd kill him . . . but you kids would go to the orphans' home." The words were mumbled in the towel. "I hate him! He's a fat turd! I wish he'd got snakebit instead of Aunt Gladys."

"He's been different since Aunt Gladys died," Charlotte said tiredly. "He yelled because the baby cried, and he slapped Clara so hard she fell down. I don't know what to do, Otis, except to be as good as we can and not cross him. I try to keep the girls quiet and out of his way."

"There's nobody to help us," Otis said. "I almost told Wally today when he asked about you."

"Don't tell anyone," Charlotte said quickly. "They'd not believe it. And it might get back to him. Wally asked about me?"

"He asked if you could slip out. I said not unless the mean old fart went to Liberal or . . . hell."

"His spies would tell him just like the Byingtons did that night Wally walked me home. We've just got to wait. If I told anyone, it would be Miss Hoover, but I don't know what she could do. He'd just say what he always says, 'Spare the rod and spoil the child,' and he *loves* his children too much to have them spoiled."

"Bullshit!" Otis shouted so loud that the boys were startled. "When I grow up, I'm goin' to tie that old man to a tree and whip the hide off him. He smiles at everybody like he's Jesus Christ, but he's more like the devil! I hate him!"

"Calm down. You and the boys get to bed and be asleep by the time he comes home. I've got to go down and see about the girls."

"Char, do you ever go in his room?"

"No. He told me he'd take care of it. He doesn't even want me to change the sheets. It's all right with me. I've got enough to do."

"Sometimes he locks the door when he leaves. Sometimes he don't. One of these days, I'm going in there."

"Good heavens! Don't even think about it, Otis. He might even lay a trap of some kind to find out if we've been in there. Don't do it. Please, don't do it."

"Don't do it, Otis," Danny begged.

"Quiet, brat," Otis said, but not unkindly. "You'd better get to sleep."

Charlotte left the boys and went back downstairs with the towel and the salve. She spread the towel to dry so her father would not realize that it was wet unless he touched it. She put the salve away and went to the room she shared with her sisters and the baby.

Her heart hurt for Otis. It was the worst beating their father had ever given him. Now she was terribly glad that she hadn't shown her brother the letter she'd found in Aunt Gladys's suitcase telling how cruel their father had been as a child. Otis, who couldn't watch a hog being slaughtered, had enough hatred for their father without adding to it.

Hod and Molly decided to put off the trip to Liberal until the first of the week. Hod was reluctant to leave Bertha at the store without the telephone or the electricity, even with George acting as watchman.

Monday morning the electricity came on, and by noon the telephone lines had been connected again. Bertha urged Molly to make the trip and get it over with. Hod made arrangements with George to come Tuesday morning and spend the day at the store.

Molly was confused by the quick change in Hod's attitude toward her. For the past four days he had gone out of his way to keep from touching her. He treated her as if he had never held her in his arms, called her honey and sweetheart, and kissed her.

Hod acted as if what had happened between them had meant nothing to him, and he was determined to make sure that she knew it. He hadn't used an endearment or said one intimate word when they were alone. He had retreated from her, putting her firmly in the place of a witness whom he was assigned to protect. She wanted to weep. His change of heart proved what she had suspected all along. He had amused himself with her.

On Tuesday morning, Hod brought the truck to the gas pump and filled the tank. He wore a white shirt and dark pants. His service gun was under the coat that lay on the seat. When he went into the store, Bertha was putting together the deposit they would leave at the bank as they passed through Pearl.

"I'm sure you'll be all right here, Bertha, or I'd not leave."

"Hell yes, I'll be all right. I've got that old double-barreled shotgun under the counter. If anyone comes in and gets smart, I'll fire one barrel to warn him and the other to *harm* him." She cut off her laugh when she saw the worried look on Hod's face.

"Don't bring out that gun unless you intend to shoot to kill. Watch every stranger who drives up to see what he takes out of the car. When a stranger comes in, stay near George."

"I will, Hod. I was just funnin'. You and Molly have fun down at Liberal. That girl hasn't had an easy time of it this summer."

"I'm going to marry her before we come back."

Bertha couldn't have been more surprised if he had suddenly sprouted a horn in the middle of his forehead.

"You're going to *what*?"

"Marry her."

"Land a Goshen, Hod. I wasn't sure you'd said that."

"I said I was going to marry her."

"I knew that you were attracted to her. But I didn't realize that marriage was on your mind."

"Do you have any objections?" Hod glanced at the stairway to be sure Molly wasn't coming down.

"Nooo . . ." Bertha drew the word out. "I want to see her happy, with a family of her own."

"It's what I want."

"She's not very experienced where men are concerned. You're a man who can be pretty overpowering at times."

"Bertha"—Hod fixed her with his piercing stare—"I'll not force her to marry me. I want her to want me every bit as much as I want her before we take that final step."

"I'm thinking that she'll not be pushed into anything she doesn't want to do."

Hod grinned. "She's gutsy all right."

Bertha reached out and squeezed his hand. "She's stubborn and has far too much pride for her own good."

"I know. I want to take care of her."

"You don't have to marry her to do that."

"That's only one reason. The other and most important reason I'm determined to marry her is that I love her with all my heart. I want to be with her every day for the rest of our lives."

Bertha looked into the dark serious eyes and realized the admission was made openly and honestly. She had heard men say they wanted a woman, but seldom did a man say that he was going to marry a woman because he loved her. The declaration was a measure of the man's character, and Bertha felt that she was an authority on men's characters after having run a boardinghouse for fifteen years.

Molly came down the stairs and walked toward them, her high heels tapping on the wooden floor. She wore an almost new dress of yellow-flowered voile. It had a round neck, short, puffed sleeves, a fitted bodice, and a four-gored skirt. At the bottom of the skirt was a twelve-inch ruffle that danced around her shapely legs when she walked.

She stopped when she realized that both her aunt and Hod were looking at her as if they'd not seen her before.

"I . . . wanted to wear something cool that wouldn't look like I had slept in it when we got there." Her high-heeled sandals were white, and she carried a small white purse.

"You look just fine," Hod said, and tried to keep the enthusiasm out of his voice. "We can go as soon as George gets here."

"He's here. I saw him go around the side to the front porch."

"I'll go talk to him."

"Aunt Bertha," Molly said as soon as Hod went out the door. "I hope he didn't think I wore this . . . for him. I've always dressed up a little when I went with Daddy."

"I'm sure he didn't, but his eyes almost popped out of his head when he saw you. You're pretty as a picture in that dress."

"You're saying that because I'm your favorite niece." Molly laughed nervously.

"You're right, sugarfoot. You're really as ugly as a mud fence."

"Ah . . . Aunt Bertha! I'll worry about you."

"Honey, there's not a blessed thing to worry about. Go on with Hod and have a good time. Here's the deposit you can drop off at the bank in Pearl."

" 'Bye. We'll be back before dark."

" 'Bye, honey. Don't worry about a thing and enjoy yourself."

Hod and George were standing beside the truck when Molly came out onto the porch. She didn't notice George gazing at her like a man thirsting for a glass of cool water, but Hod did.

"Don't worry about her, George. I'll take care of her." Hod's voice was low.

George turned his head to look at Hod and nodded.

Chapter Nineteen

It was a rough ride in the old truck over the road rutted by the recent rain. Hod could only hope that the route from Pearl to Liberal would be smoother or it would be impossible to carry on a conversation. He glanced at Molly from time to time and found her staring at the road ahead, brooding.

Hod was happy in spite of Molly's mood. He was with the woman who was dearer than life to him. He didn't care where they were going, or that they were in a rattly old truck. He loved the woman beside him beyond all reason, without reservation, without qualification. He loved every aspect of her face, the sound of her voice, her compassion for people like George and the Bonners. He loved her purely and intensely and prayed that she loved him in return, because if she didn't, there would be no hope for him, no hope at all.

Only a few words had passed between them by the time he stopped at the bank in Pearl.

"This will only take a minute." Molly stepped down out of the truck and hurried into the bank. Hod went in behind her and waited beside the door. She made friendly conversation with the teller who took her deposit. He was aware that the man's curious eyes went often to him. He took Molly's arm as they left the bank and helped her climb up into the truck.

When they were on the road again, Hod was pleased to discover that the highway to Liberal had been graded, the ruts smoothed out. The ride was not as jarring as the silence between them. After a while, he knew that if there was to be any conversation, he would have to start it.

"Have you forgotten that we're going to buy a car when we get to Liberal?"

She turned and he caught her eyes with his. "You're still going to do that?"

"Yes, we'll need one. We can't keep using Bertha's."

We. Molly's heart fluttered. *How easily he uses the word.*

"You said you'd drive it back. I'll follow you in the truck."

"I didn't say I'd do it. I'm not a very good driver. I might wreck it."

"We'll get one that's easy for you to drive."

There was silence again until Hod broke it.

"Here comes a Burma Shave sign. I always read them." He read aloud as they passed each sign nailed to a fence post. *"Don't lose your head . . . to gain a minute.*

You need your head . . . your brains are in it. Burma Shave."

Molly turned to him with laughter in her eyes. "I get a kick out of those signs. I think they're clever."

Suddenly she was happier than she had been in days. Hod was fun to be with. She would not think of how lonely it would be when he left. She would enjoy the trip.

"I do, too. There's one south of Kansas City that says, *Car in ditch . . . driver in tree . . . Moon was full . . . and so was he! Burma Shave.*"

"There's a good one up ahead." Molly leaned closer to Hod so that he could hear her over the rattle of the truck and the wind whistling in through the open windows. *"Don't stick your elbow . . . out too far . . . It may go home . . . in another car. Burma Shave.*"

The scent of her perfume reached Hod's nostrils only briefly, yet it stirred a yearning in him to hold her in his arms again. He slowed the truck to lengthen the distance between them and the car ahead, which was stirring up a cloud of dust. He reached for her hand.

"Come sit in the middle of the seat. It'll not be so windy and . . . I can hold your hand."

Molly hesitated, then slowly moved toward him until her shoulder touched his. He glanced at her, his lips broadened in a smile, and he squeezed her hand tightly before he flattened it out on his thigh and covered it with his, holding it there.

Why do I always do what he asks?

Puzzling through the thought, Molly began to analyze her attraction to this big, dark man who had come storming into her life. He wasn't like any man she had met in

Pearl or in Wichita. He was a city man, a tough man, yet he seemed to take pleasure in simple things such as the Burma Shave signs. When she was with him, she felt as if nothing in the world could harm her. She questioned herself as to why she was not more irritated by his takeover attitude toward her and could not come up with an answer.

"Did you know that it's been one hundred and two hours since I've kissed you?" Hod's voice broke into her thoughts.

"I hadn't given it any thought," she lied a little breathlessly.

"You didn't wonder why?"

"No," she lied again, turned her head, and gazed unseeingly out over the flat landscape broken only by a row of fence posts.

"It hasn't been because I didn't want to kiss you. At times I wanted so badly to kiss the worry off your pretty face that I ached all over. I was grateful for the storm damage and this old truck for keeping me outside most of the time."

"Why are you telling me this?"

"Because I want you to know why I didn't touch you, kiss you, hold you. I wanted to give you some time to sort out your feelings, and to decide if you wanted me to be a part of your future." When she said nothing, he continued. "I'll not push myself into your life if you don't want me."

"I don't know you . . . very well." She spoke with her face still turned away from him. Just the thought of not seeing him again or experiencing the excitement he brought into her life sent a chill of loneliness through her.

"Look at me, honey. Please." He felt a moment of panic when she turned a worried face to him. "Ah . . . sweetheart! I don't want you to worry. I want us to be happy today."

"I . . . don't know what to do about you." Her voice quivered, and she looked as if she would cry.

"Oh, Lord! Don't cry, honey." He turned the truck off the road and onto a lane. He stopped in the shade of a small cluster of cottonwoods. The instant he turned off the motor he had his arms around her, pulling her to him. "It tears me up to see you worry. Are you trying to decide if you want to be with me?" His deep voice was warm and strangely unsure. His arms so sheltering that she never wanted to leave them.

"It isn't that," she whispered.

"Then what is it, dear heart. I was almost sure you had feelings for me." She was pressed against his chest and her face was in the crook of his neck.

"It was like you'd had a little necking party with . . . the country girl. Then you wanted her to know . . . it didn't mean anything." Her words came out in a rush as if she had rehearsed them.

"Sweetheart! How could you think that?" He took her shoulders and held her away from him so he could look into her face. "That hour with you meant the world to me. Later, I worried that I'd rushed you. I was scared to death that you'd not want me as I wanted you."

He pulled her back into his arms and cradled her gently and lovingly.

"Honey, I'm sorry I let you think that I regretted what happened the night of the storm. I couldn't have lived through the last four days without the memory of holding you in my arms and your response to my kisses." He tilted her face so he could reach her lips and kissed them again and again.

Molly closed her eyes and lifted her hand to his face to caress his cheek.

"Do you like being with me like this?" he asked against her lips, savoring their softness.

"Yes. Oh, yes—"

"Marry me, darlin'. Marry me today," he whispered urgently, trailing kisses from her eyes along her cheeks and slowly over to the corner of her mouth.

Dazed by his kisses and his words, she leaned away from him and looked into his beseeching dark eyes.

"Marry you?" Her voice was a ragged whisper. "Why would a man who has been everywhere, done everything, even consider settling down with a . . . hick like me?"

"Marry me, Molly. Marry me today. I'll devote my life to you, take care of you. We'll be a team and share in each and every decision that affects our lives."

"I can't—" Her eyes filled and tears rolled down her cheeks. "I can't believe that you want to marry me when . . . when you've not even said that you loved me!"

"—Don't love you? Do I have to say it? My God! My love for you is eating me alive! I'm crazy about you and have been since I first set eyes on you. I couldn't understand it. But as it kept eating at me I began to realize that something very rare and wonderful had happened. Sweetheart, I love you. How could you not know that?"

"You never said it." She leaned back against him and pressed her face to his shoulder.

"I'm saying it now. Molly McKenzie, you are the love of my life. I love you with all my heart and will to the end of our days. We Dolan men are one-woman men. Our love is deep and lasting. It was the same with my father and with my brothers."

"It's too soon. You . . . don't really know me."

"I know all I want to know. You're good, sweet, and even if you were not, I'd love you and want to spend the rest of my life with you."

"But . . . where would we live?" The words were muttered against his neck. "And . . . I'm getting your shirt wet."

"My shirt is the least of my worries, honey. We'll decide together where we'll live. I'm not going back to the Bureau. I want to have a family and to be with them. I don't want my wife to worry that I might not come home to her. Marry me today, sweetheart. Let's start our life together today. We'll work everything out."

"Does it have to be today?"

"It doesn't have to be, but I want to know that you are mine and that we will spend the rest of our lives together." He kissed her hungrily, and settled his mouth gently for a moment beneath one ear. He waited with pounding heart for her reply.

"All right." He heard the words and felt the movement of her jaw when she spoke.

"Oh, sweet, darlin' girl!" He held her to him as tightly as he dared. His body, lean and powerful, was trembling. His mouth moved toward hers and took it gently, then took slow, but firm, possession. His heart pounded against her breasts.

"You'll not be sorry? You'll not miss your exciting life and want to go back to it?" she asked when she could get her breath. "I couldn't bear losing you . . . now."

"You'll never lose me. You're stuck with me for life!" He laughed happily. "We'll get married today and spend the night in Liberal. I'll tell you my dreams and you tell me yours." He stroked the hair back from her face with shaking fingers.

"I can't even think of anything now . . . but you."

"I love you so much." His whispered words now had a familiar ring. He was so dear to her. She pressed her lips to his and kissed him gently. Her eyes, when they looked into his, were sparkling.

"I'm so happy, I'm silly."

"No more so than me."

"I didn't think G-men were ever silly."

"This one is. Kiss me again, so we can get on down the road. We've got lots to do today."

Molly, sweet Molly, I'm no longer alone.

Hod backed the truck out of the lane and onto the road. Molly sat close beside him in a daze of happiness. Her hand lay possessively on his thigh. He held it when he was not shifting the gears.

"I forgot about Aunt Bertha," she said suddenly. "She'll be worried."

"We'll call her, and I'll call and ask McCabe to take Ruth out to spend the night with her. I've already asked him to go out late this afternoon and stay while George goes home to do his chores." He grinned down at her.

"Hod Dolan, you had this all planned, didn't you?" She pinched his thigh.

"Would you be mad at me if I told you that this morning I told Bertha I was going to marry you today?" His dark eyes bright with mischief held hers for an instant.

"No!"

"No, you're not mad?"

"I mean you didn't tell her *that*."

"I did. I thought as your next of kin she should know my intentions and that I should ask her if she had any objections."

"Did she?"

"She said we had her blessings . . . or words to that effect."

"If she had objected, would you have asked me?"

"I would have asked you if the whole town of Pearl had objected."

The radiance of his smile touched her heart. She laughed with pure pleasure.

"Look! This sign coming up is a good one and oh, so appropriate." She stroked his cheek with her fingertips. *"The chick he wed . . . Let out a whoop. She felt his chin . . . then flew the coop. Burma Shave."*

"I'm going to buy a whole case of Burma Shave. Maybe two cases. If I were rich, I'd buy the company." His eyes shone into hers. It was magical.

When they reached Liberal, they went directly to the courthouse. Molly had never been in one, but Hod seemed to know his way around. After they purchased their marriage license, Hod asked the clerk if she would take Molly to the ladies' room while he spoke to the judge across the hall. When she came out, he was waiting for her.

"We're to come back in thirty minutes. I told him we had some shopping to do, and he told me to think about the seriousness of what we're about to do. Foolish man! As if I didn't know that I'm the luckiest man alive."

They left the courthouse with Molly's hand held firmly in the crook of Hod's arm. He seemed to know where he was going. Two blocks down, he guided her into the jewelry store, where he purchased a pair of plain gold rings after he and Molly looked over the available selection. It was her idea to have the matching rings.

They ambled down the sidewalk oblivious to the amused glances of people around them. Hod stopped suddenly at the door of a department store.

"Do you want a new shirt?"

"No, sweet girl. I may never take this shirt off. Come. There is something else I want." He guided her inside and to the notions counter. "Buy us some toothbrushes, some Ipana, and anything else you think we'll need. I'll be right back." He placed some bills in her hand and walked quickly down the aisle.

Ten minutes later, he appeared with a box in his hands and a big smile on his face.

"What did you buy?"

"It's a surprise," he said, and grinned like a small boy. "We've just about time to get back to the courthouse."

On the walk back, reality began to intrude into Molly's happy day, and she tugged on his arm. They stopped in the middle of the sidewalk.

"Hod, I just remembered that you're Catholic. Don't you want to be married by a priest?"

"Honey, the judge will make our union legal. Later, if you want, we can have a religious ceremony in your church and in mine."

"I don't want Pastor Howell to marry us. I don't think I have a church at the moment."

"Neither do I. Do you have doubts about the judge marrying us?"

"Not if you don't."

"I don't, sweetheart. You're already my wife in my heart. This will make you my wife in the eyes of the law."

"Let's go then, husband of my heart."

Hod left the package in the truck, and once again they went into the courthouse. Fifteen minutes later, feeling as if they were walking a foot above the sidewalk, they came out into the bright sunlight as husband and wife. Hod couldn't keep the grin off his face or his eyes off his new wife. They stopped in front of the truck. He looked at the ring on her finger, then bent his head and placed a quick kiss on her lips.

"Hod! Someone will see!"

"I don't care if they line up along the curb to watch, Mrs. Dolan. I'm going to kiss my wife whenever and wherever I want to. Kiss me, wife. Remember you promised to obey." His eyes were shining with love and pride.

"Oh, my. Did I?"

"You sure as heck did. What shall we do now?"

"Go call Aunt Bertha."

"Good idea. I have a few other calls to make, too. Let's get our hotel room and make them from there."

Hod parked the truck alongside a brick building on the corner.

"Windsor Hotel," Hod said, glancing up at the sign. "This looks to be pretty up-to-date."

"I've never stayed at a hotel," Molly confessed, as they entered the double doors on the corner.

"I'm glad. The first time and the last time will be with me." With the box from the department store beneath his arm, he approached the desk. "A room, please. One of your best."

The clerk, who wore round wire spectacles, a striped shirt, and bow tie, looked first at Hod, then Molly, and down at the floor noting their lack of luggage with raised brows.

"How long will you be staying . . . sir?"

"One night."

"Well, ah, sir. I'm not sure that we have any—"

"—Any rooms?" His eyes hard, Hod flipped open his wallet and slapped his Federal credentials down on the counter. "Does that change your mind?"

The man's face reddened, and his Adam's apple jumped several times. He averted his eyes and pushed the registry book toward Hod, then dipped the pen in the inkwell and held it out. In firm script Hod wrote: Mr. and Mrs. Hod Dolan, Pearl, Kansas. While he was doing this, the clerk placed a key on the counter.

"One flight up and on your right."

"Thank you. We will be making several long-distance calls."

"The telephones are around the corner beneath the stairwell."

"I'll have the operator charge the calls to the hotel and pay for them when we check out in the morning."

"Yes, sir."

"What is the name of your leading bank?"

"First National of Kansas."

Hod picked up the key, turned, and held out his hand to Molly. She put hers in it, and they walked up the short flight of stairs. Her heart was pounding so hard that she was panting when they reached the door to their room. Hod unlocked the door and threw it open. He tossed the box inside the room and swept her up in his arms. Surprised, she wrapped her arms around his neck and held on tightly.

He stepped inside the room and kicked the door shut. Holding her high off the floor, he kissed her sweetly and tenderly.

"On this first day of our lives together, Mrs. Dolan, I pledge my love for you," he said as seriously as if he were saying a prayer. "I will love you as much fifty years from now as I do today."

"And I will love you, my husband." The tears that filled her eyes made them gleam like twin stars.

He eased her feet to the floor, but kept his arms around her. At the light touch of his lips on her mouth, a small inarticulate sound escaped her. Her hands moved up to the nape of his neck and fondled his dark hair.

"I'd like to lock that door and not leave this room until late tomorrow, but we've got things to do." She stood in his embrace as his hands stroked the sides of her breasts.

"I was afraid to touch you here before. I was afraid I'd get slapped."

She laughed against his lips, then caught the lower one between her teeth and bit gently.

"—And I wanted to do that, but didn't dare."

"You can do whatever you want to me now." He laughed happily. "I'm yours, all yours, and you are mine."

He didn't just kiss her this time; he made love to her mouth, stroking, nibbling, coaxing with light sweet kisses. He lifted his head to let her take a breath, then recaptured her mouth again as if it were cool, sweet water and he was a man dying of thirst. He released her only to take a gasping breath. She looked at him, her eyes huge and melting.

"We've got to get out of here, sweetheart, or I'll disgrace myself and scare my bride to death." He held her away from him. "The bathroom is over there if you want to wash or comb your hair. We'll go downstairs and make our calls, buy our car, and take the truck to the place where you buy your goods. They'll keep it overnight, and we'll pick it up tomorrow."

"My goodness! You're so organized it scares me," she teased.

"I'll really scare you, my sweet wife, if you don't get moving," he threatened, and swatted her lightly on the buttocks. He reached up and pulled the chain to start the ceiling fan and mopped his brow with his handkerchief.

In a quiet corner of the lobby they found two tables, and on each was an upright, shiny brass telephone. Hod dialed the long-distance operator and placed the call to the McKenzie General Store, then handed the phone to Molly and sat back to watch her.

"Aunt Bertha? It's Molly. Guess what? Oh, you! How did you know? Yes, I'm happy. I have to keep pinching myself to be sure I'm not dreaming. I know that." Laughter bubbled up. "I don't care if everyone on the party line is listening. You can put a sign out front of the store if you want to." Her merry eyes flashed to Hod, and she reached for his hand. "Tell George that Hod and I are married. We'll bring you something from Liberal. Something for George, too. We'll be home tomorrow. 'Bye."

"I know just the thing for George," Hod said when she hung the receiver on the cradle. "He needs a new flashlight."

"Aunt Bertha loves Whitman Sampler candy."

Hod called the Morrison Ranch and talked to Keith for several minutes. His eyes never left Molly's face. It was as if he was afraid if he looked away, she would disappear.

"Keith and Ruth will go out to the store tonight," he said when he hung up. "Bertha won't be alone. Keith sends his congratulations and warned me that he was going to kiss my bride. I just might have to punch him in the nose." He kissed her quickly on the lips. "Two more calls, honey."

Hod placed a call to the Bureau in Kansas City and talked to the chief. He first asked about Norton and listened for what seemed a long while to Molly. She watched him as he talked, pulling his hand over into her lap so she could hold it with both of hers.

"You think that's the end of it? That sorry bastard could be lying even if he was dying. I'll not let my guard down for a good long while." Hod's hand tightened on Molly's. "Molly and I were married today, Chief." Hod laughed, his shining eyes catching those of his bride. "Thank you. I'm very happy—we're very happy. Yes, I plan to stay someplace in this area." There was a long silence on Hod's part as he listened to what his former chief was saying.

"I'll do that, Chief. We'll stop in if we come up that way. Meanwhile, I'll talk to my wife about this other thing. We'll let you know." He hung up the phone.

"Honey, Norton was killed in Chicago a few days ago. Before he died he swore that he'd not put out any contracts on his enemies. That would include you."

"Do you believe him?"

"He knew he was dying when he said it. Most men don't lie when they are dying. I'll still be cautious for a while. We still don't know who fired that shot through the window." He leaned toward her and placed a gentle kiss on her lips. "You're very precious to me, sweetheart."

"I'm glad those men who killed my parents are dead."

"So am I, honey. The chief said there may be a job opening for a Federal marshal in this territory and that if I wanted it, I could apply, and he would recommend me. You heard me say that I would talk it over with you. We don't have to decide for a few weeks."

"Do you want to do it?" It felt strange being included in this important decision.

"I don't know. This is a sparsely populated area. I'd have to find out how much time I would spend away from home. Honey, I want to sleep with you in my arms every night for the rest of our lives. But we can talk about the job later. Now, I need to call my bank in Kansas City. I've saved almost half my wages since I've been with the Bureau, and a friend invested it for me after the crash. I'm far from rich, but I'm not broke. I'll be able to support my family."

After the call was made to transfer funds to the Liberal bank, they left the hotel and went in search of an automobile agency. They found one with a half dozen cars parked out front.

At first the salesman paid no attention to the couple who drove up in an old relic of a truck and were now walking hand in hand up and down the row of cars. Finally he ambled out to where they were standing beside a three-year-old Ford that looked like Bertha's except that it had four doors instead of two.

"Help you, folks?"

Hod ignored the salesman and spoke to Molly. "What do you think, honey? Would you like something like this? I don't want to get a big car that would be hard for you to handle."

"I don't know much about cars, Hod."

The salesman saw the possibility of a sale and went into his sales pitch, while opening and closing doors, kicking tires, and pounding on the top of the car to show how solid it was.

"This is a dandy little car. Low mileage. The old lady that had it let it sit a couple of years after her husband died. It's the best deal in town. Ask anybody up and down the street, and they'll tell you that Speed Handley will treat you right."

Hod looked under the hood and turned the lights on and off. He squatted and looked at the tires, then got in and started the motor. He left the motor running and got out to listen.

"The fan belt is slipping."

"Probably dried out from lack of use. We can put on a new one in a jiffy. Our mechanic checked this car out. He changed oil and greased her. Battery is in good shape. We can give you a good deal," he said again. "You look like a man with good credit. Twenty down and five a month, and you can drive her off the lot. Care to take her for a spin?"

Hod walked around the car. "Get in, honey."

The salesman got in the backseat. "This little car is a dandy. It'll not last long, I tell you. Only been on the lot a couple of days. To tell you the truth I'm surprised it's still here."

Hod looked at Molly and winked. They drove a few blocks up the street and then back.

"How long will it take to get that fan belt on?"

"About two shakes of a dog's tail."

"We'll take it."

Twenty minutes later the car was theirs. Hod made arrangements for the car to be taken to the grocery distributor where they were going to leave the truck. On the way there they laughed at how hard the salesman had worked to sell the car and how his jaw dropped when they said they would take it, and Hod paid with a check after a call to the bank to see if his funds had been verified.

"I hope I don't wreck it on the way home," Molly said.

"I've been thinking about that long trip without my wife beside me." Hod eased the truck into the parking area, turned off the motor, and put his arm across her shoulders. He picked up her hand to look at his ring on her finger. "Sweet Molly, this is the happiest day of my life."

"Mine, too," she whispered.

"I'm going to see if I can get someone here to drive the truck back to Pearl and catch a ride back. When we get home you can practice driving our car. Are you hungry?"

"I've been too excited to be hungry but not too excited to wonder what you have in the box back at the hotel."

His laugh rang out. "Curious little critter, aren't you?"

Chapter
Twenty

It was still light when Hod and Molly entered the hotel, asked the desk clerk for their key, and climbed the stairs to their room. The meal they had just eaten at the restaurant could have been corn bread and beans and they would not have complained. The night ahead was what was uppermost in their minds.

Hod opened the door and stepped aside for Molly to enter. He dropped his hat on a table, turned on the lamp, then the light in the bathroom. Molly stood in the middle of the room holding her purse to her chest.

"Honey?" Hod put his hands on her shoulders. "Are you scared of me?"

"Scared of you?" she repeated, her eyes large and questioning. "Of course not. I just ... don't know ... what to do."

"There aren't any rules, honey. You don't have to do anything you don't want to do. There's no law that says we have to consummate our marriage tonight." He placed a gentle kiss on her forehead. "Do you want to see what's in the box?"

"Oh, yes." She dropped her purse on the bed. "Is it for me?"

"It's mostly for me. You'll find out soon enough that I'm a very selfish fellow."

"Ho, ho! Now you tell me. Well, selfish fellow, let's see what's mostly for you." She sat on the bed, opened the box and lifted the folds of tissue paper. "Oh, my!" she exclaimed as she lifted out the white-satin nightgown and the peignoir made of thin white voile and trimmed with lace. "Oh, my," she said again. "It's beautiful." She looked up at him, her violet eyes shining and her lips turned up in a saucy smile. "If it's too little for you, may I have it?" She stood, and holding the gown and robe in one arm, she wrapped the other around his neck and pulled his mouth down to hers. "Thank you."

Hod hugged her to him. She was delightful. With a savage sound, he pressed her so close to him that their hearts seemed to be beating as one. Her mouth was soft, welcoming his, trying in every way to let him know how very much she loved him.

"Hod! Oh, Hod!"

She spoke his name with such an imploring inflection that he raised his head to look at her.

"Sweetheart—" He touched her lips for a brief moment, then put her away from him. He loosened his tie and pulled it off. "I'll wash, then the bathroom is all yours." Turning quickly before she could see the evidence of his erection, he went into the small room, closed the door, and turned on the cold-water faucet.

Oh, Lord! She's as innocent as a child when it comes to sex. God help me to do this right. So much of our future depends on it.

When Hod came out of the bathroom, his head was wet and his chest was bare.

"Your turn," he said lightly while rubbing his head with a towel. "There seems to be plenty of warm water if you want a bath."

He heard the click of the door, then turned to see that she had taken the gown and robe with her. Hod sat down on the bed and looked at his feet for a long while before he took off his shoes and socks. He wasn't sure how to proceed from that point. After turning down the bed, he switched off the light, hoping that she would be more at ease with only the light from the bathroom when she opened the door. Still in his britches, he went to the window to look out onto the street. He waited there for what seemed like a long while before the bathroom door opened and a ribbon of light flowed out into the room.

She stood in the doorway, silhouetted against the light. The neckline of the gown and the peignoir were low, just covering the tips of her breasts. The thin material flowed from her shoulders to her bare feet. Her dark hair swirled around her pale face. She was a picture of virginal beauty.

Hod's feet moved without his being aware of it. When he reached her he took her hands and held them out from her sides while his dark eyes devoured her.

"No man ever had a more beautiful bride." His words sent a shower of joy through her.

"I've never felt beautiful before."

He pulled her to him. She looked into his eyes, and the world danced, then faded away, leaving only the two of them. He drew her hand to his chest. She could feel the thud of his strong heart as his open mouth moved on hers, as if it would be too painful to stay away.

She felt his need, his desire pulling her. She felt the hunger in her heart echoing the hunger in his, and she knew a fierce longing to discover every inch of this wonderful man who had come storming into her life. Her hands explored him—his upper arms, his shoulders, broad enough to shield her from every storm. Her hands traced a tender path over his chest and found their way up to his face.

"I love you so much." Her words ended with an indrawn breath as Hod's lips slid down her cheek and his tongue delved into the corner of her mouth. The caress was inviting, exciting.

"Molly, sweet Molly, you know I want to love you!" His voice trembled with raw emotion. He spoke with his lips pressed against hers. "Don't you?"

"I want you, too." She could not deny the rigid evidence of his need, for it was pressed tightly to her belly. Her unschooled body moved instinctively and met its masculine, urgent thrust by rocking back and forth against it.

Suddenly Hod needed to feel more of her. He loosened her peignoir, opened it. His palms outlined the sides of her breasts, his thumbs provoked her nipples to hard points, then his hands spread wide over her back, pulling her so close that her breasts were flattened against his hammering heart. Her breath quickened. Her mouth clung to his, opening so he could drink more fully of the passion burning between them.

"Darlin', let's go to bed," he whispered hoarsely, slipping the robe off her shoulders and dropping it on a chair. He stepped to the door of the bathroom and switched off the light. In the dark he removed his trousers and folded them over the seat of a chair. After a brief hesitation, he took off his underwear, too.

Molly slipped into the bed and moved to make room for him. He lay down beside her and drew the sheet over them. Then, turning on his side to face her, he reached for her and pulled her into his arms. His groan of pleasure mingled with hers as her soft body met his and his mouth found hers. He was warm flesh, hard muscle. She was soft, sweet-scented woman.

I love you, I love you. The words echoed in her heart and mind. She thought that surely she had said them aloud and that he had heard them when she felt him tremble violently. Her fingertips raked across the soft fur on his chest. She had felt his throbbing hardness through his trousers, but feeling it through the thin gown as she lay against him, she realized how huge it was and wondered . . . how they would ever do what couples had been doing since the beginning of time.

"What do we do now?" she whispered against the corner of his mouth.

"Do you want me to come inside you?"

"It's what you want, isn't it?"

"God, yes! But only if you want me to."

"I do."

"I'll be careful. Oh, love, you're too fragile for a rough man like me." He buried his face in her hair and quietly held her as if he was holding something far more precious than life.

Go slowly, don't frighten her. God help me not to hurt her. Help me give her pleasure, not pain.

"You're not going to frighten me," she said as if reading his thoughts. She cupped his cheek with her hand and turned his lips to her. "I love you. I could never imagine doing this with another man. With you it seems natural and . . . beautiful."

His hand moved slowly under her gown to stroke her thigh, her hips, then slid up to her breast. Consumed with the need to feel her soft flesh, he tugged at the gown until it was above her breasts. She lifted herself up and slipped it off over her head, then wound her arms around him, pressing all of herself to him.

Sighing, they came together with nothing between them, body to body, soul to soul. When he felt the soft down of her mound against his thigh, he was so filled with love for her that he thought he would burst.

Her hands fluttered over his smooth, muscled shoulders and down along his rib cage with a freedom that was new and wildly exciting. A choked moan escaped him as her fingers touched the sensitive quivering flesh that lay rigid on his belly. He had not expected this sweet willingness, the passion that lay slumbering beneath her innocence.

"I've heard about this. Oh, my," she said with wonderment in her voice. Her fingers moved over the tip and down the shaft of his aching hardness. "Oh, my. Does this hurt you?" she asked in response to the low strangled sound that came from his throat.

"It's the sweetest hurt . . . in the world."

He rolled her over on her back and raised himself on quivering arms to hover over her. He kissed her lips, then unable to restrain himself, he positioned himself between her thighs with firm but gentle insistence. Abandoning all inhibitions, she opened her legs to welcome him when she felt the first firm, velvet touch of his probing flesh at the moist opening in her body.

"My love, my . . . sweet love—" His endearments were almost inaudible.

Holding her buttocks in his hands, he slowly slid into her until he felt the membrane guarding her virginity. He held himself there for endless seconds while little spasms of exquisite pleasure rippled through her. A low, growling sound came from deep in his throat as she rose to meet his driving shaft. At the sharp unexpected pain, she cried out his name and then found herself floating on a mighty wave, seeking more and more of the delicious pleasure, the joy of being filled where only emptiness had been.

"Molly, love!" he whispered helplessly, and with a long breath he thrust in frenzied urgency.

Molly held him tightly as his body shuddered, then relaxed, filling her with a healing warmth. From some far-off place she heard him say, "Dear God! Thank you for this sweet wife!"

Feeling wonderfully loved and fulfilled, they lay, their arms around each other, while their breathing slowed. Finally, Hod stirred and pulled the sheet up to cover them. With her still cradled lovingly in his arms, her body pressed tightly against his, he solemnly kissed her fore-head, her eyelids one after the other, and smoothed the tangles of hair from her face with gentle fingers.

"Did I hurt you, darlin' girl?"

"Just a little."

"It won't hurt the next time."

"I . . . don't care, it was so . . ." Her voice trailed.

"Then you liked what we just did?"

"Oh, yes. It was . . . wonderful . . . wonderful—"

Bertha stood on the porch at the store saying good-bye to Ruth. Keith waited in the car.

"Come on, slowpoke. You'll be late for school," he called. "George is coming across the field."

"Holy cow! Did you ever see such a bossy man, Aunt Bertha?" Ruth rolled her eyes.

"I kind of like him. If you decide you don't want him, I get first dibs."

"You'll have to stand in line behind Jennifer, the hussy, Bruza. That little heifer switches her tail at every man in town. She's hot for Keith."

Bertha laughed. "Down through the ages there's been flirts like her. They always want another woman's man."

Ruth tossed her head. "Ha! If that big lunk in the car wants her, he can have her. I'd sure not fight her over him."

"Well, I would!"

"Hey, slowpoke. Get a wiggle on. Push her off the porch, Bertha."

"She's comin'," Bertha called. "Thanks for staying with me, Ruth. I was prepared to be alone here, but I wasn't looking forward to it, considering."

"When Hod called Keith and told him the news and that they didn't want you to be alone last night, he beat it right for the school to tell me. It was fun for a change even if we did have to put up with . . . Big Mouth."

Bertha laughed. "He wasn't so bad, even if he does eat almost as much as Hod. They'll be back today. I'm still in shock about them getting married. I really didn't believe him when he told me he was going to marry her before they came home."

"If Molly wasn't in love with him, she wouldn't have married him. That girl has a stubborn streak a mile wide and when she's against doing something, she bows her neck." Ruth went down the steps to the car. "I'll call later this afternoon. If they aren't back, I'll come out. On second thought, I'll come out anyway and wait to greet the newlyweds."

After Keith and Ruth left, George came into the back of the store.

"Mornin'," Bertha called. "Let's have a second cup of coffee here at the counter. I brought it down and some of those flapjack cookies you like."

Bertha had decided that she liked the big quiet man, though he was a strange one. Yesterday when she told him that Hod and Molly had been married in Liberal, he nodded his head as if it were no surprise to him and made no comment until she pressed him.

"What do you think, George? They've not known each other very long."

"Long enough, I guess."

"It's a big step to take with a man you've only known a few weeks."

"He'll do right by her."

"I hope you're right."

"I am."

Yesterday when the postman came, George had asked him for his mail. He'd been given several legal-looking envelopes and a small package. He'd put the unopened letters and the package in the bib of his overalls after taking out the pistol he carried and placing it beneath the counter.

Bertha had been fairly busy with customers. All had been surprised to hear that Molly had married. The party line buzzed with the news after Hod's call. George left his place beside the window only to pump gas. The regular customers who knew him by sight spoke to him. It seemed to Bertha that this morning he had loosened up a little and was a little freer with his conversation.

In the middle of the morning Archie Howell arrived. George watched the car come down the road at a pretty good clip, turn in, and stop abruptly.

"Preacher's here," George muttered.

Archie walked quickly up the steps and into the store. After glancing at George, he went back to where Bertha was running her dustcloth over the shelves and rearranging canned goods.

"Mornin'," she said cheerfully, relishing the fact that if he didn't already know the news, she would have the chance to tell him that Molly was married.

"Is it true that Molly married that . . . man?" he demanded in a strident voice.

"It's true that she married Hod Dolan, her fiancé."

"She said nothing to me about . . . marrying so soon, and I'm her pastor."

"Poo," Bertha snorted. "She's of age. Even if she wasn't, she'd not have to ask *your* permission."

"I say she would. She has no parents." Open, naked hatred flashed from his eyes. It frightened Bertha and angered her as well.

"Well, she's got a husband now, and let me tell you something, Preacher. That man won't stand for anyone *bothering* his wife. And that includes you."

"Bothering?" Archie repeated, his voice raised in wrath.

You stupid bitch! You don't know it, but you've sealed your own fate. No one talks to Archie Howell like that. You'll wish you'd been more respectful to me when you reach the Pearly Gates, and are turned away to spend eternity in the fiery furnace.

Suddenly, his face changed, wiped clean of the rage it had revealed. For an instant it was devoid of expression. Then he smiled.

"I'll have to stop by and congratulate the happy couple." He stood by the counter and looked back toward the window where George sat.

"Was there something you wanted?" Bertha asked.

"Well, yes. Charlotte would like a spool of white thread."

"Right over here."

Archie placed a nickel on the counter; and as he followed Bertha down the aisle, he drew a small snuff tin from his pocket, opened it, and when she bent over the thread cabinet, he dumped the contents on her back.

Vengeance is mine, sayeth the Lord.

"Here it is. Number fifty." Bertha straightened and handed him the spool.

"Thank you. I left the nickel on the counter."

Archie walked slowly to the door, glanced at George, and saw what he thought was a sneer on his face.

You, too. I know just how to take care of you, I've had it planned for days.

Bertha followed the preacher to the door and watched him drive away. "He was madder than a hornet when he came in here."

"About Molly?"

"About Molly. That man is downright weird, George. For a minute I thought he was going to explode with rage, and the next instant, he was mild-mannered as you please. There's something about him, and has been since the first time I saw him, that makes my flesh crawl."

Shaking her head, Bertha turned and walked away. George glanced out the window, then back as she spoke over her shoulder.

"Let's have a glass of tea. That little squirt leaves a bad taste in my mouth."

George suddenly sprang from behind the counter, jerked up the dusting cloth Bertha had been using, and swiped it across her back. By the time Bertha turned around he was swatting at something on the counter. He knocked a black spider to the floor and crushed it with his boot.

"What in the world?"

"Black widow." George bent over so he could get a closer look. "No mistake. Has a red hourglass on its stomach."

"For ev . . . er . . . more! Where in the world did it come from? I've never seen one in the store before. Oh . . ." Bertha began to shake. "How did you happen to see it?"

George shrugged. "White dress. Saw it crawling up—"

"Don't say it!" Bertha was quivering violently now. "They're deadly!" She went to George on wobbly legs and, holding to his arms, leaned her forehead against his chest. "Oh, George, thank you. I'm so glad you were here. You're a sweet man. If you hadn't been fast . . . oh Lord, I hate to think of it."

Stunned, he stood there. He couldn't remember a time when any woman had leaned on him or called him sweet. He patted her shoulder awkwardly, not knowing what to say or do. It had given him a fright to see the deadly spider crawling toward her neck.

After he sat back down, he looked up at the goods that hung from hooks along the ceiling and tried to remember everything he had ever read about black widows. They were shy creatures, so tiny that one could have come into the store in a hundred different ways, but he'd heard that they liked to build their webs in dark places. Something wasn't right. He had to think about it.

He loved this store. He knew where each item was kept from the 20 Mule Team borax and Lava soap to the hairnets and corn brooms. This is the place he escaped to when life became unbearable at the farm. He had always felt welcome even if he just stood in the corner and watched Roy and Velma wait on the customers.

One time, when Molly was little and he had been in high school, she had taken his hand and shown him where a house finch had built a nest in the bridal wreath bushes. But as she grew older, she seemed to notice him less and less. When Roy and Velma were killed, he felt compelled to watch over her, to see that no harm came to her. Now she had a man who would take care of her. It saddened George that he was no longer needed.

Archie Howell left the store with a purpose firmly in mind. God had shown him the way. He had helped him to locate the deadly spider as He had guided him when he searched for the snake. It would not take long for the nosy, brassy bitch to sicken, then go into a coma as Gladys had done.

He felt clever, very clever. He turned and headed north away from town. He knew exactly where he was going and the road that would take him there. He felt strangely at peace for the first time since hearing about Molly's marriage. The ungrateful little twit! He would make her sorry by destroying those close to her; then if she didn't accept his generous offer, soiled as she now was, he would destroy her, and he would not make her passing easy.

He was suddenly sure that things would work out to his advantage after all. Wasn't he God's chosen one? Did not the Lord use him to perform His wonders? Someday the world would know of his generous deeds, and he would be praised by man as well as by God.

> *"Yes, we'll gather at the river,*
> *the beautiful, the beautiful riv . . . er.*
> *Gather with the saints at the river*
> *that flows from the throne of God."*

Archie sang hymn after hymn as he drove five miles north, veered west, then back south toward Pearl. He had not passed a car. He turned onto a trail that was just two dim tracks through the woods. It ended a half mile behind the Andrews' farm. Humming to himself, Archie parked his car in the concealment of thick jack-oak scrub and, leaving his hat on the seat, headed for the farmhouse.

The timing was perfect. George had been assigned to guard the old lady in case the Kansas City killers returned for Molly. He'd not return to the farm until chore time, unless Molly and her lover returned early. That wouldn't happen. The whore would wallow in bed with her stud most of the day. He felt a tightening in his muscles at the thought and had to force himself to relax for the job ahead. It always soothed him to sing. And he did, softly.

> *"'Tis so sweet to trust in Jesus,*
> *Just to take him at his word,*
> *Just to rest upon his promise—"*

It was a lovely day to help a poor soul to pass over, Archie thought. A cool breeze blew from the southwest; his children were in school, and Charlotte, his eldest daughter, a source of great pride, was home with the two little ones. His dinner would be on the table when he returned home.

Deep in thought, he was in the Andrews farmyard before he knew it. The house looked closed up. Not a door or window was open. An old red rooster ran at him, but found a choice morsel along the way and stopped for a tidbit. The place was as quiet as it had been the last time he was here. The door stayed closed this time as he approached, and he had to knock. He saw the blanket at the window move, then the door opened. He assumed his most angelic expression.

"Hello, dear lady. I'm back. I told you that I'd come back for you."

"Who'er you?" Gertrude squinted at him.

"Matthew. I was here the other day and spoke to your papa about courting you."

"Spoke to Papa?"

"Yes, we had a long visit. May I come in and speak to him again?"

She hesitated, then said, "I guess so."

Archie's eyes adjusted to the gloom, then swept the room quickly. A meat cleaver lay on the work counter, a hammer on the floor beside a pair of work boots. A churn full of milk stood beside the rocking chair where she had told him her father sat. His eyes went to the padlocked door leading to the room at the end of the kitchen.

"I'm going to Chicago." Gertrude moved close and peered at him.

"No, dear pretty lady. You're going to heaven."

"Where's that? Are you goin' to take me in the car?"

"I'm going to take you there, but not in the car."

"The buggy?"

"Not the buggy. It's a surprise."

"A surprise? Oh, goody! I'll get my sunbonnet."

When she turned her back, Archie picked up the weapon he had chosen when he first came into the room.

It was over quickly and was far easier than he imagined it would be. He looked down at the pile of flesh and bones on the floor.

"Good-bye, dear lady. You will be happy now. You may have had an instant of pain, and I regret that."

Stepping over her, he crossed the room and picked up the hammer. With the claw end he began to carefully pry the nails from the hasp that held it to the doorframe. What he needed was a piece of George's clothing, but what he saw when he stepped into the room made him almost forget his mission.

The room was neat and nicely furnished. Even the bed was made. What caught his eye immediately was that the walls were covered with snapshots of different sizes. Some were small, some had been enlarged. But what really boggled his mind was the subject of the photographs. He circled the room twice; then, after choosing carefully, he plucked six pictures from the wall and put them inside his shirt next to his skin, leaving his hands free.

Archie lifted a shirt and a pair of overalls from the pegs on the wall and went back into the kitchen. Squatting down beside the dead woman, he dipped the garments in the pool of blood surrounding her head, being careful to stain only the front of the shirt and the front of the overalls. He then rolled them up, and took them back into George's room and dropped them in a corner.

Ten minutes later, the hasp was so skillfully secured once again with the nails that it would be difficult to see that they had ever been removed. The hammer was replaced beside the boots. Archie looked down at the woman once again and at the meat cleaver buried in her skull. He had been merciful. Death had come almost instantly. This was the first such blow he'd delivered, and far too messy a method for his taste. But it had been necessary under the circumstances, and he was pleased to know he had the ability should he need to do it again.

When he opened the door, sunlight blinded him for an instant. He looked around, then slipped out the door. Several pups frolicked in front of the barn, but they didn't notice him; and he walked quickly across the yard and out through the pasture to where he'd left his car.

> *"I am bound for the promised land,*
> *Oh, won't you come and go with me.*
> *I am bound for the promised land."*

Archie sang softly on his way back to the car. He was pleased with how smoothly he had been able to accomplish this part of his plan. He started his car, backed out of the lane and onto the road, wondering what Charlotte had prepared for his noon meal.

Chapter
Twenty-one

In late afternoon Molly and Hod arrived back at the store. They had lain in bed half the morning, gazing at each other, touching, and making love. His eyes held hers tenderly, and there was something in his face she hadn't seen before—love and contentment.

They had made love deep into the night, until sheer exhaustion sent Molly into a sound sleep and Hod into that void between sleep and awareness. Her naked body lay molded to his, her cheek rested in the warm hollow of his shoulder. She had touched him profoundly, and the strength of his passion for her had left him shaken.

On the way back to Pearl, Molly could hardly contain her bubbling spirit. That morning she had held a cold wet cloth against herself to ease the soreness. Her body looked the same, but it would be forever different. It had experienced intense, intimate union with the body of the man she loved with all her heart. She was now a woman in every sense of the word, his woman. Nothing in her life had prepared her for the emotions that churned inside of her when she opened herself to the man she loved.

Cuddled against him, she looked at his profile, sighed contentedly, and kissed the side of his neck.

"If you keep doing that, I'm going to have to stop the car, and you know what'll happen. It'll be dark by the time we get home."

"You can't do that. We've got to get back so that George can do his chores." Her smiling face was radiant, her eyes like bottomless violet pools reflecting her love for him. "I'll try to resist you . . . until tonight." She exaggerated a pout and caressed him with her eyes.

When they reached the store, Hod passed by the gas pump and parked the car beneath the cottonwood at the side where he had worked on the truck. Stella trotted from the shade of the shed, but when she saw who had driven in, went back and lay down. Bertha came from the back of the store to meet them. George stood next to the counter.

Grinning like two kids, Hod and Molly went up the steps. Bertha hugged first Molly, then Hod.

"Congratulations, you two. My goodness gracious me! This is wonderful, just wonderful."

"Thanks, Bertha." Hod hugged her back.

"*Aunt* Bertha from now on, young man," she retorted.

"George?" Molly took his arm in her two hands and shook it. "I never thought when we left yesterday morning, that we'd come back married. Thank you for staying with Aunt Bertha."

" 'Twas nothin'."

"We decided on the way home that we were going to have a picnic and invite all my friends here to meet Hod. You'll come, won't you, George. You're one of my dearest friends."

"Already met him."

"George Andrews! I want you to come. Say you will."

"Honey, stop nagging George." Hod held one hand out to shake hands with the big silent man, and with the other pulled Molly close. "We've got to keep her in line, George, or she'll run us ragged."

"Guess so." A faint smile hovered over his mouth.

"We brought you a present, George."

"Huh?"

Molly drew a small sack out of the big one Hod had brought in and pushed it into his hands. He hesitated, then pulled out a long shiny flashlight. His fingers were trembling.

"The batteries are already in it," Hod said.

"It's a . . . good one." He started to lay it down on the counter. Molly stopped him by putting her hand over his.

"It's our present to you. Hod thought you'd like it. We've got something for Aunt Bertha, too."

Hod passed the box of candy to Bertha.

"Law. I can't remember when I last had a Whitman Sampler. Thanks, kids. Don't expect me to pass them around."

Hod watched George. He knew that he was uncomfortable and didn't know what to say about the flashlight.

"Anything happen I need to know about?"

"Naw."

"That little squirt of a preacher came this morning."

Bertha grimaced. "He already knew that you were married. He was madder than a wet hen that you wed without talking it over with him, he said, because he was your pastor. I set him straight on that and told him that you had a husband who'd not take kindly to any man bothering his wife. Golly bum! He was mad. I've got to give the smiling little weasel credit, he got over it dang fast and was nice as you please by the time he left."

"He put a black widow on Bertha."

Three sets of eyes turned on George after he dropped the words into the silence that followed Bertha's tale. He had blurted them out as if he had to say them before he changed his mind.

"When did you decide that?" Bertha asked.

George's weathered face turned brick red, and he looked out the window.

"Aunt Bertha, are you talking about a . . . black widow *spider*?"

"Today George knocked one off my back. It scared the waddin' outta me. He said it was a black widow because it had the red hourglass on its underside."

"What makes you think the preacher had anything to do with it?" Hod asked quietly.

George spoke to Hod as if he'd be the one to understand. "Black widows like dark places—wood or rock piles."

"Could it have come in on something? The bananas or feed sacks?"

"Females don't hardly leave the web. I read it somewhere."

"It could have dropped down from the web."

"No web up there." George pointed up to the hanging baskets.

"Why do you think it was the preacher?"

"He'd a saw it when she got the thread. I got to go."

"Wait, George." Bertha took a step toward him. "You're right. I was at the thread cabinet. He was behind me and would have surely seen it. If he put it on me, he wanted to kill me or make me real sick. Why?"

"Don't know." George walked through the store to the back door. He whistled for Stella, and the two of them started across the field.

"That George is awfully annoying when he won't say anything, but he's a good man and a deep thinker. I'm doggone glad he was here." Bertha nodded with a jerk, as if to add a period to her statement.

Minutes later Keith and Ruth arrived with hugs and laughter and congratulations. Keith shook Hod's hand, then grabbed Molly and kissed her soundly on the lips.

"Put my woman down. Hell! You're taking advantage of a friendship that's about to end." Hod pulled Molly out of Keith's arms.

"Don't be so stingy," Keith teased. "I'll let you kiss Ruth when we get married."

"Whoa, hoss!" Ruth's fist landed on Keith's upper arm. "You're gettin' the cart before the horse."

"Don't get in a snit, Ruthy." He looked over her head and winked at Hod. "She's already asked me. She's mad because I haven't given her an answer."

"Keith McCabe, you're lying!"

"Bertha! Save me."

"Save yourself. A car just pulled in for gas."

"On my way." Keith escaped out the door.

"Aunt Bertha, he's . . . a guest—"

"Don't worry about it," Ruth said with a laugh. "He's pretty handy when he sets his mind to it. Is that your car out there?" she asked Hod.

"It's our car. The truck will be here tomorrow, *Aunt Bertha*."

"I was wondering if you two had your heads so high in the clouds you'd forgot to bring it."

"Come look at the new car. It isn't as new as yours, Aunt Bertha. It sat in a little old lady's garage for a couple of years after her husband died." Molly's eyes were dancing with laughter. "That's what the salesman said. Not even anyone dumb as I am about cars would've believed that."

An hour later they were still standing around the car. Hod and Keith had looked under the hood, and now they leaned against it and Hod told them about a 1917 Chalmers that had been the pride of his uncle in Nebraska.

"The rods leading to the windshield, the radiator cover, and the headlamp covers were all shiny brass, and my uncle polished them every Saturday. He loved to sound the Klaxon and, believe me, it was loud."

"Klaxon? What's that?" Molly moved to the shelter of his arm.

"A horn. Uncle called it a Klaxon; an electrically operated horn."

The sound of a barking dog drew their attention.

"Goodness," Bertha exclaimed. "Here comes George, running. Stella's running and barking. What in the world?"

"Something's happened," Molly said worriedly. "George never runs."

Hod crossed the yard to meet him. The rest followed. The big man was wet with sweat and panting so hard he was almost unable to speak.

"Hod . . . Hod . . . come—" They were the only words he could utter.

"What's happened, George?" Hod reached him and took his arm to stop him.

"Gert . . . rude! Oh, God—Gertrude!"

"Has something happened to your sister? Calm down, man, and tell me so I can help."

"Did chores . . . then went in. She's . . . killed—" The words came out on a burst of breath. He was shaking from exhaustion and shock.

"She's dead? You're sure?" Hod was propelling him toward the car.

"The meat cleaver . . . in her head—" he said in a desperate whisper.

"Come on, Keith. We'd better get over there." Hod opened the back door of the car. "Get in, George. Honey"—he turned to Molly—"lock up the store and you women stay together . . . upstairs."

Hod backed the car out onto the road and sped toward the lane marked with the bedstead gate. George said not a word, even when they reached the homestead minutes later. Hod stopped beside the windmill. At a glance he could tell that the farm was well kept. No debris littered the ground, and the weeds were cut.

George got out of the car. He swiped his hand across his face. He seemed to be in a state of shock. Hod waited for him to lead the way to the house, but his feet appeared to be frozen to the ground.

"In there—" He nodded toward the house.

In the twilight's dimness, all Hod could see through the open door was a cave of darkness.

"Is there a light switch, George?"

"She takes out . . . bulbs."

"We need a light. Where's the flashlight?"

"Barn."

While George was getting the flashlight, Keith and Hod went to the door and peered in.

"Smells in there," Keith said. "A blood smell like in a slaughterhouse."

"Windows are covered. Molly said George's sister was strange. She hasn't left the farm in years."

George returned with the new flashlight Molly and Hod had given him. He handed it to Hod and turned away. Hod entered the kitchen with Keith behind him. The ray of light shone on the body on the floor. A meat cleaver was buried in the back of Gertrude's head. The blood had seeped into the cracks of the floor and was a dark color, evidence of drying.

Hod bent down for a closer look.

"She's been dead for a while." He glanced up at the socket hanging from a wire in the middle of the kitchen. "Ask George if there are any lightbulbs in the house."

George avoided looking at the body on the floor when he came into the kitchen. With help from the flashlight, he put the key in the padlock, opened the door to his room, and turned on the ceiling light. After unscrewing the bulb in the lamp on the table, he passed it to Keith and sat down on the bed.

"Take a look in George's room," Keith said, after the kitchen was illuminated and they had covered the body on the floor with the blanket Keith had taken from the window.

"One of us will have to go back to the store and call the sheriff."

"I'll do that, but come take a look first."

Hod noticed immediately that the room he stepped into was nicely furnished and neat. A nearly new radio sat on a table. There were two bookcases of books, lamps and . . . pictures. Above the bed was what looked to be a family portrait in an oval frame: a man, woman, and small girl. The child had on a white dress and black shoes. There were several other framed family pictures and dozens that were merely tacked to the wall.

"Good Lord!" Hod muttered.

"Yeah," Keith whispered. "I thought you'd be surprised. They are all of Molly and her folks."

The pictures on the wall were like a photograph album. The first one was taken when Molly was three or four years old. As she grew older, the quality of the pictures improved, and the recent snapshots were very good. There was a picture of the store and a man with a white apron tied about his waist. Molly's father. A sweet-faced, slender woman standing on the back porch of the store. Molly's mother.

Hod glanced at George. He sat with his elbows on his knees, his face in his hands while the two men looked at his treasures. Several of the later pictures had been torn off the wall. The corners were still under the tacks. Hod wondered why George had removed them.

He heard the sound of a car driving in and went through the kitchen to the door.

"Ruth," Keith said from behind him. "That woman never does what she's told to do."

Molly got out and came toward Hod. "What happened? We couldn't wait."

"George's sister has been killed. Someone buried a meat cleaver in her head. I told you to stay at the store . . . upstairs. There's a killer loose. He could be anywhere."

"We . . . stayed together, like you told us."

"Is there anything we can do for George?" Bertha asked.

"Nothing yet. We've got to get the sheriff out here."

"I'll go back with the women and call him." Keith opened the car door for Ruth to get back inside.

"Can we come back with Keith?" Molly asked. "We'll stay out in the car. We just don't want to be at the store . . . alone."

"That makes sense. Bertha, give Keith the keys to the store so he can use the phone. You and Molly stay where I can keep an eye on you."

"The party line will buzz, and you'll have more people here than you can shake a stick at." Bertha dug into her pocketbook for the keys.

"We can fix that. When you come back, Keith, park the car there across the lane. We'll not let anyone in but the sheriff."

"Can we see George?" Molly asked, after Keith and Ruth drove away.

"I don't want you going in there. I'll see if he wants to come out. You and Bertha stay in the car, and if you see anyone, sound the horn."

George looked up when Hod came into his room.

"Keith went to call the sheriff. He had to be notified."

George nodded, then shook his head. "Who'd a done it?"

"Maybe a tramp. Have you seen any around?"

"Naw. She'd not hurt nobody—"

"Why did you have the lock on your door?"

"She hated my pictures."

"Did she tear some off the wall?"

"No. She'd not been in here for a long time."

"Molly and Bertha are outside. Do you want to go out and see them?"

George's head came up with a jerk. "Don't let her in."

"She won't come in." He put his hand on George's shoulder. "It'll be an hour before the sheriff gets here. Why don't you go out and sit in the car with Molly and Bertha? They're concerned about you."

George got to his feet. He was as tall as Hod, but much heavier. He looked tired and pale beneath the day's growth of whiskers. Hod steered him to the door, where he stopped and looked at the blanket-covered body on the floor.

"She'd not hurt nobody."

"Are you saying that your sister wasn't . . . right?"

George looked at him. "I always knowed it."

"Come on out. It'll be cooler outside."

Molly got out of the car and went to George. "I'm sorry, George." She put her arms around his waist and hugged him. "I'm so sorry."

He stood as if paralyzed.

"Me too." Bertha took hold of his arm. "We're your friends, George. We're here to help you in any way we can."

Stella came to George and whined.

"Poor girl ran all the way back," Molly said. "She was going to chase the car when you left, but I called her back."

Everything seemed unreal to George. He couldn't be standing in his yard with Molly, Bertha, and Hod. The gruesome sight of Gertrude dead in there on the floor had rocked him to the core. His world had suddenly been turned upside down. What would he do? He'd always had *her* to take care of.

He walked to the fence and leaned against it. The cow mooed, the chickens stirred in the chicken house, and Stella whined and nudged his hand. All familiar sounds, yet tonight they were different.

"Who could have done it, Hod?" Molly asked, and snuggled in the crook of his arm.

"I don't know, honey. I'm glad George spent the day at the store. What time did he get there, Bertha?"

"Ruth was leaving for school. I don't remember the exact time. The sheriff won't accuse him, will he?"

"I'm not sure. She's been dead for eight hours or more. The sheriff may think he killed her before he came to the store."

"He didn't do it," Molly said. "No one can ever make me believe that!"

"I'm not accusing him. I'm trying to see this as Sheriff Mason will see it."

"The man is gentle as a lamb, Hod." Bertha stared at George's bent back and bowed head. "I admit that I didn't like him much at first. I thought he was strange, but I've gotten used to his ways. He's shy. He's the most bashful man I ever saw. Just today I got him to eat a sandwich and drink a glass of tea. He'd sit there all day and not eat a bite nor drink a drop if I didn't insist."

"Here comes a car. It's got to be Keith and Ruth coming back."

Keith left the car in the lane. When he and Ruth reached them his arm was around her.

"We were lucky. Mason was over near Kismet. He'll be here soon. I told him the first place south of the store. He'll find it."

"The party line will be busy," Bertha said. "Don't be surprised if a bunch of nosy folks arrive."

"I'll see that no one comes in but the sheriff." Keith then asked Hod, "Has he said anything?"

"Nothing much. He said several times that she wouldn't hurt anyone."

George looked so lonely standing beside the fence that it touched Molly's heart. She left Hod's side and went to stand beside him. After she wiggled her hand into his, she stood by him without speaking, giving as much silent comfort as she could. Hod watched her with love and pride.

Keith turned two cars away before the sheriff arrived. Hod talked to him for several minutes before the two of them went inside the house. A deputy who had come with the sheriff stayed beside the door. He was a short stocky man with a cowboy hat and a gun that rode low on his thigh, Old-West style.

It seemed to the group beside the car that they had been waiting for a long while until Hod emerged. He asked George to come inside so the sheriff could talk to him. George went with Hod, and Molly joined the others at the car.

Another long wait.

When the men came from the house again, George's hands were handcuffed behind his back. The sheriff held him by the arm. Molly was shocked into action.

"What are you doing?" she demanded. "Why did you handcuff him?"

"Honey, I'll explain—"

"You know he didn't do it. He was at the store. Tell him, Aunt Bertha."

"The sheriff is doing what he has to do, Molly. I'll explain later," Hod said patiently.

"I know you didn't . . . hurt your sister." Molly grabbed handsful of George's shirt. "I know you didn't."

"She was my . . . my mother." The sob that came from his throat was the saddest thing Molly had ever heard.

There was a silence after he spoke.

"Oh my goodness gracious! Your mother? Not your sister as we all believed? Hod, what can we do?" Tears were streaming down Molly's cheeks.

"We'll do everything we can. Don't worry about the place, George. We'll see to it that your animals are fed."

"We'll take care of things here until this is straightened out," Molly promised. "What about . . . what about—"

"The undertaker is on the way," Sheriff Mason said. "Hod said he'd stay until he gets here. We have a long drive. Give that bundle of clothes to Deputy Glenn, Hod. I put them in a pillowcase."

George stood in the sheriff's grasp as if he was not sure where he was or what was going on.

"Do you really have to do this, Sheriff?" Bertha asked.

"Yes, ma'am, I do. He'll have a fair trial."

"Count on me to swear he was with me *all* day."

"You'll get a chance. I'll take him on down to Liberal, Hod. If you turn up anything, let me know."

George seemed to come out of his stupor when he was being led away. He tried to turn to come back to the house, but the sheriff and the deputy held him.

"I . . . can't leave Gertrude!"

Hod hurried to him. "We'll stay right here until the undertaker comes. She'll not be left alone. Go on with the sheriff. I'll be down to Liberal in the morning."

Molly cried softly as she watched the lights of the sheriff's car go down the lane. She hadn't realized how much a part of her life the big, quiet man was until she saw him being taken away. George had always been almost invisible, but since her mother and father had gone, he had been near her most every day. Small things had been done quietly by his huge hands: the potatoes dug, the chicken house fixed, the windmill greased.

"Everyone thought she was his sister," Molly said. "Mama said something about Gertrude having come home in disgrace and that after that she never went out anywhere. Her parents raised George as their son. They'd only had Gertrude."

"When I came by the day after the storm," Keith said, "she came at me with the gun. George said there weren't any shells in it. I knew right away that she wasn't right. He seemed to be very patient with her.

"Sheriff Mason had no choice but to arrest him. He admitted that the meat cleaver was his, and more than that, a shirt and a pair of overalls with blood on them were found in his room. It was locked when we got here. He opened it with a key."

Bertha snorted. "If he killed her, why would he leave bloody clothes around? He had plenty of time to get rid of them before he came running back to the store."

"That's right, and he didn't have to run. He could have walked over," Ruth said.

"We've got a couple of detectives on our hands, Hod," Keith remarked. "Maybe we can hire them out to the Pinkerton Agency."

"Stop making fun, Keith McCabe. I'd bet my life George wasn't acting when he came to the store tonight. The man was in shock."

"Don't be betting your sweet life on anything, sugarpuss. It's too important to me." Keith wrapped Ruth in his arms. "I'm stumped by a couple of things, and that locked door is both of them."

Hod looked toward the house. The lights were on in the kitchen and in George's room. In a day or two he would show Molly the pictures. Mason had grasped the significance of them after Hod had pointed out that they had been placed in chronological order. The McKenzies were George's adopted family. There was nothing sexual in his feelings for Molly. She was the little sister he adored.

It was after midnight when they left to go back to the store. At Keith's suggestion, they had nailed the door shut, and Hod put the hammer in the car.

"The news will be all over the county by morning, and some yahoo may come out here out of curiosity and take a few things while he's at it."

On the way out they closed the gate at the end of the lane and wired it shut.

Chapter
Twenty-two

Bertha was right when she said the party line would be buzzing. She had answered six calls before sunup. People who didn't know Gertrude Andrews or care about knowing her were stirred up over the most gruesome crime that had been committed in Seward County in many years. Everyone who called was sure that George was guilty.

"It's just not possible," Molly said at daybreak, when Hod was getting ready to go to the Andrews farm to do the chores.

"I would agree if not for the bloody clothes in that locked room."

"The one who did it wants George to be blamed."

"Honey, I'll hurry back. I don't like the idea of you and Bertha being here alone with a killer running loose."

"See there! You don't think George did it."

"Be careful even of the people you know. George's sister didn't fear the one who killed her, or she wouldn't have turned her back."

"His mother. I feel so sorry for him. They passed her off as his sister because he was a . . . because he didn't have a father."

"He had one, sweetheart. It takes two to make a baby."

"He probably took advantage of Gertrude because she wasn't quite right in the head."

"That's likely, but maybe he got run over by a train on the way to the wedding." Hod kissed Molly's nose.

"Oh, you! Are you going down to Liberal today?"

"Not if I don't find someone to stay here while I'm gone."

When Hod returned, Stella and all her pups were in the backseat of their new car. He stopped by the shed, and the dogs bounced out and began happily sniffing the ground.

"There's dog hair all over the backseat," Molly wailed when she saw it.

"I couldn't leave them over there, honey." Hod grinned sheepishly.

"I know that. I'll get you the whisk broom."

A little later the Bonner family drove in with a wagonload of stove wood. Molly went to greet them.

"Hello, Mr. Bonner. Hello, Mrs. Bonner. Hey, kids, didn't you go to school today?"

"I got chicken pox," Becky said. "Willy, too."

"Oh, my. You're better now, I hope. Were you very sick?"

"I was. See, I still got red marks on my arms."

"They'll go to school Monday." Mrs. Bonner smiled

shyly from under the stiff-brimmed sunbonnet she wore. She was a neat woman with soft blond hair.

Hod came to stand behind Molly. He put his hand on her shoulder. She looked up at him lovingly.

"You met Mr. Dolan when you came by last week," Molly said to the Bonners. "We were married the other day." She made the announcement proudly.

Mr. Bonner grinned and held out his hand. "Congratulations."

"I hope you'll be happy," Mrs. Bonner said.

"Come on in out of the sun," Molly invited. "That stack of wood is growing, Mr. Bonner."

Hod reached up and lifted Becky down from the wagon. He swung her high and she giggled.

"Take them on in the store, honey. I'll help unload the wood."

Inside Bertha was talking on the phone and by the sound of her voice she was angry.

"If you think that, then you've not got sense enough to come in out of the rain." Bertha snapped. Her eyes sparkled angrily as she listened to the tirade coming from the other end of the line. "I know that man far better than you do, and I say he didn't do it." Bertha took a deep breath. "Bullfoot!" she yelled. "A woman who claims to be a Christian would never suggest such a thing. Good-bye."

Bertha slammed up the receiver and jerked the dust-cloth back and forth across the counter.

"Who was that?"

"Evelyn Bruza. She's nutty as a fruitcake. She thinks they should take George out right now and hang him."

"Hang him? There's no proof that he killed Gertrude."

"Folks are stirred up," Mrs. Bonner said. "When we came through town they were gathering on the street talking about it."

"Oh, my goodness."

"Evelyn said she heard talk that they might burn his place down."

"That would be terrible!" Molly exclaimed.

During the next half hour several customers came into the store. All had something to say about the murder, and one of them declared that she wasn't a bit surprised because that big ugly man looked like a killer to her.

It took all Molly's willpower to keep from screaming at her. Instead she spoke calmly and told her that George had worked at the store all day and that he couldn't possibly have killed his sister.

Later, when Hod came in, she told him there was talk of burning down George's farmhouse and farm buildings.

"It's mostly talk, honey. Keith is coming out to stay over there. Bonner has agreed to stay here while I go to Liberal. I explained to him that if George wasn't the killer, there was one on the loose, and I didn't want to leave you and Bertha here alone. If I leave now, I'll be back in the middle of the afternoon."

"I wish I could go with you."

"I wish it, too, honey. But I think I'll have a better chance of seeing the sheriff and talking to George if I'm alone."

Time passed slowly for Molly, although a constant string of people came to the store seeking information about the killing. Mr. Bonner stayed in the store. Molly took Mrs. Bonner and the children upstairs so they could listen to the radio or play the Victrola.

Noon came and Bertha made sandwiches of egg salad to which she had added a can of tuna. She invited Mrs. Bonner and the children to come to the kitchen table. The children were eager, but the shy woman hesitated.

"Now looky here, lady." Bertha stood with her hands on her hips. "If I was in your house at mealtime, would you invite me to eat?"

"Why, of course."

"Well. The wash dish is there in the kitchen. The kids can wash up while I take a plate of sandwiches down to Molly and Mr. Bonner."

"Yes, ma'am." The shy lady smiled. "It's a treat for the kids to eat away from home."

"Was the same in my day, and my name is Bertha."

"You're a good cook, Charlotte. You'll make some man a fine wife."

"Thank you, Daddy. Did you hear any more about the woman who was killed?"

"Only that her brother is in jail where he ought to be. I heard talk that a group might go down there and try to lynch him."

"That would be terrible. He should have a trial."

"He'll get a trial." He looked at her sternly. "That's not something young ladies should think about or talk about. It was the Lord's will the woman would die, and it's the Lord's will that her brother be jailed. Now, I'll hear no more about it."

The children were used to their father's mood changing in an instant. It did so now. He complimented Otis, telling him what a good job he and the boys had done picking up the debris after the storm and declaring how proud he was that *his* boys had dug the potatoes and put them in the cellar and that he could depend on *his* boys to do the chores before school and after.

Charlotte worried about her brother. He was becoming more and more resentful. He answered his father when spoken to, but with as few words as possible. Their daddy didn't seem to notice. The boys were at the door, ready to go back to school, when Archie called them back.

"Don't ever leave this table without thanking your sister for cooking the meal," he thundered. His mood had changed again.

"Thank you, Charlotte."

"Thank you, Charlotte," Harley said.

"Thank you, Charlotte," Danny echoed.

"Thank you." Hester kept her eyes on the floor.

"Train a child in the way he should go and when he is old, he will not depart from it," Archie declared as he watched his children head back to school. As he passed the table to go upstairs he looked down at his youngest daughter. "Wipe your mouth, Clara. No daddy wants a little girl with a nasty mouth."

The comment brought tears to the little girl's eyes and deep resentment to Charlotte. The remark was unnecessary and cruel. She hugged the child to her and tried to convince her that he didn't mean it.

Charlotte hoped that her father would go to town; then she could lie down with the baby and Clara and take a nap. She was so tired. She could handle the cooking and cleaning if she had a night's sleep, but the baby was teething and restless. Kept awake last night, she had rubbed his sore gums with her finger.

When Archie finally came downstairs, he paused on the back porch where Charlotte was washing diapers in the washtub.

"Tell Otis there's a hog out in the field. I want it in and the fence fixed by suppertime or he'll get the strop. Have supper ready early. I have prayer meeting tonight."

Charlotte was swamped by a feeling of anxiety so acute that she began to shake. She was sure that Otis would not accept another whipping. He would fight, then what would happen? He was only twelve, but he was big for his age, and hard work had made him strong. She hurried with the diapers, then put the baby and Clara down for a nap. When she was sure they were asleep, she went out into the field to look for the hog.

A half hour later she trudged back to the house. She hadn't found the hog, but she couldn't stay away from the baby and Clara any longer. She took a long drink of water, then washed the sweat and the tears from her face. The children were still sleeping. Charlotte sank down in a chair at the table and rested her head on her folded arm.

She was sound asleep when the screen door slammed.

"Charlotte, guess what?" Danny came into the kitchen. "I got to draw a squirrel on the blackboard. Teacher said it looked like a real one."

"I bet it did. Where are Otis and Harley?"

"They're comin'. Hester's comin', too. She got a star on her spelling paper."

"Run up and change your clothes. Don't wake the baby. Clara, honey, I didn't know you were awake." The little girl was sitting in the rocking chair beside the window."

"I was . . . bein' a big girl."

"Will you be a big girl a little longer and listen for the baby while I talk to Otis?"

"Uh-huh."

Charlotte went to the porch and watched Otis and Harley come across the yard. They were laughing. It was good to see her brothers laugh.

"Hurry up, Otis," she called. Then when they reached her, "Daddy said a hog was out in the field. I went out to look for it, but I couldn't find it."

"I know where it is. It found a mud hollow out past the field where we planted the pumpkins."

"Daddy said to get it in before supper and to fix the fence."

"Why? It's not hurtin' anythin' out there. Who knows when it'll rain again."

"Please, Otis. Don't cross him. Go change out of your school clothes and get the hog in the pen. I've got to have supper ready early so he can go to prayer meeting."

"Oh, all right. Go on, Harley, I've got something to tell Charlotte."

After the small boy raced up the stairs, Otis said, "Wally wants you to meet him tonight."

"Otis, I can't."

"Why not? He'll be gone."

"I can't go and leave the kids. The baby is teething and running a fever."

"Well, think about it. He'll be out back of the barn as soon as it's good and dark."

"I wish I could. I don't know—"

Otis went to change clothes, and Charlotte went to the cellar to get potatoes for supper. *Wally wants to meet me. Oh, if I only could!*

When she returned with the bucket of potatoes, the baby was crying. She hurried to the bedroom, changed his diaper, and brought him to the kitchen. Hester was coming in the door waving a school paper. Charlotte looked at the spelling test with a red star on it, told the child how proud she was of her, and sent her to their room to change clothes.

"Clara, honey, if I tie the baby in the rocking chair, will you rock him while I get supper. Hester will take over after she gets out of her school clothes."

Charlotte had peeled six potatoes and had covered them with water when Otis came down and motioned her to come to the back porch.

"You'll never guess what I saw tacked on the inside of the old man's wardrobe."

"Otis! Oh, my goodness. You didn't go in there?"

"Yes, I did. Don't worry. He'll never know it. Don't you want to know what I saw?"

"I don't know if I do or not. Otis, he'll whip you if he finds out. He's going to whip you if you don't get that hog in and fix the fence."

"Let him try!" Otis said with a snarl. "I've got a knife. I'll stick it in his belly if he starts to whip me again."

"Otis, please!"

"On the inside of his wardrobe he had six pictures of Molly McKenzie. Where'd ya reckon he got pictures of her?"

"I don't know. Please don't tell the boys. They might let it slip."

"I won't tell them." The screen door opened, and Harley came out onto the porch. "Come on, Harley, let's go get that old sow and put her in the pen or the old man will have a shit fit."

Charlotte caught her breath. Her brother was getting more and more rebellious. The younger boys copied everything Otis did. If they said that word and Daddy heard, they'd really get a whipping.

Archie walked down the street of Pearl and turned into the doctor's office. Dr. Markey was not only the only doctor in Seward County, except for the ones in the county seat at Liberal; he was also the coroner.

"Afternoon, Reverend."

"Afternoon, Mrs. Markey. Is the doctor in?"

"No. He went on a call about an hour ago." The doctor's wife was a pretty young woman with a pleasant smile. She was also his nurse.

"Will he be back soon?"

"I hope so. He went to the Gordons'. Their little one has a high fever. Doctor's afraid of diphtheria."

"The poor little thing. Maybe I should call on them."

"I don't believe you should, Reverend, until you talk to Doctor. You could take something home to your little ones."

"I hadn't thought of that." Archie hit his forehead with

the heel of his hand. "Thank you for reminding me. I wanted to ask the doctor if anything was said about a service for that poor woman who was killed."

"Doctor wouldn't know anything about that. You could find out from the sheriff if her brother has mentioned a service. Mr. Andrews had been to the office several times for different things. He was so shy he'd hardly look at me. I guess you never know what people are capable of doing."

"The sheriff must think he was capable, or he wouldn't be in jail. Nice talking to you, Mrs. Markey."

"You, too, Reverend."

Out on the walk, Archie's brows puckered. Well, he hadn't found out what he really wanted to know, so he'd have to nose around for himself. He got into his car and headed out toward the McKenzie store.

If the "widow" hasn't done the job, Lord, tell me what else to do.

Archie turned in at the store and pulled up beside the gas pump. To his utter surprise, a farmer by the name of Bonner came out and down the steps.

"You want gas?"

"Two gallons. Are you working here now?"

"Just today while Mr. Dolan went to Liberal."

"Miss McKenzie sometimes pumps gas. Is she sick?"

"You mean Miss Molly? She's all right. Mr. Dolan asked me to pump the gas."

"No, I meant her aunt."

"She's all right, too. Workin'est woman you ever saw. Always busy." Mr. Bonner watched the gauge. When two gallons had run into the tank, he hung up the nozzle, and replaced the cap on the gas tank. "You can pay inside."

"I know how much. I'll just pay you."

On the road back to town again Archie let himself go and pounded on the steering wheel.

"Bitch! Bitch! Bitch!" he shouted.

After a mile, he calmed himself and lifted his eyes from the road to the heavens. *Lord, I know You are testing me. The weapon You gave to me to smite my enemy failed. Help me, oh Lord, to succeed. Show me the way.*

He went into town and saw that school was out. The children were headed home. The boy from the cafe was walking with Margaret Jenson. Archie debated about whether or not to warn Mrs. Jenson about the dangers of a young girl and a boy who, if his mother was any example, had nothing but fornicating on his mind. He decided against it. He couldn't be caretaker of the world. That was God's job.

Archie drove to the edge of town and stopped at the home of the head deacon of his church. He told him that he was running a slight temperature and not feeling well. He asked him to take charge of the prayer meeting that night. He brought out his Bible and showed him a verse in the book of Revelation that he had planned to use: *Be thou faithful unto death, and I will give thee a crown of life.*

"Use it if you want to, Brother Finch. I've made notes on the subject and will leave them with you."

"You go right home and to bed, Reverend. We don't want you coming down with something. You're too valuable to all of us."

"I don't know about that, Brother Finch. I do my best. It's all I can do." Archie sighed heavily.

"And that's a plenty. I'll not be able to take your place, but I will fill in the best I can."

"Thank you. I must get on home and lie down."

Charlotte heard the car drive in and her stomach lurched. He was early. Otis was still working on the fence, and supper wasn't quite ready. She cautioned Hester and Clara to be quiet and waited for his footsteps on the porch.

"No need to hurry, Charlotte. I'm not going to prayer meeting. Call me when supper is ready."

"Yes, Daddy." She held her breath until he had passed through the kitchen. *What has happened? He always goes to prayer meeting.*

Charlotte heard him go up the stairs and removed the spoon she was using to stir the brown beans left over from the noon meal. She had added tomatoes and onions and made a batch of corn bread. If he had laid a trap to catch anyone entering his room, she would hear the explosion now.

She waited, breathing shallowly, and prayed. This could be the night that he and her brother came to blows. She had no doubt that Otis would beat him unmercifully if driven to it. She had stopped praying recently, but, she did now. *God, don't let him know Otis has been in his room. Please.*

Time passed, and Charlotte began to breathe more easily. The boys came in and washed up for supper. When they were all sitting at the table with their hands in their laps, she went to his door and knocked.

"Daddy, supper's ready."

"I don't think I want anything right now, honey. You go ahead and feed the children. I'll come down later."

"I'll put something back for you."

Supper was over and the kitchen in order when Charlotte finally had a chance to talk to Otis alone.

"You can go out pretending to check on the hog. Tell Wally I'm sorry I can't meet him and that . . . that I wish I could."

"I'll tell him, sis."

Chapter
Twenty-three

Hod returned at sundown. Molly had looked down the road every chance she had had for the past hour. When he parked at the side of the store under the cottonwood trees, she went out the back door to meet him, Stella at her heels.

"I was getting worried." She went into his arms. "I missed you."

"Missed you, too, sweetheart." He kissed her again and again. "Is everything all right here?"

"Fine. A lot of people came by. All of them wanted to talk about what happened at the Andrews place. How is George?"

"He's confused. He has never even seen a jail, and now he's in one. I've a lot to tell you, but I don't want to tell it in bits and pieces."

"I can wait. I'm so glad you're home. Stella's glad, too. She misses George." She reached down and stroked the dog's head.

"Honey, I'm going to pay Bonner. I don't want to do it in front of you or his family. When I asked him to stay, he waved aside any talk of pay. That man has enough pride for a dozen men."

"Yes, he does. If he won't take cash money, tell him we'll take it off the bill here at the store."

"You're sweet, honey. I love you."

"I love you, too."

"I've got to get over to George's and do chores. Close the store so you and Bertha can go with me. I don't want to ask Bonner to stay any longer. He has his own chores to do at home."

"Emergency situations require emergency measures."

After the Bonners left in their wagon, Molly put a closed sign on the door, and they got into Hod's car.

"Bonners are real nice folks," Bertha said. "The kids had a great time today. They got to listen to *Jack Armstrong, the All-American Boy*. Willie came downstairs singing, *Wave the flag for Hudson High, boys. Show them how we stand*. I wanted to give him a box of Wheaties, but didn't dare for fear of offending his daddy. That man has pride he hasn't used yet."

"So you gave them candy. They had more candy today than they've had in a year." Molly, sitting between Hod and Bertha, nudged Hod's thigh with hers and winked when he turned to look to her.

"I'll tell you what we can do, honey. This Christmas we'll get a Santa Claus suit for Bertha and she can give out candy at the store."

"You know that's not a bad idea." Bertha looked

around Molly to see Hod. "Kids wouldn't care if it was Mr. Claus or Mrs. Claus."

At the Andrews farm, Hod started the windmill to fill the stock tanks, then took a pail from the barn and went to milk. He'd left the cow in the barn lot all day with a pile of hay to munch on. After milking, he poured the milk in the trough for the hogs. Molly and Bertha fed the chickens, watched the tank fill, then moved the tin water conduit to another tank.

When the chores were done they went into the barn. Hod took a key from his pocket and opened a stout chest that sat in the corner.

"George gave me the key to this chest and told me to take out a packet of papers in a leather pouch."

Hod lifted the heavy lid and leaned it back against the wall. Inside the chest was not only the leather pouch, but a handgun, three cameras, a tin box full of negatives, and several other bundles carefully wrapped in cloth. Hod removed the cloth from one. It was a copy of *Leatherstocking Tales*, by Cooper. In the dim light they were barely able to read the inscription: *To George from Roy and Velma. Christmas 1919.*

"That was sixteen years ago," Bertha exclaimed. "It was one of his treasures."

Hod rewrapped the book and put it back in place. He took out the leather pouch and locked the chest.

"I want you to see George's room, then I'll tell you what I found out today."

He pried the nails from the back door with the claw end of the hammer, went inside, and turned on the light. It seemed strange to Molly to be going into George's home. The kitchen was sparsely furnished; table, chairs, washbench, stove, and cabinet. An old-fashioned rocking chair sat by the window. Hod had moved the table over the dark stain on the floor.

It was terribly hot in the house. Molly and Bertha waited in the kitchen while Hod opened doors and windows. He turned on the light in George's room, opened the windows, and switched on an electric fan that sat on the floor.

"Come in here," Hod called.

At first Molly saw only the bookshelves, the desk, the radio, the bed, and the lamp. Then her eyes were drawn to the pictures on the walls. Her mouth opened in surprise, but no sound came out. Bertha, however, was never speechless.

"For . . . the love of Pete! Looky there. Why, sugarpuss, they're pictures of you and Velma and . . . Roy. But mostly of you."

Molly walked around the room looking at the pictures. In one she looked to be four or five years old. In another she was waving as she climbed into the buggy her mother drove to take her to school. One picture was taken when the truck was new, and one on the day she left to go to Wichita to business school. She was standing by the truck with her suitcase. The picture taken when she came home showed her mother going to a car to meet her. There were pictures of her parents' graves and the framed clipping of her on the porch of the store. At the end of the row of photos, it looked as if some had been torn off the wall.

"Did you notice the one over the bed?" Hod put his arm across Molly's shoulders. "You were pretty even then, sweetheart."

Tears blurred Molly's vision as she gazed at the picture of her with her mother and father. She remembered going to a photographer in Liberal and posing for the picture. There was a smaller one in the living room at home.

"How do you suppose he got it?"

"I'm thinking that he wrote to the studio and ordered it. You're going to discover that George was quite a correspondent. He was a good photographer, too. He took his pictures and sent them off to be developed. He lived by the mail."

"I wonder if Daddy knew about the pictures."

"I would think so. George adopted your family as his, since he had none of his own. It was probably his way of keeping his sanity living here in this house with grandparents who were ashamed of him and with an unstable mother who claimed to be his sister."

"There was talk in the store today that his granddaddy was very strict and that his grandma and his sister were a little strange," Bertha said. "It's no wonder the boy grew up to be a man who kept to himself."

"Sit here on the bed, honey. I've more to tell you." Hod moved a chair away from an old-fashioned rolltop desk for Bertha.

"I'm almost sure that George didn't kill his mother. The sheriff showed me the bloodstained shirt and overalls they took from George's room. I spread them out on the floor side by side to study them. The overalls were stained from the middle of the bib to the crotch. The shirt-front was soaked in blood but there was none on the sleeves. The shirt was under the overalls, and I don't see how it could have gotten so much blood on the front. The duck overalls were heavy, and the blood hardly went through to the other side.

"It's reasonable to assume the shirt and the overalls were dipped in the blood on the floor. By the time we got here most of the blood, what hadn't been sopped up by the overalls and the shirt, had dried."

"What did the sheriff say?"

"He said it was interesting, but not enough to prove that George was innocent."

"What can we do to help him?"

"Get him a good lawyer. He asked about his dog today and was worried about his livestock. He said to tell the postman to leave his mail at the store."

"He left it today. I put it under the counter," Bertha said. "Mrs. Skellinger was in the store when Mr. Bruce came in. He was upset with her for talking about how mean George looked. He said that George was a private man and a heck of a lot smarter than folks gave him credit for."

"I think we'll find that out when we look in the pouch."

Hod removed a dozen or so envelopes from the bag. Most of them were from a stockbroker in Kansas City. One or two were from a stockbroker in Chicago, a couple from a law office. Hod opened one and scanned the contents.

"This is from a broker who says the balance of

George's account with his firm has reached ten thousand dollars."

"Ten . . . thou . . . sand?" Molly gasped.

"It's what it says. They are going to roll over the profits and invest in Bell Telephone. The letter was sent several months ago."

"Good grief!" Bertha exclaimed with glee.

Hod opened another envelope. "He has five thousand dollars' worth of stock in Sanford Electric and five thousand in Northwest Railroad. Each one of these envelopes has stock certificates. It's no wonder that he was worried about these documents getting into the wrong hands."

"George is rich. Isn't that a lark? Folks that've looked down their noses at him will now be licking his boots," Bertha said.

"He's got money to pay for the best lawyer we can find," Molly said. "Which one is the best, Hod?"

"I'll have to think on it, honey." He picked up another envelope and read: "The last will and testament of George Cleveland Andrews."

"He even had a will? Daddy had one, too. It sure made things easier."

Hod read the document. When he finished he handed it to Molly. She read it through quickly. By the time she finished her eyes were full of tears.

"Why would he do such a thing?" she asked.

"Because he loves you and trusts you. He leaves all his worldly possessions to Molly McKenzie with the understanding that she will take care of Gertrude Andrews for as long as Gertrude lives. The will was dated only a month ago. I imagine that he had another will and made this one out after your folks were killed." Hod folded the paper and returned it to the envelope.

"I knew right from the first time that he was crazy about you. I thought he was a man with a crush on a pretty girl. After a while I realized that he didn't love you in the way a man loves a woman he wants for his life's mate or he would have been jealous of me. I told him about telling the preacher I was going to marry you. He said something that I thought very strange. He told me that he'd already decided that the preacher wasn't going to have you. I got the impression that he would kill him if he had to."

"My goodness! Do you think he meant it?" Bertha asked.

"At the time I was sure he meant it. Then I asked him what he would think if I really wanted to marry you. He never showed any sign of being jealous, just shrugged and said he'd think on it."

"Isn't it sad?" Molly bent to wipe her eyes on the hem of her dress. "He didn't have anyone but Gertrude. I wish he'd told us. I feel bad now that at times I didn't pay any attention to him at all."

During the day Molly had moved Hod's things from the storage room to her bedroom. Bertha had suggested that they take the larger bedroom, the one she occupied, but Molly had refused. Bertha mentioned it again after they returned from the farm.

"Why don't you and Hod take the room I'm in? It was Roy's and Velma's. It's bigger. Now, you two know that

I'll be heading back to Wichita when this thing is settled with George."

Molly gripped the back of the chair with both hands. She looked as if she had been splashed with cold water.

"You can't go back there, Aunt Bertha. You've sold your house. We agreed when you came here that this would be your home now. I don't want you to go."

"Sugarpuss, I came here because you were alone and needed me. Things are changed now. You don't need me. You've got a husband who'll take care of you."

"Hod and I haven't had time to talk about what we'll do with the store. But he knows that I don't want to close it."

"Maybe we should talk about it now, sweetheart." Hod sat down in a chair and pulled Molly down on his lap.

"Hod, I don't want to lose the store. But I'd rather lose it than to lose Aunt Bertha."

"I know that, sweetheart. This store has been in your family for a long time, and I know you don't want to give it up. I also know your aunt is very dear to you. Let me run this idea by you. I want to know what both of you think.

"Honey, you said your daddy owned a section of land here. Keith said he'd heard that the section just north of here was for sale. With your land and the section we could buy, if the price is right, we'd have enough land to start a small ranch. Maybe later we could add to it. It will take most all of my money to buy the land and a small herd, but I think we'd have enough left to build a small house nearby. I'm thinking the price of beef has got to go up soon; and as this is land that hasn't been plowed, it would be good grazing with a rain now and then."

"You've been talking to Keith."

"His family have been ranchers in Texas for years. He says, and I agree, that all this land someday will be grassland, or some kind of controlled wheat land."

"You and Keith have become quite friendly."

"I'll still punch him in the nose if he kisses you like he did the other night. Bertha, Molly and I want you with us. You'll always be a part of our family. You could live here and run the store, with some help, of course. My wife will be busy having little Dolans."

Molly wrapped her arms around Hod's neck. "You're the most wonderful man in the world."

"No, I'm not. I'm selfish. Remember when I told you that?"

"Yes." She laughed softly. "When you bought yourself a beautiful nightgown and robe."

He reached for her lips with his and gave her a quick kiss. "I want my two ladies with me. What do you think, Aunt Bertha? Could you stay here and put up with a G-man turned rancher?"

Tears ran down Bertha's cheeks. "You know what I think, ya big ox! I wanted Molly to marry and be happy, but . . . I hated the thought of going back to Wichita alone."

"Aunt Bertha, I never dreamed that you'd think of leaving us and going back there."

"If it's agreed, we'll keep this plan in mind," Hod said. "Now I need to go down and take a bath before I take my bride to bed."

* * *

Keith sat at the table with Jim Morrison. The house was quiet. Jim had brought out a bottle of bootleg whiskey. They had been discussing the murder of Gertrude Andrews, a subject that had been the talk of Pearl all day.

"Seems to be no doubt her brother did it. Back in my daddy's day he'd a been hung up before he could take off his hat." Jim ran stubby fingers through thick gray hair.

"The woman was George's mother, not his sister," Keith said.

"Times is changed. Now they keep 'em in a good dry place and feed 'em good, like they're doin' with that Capone feller. He's got all that money stashed away someplace. When he gets out he'll live high on the hog."

"I feel sorry for the poor bastard," Keith said, ignoring Jim's musings. "He stuck there and took care of her. You've got to give him credit for that."

"Maybe he got tired of it."

"Maybe. I'd argue with you if not for the bloody clothes in the locked room. Yet it doesn't make sense that he'd leave them there all day. He had time to get rid of them before he went to the store. I'd swear he was in shock when he came running across that field."

"Ya say Dolan went to Liberal today?"

"Yeah. I'll go out in the morning and see what he found out."

"Have ya found out anythin' new about that other matter?"

"It's the damndest thing, Jim. I've not talked to anyone who has a word to say against him. I take that back. Wally, the boy whose mother runs the cafe, doesn't like him because he says he's downright mean to his kids. From what the kid says, the preacher is pretty handy with the strop."

"He's a cagey son of a bitch. I'm puzzled as to why he'd want to get rid of his sister, if he did. I've heard a few folks wonder how that rattler bit her on the neck, but no one blames him. It sure as hell didn't fall out of a tree. It'd naturally curl around her neck to keep from falling if someone threw it on her."

"He said she was lying on a quilt." Keith grinned at the older man. "The snake sneaked up on her."

"That makes about as much sense as puttin' socks on a rooster. He divorced one woman, four others just up and died, and a snake bit his sister. It's all fishy as hell."

"You've got to have proof, Jim. There isn't any."

"My wife knew Edna Howell. She was a nice, mild-mannered woman who caught a bad cold and died one night. She'd come through childbirth and had a month-old babe. The doctor said she must have got so clogged up she couldn't breathe and died in her sleep. Bullshit. I never heard of such."

"The others died suddenly, too."

"It could be that he'd picked out another wife and thought he'd have better luck getting her if his poor little children didn't have a woman to take care of them."

"I've not heard of him courting another woman."

"People I've talked to feel sorry for him because he's

had such bad luck with his wives. Even Ruth's folks believe that."

"Have you told Ruth why you're here?"

"I told her. And I told her about Jackson Howell and his suspicions of the old man. It wasn't until Jackson and Stuart left here and talked to a relative that they discovered they'd had different mothers. When they found out how many more women had died and that he had a houseful of kids they asked me to look into it. I had told them about a year ago about having a distant relative here. I guess that's what gave them the idea."

"I'd a thought that one of them would come here to see about the kids if nothing else."

"What could they do? They have no legal right to them. If they tried to take them, it would have caused a stink with folks feeling about the preacher like they do."

"Guess you're right."

"We can't blame this last killing on him. As far as I know he'd never been to the Andrews place, and he'd have no reason to kill her. It's not his style anyway. None of his victims, if what we think is true, had a mark on them."

"You're forgetting the sister."

"Maybe he's been so successful that he's getting careless."

"I wonder if he's the one who shot into the McKenzie's upstairs the night Ruth and I were there."

"Well, that's one you can't blame on the preacher. Your blabbermouth cousin did it."

"Marty? That stupid fool? How did you find out?"

"I'm not proud of being an eavesdropper, but Marty

should know better than to brag to someone about it when he's on the party line."

"I'll have to tell Hod. It'll ease his mind about Molly's safety. Having one killer on the loose at a time is bad enough." Keith brought his fist down on the table. "That stupid, little . . . chicken shit! Someday I'm going to break his neck!"

Chapter Twenty-four

Hod leaned up on his elbow next to Molly and traced the features of her face with his fingertips.

"My wife is the most beautiful woman in the world," he whispered.

She smiled, and he saw the dimple play hide-and-seek in her smooth cheek. They had loved long and rapturously the night before and had slept soundly in each other's arms.

"If I had known what it was like to feel your sweet breasts against me"—he kissed the tips of each and ran his mouth over her face, his lips teasing her lashes—"I would've kidnapped you the first day I saw you and kept you locked in my dungeon."

She opened her eyes. Morning light from the window filled the room. His face was inches from hers. She ran her fingertips over his lips as he smiled.

"Have you been awake long?"

"Uh-huh. I wanted to look at you and think about all the time we wasted waiting to meet each other."

"We could make up for it now," she whispered.

A large hand cupped her buttocks and pulled her tightly against the hard, elongated, aching part of him.

"I may be in this condition every morning for the next forty years," he teased.

"Don't tell me your troubles, Mr. Dolan. Do something about them." She moved and straightened her legs to get closer to him.

His arms held her so tightly she could feel the thundrous pounding of his heart. "I'll always love you, sweet Molly," he said in a voice trembling with emotion.

From then on nothing mattered except satisfying their desperate need for each other. Their bodies came together perfectly, and they blocked out everything, but this moment, this time. They floated in a world of caressing fingertips, nibbling teeth, and closely entwined limbs. Each time his lips left hers, he murmured softly of the love he had for her and vowed to devote his life to taking care of her.

Molly couldn't speak, but she kissed his face with quick, passionate kisses and clutched at his buttocks to keep his throbbing warmth inside her. At the summit, she cried his name. It was the sweetest music he had ever heard.

When reality returned, Hod's weight was pressing her into the bed. She lay molded to his naked body, her cheek nestled in the warm hollow of his shoulder. Her mouth moved, tasting the salty tang of his skin. He moved his head to kiss her lips, his mouth so tender on hers, so reverent, that it almost brought tears. She wrapped her arms around him in a wave of protective love, and her lips sought the scar on his forehead and kissed it gently as if to take away the pain he had suffered when he received the wound.

They had breakfast alone in the kitchen. Bertha had gone downstairs to open the store. Hod sat at the table watching Molly as she toasted bread in an iron skillet. He felt a surge of pride. She was his.

Molly reveled in the tenderness in Hod's eyes. Could this relaxed, smiling man be the stern-faced G-man who had come to the store that hot afternoon to ask her to be bait so he could catch a couple of gangsters? She watched the smile lines fan out from his eyes and wondered how she could ever have thought that he was cold and unfeeling.

Keith came to the store in the middle of the morning and told Hod about Marty Conroy.

"He doesn't have a lick of sense. He shot into that room because he was mad at me. It's no wonder I didn't catch him that night. That high-powered car of his will go sixty miles an hour."

Hod whistled his relief; and as long as he wasn't officially working on the murder of Gertrude Andrews, he felt free to discuss his observations with Keith.

"If George murdered his mother, he wasn't wearing the bloody shirt and overalls Mason found in his room."

"If that's the case, how did they get into a locked room?"

"Damned if I know. Mason won't budge. He needs positive proof that someone was there. He's sure he's got his man."

"Public pressure is on him. He's trying to save his job."

"George has the money to hire the best lawyer we can find."

Keith raised his brows in surprise. "How in the world did a dirt farmer get so prosperous?"

"He had a smart stockbroker. After the crash, he bought cheap stock. He could afford to wait for it to rebound. When it did, he cleaned up."

"You could hire a smart lawyer for him, but if you can't dig up any evidence to help clear George, it'll be a waste of his money."

"Money won't do him any good if they hang him."

"That's true."

"When I went to do the chores this morning, I looked carefully at the door to George's room. The only evidence I could see that someone had removed the lock plate in order to open the door was the nail heads were shiny, as if they had been recently struck with a hammer."

"Maybe the woman opened the door."

"That's a possibility. What puzzles me is that a killer who acts impulsively usually doesn't go to the trouble of setting out false clues to place the blame on someone else. He would do the deed and get the hell out."

"George may have done it that morning, then blocked it from his mind. When he went back home, he'd been as shocked as if someone else had done it."

"Stranger things have happened. Something else has bothered me," Hod said. "Did you notice how careful

George was with his pictures? If he was going to take some of them down, he would have removed the tacks, not ripped them from the wall, leaving some of the corners still there."

"That points to the woman again. When George was asked why he kept the door locked, he said she hated his pictures."

"My immediate problem is to get someone to stay at the Andrews farm for now and do chores. George asked me to look after his stock. I don't think the man ever asked a favor of another man in his life. Poor bastard."

"You should be able to hire someone if George has the money to pay for it."

"I'm thinking of hiring Ellis Bonner to move over there. They tell me that he and his family live in a shack that a strong wind could blow over. He stayed here at the store with Bertha and Molly while I went to Liberal. He took his responsibilities seriously. I had to force him to take pay."

Keith stayed at the store with Bertha while Hod and Molly went out to the Bonners' homestead. It was even more desolate than Molly had imagined. Hod explained the situation to Ellis Bonner and he agreed to take his family and go to the farm after Hod told him that he was sure that George had not killed his sister.

By late afternoon, the Bonner family, their wagon loaded with their meager possessions, including a crate of chickens and a cow tied on behind, had arrived and moved into George's house. Hod explained the lock on the door to George's room and that the rest of the house was theirs to use.

* * *

"It's getting to be a habit, closing the store early," Molly remarked as Hod drove her and Bertha into town.

"Like you said, honey, emergencies call for emergency measures. I want to call Kansas City and see about getting a lawyer for George, and I want to call Sheriff Mason down in Liberal and ask him to tell George that we have a good man looking after his farm. It will ease his mind some. I don't want to make the calls on the party line."

"If you did, you might as well put it on the radio," Bertha said. "I swear I didn't know I had so many *good* friends here. Half the women in the county want to talk to me or to Molly. They all say how mean and stupid George looked, and they don't even know him!"

"People are curious. It was the same after Mama and Daddy were killed."

"I'll drop you two off at the cafe, make my calls, and be back. We'll have supper."

Ruth and Keith were seated at a corner table and waved to Molly and Bertha.

"Where's Hod?" Ruth asked.

"Making phone calls. He'll be back."

"Come sit with us. I've something funny to tell you. I split my sides when I heard it."

"It must have been funny. Hello, Catherine," Molly said, when the small brightly dressed woman came from the kitchen. "My husband will be along in a few minutes and we'll order."

"It's goulash fit for a king tonight." Keith had stood and was waiting for Molly and Bertha to sit down. He grinned down at Catherine, whose head came up to his armpit. "How much would you charge to teach Ruth to boil water?"

"All right, cowboy. This isn't 'tick off Ruth' day." Ruth's voice was gruff, but her eyes were smiling.

"I'm thinking, *cowboy*, that you'll have something better to do with that one than to put her in the kitchen." Catherine winked at Keith and jerked her head toward Ruth.

"I've got several things in mind." Keith laughed at Ruth's red face.

"I bet you have." Catherine flounced back to the kitchen.

"What's this funny thing you have to tell me?" Molly asked when Keith was seated.

"Guess who came to see me at school today?"

"Santa Claus."

"Don't be funny. Tim Graham."

"Tim? Don't tell me he wants you back!"

"He apologized for not letting me know that he was going out with Jennifer before I came home from school, and he told me that he's getting married."

"Glory be! The two deserve each other."

"He's not marrying Jennifer. He's marrying Janythe. He told me that he'd been wanting Jan all along, but Jennifer wouldn't turn loose."

"What a weak-kneed excuse for a man," Bertha exclaimed. "Hasn't he any backbone?"

"Very little," Ruth said. "Jennifer is telling everyone that she jilted Tim and he had to take second best, which was Jan. Tim and Jan don't care what she says. They're too happy."

"What about—?"

"Me? I'd have been bored with that namby-pamby in a week. It was just a blow to my pride to have him dump me for Jennifer."

"Ruth needs a man who'll keep her in line," Keith said seriously. "One that'll whop her butt, keep her pregnant and chained to the cookstove. I think I know where I can find just the man for the job."

"You might find him on the moon, cowboy, but not on this earth," Ruth retorted.

"What will Jennifer do? She's got to have someone."

"She's already got someone. Walter Lovik."

"That redheaded woodpecker?" Bertha shook her head. "He'd flirt with a doorknob."

"And that'll set Jennifer's teeth on edge." Ruth was clearly enjoying the latest gossip about the Bruza twins. "If she thinks that he'll follow her around like a puppy, she's due for a disappointment."

Later, as they were eating, a man came into the cafe and walked straight to their table.

"Mr. Dolan?" When Hod nodded the man continued. "A group of us here in Pearl don't appreciate you coming in here and working to set a killer loose among us. Pearl is a peaceable town, and we want it to stay that way."

"I wish you all the luck in the world," Hod said politely, and continued eating.

"And whose idea is it that Hod is working to set a killer loose?" Molly demanded. Her voice was loud and angry. Her cheeks flushed.

"Citizens of this town, missy. You'll do well to tend to

your own good name and that of your daddy, or you'll be out of business at that store."

"Wait a minute." Hod placed his fork carefully on the edge of his plate and got to his feet. "You can speak to me in that sarcastic tone but not to my wife or, old as you are, you'll find yourself flat on the floor with a busted mouth."

"I'm a Christian, not a rowdy goin' around settlin' thin's with my fists and stickin' my nose in where it don't belong." The man headed for the door, then stopped. "I stand by my words."

"Christian, my foot," Bertha exclaimed.

"Who is he?" Hod asked when he sat back down.

"He's a deacon at the church." Molly was so angry she could hardly eat. "The stupid, stupid man," she muttered.

Catherine came to the table. "The barbershop crowd has been busy for the past couple days." She turned when her grinning son came from the kitchen carrying a white frosted cake with a cardboard bride and groom on top. "Wally, come say hello to Mr. and Mrs. Dolan."

"Oh, my," Molly exclaimed. "How did you . . . do that—so fast?"

"She already had it made. When you came in bells went off in her pretty little head," Wally said grinning teasingly at his mother. "Oops! I shouldn't have said that. I can tell by the frown on this small face."

"He likes to rub it in that he's bigger than I am."

"Ma! A kid in diapers is bigger than you are."

"See? Set the cake down before you drop it, you . . . smart-mouthed horse's ah . . . tail."

"I don't care when you baked it," Molly said. "Do I get to cut it?"

"Right this minute. I'll get clean plates."

Later the two couples stood beside Hod's car and waited for Bertha, who was in the kitchen with Catherine. Molly and Ruth were still giggling over Jennifer's new romance, and Hod was telling Keith about settling the Bonners in at George's place to do chores and guard duty.

"Mr. McCabe, may I speak to you for a moment?"

"Sure, Wally. What's on your mind?"

He jerked his head toward Ruth and Molly. "I rather they didn't hear because it might not amount to anything, and I'd . . . feel like a dumbbell."

"We can walk over to my car."

"Go ahead," Hod said.

"You, too, Mr. Dolan. It's about Mrs. Dolan."

They moved toward the car, and when they reached the front of it, Keith lifted the hood.

"We'll let those fellows looking out the barbershop window think we're talking cars and not plotting against them."

"What's this that would concern my wife, son?"

"I already told Mr. McCabe about Preacher Howell being dirt-mean to his kids. The other day he whipped Otis somethin' terrible with a strop. He couldn't even lean back in his chair at school. Otis hates him, but I don't think he made this up."

"Otis is the preacher's twelve-year-old son. He and his brothers do most of the work at their place," Keith explained.

"They do it all," Wally declared staunchly. "Yesterday I asked Otis to tell Charlotte that I would wait for her outside and to come out after the old man went to prayer meeting. Wouldn't you know? He didn't go. I waited anyway, and after a while, Otis sneaked out. He said his daddy didn't feel good and wasn't going to prayer meeting. Charlotte couldn't meet me. She'd sent him to tell me that she'd come out some other night."

"What's this got to do with my wife?" Hod asked.

"Otis and I had a long talk. He'd run off, but he don't want to leave Charlotte and the others. That old bastard is meaner than sin. The kids are scared to death of him. They aren't even allowed to go in the old man's room. He'd beat the livin' daylights outta them if he caught them. Otis was mad 'cause the preacher left word with Charlotte that he would whip him again if he didn't get one of the hogs in the pen and patch the fence before supper. When he went up to change his clothes, he went into the preacher's room, even knowing that sometimes he leaves traps in there to catch the kids."

"Go on," Keith said.

"He looked inside the wardrobe door and found six pictures of Mrs. Dolan tacked to the door. Otis thought it was strange. His daddy doesn't even keep any pictures of the kids' mothers. Why would he have pictures of Mrs. Dolan?"

Hod and Keith locked eyes. Keith was holding his breath, and Hod let his breath whistle out through his teeth.

"Wally," Keith said, "did Otis say if the pictures were Kodak pictures?"

"Yeah, he said they were Kodak pictures."

"Good Godamighty!" Keith clapped the boy on the shoulder. "Have you mentioned this to anyone else?"

"No. I promised Otis. If the old man found out Otis had been in his room, he'd horsewhip him. Otis has a knife and said next time he's going to fight him. I've not even told Mama."

"Don't breathe a word about this to anyone, Wally. This is very important information you've given us. Later we can tell you just how important it is. You know that Hod is a G-man, don't you?"

"Yes. I wish you could do something for Otis and Charlotte. It's a shame Charlotte can't come to school. Otis hates his daddy so much that I'm afraid he'll kill him and spend his life in the pen."

"We'll sure try, Wally. Thanks for passing along this information."

"I'd better get back and help Mama wash up that mess of dishes."

"Thanks, son," Hod said. "You've got a good head. You'd make a dandy G-man someday. You've got an eye for detail."

"Ya think so?" Wally looked bewildered.

"I sure do."

They watched the boy go into the cafe.

"By God! That bastard took the pictures of Molly off the wall in George's room. He's the one who killed the woman. But why?"

"I need to tell you why I came here in the first place," Keith said, and glanced at Molly and Ruth beside Hod's car. He talked fast, telling Hod about knowing Jackson Howell and being asked to look into the deaths of the preacher's wives. "I've not been able to get a handle on anything that proves the man's a killer; but I believe, as do his two older boys, that he killed their mothers. He killed his sister with the snake, but there's no way in hell that I can prove *that*. I was just about to give up."

"Godamighty!" Hod felt his heart pounding. "Somehow he had it in for George. He killed the woman so that he'd be blamed. He thought Bertha had influenced Molly against him and put the black widow spider on her back thinking to get rid of her, not knowing that the bite is not always fatal. George saw the spider and killed it. He must have thought that he'd finished off Bertha and moved on to set up George. His only connection with either of them was, in his mind, they were Molly's protectors. I would be next on his list."

"There's no telling how many people he's killed besides his wives. What do you think we should do?"

"Plenty. Let's tell the girls and Bertha to stay here at the cafe with Wally and his mother. We'll go to the telephone office and call the sheriff. I don't have any authority here even if I haven't turned in my badge."

Sheriff Mason was more than glad to make the trip from Liberal when Hod called, telling him that the matter was urgent business and that he would explain when he got here. After all, Hod Dolan was still a Federal officer even if he was on leave, and he had connections with the area headquarters in Kansas City.

"He should be here in about an hour," Hod told Keith on their way back to the cafe. "He'll meet us here. It'll cause a stir when he comes into town, but folks might as well know sooner than later that their beloved preacher is a killer."

Several men, including the one who had come to talk to Hod, were in the barbershop when they passed it. Molly and Ruth had gone back into the cafe and were sitting in one of the four booths. Hod could hear Bertha and Catherine talking in the kitchen and saw young Wally sweeping the floor.

Hod slid in beside Molly and put his arm around her. "I haven't kissed you for hours." He kissed her lingeringly on the lips.

"Hod! They can see in here from across the street."

"Let 'em. They, whoever they are, will know that I love my wife and that I like to kiss her. What's so bad about that?"

"Hey," Keith said. "I like your style." He put his arm around Ruth, yanked her close, kissed her soundly on the lips, and got an elbow in the stomach.

"What's the matter, sugarplum?" Keith still held Ruth locked to him. "Molly didn't mind Hod kissing her."

"Molly and Hod are married, you big jayhonk!"

"Is that a proposal, sugarplum?" Keith's eyes danced with mischief while he was teasing Ruth.

"Oh, you!"

"Settle down, you two, we've got important things to discuss," Hod said sternly, but he was smiling.

He was relieved. It was the same feeling he'd had when he'd, at last, nailed down the pattern of travel that would result in the demise of Bonnie and Clyde Barrow, who had robbed and murdered their way across the Midwest.

Keith went to the kitchen and spoke to Catherine.

"They'll be out in a minute or two," he said when he returned.

Wally put the CLOSED sign on the door and switched off the lights in the dining area, leaving only a dim light coming from the kitchen.

"I like this," Keith teased, nuzzling the side of Ruth's face with his nose.

Molly nestled in the curve of Hod's arm. She could feel the beat of his powerful heart against the arm and knew that he was excited about something. Bertha and Catherine slid into the booth; and at Keith's invitation, Wally pulled a chair up at the end. In the semidarkness, Hod and Keith shared in telling the reasons why they were waiting there for the sheriff to come up from Liberal.

"The information you gave us, Wally, may result in catching a man who, Hod and I think, has killed at least seven people and maybe many more."

"It's hard to believe that Reverend Howell would do . . . that." Molly was dumbfounded. "I don't like him, but even when we suspected that he'd put the spider on Aunt Bertha, I thought it was a mistake."

"I felt that there was something not quite right about that soft little man with his sweet smile and cupidlike face." Bertha shook her head. "Just goes to show you can't tell about folks."

"If it's true," Ruth said, "and we must wait to see if the sheriff will arrest him, it's going to rock this town. Most folks here think that he's kind and devoted to his children."

"Ruth is right," Hod said. "The only thing we have on

him is the pictures of Molly that Otis said were on the inside of Howell's wardrobe door. If they're not there, we have nothing."

"He'll know that Otis told," Wally said worriedly. "He'll kill him."

"When we get there, I'll keep him downstairs while Hod and the sheriff go up and search his room. If the pictures are not there, they may find something else that'll tie him to the murders. Nothing will be said about Otis."

"If the sheriff takes him to jail, will the kids go to the orphans' home?" Wally asked.

"I can't assure you that they won't," Keith said. "But they have two older brothers who are fine men, and I don't think they'll let that happen.

"Will George come home right away?" Molly asked.

"Honey, nothing here is for sure. It may all go down the drain if the pictures of you are not there. But if they are, I'm sure George will be home soon."

"It's going to be hard to wait."

Chapter
Twenty-five

Charlotte sat on a straight chair holding tightly to four-year-old Clara's hand, shaking it every once in a while to keep her awake. The little girl was tired and could hardly hold up her head. Charlotte feared that if their daddy thought she wasn't paying attention, she would be spanked.

This was the third night in a row that he had called a prayer service just as the children were ready for bed. The baby was asleep, the younger children were washed and in their nightclothes when he came down the stairs, Bible in hand, and called the family to the parlor.

Charlotte glanced at Otis and prayed that their daddy would not notice the look of resentment on his face. Harley sat beside him, nudging Danny to keep him alert. Her father's voice droned on. He was reading from Psalms and would expect them to recite *The Lord's Prayer* when he finished.

Charlotte's mind wandered. *Otis said that Miss Hoover asked about me almost every day. Will I ever go to school again? I'd be a whole year behind even if I went back next year. Soon I'll be too old. Margaret sent news that the class was going on a hayride. I wouldn't get to go if I was in school! Daddy wouldn't permit it. I wonder if Wally will sit in the hay with Irene Foote. If he does, I don't want to know about it. Irene has had a crush on Wally ever since the first day he came to school. After going to school in Chicago, he was—*

"Charlotte!" The voice broke into her thoughts. "You were not paying attention."

"Yes, I was, Daddy." Terror made her almost breathless. Her daddy's face was red with anger.

"Don't lie to me, girl. Hell is full of liars. *Bring a child up in the way it should go and it will not depart from it,*" he quoted the familiar phrase. "I intend to see that each and every one of you walks through the Pearly Gates. You are the oldest. You must set an example for the younger ones. You have a whipping coming, my girl. You've been sloppy in your duties in other ways that I've overlooked. Not this! You will be severely punished."

Suddenly, as if she had been stung by a wasp, Clara screamed. It was so unlike the child that for a second or two Charlotte was stunned.

"No! No! Char . . . Char!" The terrified little girl threw herself in Charlotte's lap and wrapped her arms around her neck and sobbed hysterically.

"Shut her up!" Archie yelled. "Or she'll get the same!"

During the confusion lights flashed in the windows as two cars drove into the yard.

"Shhh . . . shhh—" Charlotte tried to quiet her little sister.

"Get her out of here. The rest of you stay where you are. Brother Finch said he might come by. I want him to see well-behaved children."

Charlotte carried the crying child to the kitchen.

Archie was smiling when he opened the door in answer to the knock.

"Reverend," Sheriff Mason said, "may we come in?"

"By all means. Has there been an accident? Am I needed to—" He broke off his words when Hod and Keith came in the door behind the sheriff.

"No. Nothing like that. We're in the area looking around and stopped to check out your place."

"Looking around for what?"

"We're not sure yet."

"What's he doing here?" Archie's eyes went to Hod.

"He just came along for the ride. Did we interrupt something?"

"We were having a prayer service as we do every night at bedtime." Archie smiled at his children. "Charlotte," he called, "is Clara all right?"

Charlotte came back into the room. Clara's arms were wrapped tightly around her neck.

"Continue on. McCabe would like to sit in, wouldn't you, McCabe? Dolan and I will look around. Bedrooms upstairs?"

"Well . . . yes." Archie's face muscles had tightened.

"Yours, too?"

"Yes. I'll go along and show you."

"Stay here. We can find our way."

Hod and the sheriff went up the stairs. Archie placed his Bible on the library and started to follow. Keith stepped quickly to block him.

"We'll wait down here, Preacher." Keith looked past the chubby little man to the children. The girls huddled close to their older sister. A small boy stood with his hand on Otis's shoulder.

As if he suddenly realized he was losing control, Archie pointed his finger at Danny.

"Sit down. I have not dismissed you."

Danny cringed and whimpered, but sat down close to his brother.

"He isn't hurtin' anythin'. He's scared," Otis said belligerently.

Charlotte almost choked from the lump of fear that rose up in her throat. The resentment that her brother had held in check was gushing out. Her fright-filled eyes went to her father. His soft cheeks had turned a dull red, and his mouth puckered as he held his anger in check. In an instant his expression changed to one of sorrow.

"I apologize for my son's deplorable behavior. He knows better and—will be punished."

Suddenly it was too much for Otis to hold inside him. Bitterness, hatred and suppressed rage came gushing up from deep within his twelve-year-old heart. He shot to his feet.

"You'll not whip me ever again!" he shouted. "You'll not whip Charlotte or any of us! I'll kill you first."

Clara began to scream again. Hester jumped up and cowered behind Charlotte's chair. Danny and Harley clung to each other.

Hod came down the stairs and nodded to Keith before he spoke to the preacher. "The sheriff wants you upstairs."

Archie looked bewildered. Nothing was normal. Strangers were in his house ordering him around. The children were defying him.

God was testing him again. That was it.

"Charlotte, you and Otis take care of the little ones. Assure them that we will continue with our service shortly." He went up the stairs.

Hod motioned Keith aside. "Found 'em," he murmured.

"Thank God! I was sweatin' it."

"Could you keep these kids out of the way? He'll come down those stairs in handcuffs. It's not something they should see."

"I'll take care of it."

Hod took the stairs two at a time and reached the bedroom a step or two behind the preacher. The wardrobe door was open and the pictures of Molly were exposed, but the preacher didn't seem to notice.

"What can I do to help you, Sheriff?"

"I'd like the keys to your trunk, Howell. Then I'd like for you to explain why you have pictures of Mrs. Dolan on the door of your wardrobe."

"There's nothing in that little old trunk but a few old letters."

"The keys," Mason said, holding out his hand.

Archie dug into his pocket and produced the key. "Now about the pictures of Molly McKenzie—"

"—Molly Dolan," Hod corrected.

"They were left on the church steps," he said, ignoring Hod. "I assumed Molly brought them to me. I'm her pastor, you know."

Hod kept his eyes on Archie while the sheriff turned his back to unlock a small tin trunk.

"I don't know what you're looking for, Sheriff Mason. My children are upset over this interruption. I wish you'd conclude your business here and go on to your next search."

"We're in no hurry."

The sheriff lifted several layers of old newspapers out of the trunk. The headline on one was dated November 11, 1918 and read: ARMISTICE SIGNED. The rest were papers headlining important events such as the stock market crash and the election of Franklin Roosevelt. Mason unwrapped cloth from a bundle and found a bound leather book. He stood and flipped through pages of neat handwriting.

"That's personal, Sheriff."

"Yeah? It's a record of some kind, isn't it?"

"I'd rather not discuss my private affairs."

"I'd rather you did. Sit down." The sheriff let the lid fall back down on the trunk, then sat on it.

"Don't sit on my trunk," Archie said sharply.

The sheriff moved to a chair and motioned for Archie to sit on the bed. He opened the book and began to read:

"June 3, 1905. Today Helen departed for the great beyond. It was so easy. She looked so peaceful. Who was Helen?"

"My wife."

"September 5, 1908. Hilda left today with only a small

effort on my part to seek her reward in the sky. Tonight she sleeps in heaven. Who was that?"

"My beloved wife."

"November 23, 1911. Out of the kindness of my heart I helped poor old Mrs. Severson reach the other side."

"Who was she?"

"She was my mother-in-law, and she was suffering terribly from a liver complaint and longed to be with her long-departed husband."

"You helped ease her pain," Mason said matter-of-factly.

"Of course. It was the Christian thing to do."

The sheriff leafed through several more pages.

"December 23, 1934. Martha was unhappy. She cried constantly. She's happy now." Mason looked fixedly at the preacher. "Martha was your wife who died around Christmas last year."

"She no longer wished to perform her wifely duties, and she was lonesome for her mother, who was already in heaven."

"Did you help her make the trip?"

"Of course. She was my wife, and it was God's will."

"August 5, 1935." The sheriff read from another page in the record book. *"Poor old Mr. Yeager was happy to depart this world of woe."* Mason looked up at Archie. "Is that the Mr. Yeager who died suddenly on Sunday afternoon?"

"Yes. He didn't have one thing to live for. He was so afraid of the dust storms he couldn't sleep, and he longed for peace. His family had gone on ahead and were waiting for him on the other shore."

"Good of you, Reverend, to help him."

"I was sure that you'd understand, Sheriff. I am a servant of the Lord. He has given me the gift to ease suffering, and I gladly do His bidding."

"—And your sister?"

"God provided the means that carried her across the river so that she could tread the streets of gold. She was not enjoying life and is happier with our parents and her other brothers and sisters."

"Hum . . . you mean the rattlesnake?"

"It was His divine wish. The snake is also one of God's creatures. It went willingly into the tow sack."

"That's the end. What about Gertrude Andrews?"

"Well . . . she was demented, you know and—" Archie stopped speaking, and a change came over his face. It was as if he suddenly realized what he had been saying. He watched the sheriff rewrap his book and hand it to Dolan. He stood when the sheriff stood.

"I want you to explain all of this to the judge in Liberal."

"I'll do that. If he's a learned man, he'll understand that I was doing God's will."

"You'll get a chance to tell him why you . . . helped all these people. Have you kept count of how many?"

"It's seventeen or eighteen. I'd have to look at the record. I've been careful to be sure that each one was either of no use to anyone and merely taking up space, as the Andrews woman was, or anxious to go to a better life."

"You've done humanity a service, Preacher," Mason said dryly.

"Thank you for saying so, Sheriff."

Mason motioned Archie out the door and followed on his heels. Hod remained in the room and carefully removed the pictures of Molly from the door. In his almost ten years in law enforcement he had never come in contact with a man who admitted he had killed seventeen or eighteen people. The scary part of it was that the preacher sincerely felt that he was justified in doing so. It made Hod's heart quake at the thought of the madman having had designs on his sweet Molly.

At the bottom of the stairs, Archie looked toward the kitchen, where he heard voices.

"I'll come down to Liberal in the morning and talk to the judge."

"No. We'll go down tonight."

"I'll come in the morning. I'll not leave my children here alone."

"They won't be alone. I'll have someone come stay with them."

"I'll tell them that I'll be back in a few hours."

"Don't say anything to them. You might have to stay all night."

"Then I want Molly McKenzie to come stay with them. They were to be her children and would have been if not for Dolan."

The sheriff nudged Archie out the door. His deputy stepped out of the shadows and took his arm.

"What's this?" Archie demanded.

"We don't want you to fall down the steps, Preacher. Take him to the car. I'll have a word with Dolan and be along. If he gives you trouble, cuff him."

* * *

"What's goin' on, Mr. McCabe?" Otis asked the minute the children had been herded into the kitchen.

"It's a story that'll take some tellin', son. Why don't we wait till the little fellows are in bed. They look worn to a frazzle."

"They're tired. The old man's been acting strange lately. He's dragged them out three nights in a row to listen to his preachin'. I meant what I said about the whippin's. He's going to have a fight on his hands this time if he gets out that strop to whip me or any of them."

"Otis . . . please," Charlotte said beseechingly. "If you fight him, he'll run you off. Where would you go? What would we do without you?"

"Otis . . . don't go—" Danny began to cry.

"Ah . . . dry up, brat. I've not gone anywhere . . . yet," Otis said gruffly, but his hand went out to ruffle the child's hair.

"It won't come to that," Keith said.

"Where're they taking him?" From the kitchen door Otis saw Archie leaving and heard the sheriff say to cuff him.

"Why don't you get the little ones to bed? Come here, pretty girl." Keith tried to take Clara from Charlotte's arms, but she clung to her sister.

"She's scared . . . of men," Charlotte explained. "Come on, Hester. Help me with Clara while I see about the baby."

Charlotte carried her sister to the bedroom. Somehow she knew that from this night on her life, and those of her brothers and sisters, would be forever changed.

Keith made himself at home in the kitchen, starting a pot of coffee, while Otis and Charlotte put the younger children to bed. Hod left to go to the cafe, where Molly waited with Ruth, Bertha, and the Wisniewskis.

Otis was first to come back to the kitchen.

"Mr. McCabe, what's the old man done? Why'd the sheriff take him away? Is he coming back?" Otis sat down at the table and leaned forward on his folded arms.

"You've a right to know that your father was arrested for the murder of Gertrude Andrews, and he will not be coming back."

"Holy shit! How'd ya find out that?"

"Pictures of Molly McKenzie were taken from the wall out at the Andrews'. Only the person who killed the woman could have taken them. Your friend, Wally, told me that you had seen them in your daddy's room. Dolan called the sheriff. He said your daddy admitted it while they were upstairs."

"Lordy!" Otis covered his face with his hands. "Why'd he do it?"

"I'm not sure." Keith placed a comforting hand on the boy's shoulder.

"If I hadn't gone in his room, he wouldn't have been caught."

"And he might have done it again."

"Sometimes he'd put a paper or something in the door to see if one of us opened it. I knew I was going to fight him if he whipped me again, so I went in just to . . . be mean, I guess."

"I'm glad you did, and I'm glad you told Wally about the pictures. You may have saved lives."

"Charlotte said he called her Molly a few times. Do you think he wanted to marry Molly? She's too young for him."

"I guess he didn't think so."

"Will they send us to the orphans' home?" Otis asked. "It couldn't be worse than here if they'd let us stay together."

"I can't say for sure, Otis. I wish I could. Your brothers in Texas are good men. They asked me to come down here because they suspected that Reverend Howell killed their mothers. I was not able to find any proof, although I suspected him of killing your aunt. Snakes don't usually bite people on the neck."

"He didn't want her here, but she didn't have anyplace else to go," Otis said matter-of-factly. "I thought of runnin' off, but I didn't want to leave Charlotte and the younguns."

"You're a brother to be proud of, Otis. I'll call Jackson tomorrow. He and Stuart are your half brothers. We'll see what he has to say. You kids will be taken care of, I'll guarantee you that."

Chapter
Twenty-six

During the weeks following the arrest of the Reverend Archie Howell, the members of his church as well as the townspeople and those in the surrounding area were in total shock. At first it was disbelief. Then the opinion of many was that outsiders had come in, done the deed, and blamed their beloved pastor. Hod and Keith were treated like lepers for a while.

Gradually, as the evidence appeared, the attitude of the majority changed to anger. Several families offered to "take in" one or more of the children, even if their blood was tainted by that of a murderer. All offers were put aside as they awaited the arrival of Jackson Howell, who was en route to Pearl from Dallas.

For some reason, known only to the mind of the fickle public, George was now considered a hero. Folks were still unaware of his wealth; and as far as Molly and Hod were concerned, it was up to George to decide if they were ever to be told. He was changed when he returned home from Liberal. Hod had gone to get him while Molly and Bertha prepared a welcome-home supper at his place.

"George! Welcome home!" Molly threw her arms around him as soon as he got out of the car. "I'm so glad you're home."

"Now, now." It was all he managed to say, but he was smiling, and his eyes were unusually bright.

"Now wait a minute," Hod teased. "You're kissing the wrong man. I'm your husband."

George sent a smiling glance Hod's way, then stooped to pet Stella, who had come running. She whined a welcome and tried to lick his face. He kept his hand on the dog as he surveyed the homestead where he'd lived all his life. He didn't say anything, but nodded in approval.

Bertha met him the instant he stepped into the kitchen. "Just hold still. I'm going to hug you whether you like it or not." Her short arms barely reached around him, and her head fit beneath his chin. "Lean down here, you big ox, I'm going to kiss you." George obeyed and, to Bertha's surprise, hugged her back.

He noticed immediately the scrubbed kitchen, the clean windows with light coming in through the open doors to the other rooms. His eyes found Mrs. Bonner standing nervously beside the stove.

"Thank you, ma'am."

"Here's the key to your room, George." Hod, with his arm around Molly, had followed him into the house. George took the key, glanced at the locked door, and put the key in his pocket.

Mr. Bonner came in the door carrying a churn. He set it on the floor and held out his hand.

"Welcome back. I've been giving the milk to the hogs after I skimmed off the cream and kept it in the cellar. My wife will churn this before we go if you want her to."

"No need to hurry," George spoke firmly, and his tone took Molly by surprise.

"Can we eat the ice cream before we go, Mama?" Becky asked.

"Shhh . . . we'll see what Daddy says."

" 'Course you'll eat ice cream, sugarpuss. Didn't you help your daddy turn the crank?" Bertha flipped the cloth cover off a cake. "Looky here, George. Mrs. Bonner baked you a cake. I bet you'll like it even better than you do my griddle cookies."

George reached out and patted Becky's head. The gesture was another surprise for Molly. Becky reached up and grabbed hold of his hand and held on to it. It was George's turn to be surprised.

They gathered around the long kitchen table. George sat at the head. Years had passed since he'd eaten a meal at this table, and he could not remember ever having had company here for a meal. It was strange, but nice. Bertha said grace, thanking the Lord for letting their good friend, George, come home. The children were well-mannered and quiet throughout the meal, but Becky became excited when the ice cream was served and had to be told to settle down.

While the women cleaned up after the meal, Hod, George, and Ellis Bonner talked out in the yard.

"This is a nice house," Molly said, as she took a bowl out of the hot rinse water. "It sure looks different from the way it did when I first saw it."

"There's two rooms upstairs. I don't think they've been used in years. I cleaned them and washed the bedding. I hope Mr. Andrews don't mind."

"He's changed. Don't you think so, Aunt Bertha?"

"Yeah, I do. I saw him looking around like he'd never seen the place before."

Young Willy rushed in and pulled his mother aside. He was so excited that his voice carried throughout the room.

"Guess what, Ma? Maybe we don't have to go. Mr. Andrews is talkin' about us stayin' and Daddy workin' on shares. What's that?"

"My word! Don't get your hopes up. The man don't need us here."

"Then why'd he say it?"

"We'll know soon enough. Run on outside, son, and play with the pups." The shy woman cast an apologetic glance at Molly. "This is the nicest place the kids ever lived in. They think it's grand here."

"It is nice now that it's cleaned up. You've done a lot of work during the past week."

"It was pure pleasure working in such a nice house and seeing it shine."

"I hope Mr. Bonner can work out something with George. George is really a very nice man. He's never had a family. You know the woman who was killed was really his mother. She was demented and didn't want him here. That's one of the reasons he spent so much time at the store."

Mrs. Bonner clicked her tongue. "Poor, poor man."

Later that night Hod, with a towel wrapped around his lean hips, came up from taking a bath and paused as soon as he stepped into the bedroom.

"I don't think you realize how sweet an invitation you are, sitting there in your nightdress." Molly came to him and he drew her close, bending his head and hesitating for an unbearable moment before touching her lips with his. Her mouth clung.

Very softly she whispered, "Hod."

He lifted his head and was perfectly still, letting his eyes, soft with love, drink in her face. Then with a deep pleasurable sigh, he tightened his arms and held her close, her head buried in his shoulder, while he gently stroked her hair. He didn't say a word, but turned her face to his and kissed her mouth, fiercely, passionately. Molly closed her eyes and moved sensuously closer to him.

His lips left hers and he looked directly into her eyes, a faint smile softening his mouth.

Soft, sweet Molly, spunky and brave.

She watched as his hands slid down over her body and lifted the hem of her nightgown up and over her head. He gently pushed her down on the bed, and followed to lean over her. The light from the lamp shone on his head as he bent over her. She felt the feathery touch of his hair against her skin, then the warm caress of his lips in the curve of her neck.

She moved her hand to his nape and gently stroked his hair.

"I wait all day for my time alone with you," she whispered into the cheek pressed to her lips.

"You're my life," he said between kisses. "Without you I would be nothing now." This was not the cold-eyed G-man speaking. This was Hod, her husband, tender and affectionate, his eyes warm with love. His rigid sex nudged her belly. He was as hard and firm and as wonderful as the other nights when he had loved her.

Their lovemaking was long and rapturous. Time and again he kissed and caressed her, tireless in his desire to bring her to completion, whispering softly of the hunger that gnawed at him and the thirst for the mouth she offered so willingly.

And when together, conscious thought left them, obliterated by the need to put out the fire that engulfed them, he heard her cry his name, and felt his seed pour into her. He shuddered, striving to reach into her very soul. His heaving body was bound to hers, heart and mind. And when he could, he rolled over, bringing her with him to rest her head against his pounding heart.

He had been lonely, so lonely, and here it was, all the joy he had thought would never be his.

Molly, sweet Molly, I'll be lonesome no more.

Epilogue

December 1935

A light snow covered the plains of western Kansas. The air was crisp and cold, but, thankfully, the winds had diminished. It was a busy time at the store. Crates of oranges and apples clogged the aisles. Gaily wrapped boxes of candy vied for space on the gift counter with Coty and Evening in Paris perfume.

A Christmas tree decorated with shiny baubles, candy canes, and silver icicles stood in the window. Beneath it was a variety of small toys, slingshots, boxed pocketknives, and toy trucks for boys. For the girls there were dolls, paper dolls, and tea sets. Bertha wore a red Santa Claus hat every day and delighted in giving each child who came into the store a candy stick.

That morning the windows had been covered with frost. Molly had scraped enough off the glass in the door so that she could look out, but now the frost was melting and leaving puddles to be wiped up.

"Mr. Bruce is coming," she called. The mailman delivered packages to the store almost every day. Molly opened the door as he came up the steps to the porch. "Come in. Do you have time for something hot?"

"Not today, thanks." He set several packages on the counter and added a handful of letters from the pouch he had slung over his shoulder. "I've got the back of the car full of mail today. I see you've still got Mrs. Claus here."

"Where did you think I'd be, Mr. Pony Express man?" Bertha said sassily.

Molly sensed that the usually quiet Mr. Bruce was flirting with her aunt. These little exchanges had been going on for some time. She looked at the addresses on the packages while they continued to banter back and forth. Two of them were for George. He'd had several sent to the store lately, and Molly suspected they were presents for the Bonner children.

George had changed dramatically since his arrest. Shortly after he returned home, Hod and Molly took him to the cemetery where his mother was buried. He removed his hat, stood a few minutes, then walked away.

The Bonner family stayed on at the farm. Molly was sure that being with the children was what caused George to smile and talk more. He and Hod had gone to Liberal to pick out a car and to shop for new clothes. George learned to drive his car in almost no time at all, and drove to the store almost every day.

George was open now about his love of the Kodak and always had it with him. He teased Bertha and tried to catch her in unflattering positions. He was proud to show a new batch of pictures as soon as they arrived.

Mr. Bruce went out the front door of the store as Hod came in the back with an armful of cut wood for the Acme heater that was a supplement to the gas stove that heated the store.

"We've got mail, Hod," Molly called. "A letter from your brother Tom, one from Keith and Ruth, and one from Charlotte."

Hod shucked his coat and came to put his nose against her cheek.

"Ohhh . . . ! Your nose is cold." Molly backed away, and he followed to kiss her lips.

"I need warming up, honey."

"Like heck you do! You're hot as a pistol most every night."

"Mrs. Dolan! I'm going to tell your husband that you're talking dirty." He filled his hands with her breasts and pulled her back against him.

"Read your letter from Tom. I'm going to read the one from Ruth."

Molly quickly read the lengthy letter, then laid it aside and waited for Hod to finish the one from his brother. As soon as he looked up, she blurted the news.

"Ruth is expecting! She said Keith was acting the idiot and went around with a silly smile on his face as if he were the only man who had ever been responsible for such a miracle. She said that his grandma is almost as bad. Ruth loves being on the ranch and wants us to come visit sometime."

"We will . . . sometime. We've got to get started on our own house as soon as the weather clears."

"What does Tom say?"

"He has been writing to our brother's daughter who lives in Iowa. I told you that Duncan had been killed a long time ago. Duncan's daughter is grown-up now. Her name is Kathleen. She's going down to see Tom and Henry Ann. Driving down alone. She must be quite an adventurous girl. She may come by here and see us on the way. Her mother's folks left her money and a farm in Iowa."

"I hope she comes by. Could we write and invite her?"

"Sure, honey. If you want to." He kissed her on the neck. "What does Charlotte have to say?"

"I haven't opened her letter yet."

"Well, open it, wife." Hod put his arms around her just beneath her breasts and rested his chin on her shoulder. They read Charlotte's letter together.

Dear Mr. and Mrs. Dolan,

Just a word to let you know that we're all doing well. I was in the Christmas play. Jackson, Mary Lu, Stuart and Marge came to see me. All the kids came too except for the baby. We see the boys almost every day because Stuart and Marge don't live very far away. Otis is on the school baseball team. Harley has taken to talking nasty. Stuart threatened to wash his mouth out with soap, but he likes him a lot and I don't think he will.

I miss my friends in Pearl, but I'm glad Jackson came to get us. Back there we would always be the kids of the preacher who killed their mothers. Jackson has tried to keep us from hearing about the trial, but we know that it is over and that soon Daddy will pay for what he did. I don't want to know when it happens. The little kids don't talk about him at all, and Otis and I try not to think about him or how it was back in Pearl.

I hear from Margaret Jenson often. She told me that Jennifer Bruza had run away to Chicago with Walter Lovik who wants to enter a dance contest with her. Wally told me about it too and said her mother is fit to be tied. He writes once in a while.

We got to see Mr. and Mrs. McCabe a few weeks ago when they came to Dallas. It was so good to see her. Mr. McCabe teases her about getting fat cause she's expecting. She doesn't mind.

Merry Christmas and thanks for the Christmas card.

> *Charlotte Howell.*

Molly folded the letter and put it back in the envelope. "She still seems far older than her years."

"She'll be all right. I was impressed with Jackson Howell. It's hard to believe that he's the preacher's son. He doesn't even look like him."

"Humm . . . I thought he was quite handsome."

"More handsome than your husband? I heard Mr. Dolan would put Clark Gable to shame."

"Who in the world was telling you that . . . nonsense? Oh . . . oh . . . stop tickling me. Get your sneaky fingers out of there!"

Molly's pulse began to surge, and she could no longer speak for the giggles in her throat. She smiled up at her husband. He smiled back at her, his face younger and without that stern expression he had worn when she first met him. His arms were around her. She could feel the heavy thump of his heart against her back. She pulled his head down to whisper in his ear.

"He *would* put Clark to shame . . . but only a little bit."

He laughed against her cheek as his hand moved to caress her breast.

"Molly, sweet Molly, you're a pain in the—"

"—Neck. You did mean neck, didn't you, Clark?"

BERTHA'S GRIDDLE COOKIES

1 cup shortening
1 cup granulated sugar
½ teaspoon baking powder
¾ teaspoon salt
3½ cups flour
1 teaspoon ground nutmeg
Grated rind of one lemon or one orange
1 cup of raisins or chopped pecans or both
1 egg
⅓ cup milk

Sift the dry ingredients together. Add grated lemon or orange rind.

Cut in shortening as if making pie crust.

Mix in raisins or nuts.

Beat the egg, add milk, and stir into mixture until all ingredients are moistened.

Roll out ¼ inch thick on lightly floured board. Cut in desired shapes with cookie cutter.

Bake a few at a time on a lightly greased (not smoking) griddle until puffed on top and golden brown on bottom. Turn and brown on the other side.

Dear Reader,

Some of you may consider the 1930s as a dark and sorrow-filled time in our history. There were no jobs for twenty-five percent of the work force, and dust storms plagued the Midwest. Times were hard, but the hardships brought out the very best in Americans. Families stayed together and worked together to survive. These trying times produced the men and women who won World War II and saved the world from Hitler and his evil allies. It also produced the man who developed the Salk vaccine and others who gave us many more lifesaving drugs.

It was the era of big band music by Benny Goodman, Walter Winchell's news broadcast, Ma Perkins, Jack Armstrong, the All-American Boy radio shows and such movies as It Happened One Night. Young people jitterbugged to jukebox music in honky-tonks and sang along with Rudy and Bing.

WITH SONG, is the second of my three novels set during the Great Depression. If you have enjoyed it, you may want to read the third book, WITH HEART. The story takes place in 1938 on a ranch along the Red River between Oklahoma and Texas. It tells what happened to Johnny Henry, whom you met in WITH HOPE and again in WITH SONG. You will also meet Kathleen Dolan, niece of Tom and Hod. Keith McCabe and Ruth will appear again and, of course, Marty Conroy.

I hope you'll travel with me back to that time not so long ago, the turbulent years between World Wars I and II.

With thanks to my loyal readers,

Dorothy Garlock

CHAPTER ONE

Tillison County, Oklahoma—1938

"Bury me not on the lone prair . . . ie
where the coyotes howl and the wind blows free.
In a narrow grave—just six by three,
Oh, bury me not—"

Kathleen stopped singing abruptly when she rounded a bend in the lonely stretch of Oklahoma highway, and saw a dilapidated old car sitting crossways in the road. Her hands gripped the wheel of her old Nash and her feet hit the clutch and the brake at the same time.

"Oh Lord! Hijackers!"

She had read about them, had even written about them while working for a year at a small paper in Liberal, Kansas. Now a hijacking was

2

happening to her! She put the car in reverse and started backing up. Out of the brush beside the road a man sprang up and ran toward the car. Unable to turn and watch where she was going, she began to zig-zag. Then, to her horror, the back wheels of the car sank into the ditch beside the road. Quickly shifting the gears into drive, she gunned the motor in an attempt to go forward. The wheels spun, digging deeper into the sandy soil.

The door beside her was flung open and a big, hairy hand gripped her wrist.

"Stop it! You'll strip the gears."

Kathleen tramped hard on the gas pedal. The engine roared.

"Stop or I'll break your goddamn arm!"

She looked into a flabby, whiskered face. The man's lips were drawn back showing tobacco-stained teeth. He twisted her arm cruelly.

"All right! All right!" she shouted.

"Get out!"

She took her foot off the clutch. The car jerked and the motor died. When she was pulled from under the steering wheel, she fell to her knees and faced two pair of rundown boots planted in the red dirt beside her.

"What she got in there?" The second man peered into the back window of the car. "Jesus! It's loaded with stuff."

"We gotta get this thin' outta the ditch. Stupid-

3

ass woman! Never met one who had the sense of a goose." He reached in and snatched Kathleen's purse off the seat. "Got any money?"

"No."

"Liar." He pulled two ten-dollar bills out of her purse. "This all you got?"

"No! I've got a dozen gold bars in the bottom of that purse!" Anger was replacing her fear. She had lost one of her shoes when she was pulled from the car. She reached down to get it.

"Watch her!" The first man snarled and gave her a push that sent her reeling backward. He poked the two ten-dollar bills into his shirt pocket, tossed aside the thick pillow Kathleen used on the back of the seat so that her feet could reach the pedals, and slid under the wheel. "Get back there and push. Both of you."

"If you think I'm going to help you steal my car . . . you're crazy as a bedbug!"

"Lippy, ain't she?" The second man was shorter and had a big belly. He wasn't much taller than Kathleen who was five feet and four inches. He leered at her. "She ain't hardly got no titties a'tall." When he reached out to touch her breasts, Kathleen hit him square in the mouth with a balled fist.

"Ouch! You . . . bitch!" He dabbed at the blood on his mouth with the sleeve of his shirt and lifted his hand to hit her back. She drew back her fist.

4

"Touch me again and I'll . . . tear you up!"

"Whapsy-do! If I had time, I'd take the fight outta ya."

"Goddammit, Webb." The man in the car turned the key and the motor responded. "Stop messin' with 'er and help me get this thin' outta the ditch. Push, goddammit!"

The gears were shifted into drive and then into reverse to rock the car. The spinning wheels sent sand and dirt flying out behind. The wheels almost reached solid ground, then rolled back into the hole.

"She's not pushin'," Webb shouted, his face splotchy with anger and exertion. "Here, you girl, get back here and push!"

Kathleen had moved up onto the road and was searching the horizon for something or somebody. A few scattered steers grazed on the sparse dry grass. There wasn't a car in sight. Then she saw a man on horseback riding across the prairie toward the steers. After a quick glance back at the man pushing her car, she lifted both arms and waved.

The hijacker pushing the car went to the driver's side to talk to his cohort. Kathleen waved wildly to the horseman and pointed toward the car. The rider gigged the horse and was less than two hundred feet away when Webb came back to the rear of the car.

"Shit!" he shouted. "Somebody's comin'."

The other man got out and looked over the top of the car. The cowboy's horse jumped the ditch and trotted toward Kathleen. She hurriedly got between it and the hijackers.

"They're stealing my car!" she exclaimed without even looking at the man's face. Anger made her voice shrill.

In the brief silence that followed, the man who had jerked Kathleen from the car eyed the rifle that lay across the rider's thighs.

"Ah . . . naw. We is just a helpin' her get the car outta the ditch."

"You . . . lyin' son of a jackass!" Kathleen yelled. "You're stealing it. Make him give back my twenty dollars." She looked up at the rider and almost groaned. He looked to be not much more than a boy.

"Give it back." Young though he might be, he spoke with quiet authority.

"I don't have her damn money."

"It's in his shirt pocket." The rifle, more than the boy, gave Kathleen courage. "Two ten-dollar bills. I was trying to get away from them when I went into the ditch. See. Their car is blocking the road."

The end of the rifle moved. "Toss the money on the seat."

"She gave it to me. It's pay for getting her out of the ditch."

"Liar! You took it out of my purse."

"I'm not telling you again," the cowboy said.

"Good thing you got that gun, boy." The hijacker threw the bills on the car seat.

"Both of you move out and stand in back of the car."

"Make them help me get my car out of the ditch. It's their fault I'm stuck."

"Get under the wheel." The end of the rifle remained pointed at the two hijackers. Before Kathleen started the motor, she heard the boy say, "Take off your shirts and put them under that right wheel, then lift and push when she guns the motor."

"I'm not puttin' my good shirt under that wheel."

"No? Would you rather I put it under there with you in it?"

"It'll be ruin't."

"Don't look like it would be much of a loss to me."

"Don't I know you?"

"Maybe. Are you going to help the lady or am I going to see if I can shoot the button off the top of that cap on your head?"

A few minutes later, the Nash was up on the road and the hijackers were putting their shirts back on.

"Which way are you going, lady?" the cowboy asked.

"Rawlings." Kathleen left the motor idling and stood beside the car.

"You two stupid clods get in your car and head back up the road."

"Are you letting them go? I want them arrested."

The cowboy glanced at the girl. Her fiery red hair, thick and curly, was a halo around her head. It was what had drawn his eyes to her when he first came over the hill to see about his steers. There were not many red-headed women here in Indian country. Blue eyes sparkled angrily. She had freckles! Lord! It had been a long time since he'd seen a girl with freckles on her nose.

Ignoring her question, he walked his horse behind the men until they reached their car.

"We got flat tires," Webb complained.

"Don't you have a tire-patch, you lazy son of a bitch? It's easier to steal the lady's car than sweat a little. Is that it?"

One of them muttered something about a blanket-ass. At any other time the cowboy would have made him eat the words. Now he just wanted to get rid of the two of them. He glanced in the car to make sure that no guns were on the seats, then motioned for them to get in. He waited while they got it started and watched as the car bounced along the road on the flat tires. When it passed the Nash and headed away from Rawlings, he went back to Kathleen and spoke as

8

if there had not been a ten-minute interruption in their conversation.

"How do you suggest we get them to the sheriff? I know who they are. I'll see that he knows about this." He slid his rifle in the scabbard attached to the saddle and tilted his hat back.

He was considerably older than Kathleen had at first thought. Inky black hair, dark eyes and high cheekbones spoke of Indian heritage. He was tall, judging by the length of his stirrups, and lean. She could picture him on the cover of a dime western novel: horse rearing, guns blazing.

"I really appreciate your help. They would have taken my car and left me stranded here."

"Maybe not. They might have taken you with them."

"They'd a had a fight on their hands," she declared.

"I reckon they would've."

He smiled, and she realized that he was very attractive in a dark and mysterious sort of way. The thought entered her mind that she was out here on this lonely stretch of road with this cowboy and he had a gun. It hadn't occurred to her to be afraid of him.

"Well . . . thank you."

"You're very welcome." He tipped his hat.

Kathleen got in the car, waved, and drove away. She glanced in the rear-view mirror and saw the cowboy still sitting on his horse in the middle of the road.

Johnny Henry watched the car until it was out of sight. Why hadn't she told him who she was? Then he reasoned that she saw no need to introduce herself to a cowboy out here in the middle of the prairie, even if he had saved her pretty little hide from a couple of no-good hijackers. He had known the minute he saw that red hair and the old Nash car that she was Kathleen Dolan and that she was on her way to Rawlings to work at the *Gazette*.

A week earlier, Johnny had visited his sister, Henry Ann, and her family in Red Rock. Her husband, Tom, had had a letter from his brother, Hod, in Kansas telling him that their niece, Kathleen, would be coming down to Rawlings. She had been working for a year in Liberal and for some reason known only to her had decided to use some of the money left to her by her grandparents to buy into the paper at Rawlings.

"She wants to see and do a lot of things before she settles down," Hod had written. "She's twenty-six years old. Guess she's old enough to do as she pleases."

She didn't look to be that old, Johnny thought now. That would make her a year older than he was. She had looked to be about twenty-one or two.

Tom had told Johnny that Duncan Dolan, the

10

eldest of the Dolan boys, had gone to Montana when he was a youth and married a widow with a year old daughter he'd made legally his. Many of his letters were lovingly centered on the little girl with the red hair. After he was killed in a lumber accident, his wife and daughter had gone back to Iowa to live with her parents, and for a while the Dolans had lost track of Kathleen. Several years ago she had written that her mother and grandparents were gone and she wanted to know her father's family.

Johnny had not given her more than a thought or two . . . until today. He chuckled as he watched the car disappear. Miss Kathleen Dolan had spunk to go along with that red hair and eyes the color of his well-washed denim britches. She'd do just fine. A sudden burst of happiness sent his heart galloping like a runaway horse.

In Rawlings, Oklahoma as in most other towns in 1938, jobs were scarce. Prices had risen only a little since the bottom price for wheat was twenty-five cents a bushel, oats at ten cents and cotton at five cents a pound back in 1932. Most of the cotton farmers were allowing their fields to go to grass to save the soil from the dust storms and were trying to make a living by raising cattle. Some of them were packing up and following Highway 66 to the "promised land" in California where fertile fields held the promise of jobs.

A steady stream of hobos looking for jobs or a handout came through Rawlings daily seeking the community soup kitchen. The town had survived partly because a hide-tanning plant had opened several years ago and employed more than fifty people. Hides were shipped from the meat packing plants in Oklahoma City and Wichita Falls. There was dissatisfaction among some in town, however, because they believed that the large number of Indians working at the plant was unfairly disproportionate. Miss Vernon had said that the tanning plant was owned by a Cherokee Indian, who was not only oil-rich, but smart and decided his own employment policies.

During the past two months, Kathleen had learned quite a bit about Rawlings, Oklahoma. Miss Vernon had sent her every issue of the *Gazette* since she had answered the advertisement for a business partner in the Oklahoma City paper. The first *Gazette* had been published in 1910, just three years after Oklahoma became a state. The family had held onto the paper during the worst years of the Great Depression. Now, without an heir to take over, it was in danger of being put to rest.

Her heart pounding with excitement, Kathleen drove slowly along the street. The town was quiet beneath the hot September sun. A dust devil danced down the middle of Main Street where only a few cars were parked along the curb and not many people walked leisurely along the walks.

She stopped at a stop sign and sat there longer than necessary viewing the buildings that made up the business part of town. A number of them were vacant, but no more than in other towns she had passed through. The sidewalks on both sides of the street were new, no doubt due to President Roosevelt's recovery program. The new school she had passed was another WPA project. Even the water tower had a fresh coat of paint. The district evidently had a hard-working congressman.

Most of the three thousand residents of Tillison County resided here in Rawlings, the county seat. The tall, solid red-brick courthouse building sat in the middle of a square. An arch made of deer antlers and steer horns spanned the walk leading to the entrance. Kathleen smiled at that.

Her bright interested eyes took in everything. Rawlings was not as big as Liberal, but then she had known that. It had a large business district. Why not? It was the only town of any size for fifty miles around. The Hughes Department store was on the corner. Next to it was the Piggly-Wiggly grocery and at the end of the block the Tillison County Bank and Trust. She wondered why the phrase was usually "bank and trust" when most folks had little trust in banks since so many had gone broke.

She passed the Rialto Theatre and Claude's Hamburger Shack. Wilson's Family Market had a choice location on the corner across from the bank, and next to it was Woolworth's Five and Dime. Then, near the end of the block between Corner Drug store and Leroy's Men's Wear, she spied the *Gazette* building, two-storied red-brick, narrow, with one large window and two recessed doors; the second door leading to a flight of stairs. RAWLINGS' GAZETTE was painted in gold letters on the window.

Kathleen was not disappointed. Here she would invest her five hundred dollars and be part owner of a "real live" newspaper. Her duties would be writing news and editorials and handling advertising for the bi-weekly paper. Miss Vernon would take care of the society news, obituaries and bookkeeping. Kathleen's only concern was that she might not have time for her *other* writing, the writing that didn't bring in enough money for her to live on.

She angle-parked the Nash in front of the building and sat for a few minutes to allow her heartbeat to slow. *Thank you, Grandma and Grandpa Hansen, for making this possible for me.* Several people passed while she sat there. An Indian woman with two black braids hanging over her ample bosom and moccasins on her feet came out of the *Gazette* office. The screen door banged shut behind her and she hurried on down the street.

Kathleen climbed out of the car. The late September wind blew her hair and wrapped her full skirt around her legs. She looked through the window and saw a heavy oak desk littered with papers. A typewriter sat on a pull-out shelf at one end of the desk. The swivel chair was empty.

Coming out of the bright sunlight, she stood beside the door to allow her eyes to adjust. The familiar clanking of a linotype machine coming from the back room was the only sound. No one was in sight.

The newspaper office had an odor familiar to her: a combination of melting lead, ink and paper. The clutter was also typical. As she wasn't being observed, Kathleen let her eyes wander over the office. A few framed front pages of the *Gazette* hung on the wall: Armistice Day, November 11, 1918, the stock market crash in 1929, Roosevelt's election in 1932. Between the well-scarred desks were two four-drawer filing cabinets. Along the opposite wall on a waist-high counter, a thick book of advertising illustrations lay open. Suspended on long rods from the high ceiling, two fans turned gently.

Suddenly she noticed a leg and a foot jutting out from behind one of the desks. Shock kept her still for a second; then she rushed over to the woman who lay on the floor between the desk and the wall.

"What . . . in the world—?" Kathleen knelt down for a closer look. *This must be Miss Vernon!* There was blood on her forehead, but she was alive. "Help!" Kathleen yelled as she ran toward the back room and the clattering linotype machine. "Help! Come quick!"

The man who sat at the machine continued to type and then dropped the line of lead and started another. He appeared not to hear Kathleen's call for help. She ran to him and put her hand on his shoulder. He jumped and turned. She backed away.

"Help me! Miss Vernon's had an accident!" She took a few steps toward the front, then looked back. The big, shaggy-haired man was still standing beside the machine. "Can't you understand? I need your help!" she screamed. The man cupped his palm around his ear. *Oh, dear Lord! He's either deaf or he can't hear me over the racket of that damn linotype machine.*

Kathleen turned, ran back to the office and grabbed the phone.

"Operator, we need help at the *Gazette* office," she said breathlessly. "Miss Vernon's had an accident."

"Adelaide?"

"Yes. She's on the floor and has blood on her head."

16

"Is she there in the office?"

"Yes, yes. Get a doctor."

"I'll see if I can find him."

By the time she had hung up the telephone, the man from the back room was kneeling beside Miss Vernon. Kathleen hurried to a large tin sink in the printing area of the building. When she returned with a wet towel, he had lifted the woman out from behind the desk and was holding her head and shoulders off the floor. Kathleen pressed the towel into his hand. As he dabbed at the blood on the woman's forehead, Kathleen got her first good look at her new partner.

In her letters to Kathleen, Miss Vernon had not mentioned her age. Now, Kathleen noted that Miss Vernon's dark hair was streaked with gray and the skin on her face and neck bore fine wrinkles. She was slightly built and Kathleen judged her to be in her middle or late fifties.

Little moaning noises came from the man holding her. He was in anguish. He wasn't her husband; Miss Vernon had said she had never married. Kathleen couldn't see his face, but her first impression when she had seen him in the back room was of a big strong man, considerably younger than Miss Vernon.

The screen door slammed. Kathleen looked up to see a large woman in a white nurse's uniform. A white cap was perched on top of her bleached-blond hair. She was six feet tall or more and she looked to be a no-nonsense woman who would be able to whip a bear with a willow switch, as Kathleen's grandpa used to say. The nurse dropped a bag on the floor and knelt down.

"What the hell has Adelaide done to herself now?" Her voice was loud and brisk. "Move over, Chuck. Let me have a look."

The man lowered Adelaide gently to the floor and stepped back. As he looked up from the woman on the floor, Kathleen was startled by the beautiful amber-colored eyes deeply set in his worried, homely face. Although the dark lashes were thick and long and his brows smooth and straight, the large nose looked as if it had been flattened in a hundred barroom brawls. A deep split in his upper lip extended almost to his nose. He was broad shouldered and thick-necked. His arms were heavily muscled. He reminded her of a gentle gorilla, if there was such a thing.

"Wake up, Adelaide." The nurse waved an open vial beneath Miss Vernon's nose. The woman sputtered and rolled her head. "Wake up. You're all right. You've just had a little crack on the head."

"Maybe not," Kathleen said. "She may have had a stroke . . . or something." The quelling glance the nurse gave her would have sent a more timid person running. Not Kathleen. She looked the nurse in the eye and said, "Shouldn't she be examined by a doctor?"

18

"Are you her long-lost daughter?"

"No, but—"

"She's awake," the nurse said, ignoring Kathleen. "Help her into the chair, Chuck."

With his hands beneath her armpits, Chuck easily lifted Adelaide into the chair. Her eyes were glazed as she tried to focus on the man kneeling beside her. She flinched when the nurse dabbed at the cut on her forehead with a pad saturated with alcohol.

"You'll not need any stitches if I put a tight tape on it. What happened, Adelaide? Did you drink a little too much of that bootleg whiskey and fall out of the chair?"

Kathleen could tell by the snort that came from Chuck that he'd heard the nurse's comment and hadn't liked it. Kathleen hadn't liked it either. She thought it very unprofessional. Adelaide continued to try to focus on Chuck and said nothing.

"Don't get so huffy, big fellow," the nurse continued. "You know as well as I do that Adelaide is fond of the bottle."

"I didn't smell anything," Kathleen said.

"Who are you?" The nurse straightened to her full height. She was a very intimidating figure, a foot taller than Kathleen with that cap perched on top of her henna-reddened hair. She was *big*, rangy big: like a football player. Her lashes were heavy with mascara. She had applied lipstick to her small mouth to make her lips appear fuller. It was smeared at the corners.

"Kathleen Dolan."

"You're new in town." Strong, quick fingers taped the bandage to Adelaide's forehead.

"You might say that."

"How long are you staying?"

"A long, long time."

"I see. Then you're the one who is taking over the paper."

"No. I'll be working with Miss Vernon on *our* paper."

"Here in Rawlings we don't butt into other people's business, but I'll tell you you've got a lot to learn, girl." The nurse picked up her bag. "And for your sake, I hope you learn it fast." With that, she left the office, letting the screen door slam behind her.

Watching her leave, Kathleen had the feeling that she had just met an enemy. She was certain of it when she looked down to see the scowl on Chuck's face. She leaned closer so that she could speak close to his ear.

"What put a bee in her bonnet?"

"She don't like Adelaide."

"Well for goodness sake. Why not?"

"She's afraid Adelaide knows too much." Chuck spoke very softly, unlike the hard-of-hearing people she knew who spoke loudly. His eyes were still on Adelaide's face.

20

"Too much about what?"

"'Bout that clinic she and Doc runs."

"Chuck!" Adelaide cast fearful eyes up at Kathleen. "Shhh . . ."

"It's all right," he said soothingly. "She's the one from Kansas."

"Kathleen Dolan?" Adelaide stretched out a hand. "Oh, Kathleen, thank God, you're here."